The Price of a Kiss

"Give the gun to me." He spoke gently, but in a firm command.

In desperate rebellion, she cocked the hammer.

He watched her as if he heard the calculations in her head. "How badly do you want this information?" he asked. "You are so pretty that I may give it to you in exchange for a kiss."

"A kiss! Only a charlatan would accept such little payment."

"You value your kisses so poorly?"

"The value of any kiss is fleeting."

"What a sad moral. Also an untrue one, I hope. The poets say there are some kisses that can sustain a person's soul forever."

"The poets are idiots." This conversation had taken a most peculiar turn.

"I fear you are correct, but I hope not."

His head angled and dipped. His lips brushed hers.

Shock paralyzed her. A thousand flutters beat in her chest.

Within her daze she felt him gently grasp her wrist. He moved her arm aside so the pistol aimed at the wall to her right.

The weapon no longer separated them or protected her.

Ravishing in Red

MADELINE HUNTER

JOVE BOOKS, NEW YORK

THE BERKLEY PUBLISHING GROUP
Published by the Penguin Group
Penguin Group (USA) Inc.
375 Hudson Street, New York, New York 10014, USA
Penguin Group (Canada), 90 Eglinton Avenue East, Suite 700, Toronto, Ontario M4P 2Y3, Canada
(a division of Pearson Penguin Canada Inc.)
Penguin Books Ltd., 80 Strand, London WC2R 0RL, England
Penguin Group Ireland, 25 St. Stephen's Green, Dublin 2, Ireland (a division of Penguin Books Ltd.)
Penguin Group (Australia), 250 Camberwell Road, Camberwell, Victoria 3124, Australia
(a division of Pearson Australia Group Pty. Ltd.)
Penguin Books India Pvt. Ltd., 11 Community Centre, Panchsheel Park, New Delhi—110 017, India
Penguin Group (NZ), 67 Apollo Drive, Rosedale, North Shore 0632, New Zealand
(a division of Pearson New Zealand Ltd.)
Penguin Books (South Africa) (Pty.) Ltd., 24 Sturdee Avenue, Rosebank, Johannesburg 2196,
South Africa

Penguin Books Ltd., Registered Offices: 80 Strand, London WC2R 0RL, England

RAVISHING IN RED

A Jove Book / published by arrangement with the author

PRINTING HISTORY
Jove mass-market edition / February 2010

Copyright © 2010 by Madeline Hunter.
Excerpt from *Provocative in Pearls* copyright © by Madeline Hunter.
Cover design by Rita Frangie.
Cover photograph by Claudio Marinesco.
Text design by Laura K. Corless.

ISBN: 978-0-515-14754-4

JOVE®
Jove Books are published by The Berkley Publishing Group,
a division of Penguin Group (USA) Inc.,
375 Hudson Street, New York, New York 10014.
JOVE® is a registered trademark of Penguin Group (USA) Inc.
The "J" design is a trademark of Penguin Group (USA) Inc.

PRINTED IN THE UNITED STATES OF AMERICA

10 9 8 7 6 5 4 3 2 1

Ravishing in Red

Chapter One

An independent woman is a woman unprotected. Audri-anna had never understood her cousin Daphne's first lesson to her as well as she did today.

An independent woman was also a woman of dubious respectability.

Her entry into the Two Swords coaching inn outside Brighton garnered more attention than any proper young woman would like. Eyes examined her from head to toe. Several men watched her solitary path across the public room with bold interest, the likes of which she had never been subjected to before.

The assumptions implied by all those stares darkened her mood even more. She had embarked on this journey full of righteous determination. The shining sun and un-seasonally mild temperature for late January seemed de-signed by Providence to favor her great mission.

Providence had proven fickle. An hour out of London the wind, rain, and increasing cold had begun, making her deeply regret taking a seat on the coach's roof. Now she was drenched from hours of frigid rain, and more than a little vexed.

She gathered her poise and sought out the innkeeper. She asked for a chamber for the night. He eyed her long and hard, then looked around for the man who had lost her.

"Is your husband dealing with the stable?"

"No. I am alone."

The white crepe skin of his aging face creased into a scowl. His mouth pursed in five different ways while he examined her again.

"I've a small chamber that you can have, but it over-looks the stable yard." His reluctant tone made it clear that he accommodated her against his better judgment.

An independent woman also gets the worst room at the inn, it seemed. "It will do, if it is dry and warm."

"Come with me, then."

He brought her to a room at the back of the second level. He built up the fire a little, but not much. She noted that there was not enough fuel to make it much warmer and also last through the night.

"I'll be needing the first night's fee in advance."

Audrianna swallowed her sense of insult. She dug into her reticule for three shillings. It would more than cover the chamber for one night, but she pressed it all into the man's hand.

"If someone arrives asking questions about Mr. Kelms-ley, send that person up here but say nothing of my pres-ence or anything else about me."

Her request made him frown more, but the coins in his hand kept him mute. He left with the shillings and she assumed she had struck a bargain. She only hoped that the fruits of this mission would be worth the cost to her reputation.

She noted the money left in her reticule. By morning she expected most of it to be spent. She would only be gone from London two days, but this journey would deplete the savings that she had accumulated from all those music lessons. She would endure months of clumsy scales and whining girls to replace it.

She plucked a scrap of paper from her reticule. She held the paper to the light of the fire even though she knew its words by heart. *The domino requests that Mr. Kelmsley meet him at the two swords in Brighton two nights hence, to discuss a matter of mutual benefit.*

It had been sheer luck that she even knew this advertisement had been placed in the *Times*. If her friend Lizzie did not comb through all such notices, in every paper and scandal sheet available, it might have escaped Audrianna's attention.

The surname was not spelled correctly, but she was sure the Mr. Kelmsley mentioned here was her father, Horatio Kelmsleigh. Clearly, whoever wanted to meet him did not know he was dead.

Images of her father invaded her mind. Her heart thickened and her eyes burned the way they always did whenever the memories overwhelmed her.

She saw him playing with her in the garden, and taking the blame when Mama scolded about her dirty shoes. She called up a distant, hazy memory of him, probably her oldest one. He was in his army uniform, so it was from before he sold his commission when Sarah was born, and took a position in the office of the Board of Ordnance, which oversaw the production of munitions during the war.

Mostly, however, she kept seeing his sad, troubled face

during those last months, when he became the object of so much scorn.

She tucked the notice away. It had reminded her why she was here. Nothing else, not the rain or the stares or the rudeness, really mattered. Hopefully she was right in thinking this Domino possessed information that would have helped Papa clear his name.

She removed her blue mantle and the gray pelisse underneath and hung them on wall pegs to dry. She took off her bonnet and shook off the rain. Then she moved the chamber's one lamp to a table beside the door, and the one wooden chair to the shadows in the facing corner, beyond the hearth. If she sat there, she would immediately be able to see whoever entered, but that person would not see her very well at all at first.

She set her valise on the chair and opened it. The rest of Daphne's first lesson recited in her mind. *An independent woman is a woman unprotected, so she must learn to protect herself.*

Reaching in, she removed the pistol that she had buried beneath her spare garments.

L ord Sebastian Summerhays handed his mount to a drenched stable boy. The lad got in the long line waiting attendance by the grooms of the Two Swords.

Sebastian entered the inn's public room. A cross section of humanity huddled there beneath its open-beamed ceiling. The rain had forced riders to take refuge, and coaches had been delayed. Women and children filled most of the chairs and benches, and men arrayed themselves around the perimeter, taking turns near the fire to dry off.

That was where Sebastian stationed himself while the

worst of the weather dripped off his riding coat. The odor of damp wool and unwashed bodies filled the air. A few servants did their best to salvage some silk hats and crepe bonnets, while others served expensive, unappetizing food. Sebastian cast a practiced eye on the sea of faces, looking for one that appeared suspicious, foreign, or at least as curious as himself.

The advertisement's use of a code name both annoyed and intrigued him. It would make this mission more difficult, but it also implied that secrets were involved. The notice itself, addressed to Kelmsley, indicated the writer did not know the man had been dead almost a year now.

That in turn suggested the Domino was not from London, or perhaps not even from England. Since the name was not spelled correctly, Sebastian trusted that the Domino was not a good friend or close associate of Horatio Kelmsleigh. Hopefully, the Domino did not even know what Kelmsleigh looked like.

Kelmsleigh's suicide had been unfortunate on many counts, one of which was the way it offered too easy an explanation for a mystery that Sebastian was sure had many more facets. Tonight he hoped to learn if he was correct.

"What ho, Summerhays. I did not expect to find you taking refuge along with me in this sorry way station."

The greeting near Sebastian's ear jerked him out of his search of the room. Grayson, Earl of Hawkeswell, beamed alongside him with a near empty tumbler of hot wine in hand. A smile of delight stretched beneath his blue eyes and artfully clipped black hair.

"A cloudburst caught me five miles back," Sebastian said. Hawkeswell was an old friend, and had been a close companion in his wilder days. Sebastian would normally be delighted to have his company to pass what promised to be a miserable night, but Sebastian's reason for being here made Hawkeswell an inconvenient discovery. "Are you on your way up to London, or coming down?"

"I am returning. I met with an estate agent in Brighton this morning."

"You are selling the property, then?"

"I have no choice."

Sebastian communicated his sympathy. Hawkeswell's finances had been bad since he inherited the title, and most of the unentailed property was gone. An attempt to rectify the problem through marriage had gone sadly awry when his wealthy bride went missing on her wedding day.

Hawkeswell looked around their environs. "No baggage? I trust you did not leave it on your horse. Anything of value will be stolen by morning."

Sebastian laughed lightly, and noncommittally. He had no baggage because he planned to be riding back to London tonight, the weather and dark be damned.

"Do you have a chamber above? Is your baggage there? I asked for one, but the innkeeper has hired them all out, he says. Even my title did me no good. But if you have one, we can go smoke and drink and escape the stench down here."

"I do not have a chamber, I am sorry."

Hawkeswell's eyebrows rose above knowing eyes. "Not taking shelter at all, are you? And not heading for Brighton either, I'll wager. You are here to meet a woman. No, do not say a word. I understand the need for your elaborate dodges these days. All but the marquess now, aren't you? Can't be lifting skirts wherever and whenever anymore." He put his finger to his lips, mocking the need for discretion.

It was as good an explanation as any, so Sebastian let it

stand. He remained friendly and attentive while he completed his scrutiny of all those faces. None struck him as more apt to be the Domino than any other.

Hawkeswell appeared likely to hang on all night. Sebastian needed to shake him, and decided Hawkeswell's own theory would have to do.

"You will have to excuse me. I need to speak to the innkeeper about the person I came here to meet."

He made good his escape. He found the proprietor dispensing ale to a wiry fellow with a low-brimmed brown hat.

"Was there anyone here asking about Mr. Kelmsley, or inviting inquiries about that name?"

The innkeeper peered at him, then went back to taking his customer's money. "Above, in the back, last door. The guest there would be the one you want, and I'll not be wanting to know why."

Sebastian aimed for the stairs. He wished Hawkeswell had been correct. Waiting out the weather on a feather bed, dry and cozy with some feminine warmth in his arms, would be a pleasant recompense for the miserable ride down here and the one waiting at mission's end. Instead he was stuck with duty and obligation, and a long conversation with someone known as the Domino.

Audrianna huddled beneath her shawl in the shadows. The low fire could not fight the damp chill in this chamber. That was not the only reason she shivered, however.

Her vigil was depleting the renewed resolve that she had summoned by reading that notice again. She had begun to see this plan from a different perspective, that of her entire life up until the last seven months.

From that viewpoint, her behavior today was utterly mad and inexcusably reckless.

Mama would certainly say so. Papa would have agreed. Roger would be appalled if he knew too. Proper young ladies did not ride alone on public coaches to public inns, and wait in dark chambers for unknown men to join them.

This expedition had begun to feel like a bizarre dream. She forced her nerves under control and demanded that her mind regain some of its determination.

She was here because no one else would be. The world had buried her father's good name with his body. His death had been proof enough that he was guilty of the accusations against him. Everyone assumed that remorse, not deep melancholy, had caused him to kill himself.

The whole family still wore his shame. Mama mourned the loss of friends even while she valiantly defended his memory. Even Uncle Rupert had ceased to write when the scandal broke, in an attempt to wash himself of stain by association. And Roger—well, his undying love could not surmount the scandal either.

She tried to maintain a semblance of indifference about that, but deep sorrow squeezed her heart at the thought of Roger. Eventually that would no longer happen, she trusted. At least she could take some small comfort in the knowledge that she would never be so disillusioned again. With the bad turn life had taken, no other man would ever propose.

She had told her mother that she would live with her cousin Daphne in order to mitigate the financial burdens caused by Papa's death, when the family was reduced to the income from Mama's small trust. In truth she had wanted to escape an old life stuck in the doldrums, and build a new one where she would find contentment within her changed expectations.

The crowd below created a soft din that reached her ears. Up here on the second level all was quiet except for an occasional door closing. The silence provoked more ill ease. There were other travelers in those chambers, though. If this "Domino" attempted anything untoward, and she screamed, she trusted that aid would arrive quickly.

She pulled the shawl higher to ward off another chill. Beneath its woolen warmth, she closed her hand around Daphne's pistol. She had brought it to give her courage and so Daphne would not scold later that she had been unprotected.

Unfortunately, its weight in her hand only made her shiver again.

Sebastian pressed the latch. To his surprise it yielded. He eased open the door to the chamber.

A lamp just inside flashed its light up at him. The strong glow made the rest of the room a sea of darkness. He stepped inside so he could escape the harsh illumination. His eyes slowly adjusted.

A low blaze in the fireplace created its own sharp chiaroscuros. However, much like in paintings that exploited a similar effect, the dark began to come alive with forms and shapes the longer he gazed.

The head of the draped bed that faced the fire emerged, to join its foot that the flames bathed. Pegs on the wall beside the door showed hanging fabric. The corners of the chamber finally revealed their contents. A writing table. The hulk of a wardrobe.

A soft collection of shapes in another corner took form too, beyond the light of the fire. They gathered into something he recognized. A woman.

Her presence made him pause. He had thought the Domino was a man. He could be forgiven that mistake, he supposed, but it had been an unfounded assumption.

The discovery that the Domino was only a woman immediately raised his spirits. He would learn what he needed to know quickly, and make short work of this meeting.

He smiled a smile that had charmed many women in his day. He walked toward the fireplace.

"Please stay there," she said. "I must insist that you do."

Insist, must she? That made him smile more. She had a young voice. Not girlish, though. Her appearance became more distinct as he focused on her.

Dark hair. Perhaps that interesting color where red shoots through the brown, like a chestnut horse's hue. Hard to judge her age, but he guessed middle twenties. Her face looked pretty, but in this light most women would be attractive. A dark shawl draped her lap and chest. Her dress appeared to be either gray or lavender, and was fairly plain from what he could see.

"I was only going to warm myself by the fire," he said. "The ride here drowned me."

Her head tipped back while she considered his explanation. "The fire then, but no closer."

He shed his riding coat. She visibly startled.

"So I can hang it to dry, if you do not mind," he explained.

She nodded.

He set it on one of the pegs. Accustomed now to the room's lighting, he could tell that the other garments there were a woman's mantle and pelisse. He took position at the fire and pretended to concentrate on its comfort, but he watched her out of the corner of his eye.

He smiled at her again while he turned his back to the warmth. She fidgeted under that shawl.

"I should warn you that I have a pistol." Her voice shook with anxiety.

"Rest assured that you will not need it."

She did not appear convinced. Green eyes, he thought. They expressed determination and some fear. The latter was a good sign. It indicated she was not stupid, and a bit of fear would be useful.

"I expected a man," he said.

"Mr. Kelmsleigh was not available, so I am here instead. I assume that you want compensation for your information, and I am prepared to pay if the sum is reasonable."

He masked his stunned reaction. She thought *he* was the Domino. Which meant she was not, of course.

He had never believed that the bad gunpowder that reached the front had been a matter of mere negligence on Kelmsleigh's part, although such negligence was bad enough to ruin a man. Instead he suspected conspiracy and fraud, and he doubted Kelmsleigh had devised and controlled the scheme. All the same, he had never expected to learn that any women were involved. Now this accomplice indicated at least one had been.

Only who the hell was she? Her identity might provide a link to the others involved in that plot.

She watched him cautiously. He could see her fear better now. She was not what he expected, but he guessed he was a surprise to her as well.

He had come here to pass himself off as Kelmsleigh. Instead someone else had read that advertisement and had come to buy information too.

He changed plans. He could not be Kelmsleigh anymore. But he could be the Domino.

Chapter Two

Oh, goodness. Oh, heavens.

This day was definitely not unfolding the way she had pictured.

She had not expected the Domino to be a gentleman. She had certainly not expected a tall, handsome young gentleman with such a winning smile.

She was not sure what she had anticipated instead. She only knew that it was not this.

He seemed not at all concerned by her presence instead of her father's, or by her declaration of having a pistol. His manner remained amiable while he warmed himself in front of the fire. He kept flashing those brief, stunning smiles of reassurance.

They did not reassure her at all. Instead he struck her as very dangerous.

That could be due to the way the fire's light turned him into a collection of hard angles, or the way his eyes appeared much more intense and alert than his demeanor required.

It could be the result of his wealth, evidenced in the cut and make of that dark gray riding coat he had removed, and the quality of the high boots and snug doeskin that encased his legs. Even his dark hair was expensive, with the short, wispy, flyaway cut that damp and wind enhanced rather than ruined.

His appearance was the least of it, however. She could not ignore the way the atmosphere in the room had altered with his arrival, as if he gave off tiny, invisible lightning bolts of power.

"Sir, I think that we should get on with the purpose of this meeting."

"With the weather, there is no hurry. Neither one of us is going anywhere soon."

She wished that she had not allowed him to come so close. He stood no more than six feet away and towered above her. She could not ignore his size, or the way he made her feel small and vulnerable and at a bigger disadvantage than was fair.

"I would still like to finish this in good time."

One of those smiles half-formed, a private one that reflected some thought in his head. "Who are you?" he asked.

"Does it matter?"

"It may matter a great deal. For all I know, you thought I wanted to meet a different Kelmsleigh, and you will leave here with facts that you should not have. That could cause an innocent, unsuspecting man grief."

"I should say that is unlikely." Her voice sounded sharp to her own ears. He spoke as if his information would not be good news. "However, since you fear making revela-

tions to a disinterested party, I will identify the Kelmsleigh who interests me. He was employed by the Board of
Ordnance. I am hoping that your information relates to his
position there."

His smile proved less amiable this time. A tad preda-
tory, if truth be told. It could be the harsh light, of course,
but— To her dismay, he stepped toward her with his attention fixed on her face.

"I insist that you stay where you are." She hated the
way her demand came out a fearful bleat.

He continued toward her.

She jumped to her feet. The shawl fell to the ground.
She did not aim the pistol but she gripped it soundly. "Do
not come any closer. I do know how to fire this."

He halted an arm's span away. Close enough that she
could see that his eyes were dark. Very dark. Close enough
that if she did fire, she could not miss. He ignored the
pistol and instead studied her face.

"Who are you?" he asked again.

"You call yourself something as silly as the Domino,
and you demand that I reveal my name? My identity is no
more important than yours."

"What is your part in all of this? Are you an accomplice? A lover? Perhaps you are a relative of one of the
soldiers who died? I would not want this meeting to start a
vendetta."

His gaze all but skewered her and his scrutiny unsettled
her in the oddest way. For all his suspicions he kept flashing that vague, appealing smile that offered . . . friendship
and . . . excitement and . . . things that she should not even
be thinking about at this moment. He had the kind of face
that made women silly, and it annoyed her that she was

proving more susceptible than this situation should ever allow.

She raised the pistol just enough, so it did not point down but instead out from her hip. He glanced at the weapon, then his gaze was all for her face again. Only now he looked like a man who had been challenged but knew he would win the contest.

"What information do you have?" she demanded.

"How much money do you have?"

"Enough."

"How much do you think is enough?"

"I am not so stupid as to bargain against myself. Name your price."

"And if you don't have it?" He nodded to the pistol. "Do you think to force me to reveal everything, no matter what?"

Suddenly he was even closer. His body stood an inch from the pistol's barrel, and only a few more from her. She looked up at him in surprise.

Her breath caught. He appeared very dangerous now, in ways that had nothing to do with pistols. His gaze and smile were intended to charm and seduce and he had released something invisible to that end as well.

She doubted any woman would be immune to this man. It was as if his masculinity spoke to her primitive self and her mind had no say in the conversation.

She physically reacted even while she clung to a mental shield. Wicked little arrows of stimulation shot around her body. She valiantly fought to thwart his effect, but those arrows just flashed along their exciting paths, ignoring her ladylike dismay.

"It would be better if you put that gun down," he said

quietly. "We met to be allies, not adversaries. Friends, not enemies."

He spoke the word *friends* in a velvet voice. She grasped the pistol more firmly.

"Give the gun to me." He spoke gently, but in a firm command. His eyes reflected confidence that he would have his way on this matter, or on any other that he chose.

In desperate rebellion, she cocked the hammer.

"Two clicks. You do know how to use it." He scowled. No longer a "friend," he appeared hard and angry. "You are being foolish. At least point it away from me. It might go off accidentally now."

"I will use it if I must. Do not test my resolve on that."

"It is not resolve that I sense in you right now."

"Then your senses fail you."

"Where women are concerned, my senses never fail me. Not this sense at least."

He alluded to those stupid arrows and her breathless fear and the shocking stimulation. He *knew*. Worse, he had actually broached the matter out loud.

He studied her, weighing something. His gaze both lured and frightened her.

That smile again, intended to put her at ease and to flatter without words. "I dare not confide what I have unless I know your role in this. You are an unexpected player."

"If you are paid, what do you care who hears your story?"

"I doubt you have enough money to buy, even if I were selling."

She worried that he was correct. Everything about him spoke of the very highest quality. A golden chain arced on his tastefully embroidered waistcoat, no doubt attached to a golden watch. The ten pounds and gold locket hiding in her reticule would not impress such a man.

She may have come all this way, risked molestation and ruin, only to fail because the Domino's demands were too expensive.

He watched her as if he heard the calculations in her head. "How badly do you want this information? You are so pretty that I may give it to you in exchange for a kiss."

"A kiss! I am beginning to think that you are a charlatan if you would accept such little payment."

"You value your kisses so poorly?"

"The value of any kiss is fleeting, no matter what its worth."

"What a sad moral. Also an untrue one, I hope. The poets say there are some kisses that can sustain a person's soul forever."

"The poets are idiots." This conversation had taken a most peculiar turn.

"I fear you are correct, but I hope not. Hence my offer. My soul tells me that you may be the one woman whose kiss will be of eternal value."

What ridiculous nonsense. They both knew he was flattering to his own ends, and a kiss was not even the goal. His expression admitted the game even while he shamelessly played it.

She should put him in his place and let him know that she was not some silly woman who swooned and gasped just because a handsome man with stunning eyes and a seductive smile flirted.

Except, despite her mental scolds, she did feel a little light-headed and giddy, if truth be told. She *was* close to gasping. The flattery made her blood hum and sparkle.

"I must find out if you are that woman, of course," he said. "Since you do not want to trade, I am forced to steal." His head angled and dipped. His lips brushed hers.

Shock paralyzed her. A thousand flutters beat in her chest. The thrilling little arrows multiplied and aimed through her entire body. Roger had kissed her a few times, and while the kisses had been very nice, the effect had been nothing like this. But then Roger had not been a stranger and the kisses had not been scandalous, dangerous, and deliciously forbidden.

His lips did not just rest on hers. They subtly teased and moved and pressed. A wicked little nip made her heart flip and rise.

A new touch distracted her. Astonished her. A new softness, moist and devilish. Good heavens, the tip of his tongue was tickling the sensitive underside of her lower lip, evoking shivers that cascaded down her body.

Within her daze she felt him gently grasp her wrist. He moved her arm aside so the pistol aimed at the wall to her right.

The weapon no longer separated them or protected her. His grasp controlled her and the weapon, but this kiss interested her much more than the voice of caution in her mind that gave one panicked protest.

He moved closer. Her heart rose to her throat.

His right hand slowly moved around her neck with a stunning caress of physical connection. Careful, but controlling. Warm, but not entirely soft. The sensation of his skin on hers, and the slight roughness of his touch, mesmerized her. His hand evoked wonderful chills, until it cupped her nape. He kissed her again.

Harder this time. More demanding. More aggressive. He toyed with her vulnerability and asserted a dominance that, heaven help her, she did not begin to know how to resist. She no longer even noticed that she was being wicked to permit this, or note that she had inexplicably become stupid. A chaos of pleasurable sensations obscured such sensible thoughts.

His left hand moved and covered hers over the pistol grip. With caressing, careful fingers, he seduced the weapon from her hold.

Her suddenly empty hand caused one thread of sense to reassert itself.

What was she doing?

She opened her eyes, literally and metaphorically. What she saw jolted her out of her daze.

The door stood open. *And they were not alone.* Another man stood behind the Domino.

Her seducer stopped the kiss. Frowning, he followed the direction of her distraction and glanced over his shoulder. Alarm crashed through him.

"What the—?"

The intruder saw the pistol and rushed forward. The Domino pivoted and thrust her out of the way. She fell with a thump back in the chair.

A turmoil of movement blurred in front of her. The new man threw himself against the Domino, sending them both onto the floor. Another hand grasped at the gun while they tumbled and grappled in a heap.

A loud crack snapped through the chamber. Then the intruder was up and running, and the dark threshold swallowed him.

The Domino looked at his arm. Blood oozed through the scorched, torn sleeve of his shirt above his elbow.

"Damnation." He jumped to his feet and ran out the door. Audrianna gripped the arms of her chair and fought to calm her hammering heart.

Sounds. Loud ones now. Shouts from below, and cries and screams from nearby chambers.

The Domino strode back into the chamber and shut the door.

"Your arm," she cried.

"The ball is in the wall, over there." He pointed to a new dark hole in the plaster beneath the window. "A half inch more, though, and—"

More shouts. Closer now.

He peered down at her. "Are you rational? Collect yourself and do not dare faint on me."

"I am rational. Only a little breathless and shocked."

"You brought a loaded pistol with you and cocked the hammer, damn it. You should not be too shocked if it ends up fired." He lifted her face with a firm hold under her chin, to check her rationality, she assumed, and how close she came to fainting.

"They will be here soon," he said. "In mere seconds. Do not speak. I will answer the questions."

Her gaze shot around the chamber. Of course there would be questions. A shot had been fired in this inn, and everyone had heard it.

Confusion rolled toward the door. Voices and heavy steps and excitement. Then, suddenly, silence. The door opened a crack.

"Do not speak," the Domino commanded again.

The door flew wide to show the innkeeper wearing an expression of worry. Relief replaced it, then anger. Behind him a thick collection of faces angled to see into the room too.

"No one is dead," the innkeeper announced over his shoulder. While that news spread down the corridor, he stepped inside the chamber and folded his arms. He eyed the wound on one guest's arm, then the chair where Audrianna sat, then the pistol still on the floor.

His attention returned to Audrianna. "I knew you were trouble when you arrived. I have a respectable inn here, and I'll not be—"

"Summerhays! What the hell . . . ?" A new face joined the crush outside the door, a handsome one with blue eyes and waves of very dark hair.

This new man pushed his way past the others until he popped through the threshold. He took in the scene, then shook his head. "Badly done, Summerhays. Badly done."

Audrianna realized with alarm how this must look. A man and a woman alone in an inn . . . The man wounded by a pistol . . . They all thought she and the Domino were lovers, and there had been a quarrel and that she had shot him!

"You are bleeding, Summerhays," the new gentleman said. "Did you take a ball?"

She realized that this imposing gentleman was addressing the Domino, not the innkeeper. *Summerhays.* There had been an MP named Summerhays involved in investigating her father. Lord Sebastian Summerhays. He was the brother of the Marquess of Wittonbury, and he had been uncompromising, cruel, and relentless.

But how could he be the Domino? He of all men would know her father was dead and—

She stared at him as the truth sank in.

"The ball is in my wall here." The innkeeper bent down to examine the damage. "But it was aimed at that arm or worse, that is clear. This woman here no doubt shot at him and he is fortunate she has bad aim."

The crowd outside the door agreed with that opinion. Voices passed on the news that a woman had tried to shoot her lover. The accusation moved like an echo through the building.

"That is not what happened." Lord Sebastian tore off what remained of his sleeve and used the remnant to press the large, dark slash on his upper arm. "There was an intruder. A thief. I attempted to defend myself and he rushed at me. In the struggle the pistol went off."

"That is an unlikely story," the innkeeper muttered.

"Do you question my word as a gentleman?" Lord Sebastian asked dangerously.

"I'll not be doing any questioning, sir. I'll leave that to the magistrate, if you don't mind. You can tell him about this bold thief who intruded on an occupied room, only to shoot and flee with no money." The innkeeper treated Audrianna to a glance of disdain. "Will you be wanting us to send to Brighton for a surgeon, sir? Or can this woman here tend that wound sufficient while you wait for the justice of the peace? I'll be taking your word as a gentleman that you will indeed wait, and not slip away first."

Lord Sebastian removed the rag and checked his arm. "You have my word. We can deal with this wound. Send up fresh water and clean cloth. Also, the lady will need another chamber for the night, so see to it."

"The other chambers are taken, and I'll not be putting others out to accommodate her. Nor do I want her wandering about my property, considering what she has done here. I do not have time to serve as gaoler, so I'll be leaving that to you, sir. I'll be taking your word on that too, that you will keep her nearby and see that she remains here until the justice of the peace arrives."

"So be it, if you insist. Leave now."

His command came quietly, but with such authority that

the innkeeper immediately turned to the door. The bodies there began dispersing, making way.

"You too, Hawkeswell," Lord Sebastian said. "I require some privacy. I also ask for your discretion, not that I expect the latter to help much. I am sure that you understand."

"I will gladly give you both. I also have an extra shirt in my baggage. I will have it brought up to you." He made a little bow to Audrianna, and followed the innkeeper out of the chamber.

Chapter Three

L ord Sebastian closed the door on the curious stragglers who kept peeking around the doorjamb. Then he walked to the fire and examined his wound more closely.

"Why is it so black?" Audrianna asked.

"Hot gunpowder. The ball only grazed me but I am well scorched." He turned his attention to her. "Your name. I need it now, and do not think to lie to me. The justice of the peace will have it out of you for certain, and I'll be damned if I will remain unaware of what we are facing here."

She was too shocked and frightened to lie. "I am Audrianna Kelmsleigh. Horatio Kelmsleigh's daughter."

His face fell in surprise.

"I saw a newspaper notice from someone calling himself the Domino and it appeared to be for my father," she said. "I came instead, to see if this man had information that might clear my father's name." It had all sounded so right, so necessary, yesterday. "Why are *you* here?"

"I also saw the notice, and also hoped to speak with this Domino."

"Why? My father is dead. The world has moved on."

"I think there is more to it."

"I do not see how you could learn anything from the Domino if you pretended to be the Domino."

"My intention was to pretend to be Kelmsleigh. When you assumed I was the Domino, I decided to play along and discover who this unexpected woman was, and what her role might be in the bigger scheme."

Bigger scheme?

The door opened then. A maid carried in a basin and a bucket of water. She laid some clean cloths on the bed. "A gentleman below asked that I bring this shirt too," she said, setting it aside. She gave Audrianna a good stare, then hurried out.

Lord Sebastian put the bucket near the fire. He sat on the bed, slid off his waistcoat, then stripped off his tattered shirt. He winced when the fabric rubbed over the wound.

Audrianna blinked hard, stunned anew. This man had gone beyond dishabille. He sat there, preoccupied with that wound, undressed, half-naked if one wanted to be honest. He did not seem to think it at all odd that she was sitting right here with him.

She had never seen a man without his shirt on. She tried to feign a worldly indifference, but she could not help noting that if a woman had to see a half-naked man for the first time in her life, Lord Sebastian was not a bad beginning. A boy no longer, he still possessed the taut leanness of youth, and almost no softness interfered with the way his muscles defined his torso.

"I will need that chair now, Miss Kelmsleigh. If you do not mind."

She jumped off the chair. He grabbed its back, swung it into place in front of the fire, and straddled it. Using the warm water and some soap, he began to cleanse the gash on his upper arm.

She assumed it pained him but he displayed no reaction. Perhaps he was not as oblivious of her presence as it appeared.

"I will go below while you—"

"I gave my word that you would not leave this chamber. Besides, nothing but scorn or worse waits for you down there. You will remain here until the magistrate comes, and we will decide what to say to him."

She edged closer. His cleansing had missed a good deal of the back of his arm. "Allow me to help you, then. Give me the cloth."

He handed it over. She dabbed away the black dust. She could see the gash better now. It was not deep but a bad burn surrounded it by three inches. She doubted a surgeon could have done more than clean it like this.

"Did you get a good look at him?" he asked. "The Domino?"

"Is that who you think it was?"

"I am sure of it. He must have overheard me ask for directions to this chamber and thought Kelmsleigh was here. Did you see his face? Would you recognize him?"

She turned her sight inward. She tried to slow down the explosion of action. She had caught a glimpse of the intruder's face beneath his broad-brimmed hat when the firelight washed it as he moved toward them. She remembered his shock, first at seeing she was even there, blocked by

Lord Sebastian's body, then when he saw the pistol in Lord Sebastian's hand.

"Yes, I believe I could recognize him. Do you think he is still here?"

"He just shot a man. He will be long gone from this inn by now. It is good that one of us got a look at him, however. It might be useful later."

He sounded determined and angry. She doubted his continued interest in the Domino would benefit her own cause.

He brooded while she dabbed and cleaned. He turned his attention from the fire to her with a dark scowl. "You should not have come here. What were you thinking?"

"I was thinking that no one else cares about the truth, so I had better take up the cause myself."

"You created an unneeded complication and distraction."

"I do not believe that a man of your consequence is a slave to distraction. Nor do I have illusions that I am the sort of woman to make a man forget himself. However, I remind you that any distraction that resulted in this wound was of your own making."

His eyes blazed at her accusation, but the flames lowered fast enough. His face remained set in a stern expression but he did not blame her outright again.

Audrianna's own blood was up now too. The recent events and conversations begged for explanations.

"You referred to a bigger scheme, Lord Sebastian. What did you mean by that?"

"I do not believe that your father was guilty of negligence. I do not believe that the bad gunpowder that left those soldiers defenseless was an accident."

His response appalled her. He implied that her father had deliberately sent bad powder to the front! "How dare you! Is it not enough that he was unjustly disgraced to the point of despair? To now accuse him of—"

"He was the last check on quality in a long line of checks. The distribution could not occur without his signature. Whether he was guilty of carelessness or conspiracy, attention settled on him for a reason, Miss Kelmsleigh. I am sorry, but that is the truth of it."

She wanted to hit him for the insult. She dabbed more firmly while angry tears blurred her sight. "That is not the truth. You are mistaken. My father was not guilty of anything at all."

Suddenly his hand closed over hers, stilling it against the arm that she cleaned. His hold suggested that she had been hurting him more than she realized and he now merely stopped her. However, his firm grasp of her hand, and her close approximation to the face still stoical in its countenance, produced an unexpected flow of intimacy.

Her dismay at his insinuations about her father mixed with a new astonishment. She realized that his continued hold of her hand was intended to comfort her distress.

No one had done that before. Not since the scandal first broke. Not Mama, who was so distraught, first with worry and then with grief. Certainly not Roger. Not even her cousin Daphne, who had treated the whole episode as a book whose cover would be better closed forever.

Now this man who had all but handed her father the rope to hang himself made this small attempt to soothe her. She should shake off his touch and ignore the effort. She should tell him she wanted no comfort from him of all people.

Instead she could not move for several moments. She

closed her eyes and accepted the humanity of his concern as it flowed into her like warm water. She let it touch her heart and calm her agitation. She ignored the peculiarity of the source of the comfort because she so desperately needed its balm.

He lifted her hand and pried the bloody rag from her fingers. He grabbed a clean cloth. "Help me to bind this, please, so I can dress for our guest."

Hands shaking, she tied the cloth around his arm while he held it in place.

Then he stood. Suddenly his naked chest was right in front of her nose. A stark consciousness of that chest, with the texture of its skin and the way the firelight carved its strength with deep shadows, dazed her for a slow moment.

She forced her gaze up and caught him watching the way she looked at his body. She felt herself blush hotly. She moved away and turned her back on him so he would not view her embarrassment.

There had been nothing critical in the way he gazed down at her. Nothing insinuating or leering. His expression had been far more shocking than that.

She had seen his own fascination, and a silent acknowledgment of some shared secret. Confidence too, as if he knew he was worth looking at, but also curiosity, as if he found her interest less predictable than past women's.

She heard him dressing, then the chair being moved again.

"Miss Kelmsleigh."

She forced herself to turn and face him. He appeared all proper now. Not only a shirt and waistcoat covered him, but also the dark gray riding coat that he had removed on first entering. His cravat had been retied quite well considering the pain it must have caused to move his arm.

"Miss Kelmsleigh, I am sorry that your father is dead. I am sorry for your grief and I am sorry that my pursuit of the truth hurt your family. However, sometime tonight or tomorrow morning the county justice of the peace will be posing some awkward questions. I must ask you to trust me and allow me to answer him for both of us."

His reference to her father's death enflamed the anger that had sent her on this miserable journey. She was grateful for that moment of comfort, but it really changed nothing.

"You hounded my father to his grave, Lord Sebastian. You and the other members of Parliament who kept talking about that gunpowder. You would not accept any explanations, and insisted that the Board of Ordnance find a scapegoat for you to pillory in public. I think that I would be stupid to trust you."

"Your view is understandable. However, I am the only protection that you will have in this. My word as a gentleman, my brother's title, and my position in the government might spare you."

"Spare me? Scandal will find me no matter who you are if word gets out that we were alone here. Your station will only make me more notorious."

"That kind of scandal is the least of what you face. In fact, it would be best if the magistrate accepts this as a lovers' quarrel. Because when he learns that you are Horatio Kelmsleigh's daughter, he is going to think that you arranged to meet me here, so that you could kill me to avenge your father."

She wanted to laugh at his dramatic prediction. Only in a flash she saw the sordid scene from the innkeeper's eyes again. Lord Sebastian was correct. Her identity would put a different and far worse interpretation on the night's events.

The thought left her nauseous. She should never have left the safe obscurity that she had found in Daphne's house. She should never have rebelled against the unjust turn that life had taken, or been so stupid as to think she could alter the course of fate.

Lord Sebastian gestured to the bed. "There is no telling when he will arrive. We will arrange it so you can take some rest in privacy, while I contemplate the best way to keep you from being transported for attempted murder."

He pulled the bed's drapes closed with his good arm. Then he lifted the hem on one side and pushed it over the bed halfway to create a narrow but serviceable tunnel of privacy for her.

"Get in, Miss Kelmsleigh, and try to sleep. I will not disturb you. You are completely safe."

She looked long and hard at that bed. "Where will you be?"

"On the other side of that drape."

"That would be most inappropriate."

"I think that we are beyond pretty proprieties, don't you?"

She grimaced in resignation. She wrapped herself in her shawl, lifted a corner of the drape, and disappeared behind it. They were in gaol for all intents and purposes, and there was no way to stand on ceremony. He could not sit out the night in that wooden chair with his bad arm, and he would probably not allow her to either, while he used the bed.

She lay down and huddled on her side and closed her eyes. Despite her exhaustion, her body felt like a taut string on a bow. She kept hearing small sounds as he moved in the chamber.

Then the mattress sagged behind her back and beyond that billowing drape. She felt his presence warm her even though not a part of them touched.

She tried to sleep. It was impossible. He was just *there*. She imagined him reaching for her and—

The notion shocked her. So did the manner in which her body flushed. She tried to turn her thoughts to other things, to Mama and Sarah, to her father. Even to Roger. None of it helped much. Instead the intimacy of this situation saturated the chamber and pressed on her.

It was worse than being in a crowded coach with strangers. Then one pretended they were not there and ignored the physical proximity that would be wrong in any other situation. And they remained strangers, even if one of them liked to talk, because the talk was about nothing important. At the end of the journey they disappeared and so did the intimacy, as if it had never happened.

Lord Sebastian would not disappear. She would have to face him in the morning and could not pretend this had not happened. He was not a stranger either, anymore, and their talk had been about very important things.

And he had kissed her. *And she had allowed it*. That was what really left her fearful and, yes, waiting. She had given him cause to think that if he reached for her, she might not mind. That was what kept deepening this awareness of his body beside hers, in that shocking, startling, never-ending *there*.

He did not sleep either. She just knew that. And so she dared not move. Not one bit, all night.

Sebastian waited a quarter hour, sitting on the wooden chair while his arm pounded. Then he lay down fully dressed, boots and all, on the side of the bed left exposed by his artistry with the drapes. He went through great pains, literally, to avoid even touching the billow of fabric that shielded her.

Just resting his shoulder and arm helped. Or maybe the feminine presence so close by distracted him from the wound. Like most men, maybe more than most, he was prone to seductive considerations. He smiled ruefully when signs of arousal stirred in him just from hearing her faint breathing.

Bloody hell. Here he was, dressed in coats and boots, in as chaste a situation as one could create out of such a disaster, and yet his body encouraged him to speculate about the possibilities.

Worse, for all her stillness, he was sure she did not sleep either. Any woman as artless in kissing as she had demonstrated would not find repose with a man in the same room, let alone two inches away on the other side of a swath of cloth.

That same artlessness indicated, of course, that any speculations were idiocy. Not to mention he had an arm that could barely move.

He forced his mind away from that billow and the woman behind it who helped to warm this bed very nicely. He eyed the low fire beyond his boots until he extinguished the alluring warmth in his blood.

With the distraction gone, his arm started throbbing again like hell's drum. He turned his thoughts to how quickly and thoroughly the night had turned into a catastrophe.

He admired Miss Kelmsleigh's courage in daring to meet the Domino, but a good deal of annoyance simmered in his head as he reviewed the night's events. If she had stayed put in London, like any other woman, he might have pulled off tonight's plan and learned the truth about that ordnance conspiracy. It would have been nice to hand his brother some resolution about that. Now, instead, there would be hell to pay.

He never lost awareness of her presence beside him. She probably never forgot he was here either. A mutual alertness affected the air in the chamber. It would not do to acknowledge it, or the way it invisibly heightened the forced intimacy that the night's events had created.

Nor would it do to reflect on those kisses. Her palpable presence kept bringing his mind to them anyway, to his body's repeated discomfort.

He had assumed that she was experienced in the game when he began toying with her. Wrong there, as with so many of tonight's assumptions.

Her surprise and dazed wonderment had charmed him too much. Drawn him in. Innocence could be very beguiling, apparently. Those kisses had enchanted him, and he would not forget them for a long time. She had distracted him so much that the real Domino had been halfway across the chamber before either he or she had realized that they were no longer alone.

He tried to remember what he could about the intruder, but it was all a blur of instinct and defense. He saw only that hat, low crowned and dark, with a broad brim. He suspected, but was not sure, that the man buying ale when he queried the innkeeper had worn a hat like that. If that had been the Domino, he would have overheard the directions up to this chamber and not had to ask for them himself.

As much as annoyance with her interference tried to win out, it never did during the hours that they waited. The kisses had a lot to do with that. He also sympathized with

her desire to clear her father's name. He understood familial love and the sacrifices it could require. He had to admit
that her reckless mission spoke well of her, even if it had
been in vain. Horatio Kelmsleigh had no son to fight for
his name, so a daughter had taken up the standard.

He cast his mind to what he knew of the man's family,
besides what he had learned tonight about Audrianna. Sebastian had watched the funeral when Kelmsleigh was buried
in unconsecrated ground due to his suicide. Few people
attended. A man publicly disgraced did not have many
friends.

He had seen the widow in her black crepe. There had
been two girls with her. One had huddled closely, all but
under her mother's arm. The other stood just far enough
away to suggest an emotional isolation. He had been some
distance from the little group, and other than dark hair,
there had been nothing else to notice about the women.

He had spied that day because he thought that the other
conspirators might be present as friends and associates.
The few men around the grave occupied his attention, not
the women.

More than a father and husband were lost by his wife
and daughters. The months since had probably been difficult financially as well as socially for the Kelmsleigh women.
In truth, he had not given much consideration to the consequences of that investigation and death to these inno-
cents. Actually, he had not thought about them at all.

Now one of them was beside him on a bed, in a chamber
where they should not be alone together.

He crossed his boots. He wondered if the justice of the
peace would be reasonable or small-minded.

The interview waiting had only two possible endings, but

either one of them would be unfortunate for Miss Kelmsleigh.

The rap on the door sounded sharply. Sebastian jolted
out of the unsettled sleep into which he had fallen.
As he rose to his feet, his wound caused red to split through
his mind for a moment. He looked at the window. The barest light leaked in around the closed shutters. Dawn would
break soon.

Miss Kelmsleigh was on her feet too. She smoothed
the skirt of her dress, fixed the bed drapes, then strode to
the pegs to fetch her pelisse. He waited while she put it
on. She quickly tried to make her hair look less disheveled
in the looking glass.

The rap sounded again. Her eyes met his. She appeared
sad and resigned, and embarrassed by their night together.
No doubt the hours of thought had revealed the impossibility of the situation to her as well.

He opened the door. Hawkeswell stood there, not the
innkeeper.

"I insisted on being the one to come up," he said.

"Good man. Thank you."

"The JP is below. Will you be coming down, or should
he come here?"

"This is hardly the best place for it, but it is better than
the alternative. We don't want an audience in attendance."

Hawkeswell nodded. "Your arm?"

"It was a mere scratch. If you would not mind helping
further, please learn the time when the first coach leaves
for London and let me know."

Hawkeswell dipped away. Sebastian closed the door
again.

"Nine o'clock," Miss Kelmsleigh said. "That is the time of the first coach. I had planned to be on it."

She hid her nervousness well. Except for the way her hands grasped each other and the melancholy in her expression, one would never guess that she faced a judgment soon.

Deciding that her manner and poise would help more than hurt, Sebastian opened the shutters completely to disperse the night shadows. He turned back to her and got the first really good look at her in the light of the breaking day.

Her hair had that deep chestnut color. Those reddish lights showed even now. Her eyes possessed an arresting green hue. Her features were very regular, and more delicate than the harsh firelight had implied. Her face possessed a mature and unique beauty that one would call handsome rather than pretty.

Handsome enough to make him pause a moment and remember that kiss vividly. Then he moved the chair so it flanked the fire but still faced it.

"Please, sit here. He will see upon entering that you are a lady, and it will affect the entire conversation."

She obeyed. Sebastian took the pistol from where it had laid on the table all night, and set it on the fireplace mantel, against the hearth wall, where it would not be immediately in view.

Another rap sounded on the door, not nearly as sharp as Hawkeswell's had been. Its somewhat tentative quality was a good sign.

Sir Edwin Tomlison was a tall, very thin fellow with steel gray starting to frost his thick black hair. The resigned set of his mouth as he entered the chamber and introduced himself told Sebastian a lot. This was a man who enjoyed being justice of the peace for the status it gave him in the county, but who did not relish the jurisdictional duties that came with the position.

"Lord Sebastian Summerhays." Sir Edwin bowed. "I had the honor of meeting your brother once, before he went to war and . . ." His voice trailed off. His face fell into sympathetic folds.

"I believe that you had your own war adventures, Sir Edwin. I remember when you were knighted for them."

Sir Edwin's face lit up. A country squire made a knight, he was pleased that a marquess's brother knew the reasons.

Sebastian introduced Miss Kelmsleigh. Sir Edwin showed surprise, and recognition, at hearing her name.

"A bad business here, sir," he said to Sebastian. "There's quite a crowd down below, all of them in high emotion about the exciting events to which you have treated them. Their stories will be in Brighton by noon, and in London by night, so we need to speak frankly."

"I intend to do so. I told the innkeeper, and I tell you now, that there was an intruder who shot me during a struggle. He fled at once."

"Can you describe him or identify him?"

"I did not see him well enough. It happened very fast. Perhaps he thought the chamber held only baggage and its occupants were dining below. He seemed as surprised to see me as I was by his intrusion," Sebastian said. "He wore a distinctive hat, however. Brown, perhaps, and not fashionable." He gave a labored description.

Sir Edwin chewed that over. He gave Audrianna a sharp look, then paced thoughtfully to the window. The light had transformed from dark gray to silver and it washed his expression of consternation.

Sebastian joined him. Sir Edwin looked out the window and spoke lowly. "Would that be Horatio Kelmsleigh's daughter, sir? No one in England is ignorant of that name. Her presence here raises questions."

"I can see how it might. Ask your questions and I will answer them as a gentleman, to the extent any gentleman would."

"Are you saying there are some questions a gentleman would not answer on the matter?"

Sebastian did not reply. He let his silence speak for him. And damn Audrianna's reputation.

"I am bound by my duty to say the innkeeper here told me that Miss Kelmsleigh fired the shot that caused your wound, sir."

"The innkeeper was not present and cannot speak to the facts. You have my word that there was a third person here, a man, as I said. I will swear to her innocence if you require it. I will attend your quarter sessions and do so, if necessary, but I would prefer to spare her the notoriety of defending herself against such a baseless accusation."

Sir Edwin flushed. To require such a thing of a gentleman who gave his word would be an insult. It dismayed him that Sebastian would even insinuate such a thing had been implied. All the same, he shot another glance over his shoulder at Audrianna's back.

"Odd that she is here, what with your role in that investigation, Lord Sebastian. I would not expect the two of you to have an . . . ongoing acquaintance."

"That oddness does not bear on your duty, does it?"

"No, sir, you are correct. If there was an intruder, it does not. I'll try to keep her name out of this, but if I cannot . . . Perhaps I should say that I think she was here to impart her own information, regarding her father's activities? That might keep some from assuming her presence was for other reasons."

"You can say what you choose, and others will assume what they will, but she did not fire that pistol."

Sir Edwin nodded in agreement. "I think that I understand the circumstances here, sir."

Sebastian checked his pocket watch. "Sir Edwin, the first coach departs in fifteen minutes. Miss Kelmsleigh wants to return to London. I ask that you escort her down and see her off safely, so the curious and vulgar do not importune her with questions."

Sir Edwin drew himself tall and straight. "Certainly. There may be quite a lot of that soon enough, I expect. It would be a kindness to spare her the worst this morning." A new light entered his eyes. A critical one, for the gentleman in front of him who would forever be spared the worst, while Miss Kelmsleigh paid any cost that was assessed for this notorious episode.

Sebastian bore the unspoken criticism. No one would ever believe that meeting her here was the result of a perverse whim of fate. The important thing was that Sir Edwin was not going to hold her over for the quarter sessions, to face an accusation of trying to murder the brother of a marquess.

Sebastian went to her chair. "Miss Kelmsleigh, Sir Edwin is done with us and satisfied. He will escort you to the coach now."

She raised her gaze from where it had remained fixed on her lap. Her stoical expression broke to show her relief. Her green eyes reflected the worry she had been hiding. *I am free?* she mouthed.

He nodded, and offered his hand to help her stand. Her soft palm touched his, resting lightly but still communicating the silent intimacy of the night. Her hand left his when she reached for her mantle.

Sir Edwin picked up the valise and waited at the door. Audrianna joined him there. Before she left, she looked back into the room, and into Sebastian's eyes with an expression that he could not fathom.

Chapter Four

It was close to midnight before the gig that Audrianna hired at the local coaching inn delivered her home.

The house appeared a high, rectangular black block in the gig's lamplight. Audrianna's spirit groaned with relief at the sight of its simple, rustic mass. Nestled away from the road, far enough from London that one could pretend the talk of the town did not exist, this house and the people in it offered the comfort and solace that one finds in a true home with a true family.

She had lived here only half a year, but she knew more contentment inside those walls than in any other place in the world.

The building was dark except for golden light visible through the front sitting room's window. It was too much to hope that Daphne had left a lamp burning and gone to bed. Her cousin would be darning or reading while she waited for the missing member of her odd household to return.

Daphne's role in the house was difficult to describe. Part mother, part hostess, part landlady, she treated the occupants as her sisters. The household rules that she had established required equality among everyone, in all things. However, in truth they were all dependent on her generosity.

Audrianna entered the front sitting room and set her valise on a chair.

Daphne sat near the fireplace, with her extremely pale hair hanging down, already brushed into a river of silk for the night. She wore a primrose-hued undressing gown that flowed around her tall, slender body.

She lifted her gaze from her book. A smile of relief broke on her delicately lovely face. Her gray eyes took in Audrianna's muddy hem and the valise.

"You are tired and probably hungry," she said. "Come to the kitchen and eat something."

It was typical of Daphne not to scold, but also not to hide that she saw enough to have cause to scold if she so chose.

Audrianna followed her cousin through the house and into the short passage that led to the kitchen. Originally a separate structure, the kitchen had been connected to the house by this narrow corridor at the same time that Daphne had the greenhouse expanded.

Only low embers burned in the kitchen's big hearth, and Daphne set about adding some fuel. "Mr. Trotter gave me some money for you when I delivered your new song to him today. Twenty shillings."

Mr. Trotter was a London sheet music publisher who had recently agreed to print a few songs that Audrianna had composed. "That is much more than I expected."

"He said that 'My Inconstant Love' has sold particularly well. He said to tell you that your sad melodies make more money than the others."

"I am not sure that I only want to write sad songs, but I will try to compose a few more."

"I am sure that whatever you write will be successful, if it comes from your heart. 'My Inconstant Love' has sold well because of that."

That was possibly true. Audrianna had composed that song while devastated about Roger's inconstancy, during the week after he threw her over because of Papa's disgrace. Tears had blinded her while she worked out the melody.

Daphne opened a cabinet and examined its contents. "I think that Mrs. Hill plans on the rest of this ham for dinner tomorrow, so we had better not steal that. Let me see what else can be pilfered."

"A bit of cheese and some bread will be enough."

"You are sure? If you have been traveling—"

"I will be fine with bread and cheese."

Daphne served the food, then sat at the worktable across from Audrianna. "Did you go to London to visit your mother?"

"You know that I only visit for meetings arranged in advance, and almost always on Sundays."

"I know nothing, certainly nothing about this adventure of yours. You left no word. No note. If Lizzie had not noticed your valise was gone, I might have thought that you fell into the river."

So, Daphne was going to scold after all. It had been inconsiderate to leave with no word, but that word would have only led to many more words than Audrianna wanted.

"I remind you of your Rule for living in this house,

Daphne. Foremost among its orders is that we do not pry into each other's histories or lives."

This household, composed of single and independent women, maintained civility and safety due to Daphne's Rule. Like the codes of the monks of old, the Rule's precepts governed their behavior and helped them avoid the sort of bickering that could easily arise in such an environment. Upon first coming here, Audrianna had found the Rule a little silly, but she soon came to appreciate its wisdom.

"You are correct. It is a good part of the Rule. An essential part," Daphne said. "However, that does not stop us from wondering about each other, or caring for each other like sisters. Which is why the Rule also includes the instruction that if we are going to be absent for an extended period, we should inform the others of that so they do not worry."

She was not scolding, despite her words. Her voice was far too soft to be called a scold. There was concern in it, and gentle sympathy, and maybe a little hurt too, as if Audrianna's secrecy implied a lack of trust.

Audrianna kept her attention on her supper. She dared not look at Daphne. Her cousin possessed a worldly wisdom that far exceeded what one would expect of a woman not yet thirty years old. Audrianna doubted she could hide her discouragement if Daphne looked right into her eyes.

A white hand reached over and gently touched Audrianna's arm. "Did you visit a man, Audrianna?"

Audrianna had to look over then. Not only did the question astonish her, but also the earnest manner in which Daphne asked it. She spoke as if it would be normal for Audrianna to have spent last night with a man.

Which, to be honest, she had.

She felt her face get hot when she realized that.

"It is not that I want to pry into either your life or the state of your virtue," Daphne said, pretending she had not noticed the blush or dismay. "In fact, I question whether virtue, in this sense, should be as highly regarded as it is. It is just . . ."

"Just what?"

"I know that you still mourn what transpired with Roger, and that you have not conquered that disappointment," she said gently. "If you visited a man, that does not concern me as much as your reason for doing so. I hope that you have not allowed sorrow to make you reckless. Neither happiness nor pleasure will be yours if you embark on an affair out of resentment, pique, or rebellion."

"Please be reassured that I have not embarked on any affair, for any reason. I am grateful for my place in your home, dear cousin. More grateful than you will ever know. I was gone these two days on a personal matter but not one of the heart. I ask that you allow me to leave the explanation at that."

Daphne bowed her head in agreement and retreat. She revealed no insult. Still, Audrianna worried that she had offended her cousin. They normally were of like mind, and this was as close to a contentious conversation as they had ever had.

Audrianna would not mind confiding in Daphne, but tonight she was not sure how to explain, or what to say. She needed a long rest before she sorted out the events and implications of her disastrous journey.

She rose and took her plate to the washbasin. Daphne continued sitting there in pale, lovely serenity.

Audrianna bent and closely embraced her cousin, who as always felt rather cool in a refreshing way. "I will retire now. I will see you in the morning. Thank you for your concern. I apologize that I worried you."

Daphne turned her head and kissed her. "Sleep well, dearest."

Just as Audrianna reached the door, Daphne spoke again.

"Oh, there is one more thing I must say, lest I forget. Audrianna, the pistol that I keep high in the library's cabinet has gone missing. If you come upon it, please let me know at once."

Sebastian winced while he slid into the blue frock coat that his valet held. His upper left arm rebelled at the movement.

A surgeon had arrived at dawn to apply salves and a new dressing. He had announced that the wound appeared uncorrupted. It seemed that the worst consequence would be this current damnable stiffness of the entire limb for a few days more.

He checked his pocket watch to make sure it was ten o'clock, then headed downstairs to his brother Morgan's chambers.

He did not have to make this visit every morning that he was in town, but he did anyway. He knew his brother looked forward to everything about their hour together. To the silent companionship while they drank coffee and read the newspapers and mail. To the discussions about the gossip and strategies occupying the government. To the respite of being normal, in a day when there would be too many reminders that very little remained the way it was supposed to be.

Dr. Fenwood came out to the front sitting room just as Sebastian entered it. Fenwood was not really a doctor, but instead a manservant of significant strength and appropriate circumspection. Morgan had first called him Dr. Fenwood as a joke, but had never stopped.

Now everyone called him Dr. Fenwood, so that Morgan could maintain the small pretense that the person who helped him in appallingly intimate ways was a medical professional. There were a lot of illusions like that in this house, as everyone tried to preserve a good man's dignity.

"The marquess's health is fine this morning," Fenwood said. The title had gone to his head a bit, and he offered his opinion as if he knew the difference between fine and not fine. "My lord's disposition is good too."

That was the information that Sebastian really wanted. His brother often succumbed to bouts of melancholy. The real physicians had warned from the start that this was often common with invalids.

He entered the chamber that served as a small drawing room in the master's extensive apartment. His brother did not hear the door open, and continued reading his mail. There was quite a stack of it. Society still sent invitations, knowing they would never be accepted. And Morgan, third Marquess of Wittonbury, read every one, as if he might choose to attend a few dinner parties.

Morgan's chair abutted a window, through which he could look down on the town. Both the table and a dark blanket obscured any view of the lifeless legs that had kept him a prisoner of these rooms ever since he was carried home from a war that he had joined nobly, idealistically, belatedly, and impulsively.

That Morgan had bought that commission so late in the war always struck Sebastian as an impossible irony. One might wonder if the French retreat in the Peninsular campaign had been timed just so fate could ruin Morgan's life.

Sebastian took his place in a chair that faced his brother and poured some coffee from the waiting pot. No servants or footmen hovered to intrude upon this daily hour that they shared.

Morgan looked up from his letter. "I am glad to see that you are back."

"I was unexpectedly delayed by the rain yesterday." Normally if he were going to miss these morning visits, he let Morgan know. Yesterday, that had not been possible, of course.

Sebastian did not mind this demand on his time. He had created it himself, by starting the habit and allowing his brother to depend on it. Morgan had so few visitors now that the company of family was all that broke up the day for him.

And yet, as Sebastian made his explanation for yesterday's absence, he did not miss how his own life had changed along with his brother's. The paralysis that kept Morgan in these chambers, living a tragically altered life, had radically changed Sebastian's fate too.

"I was down near Brighton," Sebastian said. "I was looking into something related to that ordnance matter."

"It might have just been negligence, like everyone thinks."

"You don't believe that."

"No." Morgan looked out the window, but his sight really turned inward. To the memories of war, Sebastian suspected.

Morgan had followed that ordnance scandal closely, shaking his head over the newspaper reports of a company left defenseless by bad gunpowder. The Marquess of Wittonbury wanted those dead soldiers to have justice, and Sebastian wanted his brother to know the satisfaction that his comrades in arms had finally been vindicated.

"Did you learn anything?"

"I may have discovered a man who knows something. It may turn up information that dislodges the truth in the end. Finally."

Morgan nodded absently. He picked up one of the neatly ironed newspapers waiting for his attention.

Sebastian did the same. These visits had become routine. Ritualized.

"Our mother visited yesterday afternoon," Morgan said while he perused the paper. "She wanted to talk about you."

Now, that was *not* routine. "Did she now?"

"Mmmm. She wants me to tell you that you must marry. She has picked out several girls who are suitable."

"I am sure *she* thinks they are."

"I told her that she should not fool herself that you have changed that much. I suggested that what she sees as a new leaf is merely foliage rearranged to obscure the old bark. Discretion is not the same as repentance or reform."

"Thank you."

"She became very determined and imperious—well, you know how she can be."

"Is she visiting you often these days?"

Morgan shrugged. "More than before."

"Too much, then. Tell Fenwood that you are not receiving when she comes next time. Do not allow her to make this apartment hers to enter as she chooses."

There had always been the danger that their mother would turn Morgan back into a child if given half the chance. She would intrude and coddle and dominate until he lost his right to be a separate man.

That was why Sebastian had moved back into this house upon his brother's return from war. His presence ensured that their mother could not expand her rule too much, especially when it came to her older son.

"You were always better at managing her than I was. Like so much else," Morgan said.

There was nothing to say to that, so they both returned their attention to their papers.

"You said you were down near Brighton yesterday? Did you hear anything about this spectacle at the Two Swords?"

"Spectacle?"

Morgan peered at the print in front of him. A grin broke. "Some fellow's lover shot him. Now that must have been good theater. Not dead, it seems. Still, it must have been all the talk down there."

"What are you reading there?"

Morgan flushed. "One of our mother's scandal sheets."

"From Brighton?"

"London."

Damn. Sir Edwin had been correct. The gossip had probably arrived in town before either of its victims. Evidently, no names were in that scandal sheet, however.

Yet.

T he ritual ended at eleven o'clock. Sebastian took his leave and returned to his own chambers. His valet greeted him with a sealed letter in his hand.

"The directions were not accurate, sir."

Sebastian took the letter. He had written it to Miss Kelmsleigh and sent it by messenger to her father's home. "Do they no longer live there?"

"Mrs. Kelmsleigh does, and Miss Sarah Kelmsleigh. However, Audrianna Kelmsleigh does not. The footman inquired and was told that she has taken residence in Middlesex near the village of Cumberworth."

Sebastian carried the letter into his dressing room. He opened a drawer and gazed at the pistol that he had carried away from the Two Swords. His attempt to initiate arrangements to return it discreetly had been for naught.

He could send the footman to Cumberworth. If Miss Kelmsleigh had been rusticated there, a few queries should locate her. He could pack up the pistol and give it to the footman too, and be done with this.

He saw that pistol in a soft, feminine hand. He saw a woman's green eyes flashing spirit, then sparking with fascination and passion, and finally dulled by melancholy. He pictured her walking through the inn to the coach, pretending not to notice how the other patrons stared and whispered.

He told his valet to call for his horse.

Chapter Five

Cumberworth remained a country village, but London moved closer every year. It had already been absorbed into the environs of the city, one of many small Middlesex hamlets that saw newcomers mix with old residents, and land developers carve farms into small estates for the prosperous families of its larger neighbor.

Sebastian's arrival therefore did not raise much notice. He rode down the main lane, past shops in old, half-timbered buildings and stone homes lined shoulder to shoulder. He looked for a tavern.

The Baron's Board was not busy at two o'clock, and Sebastian received his ale quickly. He stood while he drank, and submitted to the proprietor's curious inspection.

"Weather this damp in town?" the man asked while he wiped some pint mugs.

"Worse," Sebastian said.

"You be on your way to someplace drier?"

"No, I came here looking for someone on a matter of business. Perhaps you know her. Miss Kelmsleigh."

The proprietor chuckled. "I know her, and her friends. Everyone in Cumberworth knows Mrs. Joyes's houseguests."

"Do they now? I believe Miss Kelmsleigh is a cousin, not a houseguest."

"Hard to know what to call those women, now isn't it? The rest aren't relatives, I don't think. Just a collection of females who came to visit and never left."

"Does Mrs. Joyes live in the village?"

"She has property outside of it a short ways. Nice house and a good bit of land. She grows flowers there in a big conservatory. She sells them in London to fancy flower shops. Her house is back off the road some, so right where you have to turn off, she has a painted sign. The Rarest Blooms, she calls her trade." He chuckled again. "Nice enough women. Keep to themselves mostly. No reason to think anything disreputable is about them, but people will talk, won't they?"

Undoubtedly. Sebastian finished his ale and asked for directions to this sign of The Rarest Blooms.

Fifteen minutes later he turned down the private lane that took him to Mrs. Joyes's house.

It was the sort of good, solid home that could be found all over England. Handsome in its smoothly dressed gray stone, it was too big to be called a cottage and too small to be called a manor. It rose two levels high beneath its steeply pitched attics, with only carefully proportioned windows decorating its plain facade.

No groom appeared to take his horse, so Sebastian tied the reins to a post. The time he waited after his knock on the door suggested that few servants worked here, despite the way the property insinuated good fortune.

Eventually the door opened. A very thin housekeeper

of middling years peered at him from beneath her cap's ruffle. She read his card and peered again. Her gaze lingered on the oblong wooden box under his arm.

"I am told that Miss Kelmsleigh lives here," he said. "I have come to return something that she lost."

A pretty blond girl stepped into view. She also read the card. "I will take care of this, Mrs. Hill."

The older woman slipped away. The blond girl bid him to enter. "You should speak with Mrs. Joyes," she said. "She owns this house. She is in the greenhouse. I will take you to her."

She ambled off, leading him to the back of the house. They passed a library with handsome cases and many upholstered chairs. A second sitting room occupied the rear of the house. He could see a conservatory through one of its windows.

Situated twenty yards behind the house, the conservatory was much larger than the ones normally found at country homes unless they were very large estates. Glass formed the upper half of all the walls in a mosaic of rectangular panes held together with iron.

Entry to the conservatory came at the end of a corridor that gave off from the sitting room. His guide opened a door and humid warmth flowed over him. He looked up. Half of the pitched roof consisted of small panes of glass too.

"Wait here, please." She disappeared around a huge potted palm. A few moments later she stepped back into view and gestured for him. She pointed him toward Mrs. Joyes, then took her leave.

Mrs. Joyes worked at a table covered with soil-filled pots. The same soil spotted her apron, hands, and cap. As he approached, she lifted a rag to clean off the worst of it.

She had a beautiful face. Very pale. Very perfect. Dark gray eyes. She possessed a natural elegance that even affected the way she stood. If he had never seen her before, he might have struck him dumb. Except he had seen her before. He was sure of it.

"Lord Sebastian Summerhays, we are honored. We do not often have such illustrious guests. Are you seeking a special flower as a gift for a loved one? We have rare pelagoriums of our own hybridization that are always appreciated."

"I am seeking a woman who I am told lives here. Miss Kelmsleigh." He nodded to the box he carried. "I must return something of hers."

"Miss Kelmsleigh is not at home. I expect her to return very shortly, if you would like to wait. Or you can leave the box with me."

Well, there it was. He could set the box down and walk out. There was no reason not to trust Mrs. Joyes to give it over when Miss Kelmsleigh returned. If he required she not open it, she most likely would swallow her curiosity.

"If you expect her soon, I should give it to her personally."

"I will send word that she come here as soon as she returns, then." She turned her head. "Lizzie, would you— Now, where has she gone? She was here just before Celia brought you in, and even read your card . . ." She clucked her tongue and displayed exasperation. "Please wait here, Lord Sebastian, while I personally tell the others to send Miss Kelmsleigh to us."

She left him amid the greenery. The air carried a lush scent that contained a bit of everything within its moist density. Citrus and roses and even the clean hint of grass. A person could get drunk on such perfume. He poked at the soil in one pot that Mrs. Joyes had been working. His finger touched the mass of a bulb.

He ambled down the aisle, past several potted lemon trees and tables of blooming flowers. At the end of the building a grape vine grew inside the glass. It was rooted outside, but its thick core entered through a low hole in the brick wall. Its various tendrils wove up sturdy supports, then rambled across iron bars two feet above his head. A stone table and four chairs sat under this leafy indoor arbor, creating a Tuscan vignette.

"That was an experiment," Mrs. Joyes said as she rejoined him. "The grape vine. I did not think it would work."

"It must be pleasant to sit at this table on sunny days in winter. You have a remarkable conservatory here."

"It is a greenhouse. Most of what people call conservatories are really greenhouses or forcing houses. I suppose that does not sound fancy enough so the wrong word has become common. A real conservatory does just that, conserve plants over winter while they are dormant. We have one of those too, at the back of the garden."

Her face arrested his attention again. "Please excuse me, but I believe I have been unintentionally rude. We have met before, I am sure, but I cannot remember where."

"We have indeed met, years ago. I was a governess for the family of the Duke of Becksbridge. You and I were introduced at a garden party which I was allowed to attend with the eldest of my charges. You have an excellent memory for the insignificant people whose paths you cross in life, Lord Sebastian."

If she were indeed insignificant, he might deserve the praise, but he doubted any man forgot meeting her. "There were other parties where the children were present. I do not recall you at those."

"I was only with them one year before I met Captain Joyes and left my situation."

There had been no talk in the town of any man at this house. "Is your husband in the naval service?"

"He was in the army. He died in the Peninsular War." The question did not alter her graceful manner, but her eyes darkened enough to suggest the subject still brought her sorrow. "If you will excuse me again, I will go and see what is keeping Audrianna. She should have returned by now."

Audrianna stared at the card Daphne had left with Celia. Lord Sebastian Summerhays was here.

Why? And how had he even found her?

The answer came to her within an instant of the question. He must have gone to her mother's house first. Mama would be writing to her soon, wanting to know what had provoked her father's persecutor to notice them again.

"Sit, please, Audrianna. I can barely reach even standing on my toes," Celia said.

Audrianna sank into a chair so Celia could fuss with her hair. Celia was the best among them with dressing hair. She presented her own blond locks in an endless variety of styles.

"She did say right away." Audrianna reminded Celia of the message she herself had given upon Audrianna's return to the house.

"Daphne is not going to object if you take a minute to set yourself to rights," Celia said while her hands deftly worked their magic. "That is the brother of a marquess in the greenhouse. An MP too. That is right on his card."

Since Celia did not know that Lord Sebastian was no stranger to her, Audrianna decided that silence was the best response.

"He is of great consequence and his name is in the newspapers all the time. You can't receive him looking as if you stood on a ship's deck all afternoon."

Audrianna did not want to receive him at all. She prayed he had not brought bad news about that justice of the peace. What if Sir Edwin had decided that she needed to stand at the quarter sessions after all?

"It is the best I can do, unless I take it all down. It is your own fault for removing your bonnet as you walked home," Celia said, stepping back. "We should start all over and fix it properly."

"You will do no such thing," Daphne's voice responded.

Audrianna looked up. Daphne stood at the door of the sitting room, the one that opened on the corridor that led to the greenhouse. She still wore her soiled work apron and her oldest cap, but she appeared ethereal and stunning. Daphne could wear rags and look beautiful.

"You must come with me at once, Audrianna. He is determined to see you," Daphne said.

"Did he say why he is here?"

"He only said that he has brought you something that you lost."

"I have lost nothing."

"It is in an oblong box. Like a glove box. A rather large glove box."

The pistol!

Audrianna felt her face flush. Daphne leveled those gray eyes on her.

"How would Lord Sebastian Summerhays even come

upon something of yours?" Celia's sweet face puckered with a frown as she suddenly recognized the oddity of this caller.

"I have no idea," Audrianna mumbled.

Daphne remained serene. "Has anyone seen Lizzie?"

"She was here just a few minutes ago," Celia said.

"She has a talent for disappearing when it is least helpful. Come along, Audrianna. Your gentleman waits."

"He is not my gentleman," Audrianna said as they marched down the corridor.

Daphne's eyelids lowered a tiny, eloquent fraction.

Daphne paused partway down the aisle that ran between the two rows of tables that held armies of pelagoriums, forced lilies, and hyacinths. Audrianna was only too happy to take a moment to collect herself.

From their vantage point they could see Lord Sebastian. He sat in one of the chairs at the stone table, beneath the grape arbor. His handsome profile faced them while he gazed at something on the other side of the greenhouse. Relaxed and confident, he proved as remarkable a presence in this interior garden as he had in that rustic coaching inn.

"He does not appear angry or displeased. He presents himself in the most amiable manner. And yet one can tell that he is not a man to trifle with," Daphne said quietly.

"I have not trifled with him."

"That goes without saying. You have no experience at trifling. He, on the other hand, is a master of it."

"Do you know him?"

"I know of him, and we met once, long ago. He condescended to remember that. It is said he is much changed these last few years. I wonder if that is true." Her considerations over for now, Daphne escorted Audrianna to their visitor.

Lord Sebastian stood as they approached. Daphne introduced Audrianna, then eased away. "I must finish the bulbs while there is still good light," she said.

Audrianna waited until Daphne disappeared. She would not be far away, however. She would be able to hear everything except the quietest conversation.

Audrianna pointed to the wooden box on the table. "Is that it?"

Lord Sebastian picked up on her low tone of voice and her circumspection. "Yes."

"Thank you for returning it. It belongs to Daphne and she noticed it missing. I expect I will now have to explain that I borrowed it, but it will be easier to do so if I have it back."

He rested his fingertips on the top of the box. "She does not know about your adventure?"

"I hoped to spare her the details."

"Better that the details are yours and not someone else's."

"Yes, I should tell her everything. I think that she already guesses part of it."

"Which part?"

"The part about you."

He glanced in the direction where Daphne invisibly worked on the bulbs. "There appears to be an attractive garden outside. It looks to be sheltered from the wind, and the sun is warm. Will you show it to me, Miss Kelmsleigh?"

Sebastian fell into step beside Miss Kelmsleigh as they strolled into the garden.

"Did you go to my mother's house first?" she asked.

"I sent a messenger with a letter. I doubt that your mother knows the letter came from me, and it never left the messenger's hand in any case."

It appeared to please her that her mother did not know Lord Sebastian Summerhays had been looking for her. Of course it would. Not only had he been one of her father's enemies, but his reputation with women was not one that any mother would like.

"Have you lived here long, Miss Kelmsleigh?"

"Only six months. Daphne is my cousin. She wrote to me after my father died, offering me a place to live. She guessed I might want to leave London. It was very kind of her. Much kinder than we had been when she found herself in need of a home when she was younger."

"It is a handsome property. Do you help growing flowers?"

"We all help when we can, but mostly Daphne and Lizzie tend the flowers. I give music lessons to contribute to my keep. That is where I was when you arrived. Up the road, teaching a young girl the pianoforte."

They strolled an informal garden, now fallow except for boxwood hedges and ivy that obscured most of the surrounding brick wall. The paths meandered through beds and around barren fruit trees. He pictured pastels in spring and a riot of color in late summer, and Miss Kelmsleigh and Mrs. Joyes sitting in the little arbor now covered by a naked rose vine.

Miss Kelmsleigh trod on with grace, her low boots crunching the twigs and dead leaves. She politely allowed him to tour the garden, but she made no effort to converse. A slight purse played at her lips, reminding him of his mother's mouth when unwelcome calls had to be tolerated owing to the caller's consequence.

In this raking light her maturity was more obvious than in firelight or dawn's soft glow. Middle twenties, he was sure now. Late to be unmarried. Perhaps she had lost her intended in the war, like too many women her age.

"I brought the pistol personally for a reason," he said, feeling obligated to excuse his intrusion. "I wanted to warn you that the first sign of bad gossip has occurred. There was a mention in a scandal sheet this morning."

She paused and stomped her little foot in frustrated anger. Her face grimaced with worry. *"Already?"*

"Only the coaching inn gossip. No names. It may come to nothing."

"Or it may get much worse, with names named, or alluded to in ways that everyone knows who it is. How soon will we know which way it will be?"

"These things have a common pattern. In four days or so it will either die away, or be much more public. If the latter happens, I will send you a warning and, of course, do what is necessary to protect your reputation as much as possible."

"Mama will be certain to tell me first, Lord Sebastian. If she is embroiled in more scandal, I will never be able to apologize enough to her. And she will be too good to scold that my mission, although noble, was foolhardy."

She had completely missed his reference to protecting her. Of course she would. She hated him for his role in her father's disgrace. She would never speculate on what might be necessary, let alone agree to it. She would think social damnation preferable to accepting his protection, no doubt.

"Foolhardy, yes. Also ill-advised, dangerous, and as it turned out, disastrous. Also—"

"There is no need to go through the entire dictionary. I have upbraided myself plenty, and do not need scolds from *you.*"

"*Also* brave. It is admirable that you wanted to be a champion for his name, mistaken though your faith may be."

She glanced askance at him, frowning with suspicion. She no doubt thought that he was flattering her to his own ends again.

He probably was. He hadn't decided yet.

"I have been thinking about the Domino," she said. Mention of her father had opened a topic that made his presence tolerable, although it was the last one he would have chosen. "In my mind, I study what I remember of his appearance. He had red hair, I am almost positive. Also, I am wondering if he was a foreigner."

Their path turned around the corner of a simple stone structure with large windows on all its walls. This was the true conservatory that Mrs. Joyes had mentioned, he guessed. They entered a little wilderness that flourished along its side, in the garden's back corner.

"Why do you think he might be foreign?"

"His hat was odd. Soft and deeper brimmed than seen here. Perhaps his coat was odd too. The cut of it. The weight." She shrugged. "I cannot explain it, but he just did not look English."

"You may be correct."

"It would make it easier to find him if I am. There are far fewer foreigners in England than Englishmen."

"Unfortunately, men do not wear colored feathers in their hats proclaiming which they are."

"The foreigners congregate in certain places in London, though. Certain inns and taverns. Lizzie—she is another member of our household—she says that there are hotels preferred by foreigners too. If I were to visit the places such a man might be, I could—"

He stepped ahead of her and stopped walking, requiring her to stop as well. "You must not do that. It would be unsafe."

Her drawn expression made it clear what she thought of his command. "I will be perfectly safe. I will bring someone with me this time. And of course, I now have the pistol again."

He could not tell if she was teasing him or if she truly intended to repeat such recklessness. "I shall instruct Mrs. Joyes to lock it away. A weapon only increases your danger. The next time you point a pistol at a man, he may not be a gentleman about it."

"Now, that is a warning worth the words, Lord Sebastian, since you know so well of what you speak."

Her mocking eyes arrested him. And the slight curve of her mouth. And her familiar manner, which revived memories of the intimacy that they had shared in that inn.

"You refer to that kiss," he said, remembering it more distinctly than was wise. Arousal awoke, in a slowly tightening coil. "I am supposed to apologize now, even though you behaved in ways that begged for misunderstanding."

"I did not *beg* for misunderstanding. I did *nothing* to encourage you to be a scoundrel."

"You did little to stop it either. And your mere presence there alone excused my misunderstanding. However . . ." He made a little bow. "Miss Kelmsleigh, my sincere apologies for my forwardness the other evening. A lady should not have to suffer such inexcusable behavior. Please forgive me."

Her hands went to her hips. "You astonish me. It is

beyond the pale that you came here to insult me further with such ridicule."

"I came to return a pistol that you aimed directly at me, fully loaded and hammer fully cocked," he reminded her.

That checked her gathering ire. Her soft, pale cheeks flushed prettily, the way they would if she had been walking in the cold. Or suffering a kiss that she did not mind too much.

"That was wrong of me. It is true that apologies are due on my part as well. I admit that I must share the blame for almost everything that happened during our peculiar meeting together."

He smiled his best smile. "I insist that you place all the blame on me. Remember the events in any way that you choose, and I will not correct them. However, do not demand that I lie to myself, even if propriety demands that you lie to yourself."

Anger flashed again. She had a quick little temper, apparently. "I do not lie, sir. Not even to myself."

"I think that you are talking yourself into believing a lie. You are convincing yourself that you did not enjoy that kiss, and that I importuned far more than I did. I, on the other hand, freely admit that I am not sorry for it, except that my distraction got me shot."

She studied him with a gaze that reflected perplexity and astonishment and a touch of fear. The last reaction was for all the best reasons, although she probably did not realize that yet.

"My cousin said that you were infamous for trifling with women not long ago, Lord Sebastian. Preposterous though I find the notion, it appears that you are flirting with me now."

He looked past her, in a vain attempt to thwart the

compelling heat rising in him. He surveyed the far end of the garden. Only the corner of the house could be seen. The conservatory blocked the view of the greenhouse completely. The confirmation that they were out of sight of all the house's occupants hardly helped matters.

"Perhaps I am flirting, Miss Kelmsleigh. Old habits die hard."

She laughed. "I hope that in the past you did not flirt with such little hope of impressing a woman. If I was a little . . . distracted at the Two Swords, that does not signify now, so you use that smile of yours to no effect. Please remember that I did not know who you were when you importuned me."

He turned his attention back on her. On the way the breeze plucked at the tendrils of her hair, and the way those green eyes carried the memories of that night. The cool light in this little woods gave her skin a snowy cast.

"And now you do know who I am, Miss Kelmsleigh. And I know who you are. It is odd, don't you think, how little difference that makes?"

It made almost no difference, from the way she reacted. Not nearly as much difference as it should. She tried to maintain a pose of sophisticated indifference, but she was unpracticed in dissembling in such situations.

"It makes all the difference, for reasons that should be plain to you." Her words faltered, and carried a tremor.

"Does it? I sense not."

"A rock would be more moved by your flattery and flirting. I could *never* be distracted by you now."

"Really?" He stepped closer, even though he knew damned well he shouldn't. "Never? Not at all?"

Her eyes widened in charming, innocent shock. She pivoted abruptly, to bolt. He could not permit that now.

He caught her arm and twirled her into his embrace.

He intended a brief kiss, to prove his point. Nothing more. That was what he told himself at least.

She did not resist or fight. She merely stiffened for an instant of surprise, then softened under the kiss. Her body reacted as if the warmth of his arms banished a deep chill.

Soft lips. Tentative and curious and artless. He did not require that she kiss him back. Everything he needed to know was spoken by her breaths and heartbeat and pliant acceptance.

The kiss was not brief. One became two, then three. Desire's compulsion took hold and only her innocence checked him. With another kind of woman, the usual kind, he would not have bothered with seduction, but it pleased him to tease her with lures and little pleasures, and note her astonished delight when his restrained caress moved over her back and sides.

Hotter now. Flames. Images of the possibilities. Arguments for more. A war between body and mind such as he had not fought in years occurred, except there was no real contest in such things.

His embrace encompassed her completely until her breasts and stomach pressed him and her tremors echoed into him. He closed his mouth on her neck's pulse and listened to her bated gasps of pleasure. Their sounds sent him on a ruthless, determined climb toward satisfaction.

He held her head so he could ravish her mouth, forgetting she was so innocent. Shock tensed through her before she submitted to the intimacy, but submit she did. Mindless now, picturing her naked above him, straddling him and releasing the cries that she now tried to swallow, he caressed more boldly until his hand smoothed over the softness of her breast.

A cry escaped her then, a wondrous sound of female pleasure. Then another and another as he teased her hard nipple through the thin fabric of her garments.

She was with him in the delirium now, bracing herself against him for balance, arching her back to encourage him. Scattered thoughts tried to form. He needed to take her away from here and find a place, anywhere, so they could have each other. He needed to—

A howling, scorching pain suddenly blackened his mind. Then he saw red and a curse erupted out of him.

His head and sight half-cleared. His upper left arm felt as if on fire. Miss Kelmsleigh stood five feet away, her hands covering her mouth in a portrait of horrified dismay.

"I am sorry! I did not mean to hurt your arm," she said desperately in a low rush. "When I heard the door, I just pushed to get free and . . ." She looked toward the garden fretfully. Feminine laughs and talk rode on the breeze toward them.

Another pain joined the one in his arm. A much lower pain. "No matter. It is nothing."

"Are you sure? You appear very pale."

Undoubtedly. His body was giving him hell. She worried while he composed himself. It took a long minute.

She calmed as she saw his progress. "It would have been horrible to be seen by Daphne and Celia like . . . like we were. I am sure that you understand. They burst from the house quite unexpectedly. Normally they do not leave the house at this hour, but work in the greenhouse."

He imagined a very pale woman treating herself to a turn in the sunlight. He would have to remember to express his gratitude to Mrs. Joyes someday.

"We really should not have— It was very bad of you

to . . ." Miss Kelmsleigh's dismay had given way to a scold. He truly did not want to hear one right now.

"Of course we should have," he growled. "We wanted to, so we should have, so we did. And stop pretending that I am forcing you to kiss me."

If slowly ebbing pain did not preoccupy him, he would have been less blunt. As it was, he only encouraged Miss Kelmsleigh to see matters in the worst light.

She strode up the path toward the house. "I see that you are as cruel as I thought. Your goal is to humiliate me, to what purpose I do not know."

He trailed her and barely resisted grabbing her again, to prove he was right. "I succumbed to an impulse, and to the lure of a very pleasant memory. And the goal, in case you did not notice, was mutual pleasure. However, you are correct. I should not have, so I must apologize again."

"For all the good that seems to do!" They emerged at the garden's edge, near the corner of the conservatory. Two bonnets on two women stayed turned away, as if ignorant that he and Miss Kelmsleigh were even in the county, let alone nearby.

Miss Kelmsleigh pointed to the far corner of the garden wall. "I do not want an apology, Lord Sebastian. I only want you to leave. There is a garden portal over there. You do not have to go back through the house."

"Certainly. Good day to you, and thank you."

"Thank me?"

"For the tour of the garden. For your hospitality."

He bowed. She glared. He smiled. She blushed. He looked in her eyes.

She turned and ran away, toward the greenhouse.

Chapter Six

"I must leave early today," Sebastian said. "I have an appointment with Castleford in the City."

"Duty always comes first, of course," Morgan said. "I am glad to see that you are able to negotiate with Castleford. I fear that I was never able to hide my dislike of the man and his notorious behavior. That is why you have proven effective in government so quickly. You have an ability to treat with scoundrels such that they do not perceive your disdain."

"Perhaps that is because they believe I am a scoundrel too, and do not hold them in disdain. Maybe they think we are fellow travelers."

"Nonsense. Your wilder past was the norm for young men. You never did anything truly dishonorable. Not like him."

Sebastian was not going to argue about his own character, least of all to convince Morgan it had more blemishes than Morgan knew. The truth was that the Duke of Castleford did see a fellow traveler when he spoke to Sebastian, because in the past they had trod the wilder paths side by side.

Now their association, for all its amicable appearance and practical usefulness, was that of two fighters facing off, pacing around and looking for the weakness in the other. Castleford found it inconvenient that Sebastian had taken Morgan's place in public life. When Morgan had faced a political fight, he retreated.

"Kennington and Symes-Wilvert are coming by anyway, so you won't be missed," Morgan said. "My morning will be busy."

"I will leave now, then."

Sebastian's valet waited outside Morgan's apartment bearing hat and gloves. Set for the day, Sebastian headed down to the street.

Percival Kennington and Bernard Symes-Wilvert entered the house just as Sebastian was leaving. Both second sons of barons, they had been Morgan's friends since their early school days. They visited at least once a week, always together like this, always in the morning because Morgan tired by afternoon. Both blond and ruddy and battling corpulence, they could have been brothers despite their disparate sizes. Kennington was the big pea to Symes-Wilvert's small one in the pod they shared.

Sebastian had never found either man interesting, but he had grown fond of them in the last year for their devotion to their old friend.

"Are you leaving, Summerhays?" Kennington said. "We had hoped to cajole you into a game of cards."

"I regret I will have to decline today." Relief tempered by guilt struck its discomforting note in him. Those whist sessions usually stretched into tedium. Kennington and

Symes-Wilvert would pick over old social gossip, or quiz Sebastian on government doings, and he would dodge questions that were none of their business. Morgan would bask in the rare pleasure of having friends around.

"We will go up, then," Kennington said. "Perhaps we will still be here when you return."

"I will be sure to check. Yes, please go up. He is waiting for you."

Morgan's visitors aimed for the staircase. Sebastian aimed for his horse. His meeting with Castleford was not for over an hour, and he had somewhere else to go first.

"If we stay here much longer, all the inhabitants of that hotel are going to misunderstand the reason," Celia said.

"What do you mean?" Audrianna asked.

Celia rolled her eyes. "Two young women, displaying themselves to every traveler looking out those windows? Think about it."

It only took a moment to comprehend. "That is a disgraceful prejudice on their part."

On the other hand, they had stood across Jermyn Street from Miller's Hotel for only ten minutes, and already she felt conspicuous.

"What is your purpose in coming here at all?" Celia asked. "If I had known that you intended to hold a vigil outside a hotel, I would have never accompanied you into town in the first place."

"I hope to see the man who intruded at that inn." Audrianna had given a very brief version of the events at the Two Swords to the household. There was no other way to explain Lord Sebastian's visit, or to be honest with

Daphne about that pistol. "The Domino was a foreigner, I think. I am told they often stay at this hotel. I had hoped . . ." What had she hoped? That if she stared at the façade of Miller's Hotel long enough, the Domino would just appear?

Something like that, she admitted to herself. She had hoped for a miracle.

"Let us walk on," Celia urged.

Just then a man emerged from the hotel. His appearance arrested Audrianna's attention. His hat reminded her of the Domino's, with its low crown and soft brim. She peered hard at him as he walked along the other side of the street.

He did not have red hair, but she could have been wrong about that, what with the firelight. Only he looked too tall as well. Even the way he moved—

"Oh, my," Celia muttered under her breath. "Now this is an interesting coincidence."

Audrianna turned her attention in the direction of Celia's gaze. Lord Sebastian Summerhays was riding down the street.

"Let us go." She pivoted and dragged Celia in the opposite direction.

"It is very rude not to greet him," Celia said. "I am sure that he saw you."

"I do not want to speak to him. Hurry along now."

"You are blushing badly, Audrianna." Celia swallowed a giggle. "What happened when he visited? Is there more to this story than you have told us?"

"Nothing happened," Audrianna said. "He was rude and I—"

"Miss Kelmsleigh? Ah, yes, so it is. I thought that I recognized the mantle." The voice, very close, stopped Audrianna in her tracks.

She turned to see a superior leather boot flanking a very large black horse. She raised her gaze to the face looking down at her. Lord Sebastian had removed his hat in greeting. He sat there like a conqueror surveying the spoils of war.

"Lord Sebastian, what an unexpected encounter." Audrianna had intended never to see him again. She felt her face warm. Memories of those caresses in the garden poured into her head. She introduced Celia.

"Are you strolling about town for exercise, or have you come for business?" he asked.

"A bit of both."

He gazed around. His sight rested on the hotel. "It is interesting that your stroll brought you to this street. Were you intending, by chance, to inquire at that hotel for our friend?"

"Why would I do that?"

"It is frequented by foreign merchants. You told me of a plan to seek out such places in order to locate him. You are sure that you are not here for that reason?"

"Not at all."

He swung off his horse. "Well, I am."

"You stole my idea!"

"It is an idea better executed by a man. I am pleased that you have learned your lesson and were not going to do something foolish. If you had come here today to pursue some investigation, I might have to punish you for disobeying me." He made a little bow, and began leading his horse back toward the hotel.

Celia watched him walk away. "He addresses you most boldly. Does Daphne know—?"

Audrianna marched after Summerhays, ignoring Celia's questions.

"What are you doing?" Celia demanded, catching up.

"I am going to learn whatever he does."

Lord Sebastian noticed her while he tied his reins to a post. He smiled that damned smile of his. Audrianna pretended it had absolutely no effect on her. Celia's expression melted in awe.

"If you are going to stand here and see who enters and leaves, I should be with you," Audrianna said. "After all, I am the one who had a good look at him."

"Only because I was distracted." Warmth in his eyes demanded that she remember how and why he had been distracted. "I do not intend to stand here. That would be inefficient. I am going inside to speak with the owner and servants, to learn if anyone fitting your description is staying here."

"I could have done that."

"You would have never received a reply. I will."

He walked to the hotel. Audrianna followed, pulling Celia along.

Lord Sebastian stopped at the door. "I will tell you what I learn."

"I will hear it myself, thank you."

"I give my word that I will keep nothing from you."

"Your beliefs and mine are not the same. Our goals diverge in every way."

"That is not true. I want the truth."

"No, you want to be proven right. I think that you will hear what you want to hear, to that end, so I must trust only myself in learning the truth."

Not pleased, he held the door so she and Celia could enter.

The mission might not be better executed by just any man, but it was clear that this particular man could get results. His card produced a flurry of fuss aimed at ingratiating the servants of the hotel with this member of society.

"Red hair, you say," the proprietor mused upon hearing the vague description of their quarry. "Mr. van Aelst does not have red hair, although he wears a hat much as you describe. Unsightly thing, if you ask me. He just left the premises, or I would find an excuse to speak with him so you could have a good look."

"He is not the man we seek, I am certain," Audrianna said. "However, from what country does Mr. van Aelst hail?"

"The Netherlands. Amsterdam."

"Do you have any other guests from Amsterdam?" Lord Sebastian asked.

"Not at the moment, no."

"Have you had any recently? The last week or so?"

The manager shook his head.

There was nothing more to learn. Out in the street again, Audrianna prepared to take her leave. "It was a small bit of information, but something all the same. The Domino may be from the Netherlands."

"Or not," Lord Sebastian said. "Can I trust that you will not spend the afternoon quizzing every servant in every hotel and inn on the matter? You will not be well received, or successful, if you do."

"You can trust nothing because I give no promises. I do not expect any acknowledgment from you that I, having seen Mr. van Aelst, was able to cross him off the list, while you would never be able to do so. Good day, Lord Sebastian."

After parting from Lord Sebastian, Audrianna and Celia completed their business in town. They visited two flower shops in Mayfair to remind the proprietors that certain debts were in arrears to The Rarest Blooms. Normally Daphne did this duty herself, but she had remained in Cumberworth to keep a private appointment.

They then walked down Albemarle Street, toward Mr. Trotter's shop. Audrianna had completed a new song. She hoped Mr. Trotter would agree to publish it

"Did he kiss you?" Celia asked. "Lord Sebastian. Did he?"

"What an extraordinary question, Celia."

"Did he?"

"Remember Daphne's Rule. We do not pry into—"

"He did. I knew it. I can always tell."

"I doubt you can always tell."

"If you were more worldly, perhaps I could not, but you are an innocent in these matters, so I can."

"Oh, and you are so worldly yourself," Audrianna teased.

"More than you."

Something about Celia right then did look very worldly. A veil of maturity fell over her face, evoked by . . . what? A memory? A loss?

"He wants you," Celia said. "It is in his eyes when he looks at you. Surely you can see it."

"I am not sure what I see." Nothing good, though. Enough to frighten her. And excite her. And considering who he was to her family, dismay her. "What he wants does not signify anyway."

Mr. Trotter's sign came into view. It dangled on high down the street, displaying two crossed flutes over a scroll inscribed with musical notes.

"Lord Sebastian was a rake not long ago," Celia said. "Not the worst one. Not totally ruthless. But a rake. It is said he has reformed, but such men never really do, so you must be careful."

Audrianna turned to Celia when they stopped in front of Mr. Trotter's door. "It is very cynical to say a person cannot reform. Perhaps he has." Evidence indicated he had not, but she wanted to make the larger moral point so she ignored that. "And how do you know so much about him, or his reputation? Have you been reading all those scandal sheets that Lizzie buys? I would think that you would have better—"

"*Audrianna.*" Celia's attention diverted from their talk. She stared at the front of Mr. Trotter's shop. "Audrianna, *look.*"

Audrianna turned around. Mr. Trotter displayed a variety of small musical instruments in his window, along with a large, velvet-covered board on which he pinned his newest sheet music. That board contained the usual assortment of hymns and old favorites, their notes neatly printed off engraved plates. Most had little vignettes at the top, displaying songbirds or flowers or religious symbols.

Those were not what had Celia gaping, however.

A copy of the music for Audrianna's song, "My Inconstant Love," held pride of place, right in the middle of the board. Instead of the border of roses that had once graced its top, there now showed a large engraving of two people.

A man looking much like Summerhays swooned while he clutched his bleeding upper arm. And the woman holding the pistol that had shot him bore a striking resemblance to Audrianna herself.

Sebastian shifted on a chair in the Duke of Castleford's huge dressing room. In the bedchamber next door a woman giggled.

Just like Tristan to dally despite requesting this appointment. Sebastian tried to ignore the reasons for the delay. He distracted himself by looking out the window, from which he could see scaffolding going up to the rear of Apsley House at the far end of Piccadilly Street. Word was that Wellington intended to enlarge the place by half again.

The door finally opened and Castleford appeared in the threshold, half-dressed in shirt and trousers. His brown hair fell about his brow and face in disarray. The fun next door must have distracted him during his day's preparations.

"Summerhays, good of you to come. I apologize for the delay but—"

"Castleford," a woman's voice cooed.

Castleford glanced back into the bedchamber. From his chair Sebastian could see in there too. A naked, dark-haired woman lounged on the bed, crooking her finger in a seductive beckon. Sprawled behind her was another naked woman, a blonde this time, small in stature.

"I said I have no more time for games now," he chided his guests. "Dress and be off with you."

The seductress pouted. A sly expression entered her eyes. With deliberate care she stretched so her glories were on total display. Then she rose on her arms and knees and turned. Her back dipped and her bottom rose, in a blatant erotic offer.

Castleford went totally still. The blonde noticed that someone else was in the dressing room. She scooted around until she repeated her friend's position.

Castleford looked at Sebastian. "You won't mind waiting awhile longer, will you?"

"Not at all."

Castleford gestured to the bottoms. "Little Katy there

thinks to make it a party. Join me. Side by side, like old times."

Sebastian was not immune to feminine wiles and willing bottoms. At the moment his mouth was dry and his body hard. "I will decline. But go. I will wait."

Castleford walked back into the bedchamber. He gave Katy's little bottom a gentle slap. "He says no. What can I do? He has become a saint on us."

Katy looked back with a pout. He bent and gave her a kiss. "Not fair, is it? I will tell you what. While I give Janie pleasure, I will watch her do the same for you."

Sebastian got up to close the door. Before it swung, Katy had positioned herself near Janie's head, legs spread wide and hips tilted to give her prime glory easy purchase by her friend's mouth. Castleford positioned himself behind Janie's ripe, round bottom and dropped his trousers.

"I do not think so." Castleford's response came after a long pause. The conversation had gone as Sebastian planned, but now it swung awry with that statement.

Perhaps his relaxed, sated state had caused Castleford not to understand. He appeared half-asleep and beatifically contented.

Sebastian's own mood was not good right now. He had listened to more feminine moaning and squealing than any man should have to endure when he was not causing the cries himself.

"If you do not cooperate on this bill in the upper house, I will not be able to help you with your own interest when it comes up in the Commons," Sebastian reminded him.

Castleford lounged lazily in his chair, still wearing only

shirt and trousers. He gave a slow shrug. "I am not convinced that you will be able to help me in any case, so why should I spend political capital to acquire your aid?"

The man was going to demand it be spelled out. "You know the influence that I have in the Commons. You have been on the opposite side of that influence often enough to be aware of it."

"True. True. You are a strong voice, with a gift for persuasion. Whoever expected you to have the skills of Machiavelli? The world has quickly forgotten your past too. But the Commons . . . well, it is made up of small-minded men who are fickle in their loyalties. One never really knows what will cause them to be persuaded one way or the other."

"And you are willing to risk that I might still carry the day?"

"I am questioning whether you can deliver your side of the bargain. You may already be yesterday's fashion, for all I know. In the least, I intend to consider this trade that you propose, to decide what path most benefits me."

There was no purpose in arguing further. Annoyed by the waste of his time, Sebastian made his way home.

The butler approached as soon as he entered the house. "Sir, it was requested that you attend on your brother as soon as you return. He has need of you."

"Is he ill? Has the physician been called yet?" The dread of bad news broke out of its corner in his soul.

"I do not know. Your mother is with him. It was she who asked for you."

"You should have sent someone to find me," Sebastian snapped as he strode away.

He took the stairs two at a time. He threw open the door to Morgan's apartment and checked the small library and drawing room. When they proved empty, he aimed for the bedchamber, afraid of what he might find.

The scene inside the chamber brought him up short at the threshold. No physician. No sick Morgan. His brother sat in an upholstered chair, beneath the lap coverlet that shielded his dead legs, looking as well as he ever did.

In a chair pulled close to him, managing to hover despite her iron posture, sat their mother. Regal as always in a white dress that set off her dark hair, her pale face wore the pained stoicism that she always displayed when in Morgan's presence.

Esther, Marchioness of Wittonbury, turned her attention to the doorway. One perfect eyebrow arched critically over one brown eye. "Ah, here he is."

Her tone said much more than her words. *Here he is, the great disappointment. The willful, worthless one. The one so like his father in his appetites and sins.*

The one who should be dead or crippled if any son is.

Sebastian acknowledged her, but addressed Morgan. "I was given word that you required me. I am relieved to see that you appear well."

"Your brother does not only need you when he is dying, Sebastian. As marquess, he still has authority in this family, and in the state."

"Of course. What do you want, Morgan?"

Morgan fingered a paper on his lap. "Our mother brought me something. I am hoping that you can explain it. She says there are others, and not just this one. They are selling well in the shops."

Sebastian waited. His mother's delicate mouth pursed. Morgan turned the paper over.

An image showed on the other side, a crude engraving, hastily made and clumsily colored.

The picture showed Miss Kelmsleigh, appearing young, vulnerable, and fearful, submitting to the aggressive seduction of an evil-faced Sebastian Summerhays. A paper labeled "Ordnance Inventory" burned in the fireplace behind them.

Chapter Seven

"*Lady G is reported to be spending a week in seclusion at her property in Surrey, accompanied only by her closest servants and one guest, a poet of considerable acclaim. Perhaps another epic verse will be forthcoming.*"

Lizzie read the gossip notice in a flat, bored tone. She rested her chin on her hand while she held the sheet to the lamp. Audrianna was distracted by the resulting elegant profile. Lizzie's dark, upswept hair balanced just so on her crown, and the lamp emphasized her blue eye and very delicate features.

Lizzie sighed and lifted another sheet. She did not like it when Celia requested this entertainment. One might think that Lizzie found her own fascination with society gossip embarrassing.

Only her soft voice broke the silence in the library. Daphne read by the fire, and Celia darned a damaged dress. Audrianna returned her attention to a blank sheet of paper on the writing table where she sat. She groped to find words to warn her mother about that engraving on the sheet music.

"EC is said to have spent over two hundred pounds for the matched pair he bought off Lord M," Lizzie read. *"While it is general agreement that they are fine cattle, there is rumor that in fact Lord M offered them as part of the settlement for a substantial gentleman's debt."*

There really was no good way to write this letter. Audrianna wondered how little she could reveal. She would prefer it be much less than she had confided to the women in this library, and even they did not know about that long night alone with Lord Sebastian in a bedchamber at the Two Swords.

Whoever thought nice Mr. Trotter would be so greedy that he would stoke demand for her sheet music with scandalous images? Unfortunately sales had increased tenfold as a result, and Mr. Trotter had proven deaf to her pleas that he go back to pictures of flowers.

"Two farm boys in Middlesex, near the town of Trilby, found the remains of—"

While Audrianna had not really been listening, the way Lizzie broke off caught her attention, much as if a musical piece had ended before the final notes.

"I am tired of reading aloud," Lizzie pouted, setting the paper aside. "The words are blurring in front of my eyes too."

"You might at least finish with that bit, and not leave us hanging," Celia complained. "If Audrianna and I brought those papers and sheets all the way from London, seeking out every one for you, you can at least read the best parts to us."

"Why don't you entertain us for a while instead, Celia?"

Daphne said. "You might sing. Audrianna has a new song and you could teach us all."

Celia set down her darning. She rose and walked over to Lizzie and snatched the paper. "I want to know what the boys found first." She searched for the notice.

"Two farm boys in Middlesex, near the town of Trilby, found the decayed remains of a reticule snagged in the limbs of a fallen tree on the banks of the Thames." Celia hooted. "A reticule? Now that is hardly exciting. I thought it would be a body." She peered again. The text arrested her attention.

"What else does it say?" Daphne asked.

Celia startled. *"It has been recognized as the property of the missing bride of Lord Hawkeswell, according to the local magistrate—* Oh, dear, it does sound like there is a body involved after all. How sad."

Daphne returned to her book. Celia strolled over to Audrianna and looked down at her letter. "You have such a nice hand, Audrianna. I so admire your penmanship. It is clear that it is the writing of a lady."

While she admired the invisible words on the blank paper, Celia placed the gossip sheet on the writing table, and pointed. "It bodes badly, does it not, this reticule and the fate of that lost girl? I understand why Lizzie did not want to continue reading after she saw *this* tragic story."

Her finger did not point to the reticule story. It touched the one beneath it.

Recent stories out of Brighton have many wonder-ing if an illustrious gentleman, known as a wild stal-lion not long ago but recently purported to have been broken, has secretly romped in the pasture again.

The identity of the filly has many suggesting the worst kind of seduction, one based on coercion and on compromise of duty.

Audrianna stared at the words. For all its vagueness, she was sure that it was about Lord Sebastian and herself. But it was a stupid lie. There had been no coercion, and definitely no romping, just a ridiculous misunderstanding.

Audrianna looked over at Lizzie, who glanced askance in her direction at the same time. Audrianna then gazed up at Celia, unable to hide her astonishment. Maturity veiled Celia's young face again. *This is taking a bad turn*, her expression said.

"Since I am the only one who does not know the reason for all the meaningful looks and careful posing, perhaps one of you can share the secret with me," Daphne said.

Audrianna looked over her shoulder. Daphne's book was closed. She had been watching them.

"You had best show her," Celia said. "She will find out soon anyway, from the appearance of things."

Not only Daphne would find out. Everyone would.

Audrianna rose and went to the bookcase. She removed the tome in which she had hidden the sheet music brought back from Mr. Trotter's. She placed it into Daphne's hand.

Daphne unfolded the sheet and studied it. "And the scandal sheet?" she asked without raising her gaze from the image.

Celia brought over the scandal sheet. Lizzie joined them by the fire and also examined the papers.

"I fear that you have been thoroughly compromised." Lizzie's soft face communicated a best friend's sympathy even while she remained blunt in her assessment. She kept shaking her dark head dolefully. "The scandal will be insurmountable."

"What do I care?" Audrianna said. "I am already compromised by my father's ruined name and by the way Roger threw me over."

"This is much worse," Lizzie said. "There is no comparison. This will affect your sister and your mother and your friends. Women will shun you to protect their own reputations."

"I fear she is correct," Celia said. "You know she is, Audrianna."

Would these friends here shun her? She could face this down if she had the sanctuary of this home and family, but if they cast her out—

"This is much worse, that is true," Daphne concurred. "However, this also is much better."

"I do not agree with Lizzie's dire predictions," Audrianna said, even though she really did. She held a brave front, but sick worry lodged in her stomach. "However, I also do not see how this can be much better than anything, Daphne."

"Lord Sebastian may not care if he is mocked and scorned in public this way," Daphne said, waving the sheet music. "His mother and brother will care a great deal, however. And unlike with your father or Roger, there will be compensations for your suffering this time. With your mother's permission, I will see to it."

"I would rather you did not."

Daphne studied her. Then she rose as if the conversation had ended, and slid her book back into its place in the mahogany bookcase.

"It will be very chilled tonight," Daphne said. "Lizzie,

please go and light the fire pots in the greenhouse. Celia, I would be grateful if you helped her."

The two of them left. Audrianna stared at the fire, and tried to imagine what it would be like to live down this scandal. It might be a very big one, the way Lizzie assumed.

Then again, perhaps not. It could remain confined to London alone. She might still be able to maintain her obscurity out here in the country. How many people who passed by Mr. Trotter's shop had also heard the gossip, after all? When one thought about it, a woman shooting a man was not an absurd image to put on the top of a song titled "My Inconstant Love." It might all remain fairly quiet and—

"Audrianna, I fear that I must break my own rule." Daphne's voice, right behind her head, made Audrianna startle.

Daphne walked around her chair and sat once more in her own. She leaned forward and reached out to take Audrianna's hand. "As my relative, and as a young woman new to her independence, you are not merely a guest here. Your mother agreed to your staying here because she assumed you would be safe."

"And I have been."

"As you say. However, this image— I must ask you to tell me again what happened at the Two Swords, Audrianna. And this time I implore you not to leave half the story out."

Sebastian perused the stack of papers on his writing desk. Besides the engraving given to Morgan, five others had now been procured in town by the servants, at Sebastian's instruction. Yet another adorned the top of a piece of sheet music published by Mr. Thomas Trotter of Albermarle Street.

The music and song had been written by none other than Miss Kelmsleigh herself. "My Inconstant Love." Sebastian hummed the melody in his head while he read the words. It appeared a heartfelt song, ripe with the fresh ache of a broken heart. It appeared that Miss Kelmsleigh had been disappointed in a matter of the heart, and had released the pain in this sad little song.

He turned his attention to several notices in scandal sheets from the last week. He had not been named in any of them, but anyone aware of the rumor about the doings at the Two Swords—and he assumed that meant all of society now—would have no trouble following the direction that speculation was taking. It appeared that the scandal was going to stick, and stick hard.

To be accused of seducing Miss Kelmsleigh, when he had not, did not surprise him too much. He had all but invited that when he implied to Sir Edwin that he and she had met because they were lovers. The world knew he had not been a saint, so he could hardly expect anyone to view the evidence otherwise.

These engravings and notices did not imply a liaison, however. The accusation was that he had used his role in the investigation of her father to coerce her into bed. One might easily assume that he had discovered more than he had ever revealed about that bad gunpowder, but buried the evidence in trade for Miss Kelmsleigh's favors.

That made him a scoundrel of the worst kind. He was being depicted not only as a man who would cynically prey upon the innocent, but also as one who would compromise his duty to his position and to the truth in return for ill-gotten pleasure.

He noted that Miss Kelmsleigh, whose willfulness had brought all this about, was treated most sympathetically in all these images and insinuating notices. The engravings showed her as sweet, innocent, frightened, confused, dismayed, resistant, and victimized—even the ones that drew a pistol in her hand.

The assassination of his character distracted him enough that he was not ready for the day when ten o'clock came. He went to Morgan's chambers anyway, wearing neither coats nor cravat.

Morgan hid any disapproval, of which Sebastian assumed there was some. Even in his infirmity, Morgan dressed for the day.

"How does your arm fare?" Morgan asked.

"It is still stiff and sore, but is healing cleanly."

Not much was said while they ate breakfast. They had not spoken much since that interview two afternoons ago, when Morgan had revealed the engraving.

"It is getting worse," Sebastian finally said. "The scandal. It is taking an unfortunate turn."

"I know. Our mother brought me several more engravings yesterday."

"How thoughtful of her."

"Her place in society means a lot to her. It is all that she has now."

"My concerns are bigger than our mother suffering a few innuendos during her social calls. There has been a change in how I am viewed. It is subtle, but unmistakable. My influence has been compromised, along with Miss Kelmsleigh's reputation."

The reaction had not been entirely subtle. Castleford had retreated from serious negotiations at once. Among other MPs he saw, a few eyes reflected satisfied glee when aimed his way. More telling was that he had not been invited to an important meeting today that normally he would expect to attend.

Morgan pondered that. "Your arrival may have been too abrupt for some, and your rise too fast for others. There will always be those who resent a man of merit and consequence who surpasses them."

Merit may have helped that rise, but birth and blood had mattered more. Everyone knew that although active in the Commons, he was Parliament's stand-in for his brother, and his seat itself was in Wittonbury's pocket. Not only was Morgan a marquess, but he had also been one of the nobility's sacrificial lambs to the god of war, and that gave more weight to Sebastian's influence too.

Sebastian suspected this indirect attack on his character had other reasons besides envy, though. A man could not be effective in politics without making enemies. There were winners, which meant there were losers.

Since Sebastian usually was among the former, there undoubtedly were men looking to extract as much revenge through this scandal as possible. The only question was whether it would render him totally useless in the end. As Castleford had put it, would he instantly become yesterday's fashion?

"Our mother is distraught for herself," Morgan said. "As you noted, the truth is this will cause her a few moments of embarrassment and little more. There is no doubt that you can take care of yourself, so even if the worst happens, I do not fear it turning you to drink. The only person who will be truly hurt by this is Miss Kelmsleigh."

Morgan turned his attention briefly to the street below his window. Then he braced his arms against his chair and resettled himself on it a bit. Finally he reached for the coffee urn and set about completing his meal while his reference to Miss Kelmsleigh hung in the air.

Morgan had always been a bit dull, but he also had always been honest. Forthright, frank, and honorable in the simple way taught to young boys, the nuances of life often perplexed him. All of which made him ill-suited for the kind of sly manipulation of the conversation that he attempted now.

It was not clear how this good, decent man of few vices had been born into the family. He did not take after their father; that was certain. Sebastian did, to their mother's vexation. But Morgan had little in common with her either, and possessed none of her ruthless indifference to the pain of others.

"I did not do it," Sebastian said. "I have not had Miss Kelmsleigh's favors under any circumstances, least of all those insinuated by this gossip."

"I did not think you had."

"Like hell you didn't."

Morgan expressed dismay at Sebastian's sharp tone. "No matter what happened, she is a victim twice over, isn't she? Of her father's negligence, and now of these rumors."

"All criminals have families who become victims of their acts."

"That is what our mother said. I did not answer her, because she never hears anyway. I will tell you, however, that I do not like that this criminal, if he was one, had a family who now must suffer more because your enemies make sport of this . . . misunderstanding."

Morgan leveled his gaze on Sebastian. Sebastian looked straight back. The rest of the conversation passed without words. Then they returned to their coffee and mail.

"I will put out the true story of what transpired at the

Two Swords," Sebastian said when he rose to leave. "For everyone's sake, that might be best."

"The truth is always best, Sebastian."

The hell it was.

Scandal created the oddest excitement, Audrianna thought the next afternoon. The household became both funereal and charged with purpose at the same time.

Lizzie and Celia had debated long into the night just how Audrianna might be salvaged. They came to the problem from very different perspectives. Lizzie believed that at best a few decades of impeccable living and significant charitable work would be needed to redeem a fall that involved the loss of virtue. Celia opined that a confident demeanor, superb style, and one important lover could get a woman back in society faster, and at a more elevated position.

Neither asked which Audrianna preferred. She just sat there on her bed while they picked apart the disaster her life had become.

The next morning both of them walked to Cumberworth to post a letter that Audrianna had finally written to her mother. A half hour after they left, it became clear that the letter had been unnecessary. A hired carriage rolled up the lane and stopped in front of Daphne's house. Audrianna recognized its occupants from where she spied from a window.

Daphne materialized at her side and together they watched her mother and sister approach the door.

"She is distraught, of course," Daphne said. She referred to the expression on the face of Audrianna's mother.

Audrianna had never seen her mother look so weary.

Even after her father's death, even during the relentless hounding by Lord Sebastian and others, Mama had not broken completely. Now she walked like it pained her to be alive. She still dressed all in black, even though her remaining friends argued that the period of deep mourning should be shortened if a husband takes his own life.

"Your sister Sarah appears angry," Daphne said. "For you, I trust."

"Not for me. She knows what this will cost her." There had been a chance, a small one, that Sarah might escape the worst of their father's disgrace. With a modest settlement and a few years passing, she might marry decently even if not as well as she wanted. It was one reason Audrianna had left and come to live with Daphne—to allow her mother to spend what little she had on the one daughter for whom a respectable future might still be attained.

Audrianna followed Daphne to the door. When it opened, both Mama and Sarah had replaced their real feelings with masks of sympathy.

"Dear Aunt Meg," Daphne greeted, leaning in for a kiss. "It is fortunate that you have come. There is much that we must discuss."

"The most preposterous tale came to my ears, Lord Sebastian." Mr. John Pond, Astronomer Royal, peered into the observatory's new ten-foot transit telescope while he spoke. He tipped the mechanism a fraction of an inch and peered again. Above them a panel in the Greenwich Meridian Building had been opened to the stars.

"It was about that business at the Two Swords outside Brighton. A long, elaborate, fantastical tale is now being told. Something about a mysterious intruder and a coincidental meeting. Your friends should devise a more plausible explanation if they seek to absolve you."

Sebastian had known Pond for over ten years. They had met when Sebastian was still at university, and the noted astronomer had since taught him a few things about his science that could not be learned from books and lectures. A friendship had developed, which now allowed Sebastian easy access to the observatory, and also allowed Pond to speak so freely.

"I have no friends with imaginations fertile enough to concoct such a story. Or stupid enough to hope such an absurd truth would be believed faster than a more damning lie. The story that you heard came from none other than me."

Pond turned his head just enough to look askance at Sebastian with his free eye. "You are saying that is what really happened with that young woman?"

"I am. You have my word as a gentleman."

Pond went back to his study of the heavens. "No one will believe it."

No, probably not. No one would actually say it was a lie, though. That could mean a duel. But sly grins and raised eyebrows could hold entire conversations that spoke what the mouth could not.

It was a hell of a thing. The truth, which had spread faster than the scandal, seemed only to stoke speculation owing to its peculiar circumstances, and to the fact that it touched on Miss Kelmsleigh's father.

Better to have kept silent on that whole matter.

"The heavens are unusually clear," Pond said. "It was a good night for you to come. It has been too long."

Too long, like so much else. Too long without a woman unless he observed the most stifling discretion. Too long without a good ride in the country with no destination. Too long since he had indulged any of his interests that required time, like these astronomical studies that had once been his claim to displaying any purpose besides the pursuit of pleasure.

Having taken his brother's place, he should have executed those duties as his brother had, and not allowed duty and government to absorb his life. Morgan himself had never done that. But then Morgan was the marquess, and had nothing to prove.

Pond pushed away from the telescope and jotted some notes on a paper near his chair. "I am done. It is all yours. I will leave you the list of stars I am observing, and you can make notes. You can help me make Brinkley eat his theory."

Sebastian adjusted the chair, which was designed to allow a semireclined angle to match the telescope's trajectory. He settled himself into it, leaned back, and positioned himself at the end of the long, dark metal tube held firmly in place by two massive, flanking piers.

"Be sure to alert the watchman when you leave, so the building can be locked," Pond said.

Sebastian adjusted the eyepiece. He peered into the dark sky, and gave himself over to awe of the eternity that the cosmos implied. Nothing at all in his small, transient world seemed very important when he gazed at the stars. Certainly not the decision that had set him on the road to Greenwich tonight, seeking distraction.

Chapter Eight

"He has come," Celia announced, running into the greenhouse. "I was walking past the library window when movement outside down the lane caught my eye. He is on horse. He appears quite magnificent."

"Of course he has come," Daphne said. She began untying her apron. "If he had waited much longer, we would have had to go to him. He would not want that."

Audrianna wished he had not come. This was going to be horrible.

"I will not countenance this," she said to Daphne. "It is not fair to expect him to pay, quite literally, for something that was not his fault."

"Intentionally or not, unavoidable or not, you were compromised. Worse, the whole world is assuming more than is true. He knows that he cannot let it stand unaddressed."

"I will not accept payment for this scandal. To do so would make me . . ." Complicit. Truly soiled. Perhaps, to his mind, even calculating.

"Then your mother will, in your name. I daresay he intends to do it that way in any case, for appearance' sake. You will not have any choice."

Daphne beckoned her to follow into the front sitting room. Celia went to the door, to let Lord Sebastian in.

He entered the drawing room alone, looking sober, determined, and fairly hard. There could be no illusion that this was a simple social call. All the same, Celia's description had been apt. He did appear magnificent. Tall and dark and commanding, he greeted Daphne and herself.

Daphne invited him to sit. He chose to remain standing. Daphne perched her ethereal self near the window, making clear that she intended to remain as chaperon and negotiator. Audrianna sat as far from Lord Sebastian and the pending humiliation as was possible.

"You have no doubt come because of the rumors that are spreading," Daphne offered after an awkward pause.

"In part, yes."

Audrianna could only imagine the other part. Fury, most likely, that his name was being impugned so maliciously, and over the daughter of Kelmsleigh no less.

"My aunt, Mrs. Kelmsleigh, is understandably distraught for her entire family," Daphne said. "Coming on the heels of the false accusations about her husband—well, she fears they are all hopelessly ruined now. She believes that her younger daughter's future will be as compromised as Audrianna's. Aunt Meg sees destitution around the corner for them all."

Lord Sebastian smiled, but it was not one of his winning smiles. Tight and hard, his expression said that he knew where she was going and he did not care to be led to that point by anyone, including her.

"I take responsibility for the current scandal, Mrs. Joyes.

I will not do so for whatever came before the night that I met Miss Kelmsleigh, no matter how much you or her mother want to tie it together."

"Then let us confine our conversation to the night that you met my cousin, sir, and the attendant consequences."

"The conversation that I came here to have was with Miss Kelmsleigh, much as I am sure you would be a pleasant partner in any discourse."

"My cousin is too innocent to begin to know how to have the conversation that is necessary. Ideally a male relative would do this duty, but since there is none, I am obligated to—"

"I am right here, Daphne," Audrianna interrupted. "I am hearing every word. Please stop referring to me as if I am not even in the room."

Daphne looked over, as if she had indeed forgotten that Audrianna was in the room.

"Mrs. Joyes, I think that Miss Kelmsleigh will acquit herself well enough today," Lord Sebastian said. "If she can travel to Brighton alone, confront an unknown man, and brandish a pistol, a brief conversation with me will be a small thing in comparison."

"I agree that this conversation must be between Lord Sebastian and me," Audrianna said.

Her rebellion surprised Daphne. "Considering the topic, that is most indelicate."

"I lost undue consideration for my own delicacy some months ago, dear cousin. Independent women, I have learned, must put such indulgences aside."

Lord Sebastian moved his attention away from Daphne in such a manner as to indicate dismissal. "The day is fair, Miss Kelmsleigh. Shall we tour the garden again?"

Audrianna planned never to be alone in any garden with

this man again. "I would much prefer a turn along the lane, if that is acceptable to you."

"As you wish."

She fetched her gray pelisse and lilac shawl from pegs near the library, then joined him at the door where he waited for her. Daphne remained in the drawing room, her thoughts hidden behind a mask of serenity.

The morning damp had long ago dried on the grass that flanked the lane. A warm sun hinted at better weather to come, but a crisp breeze chilled enough that Audrianna was glad for her shawl.

Lord Sebastian paced beside her, his boots crunching the twigs littering the ground. His serious countenance suggested that he did not care for the day's mission, and resented that courtesy obligated him to offer apologies, concern, and the acceptance of blame.

Audrianna glanced back at the shrinking house. She assumed that she would see Daphne at a window, keeping watch. No fair head showed there, however.

"Matters have taken an unfortunate turn," Lord Sebastian finally said. "The scandal grows. I have let the truth of my wound be known, but as with Sir Edwin and the innkeeper, the truth sounds fictional compared with more commonplace explanations."

"I have seen some allusions to it in the papers, so I am aware of this. It was good of you to come and warn me, however."

"It is, I regret to say, on everyone's lips."

"It is not fair at all. However, life often is not. I will live this down as I have the other misfortunes in my life, and I am sure that you will as well."

"You are too understanding."

"If this were the normal sort of compromise, I doubt I

would be. However, the most peculiar circumstances attend our situation, and I think that the normal rules do not apply."

"The world does not care what you or I think, Miss Kelmsleigh."

"I find that I do not care one way or the other what the world thinks anymore, so it is even."

"That is very brave of you. And very foolish."

Her moral satisfaction in doing the right thing passed in a snap. Irritation took its place. She had just let this man off the hook, and he now insulted her.

"You should be glad for my foolishness, and not scold, sir. Daphne and my mother hatched a plan to demand compensation from you. Had we not taken this turn, and had I not insisted that we speak alone, I think that you would be a good deal poorer by now."

"Mrs. Joyes would have negotiated to no avail. I will make no payment."

"Of course you won't. You are not guilty. Why should *you* pay?"

Her emphasis made him smile sardonically. "Oh, I will pay, Miss Kelmsleigh. One way or another, there will be an accounting. However, laying out a sum of money to you and your family is the least promising alternative."

"Then we are agreed. We will brave it out and pay what we must to the court of gossip, and that will be that. Come, let us return to my cousin and make that clear, and be done with all of this."

She turned on her heel toward the house. A firm hold on her arm stopped her after the first step.

"You misunderstand, Miss Kelmsleigh."

She looked down on that gloved hand that so easily, and discourteously, controlled her movement. The memory flashed of him doing this in the garden, and where that had led. She ventured a glance at his face and thought she detected his own fleeting memory in the way his eyes warmed for a second.

He let her go, but his own stance, now blocking the lane, made it clear they would not be returning to Daphne just yet.

"Five years ago, even two, I would have done it your way," he said. "Or even your cousin's way. Today I cannot afford to. My character has been insulted and my honor badly impugned." He removed a paper from his pocket. "This is what I mean."

She took the sheet and unfolded it. It bore a crude, ribald engraving. A woman who looked vaguely like herself sat on a bed in dishabille with one breast already bare, resisting the groping embrace of a man who looked a lot like Lord Sebastian. Outside a window one could see the sign of the Two Swords. Beneath it, vaguely visible in the moonlight, were half-buried kegs of gunpowder.

She kept staring at that bare breast. "This is shocking. I knew Mr. Trotter had put a picture on my sheet music, but it was not anything like this."

"Mr. Trotter is the least of it. The print houses compete with each other, and worse than this can be bought for mere pennies."

She handed him back the engraving. "Perhaps I should demand compensation after all, if I am being shown so scandalously."

"That would solve nothing. It would only confirm the worst rumors, and be an admission of guilt on my part."

"So, it is hopeless all around. Thank you for being honest with me. I think the only choice is for me to go live somewhere else." She made a little laugh to hide her dismay. "Brazil, perhaps."

She ducked around him and strode toward the house. She did not want to converse with him anymore. That engraving made her face heat whenever she pictured it. She did not begin to know what "worse than this" meant. She feared that her likeness was now doing the most obscene things on a thousand images.

Twigs crunched firmly behind her. "Miss Kelmsleigh, it was not my intention to come here today, impart bad news, and leave you distressed."

"How could I not be distressed?" she snapped over her shoulder.

Again that gloved hand on her arm. "Stop. Listen to me. Allow me to speak, please."

His hold gave her no choice except to stop. She did not face him, however, but instead watched the house. She did not think she could see his face again without also seeing that engraved Lord Sebastian leering dangerously while he caressed her engraved nakedness.

"We are both compromised, Miss Kelmsleigh. We will both pay. The accounting will be much less, however, if we marry."

For a breathless moment the world stilled. Even the dead leaves ceased fluttering along the lane. Her brain emptied, unable to accommodate what he had just said.

Then she understood him all too well. She turned to face him.

"You jest, of course."

"Not at all. It is the only solution that I see. It is much better than paying you off like some milkmaid I got with child. As the daughter of a gentleman, it is your due. But for our unfortunate history, you would be expecting it, and so would your mother and cousin."

"Our unfortunate history—you do have a politician's way with words, sir—would make such a match comical. The print shops will be busy for years."

"A wedding will make our association so commonplace that the scandal will blow over before the start of the season. It will continue the fiction begun with Sir Edwin at the Two Swords. Our indiscretion will be known as an amorous one, not cynical and base."

"Very neat *for you*. You will be absolved of having coerced me, but I will still be a woman who granted her favors to a man before marriage. Worse, to a man who hounded her father to his grave. No, thank you. I prefer to go to Brazil."

His hand sliced the air with impatience. "Please be serious. You are not going to go to Brazil. You will end up living here the rest of your life, afraid to show your face in town, barely living down the scorn of the local people. You will be unable to give music lessons because of your notoriety and you will be completely dependent on your cousin. This property will become a cloister in which you age and die."

His cruel, blunt predictions came as slaps to her face. She had no trouble imagining the limited, bleak existence he described. A tide of fearful desolation submerged her self-righteous ire.

"You play to win, I see," she said.

"When I must, yes." He stepped closer so her nose pointed at his chest. "Come now. Marriage to me won't be so bad," he said more gently. "You will want for nothing and live as you choose." His soft glove lifted her chin so she gazed on his face. "And we want each other, odd though you may find that. Pleasure goes a long way to making marriage tolerable for a woman."

She hated that he knew that he affected her. She wished his face did not awe her and that her heart did not do that silly jig while she looked in his eyes.

His head dipped and his lips touched hers. He lingered long enough to ensure the arrows began scurrying. He deliberately reminded her of the overwhelming sensations in the garden.

She allowed it, half-hoping he would make her stupid again. Only this was not a surprise in a garden, and she could not forget who she was this time.

She saw lights of desire and victory in his eyes when he stopped the kiss and looked down at her. She stepped back, away from his body and hold, and faced him squarely. An unnatural calm swept her.

"Probably you are correct, Lord Sebastian, and I do not have the courage to leave all that I know behind to seek a new life in a distant land. I still have a choice, however."

"Of course you do." He did not believe that. She could see he assumed it could only go one way.

"Please do not patronize me, sir. I do have a choice. A more important one than you pose. I can live the sad existence that you describe, but in doing so, I can ensure that you lose your influence in government and society. Or I can live in luxury by marrying a man who used his position to do my father and my family great harm. I would say that the honorable decision is clear, wouldn't you?"

He displayed no astonishment. No anger. He just looked at her.

She strode away. "Good day to you, Lord Sebastian."

Chapter Nine

Audrianna decided to devote herself to finding the Domino. He still might hold the key to clearing her father's name. There was also the smallest chance that he might confirm to the world that the assumptions behind the scandal were a lie.

She did not allow herself to count on that. In walking away from Lord Sebastian's proposal, she had accepted that the worst would happen. She had no illusions that she was not doomed.

The evening after the meeting with Lord Sebastian, she sat in the library with the other women and tried to compose an advertisement for the *Times*. If the Domino was in London, he might see it. That was how he had looked for her father, after all.

She labored at it for a half hour and could not find the words to be both cryptic and plain. Discouraged, she folded the sheet of paper and set it aside. Now she had to write to Mama. That was going to be even more difficult.

It would be much easier to write a new song. She might title it "My Scandalous Innocence." Or "A Vase Chipped but Unbroken." Or "Pride Vanquished by Fate." Or—

"So?" Celia asked. Her question broke the silence of the last hour. "Isn't anyone going to explain what happened when Lord Sebastian came to visit today?"

"It was a private matter, Celia," Daphne said without looking up from her book.

"Oh, tosh. We all know why he came. Did he offer a settlement? How big? Can you buy property with it or must you live off the income? Will there be a trustee, or is it yours to do with as you wish?"

"He offered no financial settlement," Audrianna said. She made a display of dipping her pen and setting her attention to her letter.

"That is odd. He is not rumored to be without honor. I would have thought, considering some of the engravings that I have seen in town, that he would offer at least twenty thousand."

That got Daphne's attention. "There are other images?"

Celia nodded. "Rather explicit ones."

"How do you see such things, Celia? When we go to town, you are not gone from my side more than ten minutes in all," Daphne said.

Celia shrugged. "You just need to know where to look, that is all."

Audrianna could feel Daphne's curious attention on her now. She dipped her pen again.

"Actually," Lizzie offered quietly, "for a man of his station, and a young woman of Audrianna's birth, he really should have offered marriage in circumstances such as this. To offer a settlement would be insulting."

Audrianna bent over the writing table. *Dear Mama . . .*

"You are such a child sometimes, Lizzie," Celia said. "For all the *should*s that you were taught, the world has more than its share of exceptions."

"You are correct, Celia. However, Lizzie is as well," Daphne said. "I know that Aunt Meg was torn on the matter. She knew that she should demand he do the right thing, but after the scandal about her husband, she knew he never could."

Audrianna put down her pen and turned to Daphne. The way Daphne phrased that, it sounded backward. Twisted. "Are you saying that Mama believed that the lies about Papa meant that Lord Sebastian should not be expected to do the right thing? That is a fine kettle of fish, since he helped spread those lies."

"Calm yourself, dear cousin. In the least, it would be a recipe for unhappiness."

"You would be much better off with money," Celia agreed.

"If you hate him, that is probably true," Lizzie said. "I only meant that money does not cleanse the terrible stain that you now bear the way marriage does."

"Thank you, Lizzie," Daphne said. "However, such pointed reminders are hardly helpful."

Her gentle scold sent Lizzie back to her book. Daphne picked up hers as well. Celia, however, was not to be deterred. "So, how much?"

"Nothing," Audrianna admitted.

Nothing? Celia mouthed with astonishment.

"I refused any such compensation, and he was not inclined to make any to begin with."

Lizzie frowned. "How odd. He seduces you and the entire world finds out, and he is prepared to do nothing at all about it?"

"He *did not* seduce me." Audrianna looked around the

library at her friends, exasperated. "You *do* all believe that, don't you?"

Celia nodded while she checked the tie on her shoe. Lizzie nodded while she got distracted by the painting on the wall.

Daphne turned a page in her book. "Of course we all believe that, dear."

Sebastian's indignation knew no bounds. It only grew on the ride back to London. Memories of the meeting with Miss Kelmsleigh distracted him for days.

Not normally a man given to confidences, he found himself a week later at Brook's, spilling the story to the Earl of Hawkeswell, the one man who at least knew part of the truth since he was actually at the Two Swords. Hawkeswell was also one of the few men whose discretion he could trust.

"She turned me down. She did it to extract revenge."

Hawkeswell kept half his attention on the dice rolling on the hazard table. "You cannot be too surprised. She has good cause to hate you, and would not welcome such a solution to being compromised, no matter what the rules say. She is faring better than you in this scandal, and she has no reason to want to help you absolve yourself."

Except he had been surprised. Not by her first rejection, but by the final one. He had assumed that kiss would seal his victory. Her response indicated it would.

To then see her standing there, separate and straight, calmly poised but still flushed from arousal, outlining her choices—he had not thought of her as especially strong until that moment. Nor had he fully comprehended her determination to avenge her father, for all her bravery at the Two Swords.

She had ended that meeting with aplomb. She had both impressed and infuriated the hell out of him.

"You should have brought some jewels with you," Hawkeswell said.

"If she cannot be bought by marriage, she would not have been swayed by jewels."

"Tangible things have a way of making theoretical ideas solid and real. She has refused a life of luxury and security, but she does not truly comprehend what she forgoes."

"So that explains the ease with which you cut such a wide swath through women. You bribe the hesitant with rubies and pearls."

They both laughed at that, since everyone knew that Hawkeswell needed little help from jewels in his conquests, and had little money to buy jewels in any case.

"Speaking of cutting wide swaths, have you seen Castleford recently?" Hawkeswell asked.

"A week ago." Memories of two erotic bottoms invaded Sebastian's head. That led to some vivid speculation about Miss Kelmsleigh's bottom.

"It is as if I do not know him anymore. I applaud healthy hedonism, but his has taken a dark turn. He is becoming dissolute. It is as if he relishes being infamous."

"A demon drives him, but I do not know its name."

"Hell, what demon could claim him? He doesn't have our problems. Let him walk in my boots a week or two and that would give him some reason for turning into an ass."

It was the first allusion that Hawkeswell had made in over a year to his missing bride, and to the vague suspicions that hung over him about her disappearance. No one really believed he had sent her away, or worse, but a question mark still sat there, looming larger these last few days.

"Was it hers?" Sebastian asked, risking the temper that this friend could reveal unexpectedly. "That reticule found by the Thames."

Hawkeswell inhaled deeply and gazed blankly across the chamber. He ran his hand through his hair and returned to his cards. "Her guardian says it was. It is not a good sign and I fear the worst. Poor girl."

Poor Hawkeswell too. That girl had come with a lucrative settlement that he badly needed. Her disappearance on her wedding day had left him in limbo—unable to wed again, but unable to pry the settlement from her trustee, who insisted it would not be paid without a court's judgment if she were dead.

Hawkeswell grinned sardonically. "Hell of a thing, isn't it? I should be the one drinking myself to death, not Castleford."

"Perhaps he has his reasons too, but I have accepted that he wants neither counsel nor sympathy from me. Not all friendships last forever."

"True words, but sad ones." Hawkeswell lifted his glass. "To Tristan St. Ives, Duke of Castleford, that he might slay that demon."

Sebastian drank, then lifted his in turn. "To healthy hedonism, and your current lady fair whoever she may be."

"To Miss Kelmsleigh, and the hope that she can be bought."

"And if not, to all the ones who can be."

As always happened when they played this ritual, Hawkeswell raised his glass one more time. Whoever or whatever he toasted remained a private thought before he threw back the rest of the spirits in his glass.

L ady Wittonbury rarely sought out her second son. Her sudden appearance in the library while Sebastian wrote some letters therefore surprised him.

She perched her imperious presence on a settee from which she could face him. She radiated her usual authority and confidence.

Sebastian greeted her, asked after her health, and returned to his letter with an emphasis of movement that he trusted would send her away. It was not to be.

"I want you to know that I am grateful for the attention that you give your brother," she said.

"I am happy to do it."

"Of course, it is only his due."

"Certainly."

"Everyone knows that he should never have bought that commission. As marquess, it was not his place to do so, but yours if anyone's."

Sebastian put down his pen. Outside a steady drizzle turned the garden into a palette of emerald greens and steely grays. "It has taken you a long time to put that accusation into words," he said. "Perhaps now that you have, you will feel better."

She was not a woman easily cowed, least of all by a son. "If a family were going to send a son to war at all, it should not be the firstborn and lord."

"It is done sometimes. Dalhousie. Uxbridge. There are other examples we both know. He was not the only peer in uniform."

"They come from families with excessive military traditions. Do you deny any guilt in the tragedy this caused?"

If she wanted to attribute his complicated feelings about Morgan to guilt, so be it. There was little point in arguing with her.

"But what is done is done," she said.

He suspected she did not offer a mother's absolution

with that belated acceptance of fate. More likely she turned from one front in her private campaign, to another.

"I am told that you execute your duties well. That through you the Wittonbury power survives."

"I do my best."

"This business with that woman will interfere with your doing your best in the future. The *on dit* is quite damning. It gives lie to the impression that you had reformed."

Sebastian did not defend himself. That also would make no difference.

"I have been thinking for some time that you should marry."

"Your concern with my happiness is touching. I can't decide whether I welcome this next change in our conversation's topic, however. Let me see: guilt, scandal, or marriage? Guilt, scandal, or marriage. I confess that I find all the subjects unappealing. You have always had a talent for making our discussions disagreeable."

Her eyes narrowed. "I have not changed the subject at all, as you well know. You will soon have your brother's place. Considering his health, you should marry because you will be marquess soon. The scandal will only compromise your effectiveness now and then. Therefore, marriage will prepare you for your inevitable title, ensure the succession, and also distract the world from this latest seductive escapade of yours."

She used to talk to his father like this. It had not been a joyous union.

"Actually, I have been thinking of marriage," he said, after letting her glare at him for a solid minute.

Her face fell in astonishment. She frowned, suspicious at her easy victory. Then the thought of being able to meddle in his life won her over. "I am delighted to hear it.

I will see that you are introduced to the best young ladies. We will settle on one this season."

"I already have someone in mind."

Suspicious again. "She is suitable, I pray."

"Under the circumstances, she is very appropriate," he said. "Now, you must excuse me. I will be late for my breakfast with Morgan."

He walked out before she could pepper him with questions.

He entered the master's apartment and joined Morgan by the window. He drank some coffee, and opened the *Times*.

As was his habit, he scanned the notices and advertisements on the first page. His gaze slid down the long column, then halted and moved back up to one of them.

"Is something amiss?" Morgan asked.

Sebastian checked his pocket watch. "Nothing is amiss. However, I will have to leave you early today. I have an appointment at quarter past eleven."

Audrianna made a display of perusing the books in the shop. She kept her face to the spines, but shot furtive glances toward the central circular counter.

She might have misunderstood the notice, of course. It had been quite cryptic. Enough that she doubted anyone else would realize that it related to her fall from grace.

To the future partner interested in swords, black arts, and gossip, meet me below the dome in the muses' abode, half past eleven on Thursday.

Black arts referred to the making of gunpowder. The dome referred to the one atop this large bookshop on Finsbury Square commonly called The Temple of the Muses. She was almost positive that it had been another notice from the Domino.

She also believed that it had been written specifically for her attention. If the Domino knew about the scandal, he would have learned by now that her father was dead and that she had been the woman waiting for him at the Two Swords. And the one now subject to gossip.

She barely contained her excitement. She wished a man with red hair would walk in the door. She judged how they would converse once they met. If they both admired books along the counter while standing near each other, and if they spoke lowly, they could do so without any patrons being aware.

She stole a glance at the case watch that she held in her gloved hand. He should be here by now. No one with red hair was under the central dome, however. Only two women stood there, and two gentlemen who looked nothing like the Domino.

Perhaps he watched just as she did, from a corner not in clear view. Maybe he thought his notice had not been seen.

She strolled over to the large counter. It included a glass case at one end. She peered through her wavy reflection at the fine bindings in the case. An old music book caught her eye.

"I should have guessed that it would be you."

The low, displeased voice sounded right in her ear. She focused on her reflection again. Another face had joined hers. Lord Sebastian now stood right next to her.

"Go away," she whispered furiously. "You are going to ruin everything again."

"I am not going anywhere. I, too, want to meet our friend. Also, I cannot leave you unprotected."

"This is a busy and safe establishment. Besides, I have the pistol."

"Damnation, Miss Kelmsleigh. Your efforts to protect yourself will get someone killed eventually. I can only pray it will not be me."

"If you would mind your own business, you can be sure it won't be. Now, away with you. He will never show himself if he sees you here."

"What makes you think he even saw your notice? He could be in Amsterdam, for all you know."

"Very shrewd of you to think of that. Except I did not place this notice. *He did.*"

His gaze shot away from her. He intensely examined the shop, studying every other patron in it. "He is not here."

"How would you know? You do not know what he looks like."

He just shook his head thoughtfully, while he continued perusing the shop. He pulled out his pocket watch. "It is past the appointed time by over a quarter hour now."

"You *did* ruin it. He probably looked in the window, saw you, and left." Disheartened and at her wit's end, she ached to rid herself of this interfering man. "Excuse me, please. I must return to Daphne. She will wonder what has become of me."

She strode to the door. Out on the street, polished boots fell into step beside her.

"Do not interfere with me now," she said. "I am half-inclined to shoot you for real. If I am going to pay the price, I may as well do the deed."

"In a manner of speaking, you already did shoot me. You cocked the hammer. The pistol would have never gone off otherwise."

"*Please*. I do not want to be seen with you. I do not want anyone thinking that I arranged an assignation."

"You have already been seen with me. Our meeting will be all over Mayfair in an hour."

"Oh, that is simply wonderful. Thank you *very much*."

"Come now, the scandal can hardly get worse. Also, our meeting today has been most fortuitous."

"I think it has been most infuriating. Now, my cousin waits for me in there." She pointed to a milliner's shop. "I must bid you adieu."

He did not take dismissal easily. As she strode across the street, those boots kept in step beside her.

"Allow me to explain why it is fortuitous, Miss Kelmsleigh. My brother has expressed an interest in your situation. He would like to meet you. I planned to send invitations to you and your mother."

"My mother!"

"Of course. However, since you are in town today, I could take you to him now if that is agreeable to you."

"What possible interest could your brother have in meeting me?" She imagined sitting under the scrutiny of a marquess who had ample cause not to like what he saw.

"I believe he wants to condole with you, that you are suffering this cruel gossip. He is a very sympathetic person that way."

"Is he not too ill to receive guests?"

"Due to his war wounds, his movements are curtailed and his health is frail. But he is not so ill that he does not miss company."

She wavered. It would sound very harsh to refuse to visit a housebound invalid who had expressed sorrow for her plight.

"Ah, here is your cousin. Mrs. Joyes, I have just invited Miss Kelmsleigh to visit my brother. I hope that you will agree to allow it and accompany her so that tongues do not wag more."

Daphne showed no surprise at seeing him as she exited the milliner's, or at hearing the impromptu invitation. "That is generous, Lord Sebastian. However, I regret that I have several errands still to complete."

"Pity. It will have to wait for those other invitations after all, Miss Kelmsleigh."

Daphne cocked her head in curiosity.

"He intends to invite Mama and me together," Audrianna explained.

Daphne's eyes widened the barest fraction. No doubt she was imagining Mama's reaction to such an invitation, and the chilly atmosphere of such a visit if she decided to accept. Which she would feel forced to do. One did not turn down a marquess.

"I could accompany her as far as your house," Daphne said. "If the marchioness is at home, no one could question the propriety of such arrangements."

"Splendid. Once we are there, you must use the carriage to complete those other errands. I will have our man take you both home as well."

Wittonbury House was a mansion on Park Lane, facing Hyde Park and flanked by other massive homes of notable families. The façade displayed a restrained flamboyance that hinted at its construction in the prior century. Audrianna gazed up the six stories to where a large, scrolled pediment perched near the cornice, emphasizing the way the building projected out slightly in the center.

She had never visited a house this grand. Roger had some connections among the *ton*, but with him away with the army during most of their engagement, she had never enjoyed invitations to their homes for balls or parties.

They bid Daphne off in the carriage and approached the door. Once inside, Lord Sebastian spoke privately with the butler, then invited her to accompany him up to the drawing room.

"We will have to go to my brother. He does not leave his chambers," he explained as they mounted the stairs. "I hope that you do not mind."

"I pray that I am never so fastidious about etiquette as to insist that an invalid come to me at his inconvenience." She strolled around the drawing room. The chamber shimmered with costly fabrics and furniture. Even the walls proclaimed wealth, with oil paintings by Raphael, Titian, and Poussin. "Have you always lived here?"

He watched her progress around the room's edges, as if he found her gait interesting. "I returned when my brother was brought back from Spain. I lived elsewhere in town for some years prior to that."

She traced her fingertips over the luscious silk tassel holding back a drape in Vienna green. It felt as sensual as it looked. "Did you mind returning?"

This house was all luxury, but his coming back would be a bit like her returning to Mama now. She loved Mama, but did not think she could take her place there again without it chafing.

It was probably different for men, though. They were free of shackles wherever they lived, once they came of age. This homecoming's only penalty to his old life would be some inconvenience, perhaps, especially in the indulgence of his sensual appetites.

"I believed that I was needed here," he said.

"It was good of you to return, then, no matter what your preferences."

She peered out a window at a garden. "I hope that you did not tell your brother about our last conversation. The one on the lane at my cousin's house."

"I did not say a word to him about that."

"Thank you. This would be very awkward otherwise."

"My brother would find it amusing that you rejected my proposal. He might think the news the best part of his day."

He actually smiled while he said it, as if he found it amusing too. He most likely was relieved she had turned him down. The result had been ideal—he had offered to do the right thing, but had not actually had to do it.

"I did not expect you to show such good humor about it if I saw you again," she said.

"I understand your position, Miss Kelmsleigh. I did not take great offense. Some offense, but not great offense."

Again that smile. She forced clarity on her thoughts so she would not gaze upon him like a bedazzled fool.

A footman appeared in the doorway, then, and communicated a message without speaking a word.

"My brother is ready, Miss Kelmsleigh. I will take you to him."

Wittonbury's apartment was larger than most homes. They entered into a chamber that looked to serve as an anteroom.

Its pale walls and deep red upholstery made one ignore that it was a captive room with no window.

A crisply dressed man, heavyset and ruddy faced, greeted them. Lord Sebastian introduced him as Dr. Fenwood.

"My brother is well, Fenwood?"

"Very well, sir. He is pleased that you have brought him company. He is in the library." Dr. Fenwood paused. "Lady Wittonbury just arrived and is with him."

"Did my brother send for her?"

"I do not believe so, sir."

"Fortune is raining upon us today, Miss Kelmsleigh, if my mother is joining the party," he said as he escorted her to a door giving off the chamber on the left.

"You mean that *good* fortune is raining on us, do you not?"

"I doubt it."

The library proved much larger than the anteroom, and had the benefit of large windows along two walls. Twice the size of the library in her familial home, it made Audrianna wonder about the real library down below, the one that served more than one person.

Her perusal of the appointments and dark cases, the Turkish carpet and tall windows, abruptly ended when she saw the marchioness sitting near the fireplace.

Lady Wittonbury was formidable. All other descriptions would be secondary. Audrianna ticked them off anyway. Beautiful, even in her middle years, with her younger son's intense dark eyes and a tall, willowy body and a halo of midnight hair. Imperious, in the way she sat there, her back straight as an iron rod, her poise that of a queen. She arrested Audrianna's attention so thoroughly that it took a few moments to notice the man in the deep chair beside her.

Except for the marquess's face, cravat, and shirt collar,

he was all dark. His face was a softer version of his brother's, and much older looking, with a weary, dull countenance. His black coat descended to a dark blanket that covered the lower part of his body. He sat in a dark chair. One might think he would fade away into the shadows if his luminous mother did not sit nearby, shining her vitality on him.

"Please sit here, Miss Kelmsleigh," he said after introductions. He indicated a chair to his right. Lord Sebastian remained standing.

"Do you live in town, Miss Kelmsleigh?" the marchioness asked.

"I live in Cumberworth, in Middlesex."

Her eyebrows rose. It communicated disdain more than curiosity. "Cumberworth? I do not recall the newspapers mentioning that your father had property in Cumberworth."

The reference to her father and the stories in the paper was no accident. Audrianna resented this woman making a point of mentioning that, as if there were some danger anyone had forgotten it. "I live with my cousin."

"Her cousin, Mrs. Joyes, grows flowers in an immense greenhouse," Lord Sebastian said. "A grape vine grows within it."

"A grape vine?" Lady Wittonbury said. "How . . . rustic."

"We do live in the country, Madam. So, yes, it is a bit rustic."

"The garden is not rustic at all," Summerhays said. "When it is in bloom, I am sure that it would do the finest manor house proud."

Audrianna thought it kind of him to defend the garden and grounds of her home, although she suspected he enjoyed disagreeing with his mother more than complimenting her.

"So you do not live with your mother," Lady Wittonbury

mused. "Two unmarried young women living alone in the country . . . That is unusual."

"Not at all," the marquess said. "Since the war, it is too common."

"Mrs. Joyes, Miss Kelmsleigh's cousin, is indeed a war widow," Summerhays added.

That silenced Lady Wittonbury, but it did not stop her scrutiny. Audrianna felt like a disagreeable bug under her pointed attention.

"What sort of flowers are grown in this greenhouse?" the marquess asked.

Audrianna described the bulbs they forced in late winter, and the amaryllis in fall, and the many pelagoriums that they propagated and even hybridized.

"Your gardeners must be very busy," Lady Wittonbury said.

"We do it ourselves, Madam. Or rather, Daphne and Lizzie do most of it, and Celia and I help."

"Lizzie? More young ladies. Rather like an abbey."

"That is what my cousin says. Not abbey, but a home for *beguines*. They were common in medieval France. Laywomen would live together as we do. Some would take employment outside the walls, and none took vows, but they lived communally."

"Your cousin has put her property to good use then," the marquess said approvingly.

His mother stood, becoming even more formidable as she towered over Audrianna and the marquess. "I am delighted to have met you, Miss Kelmsleigh, and to have learned about your unusual home. It all sounds radical and far too independent to me, but I am an old-fashioned woman. Now, I must ask your forbearance. I have to attend to a pressing matter." She bent down and kissed the marquess on his head, as if he were a child. She gave Lord Sebastian a direct look as she took her leave.

"I will escort you," he said. "Miss Kelmsleigh, my brother will be glad for your continued company while I am gone, if you would be kind enough to indulge us both."

"Yes, do stay," the marquess said. "Tell me about the grape arbor."

"Why is she here?" The question came in a tight, low snap once the door closed behind them.

"She is here because I invited her," Sebastian said.

"Oh, give me patience. You sound so much like *him* with your sardonic dodges." She aimed not for her own chambers, but down to the library. There she paced back and forth, shooting him glares of displeasure.

"You have not done anything rash, have you?" she demanded. "It is one thing for you to dally with the daughter of a man exposed the way her father was. It is quite another if you attempt to rectify the indiscretion by—"

"By what?"

She stopped walking and faced him. "It is shocking that you brought her here, inviting more of society's scorn. She is most unsuitable, in every way. Even without this humiliating scandal, even without her father's disgrace, she would not do. This is not a situation where honor requires you do the right thing. Furthermore, whatever is between you and this woman must end. Even a continuing liaison will only damage the family and your influence."

"If I sound so much like *him*, it is because you sound so much like *you*," Sebastian said. Her criticism of Miss Kelmsleigh annoyed him deeply, more than it ought.

"I only remind you of your duty."

"I will not tolerate your rudeness to my friends."

"*Friends!* You count her as a friend now? Is it your goal to vex me to the point of apoplexy?"

"It is my goal to remind you that I am indeed too much like him, and not likely to accept your interference. In that, at least, I have not taken Morgan's place."

Her eyes narrowed and her pale face flushed. "As if you could take his place in anything."

"Of course not. I am not he."

"That is certain."

"Your vexation is of your own making, and I will leave you to stew in it now. Fill my brother's ears with your advice if you choose, but spare mine in the future."

He left the library and headed back upstairs. His mother had soured his mood more than he cared to admit. They both knew he had, in fact, taken Morgan's place in many ways. That was the true source of her anger.

And of his own sometimes.

Chapter Ten

Morgan and Miss Kelmsleigh did not notice him when he opened the door. They were too busy laughing.

The sound was so unnatural to these chambers that Sebastian paused in the threshold.

"It is good to hear my lord making merry." Fenwood spoke lowly. Sebastian turned to see Fenwood right behind him, craning his neck to look into the library now that the door had been opened.

Morgan's high spirits transformed him. His face took on color while he guffawed at Miss Kelmsleigh's joke. He appeared more animated, more alive, than he had in months.

Had merely the presence of a woman done that? Other than their mother and a few servants, no woman had entered this apartment in a very long time.

He stepped back so he could shut the door again, but Morgan noticed him before the retreat was successful. "You did not warn me that Miss Kelmsleigh possessed such a wit, brother."

He strolled toward them. "I know it to be sharp, that is true. I am jealous that you have been entertained by the cleverness of her tongue. Regrettably, I have only received its lashes."

"I would share her cleverness, but so often the retelling loses so much," Morgan said. His eyes actually twinkled while he and Miss Kelmsleigh shared a conspiratorial glance.

"Why do I think the joke was on me?" Sebastian said.

They both laughed again.

"Your company has been as refreshing as a fair day, Miss Kelmsleigh. Promise me that you will call again," Morgan said.

The suggestion took her aback. "I will try to do so. Thank you," she said.

She would not try very hard. Sebastian knew that she intended never to come here again.

"I would like you to see the house and garden before you leave. My brother will have to escort you, since I cannot."

"That is unfortunate, since the day is truly fair and might refresh you all the more. Can you not at least watch from the window while we take a turn in the garden?"

"I suppose I could, now that you mention it. I can be the chaperon watching from on high, and my brother will not have to request my mother's presence. I will call Dr. Fenwood and have him move me."

"I will do it," Sebastian said. With no further ado, he lifted his brother. Only after Morgan's surprisingly light weight was cradled in his arms did Sebastian consider that moving an invalid marquess in Miss Kelmsleigh's presence was undignified and inappropriate.

He had done this often enough that Morgan displayed no distress or embarrassment. Nor did Miss Kelmsleigh.

She positioned a chair right beside the window and Sebastian set his brother down.

"Open it, please," Morgan said.

Sebastian could not remember the last time Morgan had risked the chill of fresh air. "Are you sure?"

"Open it."

Miss Kelmsleigh opened the casement a crack. Sebastian found another of the lap blankets in a chest and draped it over his brother's shoulders.

"I will send in Fenwood. He will ensure you do not catch a chill," Sebastian said.

"Do not. He will close the window, even if I agree to wear ten blankets and a fur. Tell him I forbid him to enter for half an hour."

Sebastian could not find ten blankets, but he located one more, which he tucked around Morgan as well.

Miss Kelmsleigh watched. "I did not intend to endanger your health with my little suggestion."

"This fresh air is so delicious, I do not care if I suffer a fever later." He inhaled deeply and closed his eyes while he savored the light breeze. "Off with you both now. You must write and tell me what you think of the garden, Miss Kelmsleigh. Perhaps The Rarest Blooms will have ideas for its improvement."

The garden was magnificent, of course. Larger than most country gardens, it even had a little wilderness at its back. Audrianna had learned about garden fashions since living with Daphne, and the meandering paths and informal design of this one said a master planner had laid it out not so long ago.

"What did you think of the house?" Summerhays asked while he paced beside her.

He had given her a tour of the vast library and even larger ballroom. The most interesting chamber had been the circular music room that held an exquisite pianoforte. "It is most impressive. A more sophisticated woman might not be in awe, but I confess that I am."

"You do yourself an injustice. You acquit yourself well enough when you choose. My brother is already fond of you, and you did not allow my mother to frighten you."

So he had noticed that his mother had tried. "She was not pleased by my presence in her impressive house. I think that she was surprised to find me there. I think that your brother was too, and did not ask to meet me at all."

"Why would you think that? He delighted in your company."

"I think that because I asked him and he told me the truth."

"How like him." He cast a frown over his shoulder at the face at the high window. "You have found me out. However, he did express sympathy for your plight. It was good for you to meet him, and my mother, and see the house. You should see the life you will have when we marry. The good and the bad."

When we marry.

"I did not accept your proposal."

"You were in shock."

"It was unexpected, but I was not in shock."

"You did not comprehend what you were turning down."

"I did, most clearly. *You.*"

Only she had not truly comprehended. He was correct

about that. In showing her this house, this comfort, he had dangled a lure.

He had revealed much more than luxury too, although she did not think he realized it. Seeing him with his mother, his brother—a whole history suddenly existed, and he became more real and human. The way he had lifted his brother, the care he had shown as he fussed with those blankets—it was very hard to think such a man was by nature cruel.

"Miss Kelmsleigh, I want you to reconsider my proposal."

And she wanted to reject it again, with the same strength and certainty as the last time. Only she could not. His little strategy had worked too well.

"Lord Sebastian, my mother would never countenance such a match, after what happened to my father."

He glanced over his shoulder, to that window. Then he took her hand and firmly led her down another path that veered around a thick planting of blackthorn. A bench waited there, and he handed her down so she would sit.

"If you tell your mother about my proposal, I think that she will countenance it just fine. She will want the connections, and the financial security, and the position for all of you. It is a rare mother who demands her daughter turn down the brother of a marquess, for any reason."

"My father—"

"She will convince herself it is your due, and hers, because of that sorrow. She blames me for an injustice, and this helps to rectify some of it. You know that she will find her way to that view. It is why the notion of her being invited here caused you alarm."

"And my own view?"

"Adopt your mother's. It is practical at least. There will be no better way, no other way, to make me pay."

"I will blame you no less after we are wed, even if I think you are paying. Do you not care that this will be poison to what you propose."

"As you saw, it is a very big house, Miss Kelmsleigh. All of the others are at least as large. You can live your life tolerating my company no more than ten hours a week if you choose. Trust me when I promise that it will be very easy to be married and mostly separate. I have seen it done."

She could not deny that he made a compelling argument. There would be a type of justice if the man who so hurt her family became the agent of its rise and revival. Marriage would also dull the scandal and provide more security than she had ever hoped to know.

As for the luxury—she tried to resist its lure, but she was human. Images invaded her mind, of gowns she had never worn and balls she had never seen. He had his own boxes at the theaters, certainly, and there would be long, exquisite dinners amid flickering candles and silk and the very best company.

As for those ten hours a week—

Fingers touched her chin and guided her face to the left. No gloves this time, but the unmistakable sensation of masculine skin on hers. The contact startled her out of her reverie.

He sat beside her. His eyes said he knew where her mind had been, and where it was now turning.

"It will be more than tolerable, I promise."

His lips touched hers, making his reference clear. Under the circumstances, she assessed this kiss in ways she had not the others. After all, she needed to be very sure of what she would be getting in this marriage.

Yes, more than tolerable. Much more. She did not remain objective very long. Still, she noted that his kiss was rather firm and dry, and that the way his hands cradled her head was both sweet and controlling. She vaguely acknowledged that he then embarked on a gentle ravishment of her mouth, but a ravishment all the same. As pleasure started to cascade through her body, she dully considered that it had probably taken him a lot of practice to learn to kiss like this, and admitted that she had been primed for this by his mere presence, which still affected her too much.

Then she thought about nothing at all, except the building cravings that demanded all her attention.

Sinful cravings. Shocking ones. Her body had become more practiced in these things, and offered little resistance. Devilish titillations teased her as if invisible feathers flicked and stroked her body. Her breasts grew heavy, and impatient with the garments binding them.

Floating now, as if her body had lost its grounding. His hard arm encircled her and kept her from blowing away. The embrace brought her to earth too well.

"Your brother—"

"It is well past a half hour since we left him. Fenwood has removed him from the window."

How careless of the marquess, to leave her unprotected. "Your mother." Did she even say it? Kisses on her neck had her gasping so she did not know for sure.

"She will be receiving callers now, and we cannot be seen from the drawing room's windows."

She tried to remember what she saw when she looked out that window.

His fingertips touched her lips, as if to silence her. Except that was not his intention at all. He coaxed her lips apart. "Yes. Like that."

That other kind of kiss this time, invasive and intimate. The excitement and pleasure immediately intensified and she lost herself again, and entered a dark place of primal desire.

She did not care when his embrace pulled her closer. She wickedly reveled in the signs of his own passion. She did not object at all when he caressed her breast. She wanted him to. She almost begged him to.

It felt too good. Unearthly. Amazing. Somehow he found a way to touch her so she almost cried out. The pleasure turned sharper and raised a madness in her. A warm throb teased her horribly where she sat, causing a compelling discomfort that fed the frenzy filling her mind.

"Tolerable enough?" His dark voice spoke lowly in her ear while he teased her breasts mercilessly.

She was too preoccupied to even care he had asked some question or other.

Suddenly he was gone from her side, leaving her flushed and vulnerable in the breeze. Its cool flow made her open her eyes and blink.

He had not gone far. He knelt right in front of her. Her head cleared enough to realize he was going to propose again, on bended knee. That was too charming to bear.

Only he did not propose, and nothing in his expression suggested such honorable intentions. The way he looked, and looked at her, sent a thrilling alarm straight through her.

He lifted her left foot, slid off her slipper, and placed its arch on the front of his knee. Before she collected herself enough to object, he began raising her skirt.

Shocked, she reached to push it down again. "What are you doing?"

"What you want me to do, or at least what our circumstances permit right now."

"You misunderstand what I want." Except he really did not. As he pushed up her skirt, he also caressed her leg, and his palm's movements soon became of more interest than her skirt's.

"You are being too wicked." She tried again to push the skirt even as it inched up, but pleasure was making her the worst fool.

"Yes." He managed to get the hem over her knee so her stocking leg was bare to her thigh. He ignored her attempts to cover herself. He bent and kissed her knee, then the inner flesh right above her garter.

She almost jumped off the bench. The shock to her body left her breathless. She stared at him while he did it again, fearful of how everything had transformed suddenly, and turned most serious, and very dangerous. She suddenly found herself in deep water and she did not even care if she drowned.

His hand replaced his mouth. His caresses made wanton moans and pleas sound in her head. It was all she could do to hold them in.

He watched her helplessness while he caressed higher. Her body throbbed in response. She could feel distinct pulses down there, wanting and waiting and hot.

His fingers pushed up the bottom edge of her drawers until they bunched at the top of her thigh. She closed her eyes and tried to gather some self-control.

"You should not," she whispered.

"No, but I am not so good as to stop. Nor am I being really bad. After all, the world has already given you to me, and there really is no choice for you except to submit to what fate has decreed." His hand teased along that edge of fabric. "You should know how it will be when you do."

His fingers slid beneath the fabric of her drawers. He touched that pulse. Her breath caught as the sensation obliterated every other awareness.

He caressed and her mind split from the intensity. She closed her eyes and the pleasure overwhelmed her. He said something and she did not hear him, or could not remember if she did.

She lost the fight to contain it. She leaned back against the bench, boneless and weightless. She shifted her hips so she might feel more and succumbed completely to the pleasure.

Soon she could not bear it. The pleasure took on an angry, frustrated center. Shrieks of need began streaking through her abandon. One escaped, she was sure, sounding through the garden.

Those wicked touches stopped, replaced by soothing caresses on her thigh. A cry of frustration escaped and she heard herself this time. She pressed her hand to her mouth lest one more slip out. She let his soothing strokes do what they could, but she wanted to hit him for stopping and leaving this hungry edge of desire in her.

She rode the tide down until something like sanity returned. She still felt the breeze on her leg. She opened her eyes and straightened, embarrassed now, and at a bigger disadvantage with this man than she had ever been.

He no longer caressed her thigh. Instead he fastened a chain around it.

A gold chain, with dangling green stones. Her thigh now wore an emerald necklace.

She stared at it. "Payment?"

"No, a bribe."

She touched the green stones and they beat gently against her flesh. He was going to a lot of trouble. "Why?"

He rose and sat beside her. She worked the clasp and removed the necklace, admiring it in the sunlight.

"Because you deserve more than scandal and infamy, and because I no longer can afford to be known as a rake and a scoundrel."

"Did you ever really stop being one?"

"I would like to think that I was never a scoundrel."

That begged the question about the rake part. It was fair warning that outside those obligatory hours together, he would be going his separate way too.

She pushed down her dress and slipped on her shoe. "I am sure that Daphne has been waiting. I must go."

They strolled back to the house. She should feel more embarrassed than she did. That alone had her thinking over the various implications of both his proposal and this powerful sensuality.

She had quite forgotten for a while, within that pleasure, her resentments toward him. The anger had been obscured within that daze. That momentary timelessness, more than the sensations, might indeed make this marriage tolerable.

Would it be a betrayal of Papa to accept? Even if it gave Mama security, and Sarah a chance for a better life? She did not believe Papa would hold it against her. The question was whether she would hold it against herself.

On the other hand, she might more easily find a way to vindicate him if she had this new, higher station being offered.

"If we were to do this, I assume it would be a sophisticated union, such as one hears about among the *haut ton*," she said. "That you would have lovers and that, after a time, after a son is born, I could too." It was, she discovered, fairly easy to speak frankly with a man with whom one had shared scandalous intimacies.

He paced on a bit before answering. "Of course."

When they reached the house, she still held the necklace. "I cannot take this."

He removed it from her hand, then also took her reticule. He dropped the necklace inside and handed the reticule back. "If you reject me again, it will be the only compensation you will have. If you do not, it is an appropriate engagement gift."

Daphne indeed had arrived back from her errands. She had refused the offer to wait inside, and still sat in Lord Sebastian's carriage.

Lord Sebastian handed Audrianna to a footman at the house's door. She bid him adieu, stepped away, then thought better of it and turned for a last word. "I suppose those few hours a week might be tolerable enough."

"Today was the least of what waits in that part of our union, Miss Kelmsleigh. Perhaps you will let me know your decision about the other parts by week's end."

"Yes, I will do that."

She climbed into the carriage. Daphne appeared serene, and not at all annoyed that she had to wait.

"Did you meet the marquess?" she asked as the carriage rolled away.

"Yes, and he is very amiable."

Daphne resettled herself on her bench. "And was the marchioness home?"

"As promised. I met her too." Audrianna wrinkled her nose in distaste.

Daphne laughed. She adjusted the curtain. She eyed the carriage's fine interior appointments.

She looked out the window a few minutes, then turned a very direct gaze on Audrianna.

"So, dear cousin, when is the wedding?"

Chapter Eleven

Sebastian received Audrianna's letter accepting his proposal two days after her visit. Mrs. Kelmsleigh's letter arrived the next day, expressing restrained joy and inviting him to call on her. He did so at once and met her younger daughter, Sarah, and drank punch in her tidy drawing room near Russell Square while they passed a half hour pretending she did not hate him.

Then she got down to business. She demanded a discreet, small wedding since it would be less than a year from her husband's passing. She also asked for permission to put Audrianna's new wardrobe on his accounts, along with wedding garments for her and her daughter.

No specific amount was requested. It would be indelicate to actually talk sums. In agreeing to cover these feminine costs, he accepted that he had just given them carte blanche. Between the impulse for revenge and the opportunity for indulgence, the Kelmsleigh women would probably put him in dun territory.

Morgan expressed satisfaction at the news that Sebastion was "doing the right thing" by Miss Kelmsleigh, but then Morgan possessed uncomplicated views of right and wrong, of honor and decency. Sebastian was pleased that his brother was pleased because, when that letter from Audrianna came, he had found himself pleased as well.

She was proving to be lively, smart, and sensual, and he could do worse. And if he later decided that he had been trapped into a temporal hell, he could follow his father's example in this as in so much else. She even expected him to.

Their mother said absolutely nothing the evening that Sebastian sought her out to inform her. She did not even look at him during the announcement. A statue would display more reaction, but even an actor could not be more eloquent.

Finally, as he was leaving, she flatly said that she would see to the wedding preparations and the breakfast, so the family was not totally humiliated in every possible way. Since he had braced himself for a long, tedious row, he kissed her in gratitude before retreating from her icy presence.

The announcement of the engagement raised eyebrows and caused another gust of gossip, but the wind soon went out of the scandal's sails. There would be little breezes for years, of course, but a week after sealing the deal, a letter came from Castleford, accepting the mutually beneficial trade of favors that he had dismissed before. That signaled the return to normal in Sebastian's political influence.

One colleague in the Commons, Nathan Proctor, tried to make amends for a few reckless cuts by approaching him one afternoon as they both left Brook's.

"That boy from my county is finally coming home," he said in passing.

Sebastian's mind was on other things, and he could do nothing except smile blankly at the reference.

"That one with the third regiment that I told you about last year. All blown up, he was. On death's door and being cared for in a convent over there up until last autumn. He is finally fit to travel, and is coming home to his family. He will be staying here in London with a sister for a while."

The third included the company that had been left defenseless by the bad gunpowder. Sebastian had spent two years seeking out the few who survived, to discover what light they might shed on the business. Other than stories of death and helplessness, of cannon that misfired and muskets made useless, he had learned nothing.

His mind picked back through memories of all the evidence and facts he had learned. "He was a gunner, wasn't he?"

"He was. It is a miracle he is alive. They train their cannon on ours, of course. The lad only survived because he had been bending to open another keg to check it."

Gunners handled powder all the time. This young man might know more than the other survivors.

"When will he be in England?"

"Two weeks or so, I am told. The family finally found the money to send people over to bring him back. Not able to make it on his own, of course."

Sebastian thanked Proctor, and asked to be told when the soldier was home. He then continued on his way. How capricious of fate to offer another potential breakthrough in the case of Kelmsleigh, right on the heels of his engagement to the dead man's daughter.

Unfortunately, he did not expect to learn anything that would exonerate Audrianna's father. Rather the opposite.

Upon returning to Park Lane, he checked on Morgan

and discovered that Kennington and Symes-Wilvert were visiting. Unable to make a good escape, he was trapped into a long hour of whist. Morgan's two friends wanted to talk about the wedding.

"Damned decent of you, Summerhays," Kennington offered sonorously.

"Yes, damned decent," Symes-Wilvert concurred.

"My brother is only sorry that they could not announce their intentions before this unfortunate gossip started," Morgan said. "In attempting to allow Miss Kelmsleigh's family the entire period of mourning for her late father to pass, and in trying to let time itself blunt future gossip on the capricious direction that affection can take, they innocently opened the door for worse speculation."

Sebastian stared at his cards. Morgan had just lied. Not baldly, since Morgan did not know for certain there had not been a liaison prior to the night at the Two Swords, but . . . His brother admired Audrianna, and it appeared he would stretch the truth to help her weather this storm.

"I hear she is a handsome woman, so I am sure the match is not all caprice," Kennington said. "You met her while looking into that business about her father, I assume."

"Yes." And he had.

"I expect that you will be giving up on that now, like the others did. It did not look like it was going anywhere anyway, once he all but confessed in hanging himself," Symes-Wilvert said.

Sebastian played a card.

"If there were others involved, I do not think they should sleep easily just yet," Morgan said. "My brother can be most tenacious in the execution of his duty."

"Of course. I was not implying that he would not do his duty, you understand," Symes-Wilvert said, flushing. "Just, his bride will not be wanting all that dug up again. I thought—"

How like Symes-Wilvert not to realize that in marrying Miss Kelmsleigh, Sebastian all but forced himself to exercise that tenacity that Morgan mentioned. If he gave up his investigation now, he essentially admitted those engravings had got his character right.

He noted Morgan's serious expression now that the conversation had turned to that gunpowder. It had always been thus. Since the first reports of that massacre reached London, Morgan's interest had been very keen. He had lost his composure once, when he spoke of the horror those soldiers had faced due to negligence or worse. Morgan's fondness for Audrianna would not change any of that.

"Miss Kelmsleigh knows my views and intentions," Sebastian said. "I am grateful for your concern regarding my marital harmony, however."

"I think Summerhays here intends to keep harmony in other ways." Kennington chortled at his own innuendo. Being Kennington, however, he would not risk that others might miss his all-too-obvious point. "Time to put all that practice to good use, eh, Summerhays? Then your lady will not be caring what you do in this other matter."

Symes-Wilvert snickered. Morgan smiled with forbearance at his faithful, foolish friend. Sebastian laughed obligingly, and snuck a look at his pocket watch.

"I think we overdid it," Audrianna said.

"Overdid it? Certainly not." Her mother's soft, pale face and new lace-trimmed cap hung over the new Russian flame promenade dress that she held to her body. It, like most of her new ensembles, would not be worn until April when she put away her widow's weeds, but her anticipation of that day was in her eyes. "And why should we not overdo it? Even if we did, which we didn't. It will take more than a new wardrobe to repay us for all that has happened."

"Much more," Sarah said. Then she giggled. "Surely at least two or three wardrobes."

Mama bit back a laugh. She set down the ensemble and lifted a dinner dress of puce silk. "What do you think of this one, Daphne? I debated forever about the rollios near the hem. Do you agree I chose wisely?"

Daphne offered compliments on the dress. She watched the display from a chair. She had been invited by Mama to visit specifically to inspect the loot.

The extent of the haul stunned Audrianna, even though she had helped buy it all. Bonnets and hats, shawls and reticules, hung from the chairs and covered a table. Dresses had been unwrapped and heaped on the sofa, but many more still waited in their muslin shrouds for inspection.

"I wish that Lizzie had come with you today," Sarah pouted while she tried on an evening cap adorned with ostrich feathers. "She has such exquisite taste, and I have grown fond of her."

"Her headaches have returned now as the days lengthen," Daphne explained. "The physician says she must just bear it, and rest, unless she wants to become an habitué of laudanum. I will be sure to give her a detailed description of every dress, hat, and gown, however."

"Show Daphne the rose satin, Audrianna," Mama said. "Now, there was some penance for Lord Sebastian."

Audrianna held up her new rose satin evening dress for

Daphne to admire. "You know, Mama, in a manner of speaking, I am the one who will be doing penance for all of this finery."

Mama's face fell into a mask of tenderness. She walked over and gave Audrianna an embrace and kiss. "Indeed so, my dear. Indeed so. It is so brave of you, but then you were always the strongest among us. Except for his station, I would have never permitted this marriage, even after his unforgivable misuse of you. But he is from one of the finest families and your expectations are so improved with him, no matter how distasteful the marital duties will be."

The little speech made Audrianna blush, but not for the reasons Mama would think. "I meant that I will do penance because the bills for all of this will arrive right after we are married."

"I would not worry," Daphne said. "I doubt that Lord Sebastian will be surprised, or find the sum nearly as high as we do."

"See, Daphne agrees we did not overdo it," Mama said, even though Daphne had agreed to no such thing. "Oh, did I tell you? I have received a letter from my brother Rupert. He is overjoyed by the news of the engagement, and will travel to town to attend the wedding. It appears, Audrianna, that you have bridged that estrangement, just as you have brought so much other good fortune to us with your sacrifice."

Daphne's expression did not alter one whit. Yet Audrianna sensed a chill surround Daphne's chair on the mention of Uncle Rupert. There could be no joy for Daphne in seeing him at the wedding. After all, Uncle Rupert had left Daphne to her own devices when his and Mama's brother, Daphne's father, had died.

Audrianna set aside her rose silk gown. "Have you seen

enough? Mama and Sarah can play this game together if you have. We can take a turn on the square if you like."

Daphne found that agreeable. Bonnets and pelisses donned, they made their escape.

"I suffered Mama much better before I had some experience in not having to," Audrianna said as they strolled down the street. She entwined her arm in Daphne's. "I miss all of you."

No sooner had she accepted the engagement than Mama had insisted she return to the nest. *You must marry out of your family's home. The preparations will be inconvenient if you are in the country.*

Being here offered little real convenience. It took almost as long to reach Mayfair from this street off Russell Square as it would from Cumberworth. Mama had never liked living so far from the fashionable western neighborhoods, but the house that they let here had been convenient to Papa's duties at the Tower.

"She just wants you near her for a few final days. You will be leaving the cage soon," Daphne said.

"I fly from one cage to another, however. I think I will see my months at The Rarest Blooms among the most happy and free that I ever knew."

Daphne squeezed her hand. "We are always there for you. You will visit often."

"Will you all be with me on Saturday? It will give me courage if you are."

"I will be there, and Celia, I think."

"Lizzie?"

"I would not count on it. These headaches are too capricious."

They reached Bedford Square, with its neat, modest town houses lined in uniform rows on each side. She and Roger used to stroll here before he went to the war. After their engagement, he had spoken of letting one of these houses once they were wed. She had spent hours while he was gone picturing herself in one of them. The square held enough memories that she had avoided it for months after she released Roger from his obligation.

They entered the garden and strolled amid its barren trees, boxwood, and ivy.

"Do you mind too much that Uncle Rupert and Aunt Clara will be at my wedding?" Audrianna asked.

"Who am I to mind? Their recent slights to your family signify more than any old ones to me."

Those recent slights were not small ones, and Audrianna did mind that this rapprochement would happen with no further ado. After Papa's death, Uncle Rupert had done nothing to alleviate their strained circumstances. "I fear this means that Mama believes he was justified in breaking with us."

"It only means that she understands the ways of the world. She may not think her brother was justified, but she understands why he did it. And she understands why now he wants the connections that you bring to the family."

"It gives me heart to know I am so useful to him." She could not keep a sardonic note from her tone.

"It would give me heart to know that you welcome this wedding in some way, cousin, even if it is only for the wardrobes and connections that your family will enjoy," Daphne said. "The circumstances were such that you could make no other choice, but—"

"At the moment I do welcome it, if only to end this

month of waiting. And to escape Mama. If I am going to do this, I am eager that it be sooner rather than later."

Mama actually had little to do with her restlessness, and it was unfair to blame her. The real reason was that she did not care for the formalities now smothering her and Lord Sebastian. Their every meeting took place on stage now, on which they wore costumes of etiquette. Every word was planned and every flattery predictable. The mood was so different from the events and easy conversations that had led to their engagement.

Instead of learning to know him better this last month, she had come to know him less well. He kept receding in familiarity. She feared that if much more time passed, she would marry a total stranger.

"One part that I do not welcome is Lady Wittonbury," she admitted.

"Has she been rude to you?"

"Is the word *rude* ever applied to queens? She has let me know I am not suitable for her son with every glance and every address. She sent me a little stack of books on etiquette and behavior last week."

"Now, that *was* rude."

"I thought so. They arrived with a personal note from her. She explained that such books were written for those trying to better themselves, by those who already had, and therefore often include mistakes that the best born would recognize. So she had corrected the errors."

"She provided a gloss on the texts?"

"Oh, yes. There are little marginal notes all through them in her hand." Daphne was laughing and Audrianna had to laugh too. "Most of the comments explained that only common people would consider this or that advice accurate."

Daphne stopped to admire some crocuses poking their heads through the ivy under a tree. "Has your mother spoken to you, Audrianna, with more useful advice than the marchioness offered? You know what I mean."

"Mama believes there is no need. It would be nice if someone who knows me believed that the rumors were not true."

"It was not your character, but his, that raised the doubts, and I apologize for mine. If you have any questions, I will try to answer them, since your mother has not invited the conversation herself."

She had many questions, but not about the matter that Daphne now broached. Lord Sebastian had already shown her that part would be tolerable enough. It was not the night-by-night living that worked on her mind, but the day-to-day.

How would she hide the anger that she still felt about Papa?

How would she keep the marchioness from making her miserable?

How would she find friends in this new world that she entered?

What was the etiquette when your husband took a mistress? Those books said nothing about that. Perhaps she would ask the marchioness someday. Innuendoes the last month indicated that Lady Wittonbury had extensive experience on how the best born handled such developments.

She stopped walking and looked at a naked bush. Its many long branches had turned red and supple. Swollen nobs showed all along them, waiting to burst at the first signs of extended warmth.

It was a forsythia. The most common of blooms. That was what she was too. Ordinary, and not at all rare. If not for the progression of a series of unexpected quirks of fate, Lord Sebastian would have never noticed her, let alone proposed.

She was supposed to revel in her good luck. Nor was she so noble that she did not. She and Mama and Sarah had overdone it at the dressmakers, and she had enjoyed every minute of their orgy of self-indulgence.

"I do have one question," she said. "It is not about him, or the life I will have. It is about me."

Daphne cocked her head in curiosity. "What is it?"

"Is it wrong for me to enjoy the kisses of a man whom I will never love?"

Daphne smiled softly. "I am relieved that you asked that. You cannot know how much. No, it is not wrong. Women pretend that love is required for that excitement, but men admit it is not. And the excitement itself often breeds some affection, and that makes life endurable." She gave Audrianna a little kiss on her cheek. "Nor is it a betrayal of your father to enjoy the kisses, if that is what your question really meant. He would not want you living in dread of the night."

Daphne could be very wise sometimes. She understood the human heart without even trying. "Why are you relieved?"

"Because if you did not enjoy those kisses, you would be entering hell. I am grateful for the indication that you will not be. Now, I must go back and take my leave of your mother. I have several errands in town, so I can arrange a surprise for your wedding."

Chapter Twelve

Audrianna's wedding day did not open auspiciously. Dawn revealed that a drizzle and a biting north wind had descended on London. Mama had the fires built up and fussed about the way the rain would ruin their shoes.

Audrianna bathed and dressed, and sat for the new maid to do her hair. She had avoided asking Mama how this extra servant was being paid. No doubt when Lord Sebastian made his obligatory call after the engagement, Mama had expressed distress about preparing for the wedding day when their circumstances had reduced them to one servant.

She was ready long before anyone else, and went to Sarah's room to hurry her along. She found her sister and mother arguing over which dress Sarah would wear. That had been decided long ago, during one of their financial debauches at the dressmakers.

Audrianna inserted herself between them. She removed the violet dress from Sarah's hands, laid it on the bed, and lifted a primrose dress instead. "You will wear this one, as agreed when you ordered it, or you will not go. The coach already waits outside, and I will not have the entire day be victim to your whims."

"The other is much finer," Sarah said. "I look like a child in this one."

"The gentlemen will notice you faster if you wear this primrose," Audrianna said.

Sarah stopped pouting long enough to consider that.

"I am leaving in the coach in a quarter hour," Audrianna said. "It is my sincere hope that you will be joining me. Mama, you should finish quickly too."

"A quarter hour is far too soon. We will be at the church before anyone else, and appear ridiculous," Mama said.

"We are not going to the church right away. I want to visit Papa's grave first."

Her mother's sigh filled the chamber. "Audrianna, with the rain—really, it is not wise to—"

"I can hardly go after the church. I may not be able to go at all for a long time to come. I will wear my long cloak and change into my silk shoes after. You can sit in the coach if you like, but I will visit his grave so he knows I have not forgotten him."

Sebastian approached St. Georges with Hawkeswell by his side. Invited guests passed them, offering Sebastian felicitations.

"Fortune has chosen to give you the rawest day in weeks," Hawkeswell said. "I am not superstitious myself, however."

Sebastian was not superstitious either. He credited nature with taking no heed of mankind's doings, let alone choosing the weather for one man even though it affected thousands. He *was* a student of ironic coincidences, however. So as he and Hawkeswell stopped at the church's threshold, he noted that the last time the weather had been this bad was the day he met Miss Kelmsleigh.

All thoughts of rain and wind disappeared when he saw the interior of the church. Someone had turned it into a garden.

Curved arbors of ivy-covered wood were spaced periodically down the wide central aisle. From where he stood, the perspective created the impression that the entire length had an arched ceiling of foliage.

A cluster of pots that contained vivid tulips surrounded the entry. Another thick massing of spring flowers spilled over the altar. Nosegays of daffodils and hyacinth decorated the ends of each pew. The entire effect was an opulent, bright painting that emitted light from hundreds of blooms.

"Impressive," Hawkeswell said. "You may have a small, discreet wedding, Summerhays, but it will not be forgotten soon. Your mother will start a new fashion."

His mother had nothing to do with this. This exuberance was not her style and she probably did not approve of the theatrical notes, especially during Lent.

Mrs. Joyes had decorated this church, and populated it with the children of her greenhouse. Society would be impressed, and bring her their trade, no doubt, but he did not think that was her goal. Audrianna could not identify most of the people at this wedding, but she would recognize each pot and flower.

A little commotion behind them caused Hawkeswell to turn. "We should go down. Your bride's carriage is here."

Sebastian turned to see the carriage door open. Mrs.

Kelmsleigh and her younger daughter emerged. Sarah squealed as the wind tried to steal her hat. An elegant ankle and white hem poked toward the top step. Mrs. Kelmsleigh cried out and pointed at what appeared to be a grass stain on the snowy fabric.

"That is an extremely fine carriage," Hawkeswell mused. "It looks new. The ladies are in the very latest styles too. No expense has been spared."

"None at all, I am sorry to have cause to know." The bills had just started to come in. Mrs. Kelmsleigh had shown no restraint in bleeding him.

"I wish I had a sister, so I could have enjoyed your generosity. Hell, I am sorry there was no way for you to marry *me*."

They turned away before Audrianna was totally out of the carriage, and walked down the aisle. Sebastian's groomsman already waited there.

"Chin up there, Summerhays," Hawkeswell muttered. "This is not nearly as painful as we think it will be. More like the guillotine than a hanging, I would say."

Audrianna wept when she saw the flowers. They brightened the day and banished the chill. They nodded to her while all these strangers stared.

The building nervousness of the last few days, the melancholy from visiting Papa's grave, the irritation with Mama and Sarah—all of it disappeared as she stood at the church door and surveyed the garden that The Rarest Blooms had made for her.

Her eyes sought out Daphne. She sat to the far side of the guests, wearing the palest lilac dress that enhanced her pale beauty beyond belief. She would have upstaged Sarah badly if Sarah were not in the primrose instead. Daphne was alone. A note had arrived yesterday saying Lizzie's headaches had returned, and that Celia would be staying home too, to nurse her.

Lizzie had braved an unexpected visit to Mama's house two days ago, however. Audrianna suspected that, having been granted a day of freedom from the pain, Lizzie had really come to town to help Daphne plan this display.

A portly, gray-haired man approached, to take her arm. Uncle Rupert. Mama had insisted he be allowed to do this, despite his cruelties in the past. Audrianna had acquiesced, but in her mind it was her father escorting her and accepting the well wishes, with his good name restored and his comforting presence by her side.

Lord Sebastian waited for her. He looked splendid. No one could ever think him other than the best catch. His dark blue frockcoat made his cravat gleam in contrast, and his eyes fairly glowed in the light coming from the many candles.

He smiled as she approached. A kind smile. Reassuring, but still a smile designed to make a woman's head spin. Her own did, as it always had. The faces blurred and receded. Even the flowers turned into a watercolor wash of hues. She spoke the vows like a woman drugged.

A udrianna entered her new bedchamber. The wedding was over. They had returned to visit the marquess before attending the breakfast that he could not join. Now the guests were gone and all the rituals had been completed. Except one.

She had been given a lovely suite of rooms. The marchioness had redecorated them herself. Crisp toile fabric hung on the bed and windows. Deep blue covered the cushions of two chairs. A fine chinoiserie writing desk angled near a window. She opened it to find all the necessities for letters.

A door on one wall gave access to her dressing room. Her personal belongings had been moved yesterday. A little army of servants and maids had descended on Mama's house, to pack all those dresses into trunks. Now they inhabited the wardrobes that lined the walls of this chamber that exceeded her old bedroom in size.

A lady's maid named Nellie inhabited it too. She had been the field marshal of yesterday's army, and the new bride was her duty. Red-haired and stocky, with a dusting of freckles on her face, she bobbed out from where she ironed in a corner when Audrianna entered.

"Lady Wittonbury told me to serve you today, Madam. I was warned that you may want to choose your own woman, of course, but until then I hope that I can please you. I was told that the marchioness chose me because she believed that you would be more comfortable with me than with a French maid, and I swear I haven't one drop of French blood in my veins."

Nellie seemed to think the requirement was political. More likely Lady Wittonbury had concluded that Nellie's simplicity suited Audrianna's background. Audrianna could only imagine the other requirements that Lady Wittonbury had itemized to the hiring service. She had to admit that the marchioness was correct in one thing, however. She would be more comfortable with a maid who did not have a lot of airs.

Nellie moved to a wardrobe and removed an undressing gown. "I was in service to a lady up north, Madam. I am new to London's ways, but I can dress hair with the best of them, and I ply a fine needle. Will you be wanting to remove those wedding garments now?"

"Yes, that will probably be best. And brush out my hair as well."

Nellie went to work unfastening the dress. "Should I prepare you for bed, Madam?"

"Yes, I think so."

Summerhays had not said a word about that as he walked up to these chambers with her. Yet she was very sure that the last ritual would not wait for the night. His intention had been in the air and his presence, and it made her heart beat harder with each step beside him. The light stirring in her body was partly fear, and also something else.

"Would you like to wear this nightdress that came?" Nellie went to a table and lifted one of several boxes perched on it. She brought it over.

A beautiful nightdress lay within. A card said it was from The Rarest Blooms. Audrianna lifted the filmy, lightweight fabric. It was far more elegant than the nightdresses Mama had made her order. More mature too.

"I think that I will use this. Bring me the other boxes too."

Sebastian's valet poked his head into the dressing room. Nothing was said, but it was the sign that the lady's maid had left Audrianna's chambers.

He could wait, of course. For the night, or even several nights. He did not want to. Nor did she expect it. She had known, when he kissed her at her chamber door, that he would be coming to her.

Dressed in a robe of dark blue silk, he opened the door that led to her bedchamber. This entry had been cut once it was determined that Audrianna would use this chamber to the north of his apartment.

Her chamber's window drapes had been pulled, casting the room into modest shadows. One, however, was not closed completely. A beam of dusty light sliced through the dark, ending on the bed. He saw what it illuminated, and a hard arousal hit him immediately.

The light bathed a beautiful woman in a diaphanous, transparent gown, reclining on a flower-strewn bed.

Tiny blooms peeked out of her hair and dotted her body. Some discreetly placed lace almost made the transparent bodice modest. But not quite.

He had anticipated nervousness and awkwardness from her. He had even debated what to do if she cried. He had not expected this.

He went to the drapes and parted them a little more, so he could see this Flora more clearly. Her legs, hips, even her mound, became discernible as filmy forms within the flowing gauze. He suppressed the urge to stride over there, strip off that provocative dress, and take her at once.

"You look very beautiful, Audrianna."

"I was afraid you might think it was silly. It appeared that way when you first came in."

"Not at all silly. I was surprised, but in the best way."

"The dress was a gift. And the flowers. My friends sent them, to be waiting for me when I came up here."

"You look like a spring nymph. I would like to leave this light upon you, but I will close the drapes if you prefer."

She gazed down her body, and at his robe. He saw the moment when she calculated that he would not be the only one seeing in the light, and that he would see more than flowers and gauze, perhaps.

He turned to close the drapes.

"It would be childish of me to make this bold display, then hide in the dark where it can't even be seen."

"I would understand, but I am glad you will be a little more bold." He walked to the bed and unbuttoned his robe. Her eyes shut firmly. She turned her face away.

Not so bold after all. He cast the robe aside and slid under the sheet.

The gown proved more revealing up close. Elegantly erotic. Her dark nipples pressed against the fabric, already tight and hard. Not an innocent girl's wedding garment, but then she was not a girl.

He kissed where the gown met her shoulder. "Mrs. Joyes has excellent taste."

"I think that perhaps Celia chose the dress. The card did not say, but . . . I think so. Not Lizzie, that is certain."

The small talk seemed to calm her. For all her inviting, theatrical welcome, she was palpably nervous. "Why not Lizzie?" He used kisses and words to soothe and lure her. And to control himself. "Because she has been ill?"

Her breath caught when he kissed her breast. But she also shifted a little, toward him. It was not clear that she even realized she did that. A bloom resting on her breast fell onto the sheet. "No, although her illness means she would have no time to order such a garment. I am certain it was not Lizzie because she has memorized the kinds of books your mother sent to me, and this dress is a little scandalous."

"So you knew it was, and you still donned it."

She looked up at him. "Is that shocking?"

"Yes, but it bodes well for us." He claimed her mouth in a kiss and released some of the desire burning through him. She responded tentatively at first, but the sounds and breaths and moves of her excitement soon swept her along. He unfastened the tiny buttons conveniently placed on the front of her bodice.

Barely breathing, she looked down at his hand. Little flexes tightened her body, giving subtle evidence that this excited her more.

"No?" he asked when his fingers reached the last button. He wanted to hear her acknowledge her anticipation.

She did not answer at once. She just looked at where his hand rested. "Yes," she finally said.

He parted the dress to reveal her breasts. They were lovely, high and firm, with erotic tips. He flicked his tongue on one of them and her gasp of pleasure almost undid him.

He teased her breasts with his mouth and hands until she slid into abandon. Lost in her own sensuality, she did not react badly when he peeled the dress off so she was naked. He eased on top of her and tensed against the way her softness and warmth sharpened his hunger to the point of pain.

He tempered his hardest urges and blunted the sharpest edges of his need. Resisting the darkest depths of the sea of pleasure, he set about making her more crazed yet, so she would find the rest tolerable enough too.

Skin on skin. Shocks of vulnerability and intimacy, one after another. Knowing hands and confident guidance and masterful power. Perfume everywhere, of bodies and crushed flowers.

The astonishment never ceased but her body's resistance eased. Pleasure spoke louder than any caution. Pleasure so sweet and torturous that she found it unbearable, but also never wanted it to end.

He awed her more than he ever had, in ways she could not fight. She wondered at the sensation of his taut shoulders and back under her palms as she instinctively embraced him. He was both new and strange and old and familiar to her, in body and spirit and everything else.

He shifted and rose on an extended arm and her embrace fell away. He lifted her right leg and bent it at the knee. He looked down her body, his hair falling over his brow and his eyes hard in their intensity. She did too, and wondered if he could see what she thought he could see.

The touch from the garden, so welcome and necessary. She had been waiting for it, wanting it. Still it stole her breath. She closed her eyes so she would not see him watch her madness. He did wicked things. So wicked that she cried out, and bit her lip so she would not again. Except she did. He kept making it worse and soon cries filled her head so all thought was gone. Then nothing existed except that pleasure making her desperate for something she could not name.

He moved again, up her body until his chest hovered above her and his hips spread her thighs. He pressed into her and awareness sliced through her daze.

She looked up at his face, serious and hard. The dark of his eyes went on forever in his passion, and his tight jaw showed how he fought for restraint.

He tried not to hurt her, she was sure. He did anyway. She closed her eyes so he might not see how much. Then it was over and they were joined and the pain eased, but the reality of this, of him and her and what was happening, overwhelmed her.

Remnants of the pleasure stirred while he moved in her. His physicality again impressed her palms and fingers. The moments turned long, and too real.

His careful thrusts beckoned the pleasure forward again, so it was not horrible. No daze or distance developed again, however. Pleasure did not obscure the truth now. Instead an unbidden intimacy overwhelmed and awed her during her vulnerable submission.

He did not leave once it was over. She thought he would, to spare them both the uncompromising reality that kept assaulting her in the aftermath.

No anticipation now. No excitement obscuring how it was. She lay beside a naked man whom she barely knew.

She was unable to set aside how defenseless he made her feel. Powerless really. His possession of her had disadvantaged her, and at the start of a long game that she had not fully realized that she had agreed to play.

She closed her eyes so she might find some privacy. She had been stripped of it completely in this bed, as surely as he had removed that nightdress. That dismayed her more than anything else. Much more than any pain. Her separateness had been breached without her ever agreeing to it.

"You appear very thoughtful." His voice, so close, forced the intimacy to reassert itself.

"I am doing some ciphers in my head. Addition. Subtraction."

She felt his low laugh on her cheek even though it made no sound. "What do you cipher?"

She opened her eyes, to his naked shoulders and chest. That had not mattered while immersed in the pleasure, but it shocked her now. "I am calculating how often this can be done in ten hours, and whether you will want to do it again soon."

His eyes were kind, as if he knew how awkward she felt. How confused and exposed. "Not too soon. Not for a few days."

He sat up. She knew he would leave. He did not do so at once. He gave her time to close her eyes. Someday perhaps she would not.

She heard him move in the chamber.

"Call for your maid. She will prepare a bath for you. We will dine with my brother tonight in his chambers. I promised him we would, since he could not attend the wedding breakfast."

She felt him standing right beside her, then a light kiss on her cheek. "I am sorry that I hurt you. I tried not to. I will not again."

It touched her that he had tried. She imagined this could have been hellish if he had not.

She opened her eyes to see that dark robe near the door to his chambers. He needed no absolution from her. He had not asked for it, but only spoken to reassure her. Yet a new sense about him had entered her while she was stripped of all protection, and it whispered to her instincts now.

"You did not hurt me very much."

He paused and looked at her through the shadows.

"I am more shocked than hurt, and more confused than shocked. It was as you promised. More than tolerable enough."

Chapter Thirteen

He did not come to her for two nights. Then he came every night. Audrianna calculated that those hours, in addition to the time spent in each other's company but not in bed, indeed came to about ten hours the first week.

By the end of that week she grew accustomed to having a naked man in her bed afterward. He did not linger long, but he did not leave immediately. She had assumed this was something done in the dark and in silence, a duty performed on the sly. Perhaps Lord Sebastian took a more liberal view because of all those experiences as a rake.

Allusions to his past showed up at every social event she attended. No one actually spoke of it, but she perceived a merry astonishment that he had married at all, and only to make such a bad marriage at that. A few ladies' clever barbs insinuated that she had all but trapped him. It became clear that Lady Wittonbury was of that view.

She mostly managed to avoid Lady Wittonbury. As Sebastian had said, it was a very big house. The library and

music room became her havens when she left her own
chambers. And the garden, of course. It was so large that
one could disappear in it, and if she felt the need for different environs, she took Nellie and walked in the park or
down Oxford Street.

She usually had to suffer Lady Wittonbury's presence
at breakfast, however. They would open their mail and Lady
Wittonbury would advise which invitations to accept. Some
of the events would not happen for weeks, even months,
when the season was in full bloom. Lady Wittonbury explained several times that this season would be fairly quiet
compared to others, owing to the court mourning of Prin-
cess Charlotte that still stretched in front of them.

After the mail, Audrianna would read the newspapers
that had been set out by the servants, starting with the *Times*
advertisements and notices. She had taken up Lizzie's habit,
but for a purpose. The Domino had twice now used such
communication, and she hoped that he would again.

Sebastian was never at those early meals. On the eighth
day of her marriage, Lady Wittonbury explained that the
two brothers broke their fast together in the marquess's
chambers.

"Wittonbury needs to instruct him, of course. He only
wields my elder son's power in government, not his own."

Audrianna had difficulty imagining Lord Sebastian taking instruction from anyone, or wielding secondhand power.
She was about to defend her husband, when the marchioness changed the subject.

"We must do something about your wardrobe, dear. I
have held my tongue about this as long as I can bear it. I
will take you to my dressmaker this afternoon."

"My wardrobe is new. It would be wasteful to replace
it so soon."

"You can give it away. It will not be wasted."

"Forgive me, Madam. My attempt to dissemble was clumsy. The truth is that I do not want to replace it. There is no need to, and I like it as it is. However, I thank you for your concern for me." She especially loved the primrose India muslin dress and aurora sarcenet spencer that she wore today, and resented that the criticism appeared to have been provoked by these specific garments.

A lesser woman would stand down. Lady Wittonbury felt no need to. "My concern is for me, and my son, as much as for you. Some of your dresses are not the best choices in color or style."

Her tone remained cajoling even as her words became more pointed. Her face wore the smile one might use when indulging a recalcitrant child who would be forced to obey if reasoning did not work.

"Every dress was obtained from a top dressmaker, Madam. The styles are from the latest plates, and visible on other ladies of the *ton*. I did not just ride in from the country on a wagon, and there is nothing inappropriate about my wardrobe. Some dresses might not be to your taste, but that is another matter."

"My taste has been celebrated since I was younger than you. Ask anyone. I sought to help you by offering my advice, but I can see that was an error."

"You have been a marchioness since you were younger than I am. No one would criticize your taste no matter what they thought."

The implication that the praise had been mere flattery astonished Lady Wittonbury. "You are a bold, ungrateful girl, I see."

"I must disagree again, Madam. I am not ungrateful,

and I am not a girl at all. I am old enough to choose my own wardrobe, for example."

Lady Wittonbury's indignant stare could have frozen an ocean. She rose to her feet with purpose and sailed out of the room.

Audrianna scolded herself, but her own heart rebelled against accepting blame. She had not insulted Lady Wittonbury. Quite the reverse. She suspected that a story was being told upstairs that would sound as if she had, though. She braced herself for a request from Sebastian for her attendance once his breakfast was done.

It came soon enough. Her stomach turned at what might be coming. She found him in his bedchamber, gathering some papers. He had dressed for riding and appeared distracted. He barely looked at her as he shuffled through some pages, checking their content.

"I am told that you had a row with my mother."

"We had a disagreement, not a row. I was not disrespectful."

"But you refused her wishes, she said. You refused her instruction."

"Yes."

He shuffled some more, than laid the stack down and gave her his attention. He reached for her and held her at arm's length. "Is this one of the dresses?"

So he had received a full description of the episode. She suffered his inspection. If he told her to give this favorite ensemble away, to submit to his mother's fashion whims, there really might be a row in this house this morning.

"I am no expert, but this dress and your others appear fine to me," he said. "She will try to tell you what to do. It is her way. She can be a help in some things, if you want her help. Use your own judgment. Show her the respect she deserves, but I am the only person in this house who can command your obedience."

He surprised her so much that she impulsively embraced him. She stretched up and pressed a kiss to his lips.

His arms enclosed her. He looked down, half-amused and half-serious as sin. Then he released her, and picked up his papers. "I may have to tell my mother to argue with you more often."

"I hope not! Why would you do that?"

"If I want the denouement, it may require the first act."

She laughed. "It was only a kiss. You have those whenever you want."

He gave an odd little smile and turned his attention back to the papers. "Yes, I suppose I do. Whenever I want."

No sooner had Sebastian left the house than the marquess sent for her. She found him in his library, in the same deep chair where she always saw him. He set aside a book upon her arrival.

"I have been told that there has been a row," he said.

Lady Wittonbury must have given a very dramatic report if both brothers felt obliged to speak to her. "It was merely a disagreement, I promise you."

"My brother should move you to your own house. He will not do it on my suggestion. However, if *you* tell him that you are unhappy here, he will reconsider."

"If you say that he will not do it, then he will not change his mind, least of all at my request."

"I will speak plainly to him on your behalf."

"Please do not. I do not want my presence to cause strife, least of all between the two of you."

He sighed deeply, and gazed down at the cover on his lap. His head then jolted up, as if he did not like where his thoughts had wandered.

"He is only here at all because of me. But he has other responsibilities now. Tell him that you prefer your own household if you do."

She sat down in the chair right beside him. The one the marchioness normally used. "And what of your preferences? They matter too."

His face fell into an impassive mask. "I have learned to accept many things. Foremost among them is that almost everything that I would prefer is no longer possible."

His quiet, frank admission touched her. "Must you be accepting? Have you no choice?"

A spark of anger showed in his eyes. "Should I rave against cruel fate? Be forever angry at my infirmity and uselessness? In that direction lies madness, my dear sister."

"You are not useless. That is melancholy speaking. Your brother depends on you for advice in his duties, and guidance in politics and finance."

"Did she tell you that?" He leveled his gaze on her. He looked more like his brother than he ever had, and his eyes showed more intelligence and depths than she had ever seen.

"Yes. Your brother did as well."

"Well, here is the truth of it. He needs no advice from me. He is smarter than I am by a measurable sum, and shrewder again by half. He charms while I plod, and he can walk the finest edge of the highest cliff in society without blinking or falling. I do not believe my mother's long lie about his reliance on me, or his own pretense of the same. I would be grateful if you do not strive to believe it either. It would be nice not to have to pretend, with *someone*."

His stark honesty surprised and flattered her. His lack of pretention disarmed all formalities. She felt much like she did when talking to a friend who offered a secret confidence.

"He is certainly an admirable man," she said. "However, he is not infallible as he walks those cliffs. After all, he had to marry me."

He smiled to acknowledge her little joke. "Perhaps the invisible hand of justice was at work there. However it happened, I do not think he will regret it."

His approval went far to soothing the scorching his mother had given her pride. At least one person in the family did not think Sebastian had been trapped by someone unsuitable. She warmed even more to this unpretentious man at his reference to justice. It sounded as if he believed her family had been wronged.

"Even if it is as you say, and he does not require your advice, I will not ask him to leave here. I cannot do that."

His relief showed more than he knew. That tugged at her heart. He probably dreaded losing the company of his brother, and those consultations too, even if they were a pretense. He had offered to make a noble sacrifice, but she could tell he was glad she would not accept it.

He reached over and patted her hand. "He said that you would acquit yourself well with our mother. He said I should not worry about your odds in that game. I think perhaps he is correct."

So Sebastian thought her a worthy opponent of his mother, if necessary. One might even say that he had spoken well of her. That lifted her spirits more than she expected.

She spied a chess set on a far table. "Would you like to rest, or would you prefer company a little longer? I would not mind hiding here, until Lady Wittonbury is thoroughly occupied with her day's plans. We could have a match."

"I would be glad for your company. And you may hide here whenever you need to."

"I might turn into a coward if given carte blanche to hide, so I will only accept your offer when I absolutely must. However, if there is another little row, perhaps you will allow me to tell you if I feel I must tell someone. I do not want to be a wife who is always complaining to her husband, and there are times when just speaking of a hurt makes it go away."

"I am always here if you need a sympathetic ear." He called for Dr. Fenwood, to have the chess set moved close to their chairs.

Sebastian passed through the Tower gate. The meeting he was about to have had been a long time coming.

When word about that massacre had finally become public, the Board of Ordnance had done what any government entity would do when under attack. It had turned inward for protection, and denied all responsibility.

The integrity of gunpowder was vital to any war effort, and the Board prided itself on its protocol for ensuring the military's gunpowder was manufactured correctly and had the necessary firepower. According to them, processes and checks were in place to ensure just such a mishap could not occur. Since it could not happen, it had not happened.

Sebastian's conversations with the officials of the Board

had never yielded much besides frustration. They took the position that until there was some proof that gunpowder tested by them had been the cause of the problem, they had nothing to say. They dismissed reports gathered from survivors that the British cannon could not return fire, and ignored opinions from gunners and suspicions from the army itself that only bad ordnance would explain that.

Short of physical evidence, they held themselves untouchable. Since the gunpowder in question was not available for examination, but scattered on a Spanish hill, they were safe.

On the other hand, they had done nothing to protect Kelmsleigh when attention focused on him since he had given the final approval on the quality of gunpowder prior to its distribution. Their lack of defense only encouraged more attention on this most likely source of negligence. Kelmsleigh's superiors had left him alone and exposed while arrows aimed at him, instead of them.

Sebastian had long ago accepted that he would learn nothing at the Board's offices, and he had not arranged this meeting. Instead the request for a conversation had come from Mr. Singleton, the Storekeeper, who had been Kelmsleigh's ultimate superior.

He was directed to a chamber in the old medieval structure. It contained no evidence of regular use. The table was bare and no records could be seen. The soldier who escorted him left him there, and closed the heavy door as he departed. Sebastian imagined prisoners over the centuries hearing that sound upon their incarceration.

He looked out the small window. He could see the yard where, in ages past, axes had severed heads from bodies. The Tower had served many functions over time, but it was most known for that one.

He checked his pocket watch. He would not have put Audrianna off so quickly if he had known there would be this delay. Images of the morning came to him, of his mother's umbrage and tears, and of his wife's expression when she entered his chambers.

With one glance he could tell that she was a little afraid. She had been concerned that he would place her under his mother's dominance, quite likely. She might have been worried that he would scold, or even chastise her physically.

Oh, yes, that last possibility had been in her eyes, and it disturbed him. For all of the passion, for all of the sensual closeness of the last week, she did not know him well at all.

Nor was she much aware of what had or had not passed between them. Her happy kiss today had been the very first one she had ever offered him, given of her own impulse. She had not realized that.

He had.

He could have no complaints about Audrianna's willingness or behavior in bed. She did not protest or deny. She did not require modesty. She was passionate and agreeable, and she would most likely continue to be when, with time, there were new initiations.

However, he wondered sometimes if, after he left her and the pleasure had faded, she got out of bed and sat at her writing table and noted down in an account book just how long he had been there, and how far toward ten hours she had progressed this week.

It was one thing to have a woman accept you, but under obligation. It was quite another to have a woman offer even the smallest intimacy totally of her own inclination. Audrianna's little embrace and kiss today had surprised him, and pleased him to a ridiculous extent. The memory of it still did.

He would have liked to stay with her and not run off. It would have been interesting to see what the next ten minutes might have wrought.

Now, for all he knew, she might not kiss him again on her own accord for another five years.

"My apologies, sir. A serious matter of safety interfered with seeing you at once. I hope that you understand that the nature of our stores can create such eventualities." Mr. Singleton offered the excuse in a rush. His flushed face said he truly hoped Sebastian would not take offense.

That was a good sign, and Sebastian was happy to reassure him. "I am curious why you requested this meeting at all, Mr. Singleton. I have sought one in vain for almost a year."

Singleton's nod acknowledged the truth of that. "My apologies on that too, sir. I am, as I hope you know, a servant of the state."

It was not clear if that was a slip or a warning. In either case, he had all but said that he acted under orders, in this as in all else.

"I hope the marquess is well, sir."

"My brother is fine, thank you."

"Please give him my greetings. And your new wife? My sincere felicitations to both of you."

"Thank you."

"Splendid." Singleton gathered his attention and thoughts. "If I may speak frankly, sir, and please believe that I intend no disrespect—"

"Of course."

"Considering your zeal in a certain matter, the identity of your intended caused some interest here."

"You mean because of her father. Well, Mr. Singleton, both my bride and I would be the first to agree that fate can be capricious."

"Quite so, quite so. Capricious. However—we are wondering if your continued interest in that matter will now be relinquished."

It was not clear which answer he wanted, which was curious considering their prior unhelpfulness. "Tell me, Singleton, do you have an opinion on whether it should be relinquished? Do you consider the current assumptions about Horatio Kelmsleigh both a complete explanation, and a just one?"

A pursing smile tightened Singleton's face. "We maintain that nothing happened within these walls or under our jurisdiction to give me cause for any opinion."

"And yet I sense that you have one."

"Privately. Confidentially. I can only say that it is my feeling that if you pursue this matter, you will not exonerate your wife's father, if marital bliss has inclined you to try."

They knew something. Of course they did. Ordnance did not move without careful monitoring and records.

Sebastian took his leave soon after. The peculiarity of Singleton's confidence occupied his mind while he rode down Tower hill. Singleton had spoken as if the investigation had reached a crossroad, not a wall. Which meant that the Board of Ordnance anticipated new information coming out that would stoke one MP's interest again.

Two nights later, while Sebastian dressed for a ball, a gentle rap sounded on the door to Audrianna's bedchamber. The door opened a crack and her head angled around its edge.

Her hair was dressed already. Her chestnut locks formed an intricate topknot and delicate spirals that framed her face. Her eyes, forest green in the candlelight, sought him.

"May I enter? I need your judgment."

He set aside his cravat and gestured for his valet to leave. Once he was alone, she stepped into his dressing room.

His mouth went dry.

She wore a red gown. More a deep crimson. The hue was actually subdued, and the cut quite modest. But something in the way it fit her, and in how the silk fell along her form, made her appear worldly and confident.

"Is it a bad choice? I ordered it on the best advice, and I love it, but after that conversation with your mother, I am having second thoughts."

His mind wandered, to images of turning her and bending her and that red silk rising, rising . . .

"You don't approve."

"You are wrong there. You are entrancing in it."

She liked the compliment, but began inspecting herself again. "Are you sure it is not vulgar? I fear she will say so. The color is fashionable, but she will want me in white, always white. Like a girl. But I am not a girl, am I?"

No, she was not. She was all woman in that gown. He could not keep his hands off her, and he stopped trying. He pulled her into an embrace. Her slight, pliable warmth aroused him more. He calculated the hour, and how long this ball would last and whether attending at all was really necessary.

"It is generous of you to care what she will think. However, I command you to wear this dress. There, does that make it easier to be sure again?"

She appeared sultry and fresh at the same time. "It does restore my confidence. I will not care what anyone else thinks. It is good to know that you like it, however. This is my first ball among the *ton*, and I know they will be judging my fitness to be your wife." She stepped away from him and looked down at the draping crimson. "He said that you would approve, but I wanted to be sure."

"He?"

"Your brother," she said as she left.

The strangest reaction sliced through him. She was gone before he subdued it.

The reaction had not been foreign or new, but having it right now was odd.

Jealousy. That was what flared in him. Jealousy that she had gone to Morgan with her worry before coming to him.

Chapter Fourteen

She refused to be intimidated by Lady Wittonbury's dramatic expression of forbearance upon seeing the gown. Summerhays liked it. That was all that mattered.

The ball almost overwhelmed her. The silks and flickering lights, the laughter and the music, cluttered her senses. She had met enough ladies through the marchioness and Sebastian that she kept herself occupied on the fringes of conversations. Mostly she admired the gowns and headdresses and concluded that her own ensemble was appropriate enough.

Sebastian danced with her twice, but then Lord Hawkeswell lured him into conversation. She went in search of another familiar face. Suddenly the last one that she ever expected to see was right in front of her.

Roger froze at the same moment she did. They stood there like two porcelain figures on a shelf.

He had not changed at all, and yet he appeared different. Separation allowed her to see him more clearly, the same way time had permitted when he came back from the war.

Love and excitement could not bridge the strangeness now, however. She found herself itemizing the details of his appearance while she waited for hurt and disappointment to twist her heart. Some did, emerging from wherever she had buried it. A good deal of resentment joined it too.

"Audrianna." His blue eyes warmed in a way that once made her breathless. "You are looking well. You have grown more lovely, I think."

He looked well too, but then a uniform did that for a man. She wanted to think that his thick, tawny hair had thinned, but it probably had not. "Have you been in London long, Roger? Or are you just visiting?"

"The regiment was moved to Brighton in January, and I availed myself of a short leave."

Mention of Brighton made her face warm. If he now lived there, he would be aware of every detail of the scandal. He had probably been congratulating himself on his narrow escape.

"Your mother is well?" he asked.

"Yes, most well. You should call on her. Our situation has changed considerably, as you probably know. She no longer holds any anger for you. She would be delighted to see you again."

His smile wavered on her mention of anger. He stepped closer. "And you, Audrianna? Has your new situation dulled your own anger with me? I hope that it has, and that we can be friends."

Why? she almost asked him, only she knew the answer. She no longer was a fiancée whose disgraced father would stain an officer's career and subject him to suspicions or worse. She had become a path to valuable connections.

That disheartened her. It implied that, from the start, Roger's interest or rejection had not been about her. Even his attentions and proposal were not about love. Roger probably saw the offices of the Board of Ordnance as a good place to go once the war ended, and her father as his means of getting there.

Suddenly he was closer yet. Not too close, but almost. He spoke fast and low. "Please say that you welcome a friendship. You are so beautiful tonight that I can barely think. I have been miserable since you withdrew from our engagement."

His boldness astonished her. She darted glances left and right to see if someone might overhear. "I can do nothing about your misery, if indeed you experience any. And let us not forget, as we share the memories, that you *asked me* to break with you. Most cruelly."

That memory loomed large suddenly. She had anticipated his return home with excitement and relief, only to have him dodge a reunion. When it finally came, he had been formal, hard, and unloving. He had itemized the ways in which her father's disgrace would reflect on him. He had expressed impatience when she wept.

"Yes, and I have no right to expect other than cruelty from you now in return. I had no choice, however. I think you know that."

"I do know that. I realized that my belief that you would be better than the world was childish." She had never hated him for that day, much as she tried to. She'd wept in the weeks that followed for dashed dreams and a hopeless future, but she had understood completely.

He dipped his head and spoke secretively. "I have never stopped loving you, Audrianna, or stopped regretting my cowardice. I lament it all the more seeing you here tonight, looking so . . ." He laughed at himself and gave his head a little shake, as if to clear his dazed brain.

"That is unfortunate for you, and beyond my remedy. If you ask for friendship alone, however, it is yours. If we see each other again, I will not cut you. And if my friendship can benefit you in some way, without my direct agency, I will not deny it if asked about you."

She walked away, and sought the thick crowd. She hoped her forced poise obscured her dismay at what he had really been requesting.

*W*ho the hell was he?

The tawny-haired man stood one step too close to Audrianna for comfort. Nor did she look like a woman talking to a stranger.

"Did you hear one word I just said, Summerhays?"

"Of course. You were telling me that the Thompsons have hired a runner." He could not be certain from this distance, but it appeared Audrianna was blushing.

"That was five minutes ago. I was just now saying that this fellow has been asking questions about *me*. They are making their suspicions explicit, and I am half-inclined to bring suit for criminal slander."

That captured Sebastian's attention. Some of it, at least. He kept one eye on the conversation taking place across the ballroom. If that man did not step back, he was going to go over there and—

And what? He noted the anger sparking in his head. Jealousy again. Unwarranted and unexpected. Only this was not with an invalid relative offering reassurance, but over a handsome man with blue eyes that were enjoying that red gown more than they should. Every instinct, especially the ones honed by experience in these matters, said that fellow was bent on seducing her.

"I expect they will want another inquest," Hawkeswell said. "I do not fancy one where someone impugns me, and accuses me of hurting her."

"They may only want to have her declared dead."

"It won't happen until at least seven years pass. Everyone knows that."

"Evidence is accumulating that will permit an earlier determination. The shawl last year, and the reticule now. If the runner finds anything else, this will finally end."

"As long as he does not try to blame me, I will welcome it."

"He cannot find a way to blame you, so his efforts are for naught if that is the goal. You should ignore him."

Audrianna was saying something. She appeared much as she had when she rejected his first proposal. The man was not taking it well. *That is right. Put the damned scoundrel in his place.*

"What the hell is distracting you?" Hawkeswell peered in the direction of Sebastian's repeated glances. "A new pursuit? So soon? You might let the ink dry on the wedding license first."

"That fellow over there is after my wife."

Hawkeswell peered harder. "It is hard to tell from here."

"I can tell."

"Recognize the scoundrel's game, do you?"

"I never pursued women married just a week."

Hawkeswell laughed. "Ah. *Standards*. He offends yours, I can tell from your indignant tone. Do you really care, or are you just being one of those boring, possessive apes who is jealous of all his property?"

Did he care? Or was it just possessiveness over a new acquisition? The question caught him up short.

Hawkeswell stepped around, and deliberately blocked the view of Audrianna. "If ever there was a match made at the altar of obligation, it was yours, Summerhays. For her and for you. You know that you will both take lovers sooner or later. My money is on sooner for you, and much later for her. That is how it usually goes."

"Not always."

"True, not always. Sometimes the wife remains faithful and bitter. Well, go over there and thrash him, then, so she learns how you expect it to be."

That would not be necessary. Audrianna came into view again, walking across the chamber's corner. Alone.

"Sometimes you are an annoying bastard, Hawkeswell."

"Only when you want to be an ass, Summerhays."

Audrianna reviewed the ball while Nellie unfastened her gown. It had gone well, she thought. In a crowd of that size, her insignificance became a form of protection. Even so, there had been introductions and even some kind smiles. Perhaps in a few months she would not feel like an intruder at such assemblies, even if she never really believed she belonged.

She reached for the gown's shoulders, to slide it off.

"Not yet."

Startled, she looked over her shoulder. Nellie was gone. Sebastian stood in the doorway leading to her chamber, leaning against the jamb, his arms folded and his coats and cravat removed. The candle glow picked out the white of his shirt and the dark of his eyes as he watched her.

If he did not want her to remove the gown, she would not. She could think of nothing else to do instead, so she just stood there with the red silk gaping on her back.

"You are ravishing in that dress. Everyone thought so."

"In that crush I do not think many noticed me at all."

"I noticed. I could hardly keep my eyes off you."

She wondered if his eyes had sought her while Roger pressed his attentions. The notion flustered her enough that she reached back to unclasp her necklace, to hide her dismay. "This gold that you gave me worked well with it, I thought. The emeralds did not, much as I wanted to wear them."

He came over to help her. His presence warmed her back and soon the necklace dripped into her hand. She took a step toward her dressing table. His arm encircled her and pulled her back. A hot kiss on her neck made her gasp. Slow caresses on the silk covering her breasts made pleasure course through her in fast, rippling currents. The necklace escaped her fingers and fell to the floor.

His hands moved all over that silk. All over her. Firm strokes claimed her stomach and hips and thighs, while his hard body pressed her back. Pleasure crashed into her in high, fast waves that left her without strength. When he teased at her nipples, she could only arch against him for support while her body begged for the torture.

Biting kisses. Feverish, hard, and impatient. He scorched her neck and shoulder and she turned her face to accept more.

Then she was floating, being carried in her daze to her bed. He did not put her in it, but set her feet on the floor. Her legs almost did not hold, and she staggered.

Still embracing her with that controlling arm, still supporting her, his other hand reached for pillows. He made a stack in front of her.

He lifted her slightly. "Kneel here."

She did not understand, but she obeyed. Then he pressed her body forward until she lay on the bed with the pillows under her hips. She realized the implications of her position. Surprise jolted through her. Deep and low in her body a potent thrill of anticipation coiled tightly.

The silk slid up her legs slowly in a sensual tease. Higher yet, until its watery red bunched at her waist and draped on the bed. He pulled her drawers down to her knees.

A touch. One sure, deep stroke. She could not contain her moan.

He left her like that, exposed and waiting. She pulsed with impatience. The craving was unlike anything she had experienced before. She looked back to see his shirt dropping, then his naked body coming over her.

He took her hard, and she wanted it even harder. He filled her to where that was the only sensation she knew. His thrusts stroked a new hunger that got worse and worse, growing within the pleasure. She wanted this, wanted him and his own angry craving finding release in his lack of restraint. It was mad, feral, and as red as the silk flowing between them.

Sensations tightened and sharpened. Wanton now, mad with need, she lost control. Crying out, urging more, she soared to an unearthly point of intensity that burst in a long, dark scream of exquisite relief.

He slipped the gown off her boneless, sated body, and tossed it aside. It was probably ruined. He did not care.

He pulled the pillows away and set her to rights on the bed, then fell down beside her. He did not sleep. The contentment was too perfect to give up just yet.

She sought his side as if by instinct. He embraced her with his arm and drew her closer still.

The bliss was heavenly, but fleeting. She began stirring in the world again. His mind started thinking once more. It sorted through the night's events. He lingered on memories of her naked bottom erotically bared and raised, surrounded by a froth of red silk, and her gartered thighs parting in invitation while she waited for him.

Images from the ball pressed on him. One in particular. Two hours ago he would not have asked, and two hours hence he would not either, but raw eroticism forms its own bonds, even if they are temporary.

"Who was he? The man at the ball?"

She went still, right in the middle of a catlike stretch. She might have stopped breathing. He could practically hear her mind snapping alert, choosing her words, deciding whether to lie. Her caution told him everything he needed to know to want to kill the man.

"He is an old friend. He is an army officer." Silence quaked during a long pause. "We were engaged before he went to France."

"And then you were not after he returned. What happened?"

"I released him. Time changed things."

"For you or for him?"

"For us both. It is a common story, I think. Alliances made before a long separation often do not survive it."

Hardly. They almost always survived it because the woman would not accept the change. Furthermore, she was lying. The scoundrel had broken her heart. That song she had written was about that pain. "Did you release him recently?"

"Over a year ago. Before Christmas last. Is that recently?"

Recent enough for this man to still be a rival.

He would not force her to speak of it any more. He knew how it had been. That coward had asked to be released, so he would not be tainted by her father's disgrace.

In all her accusations, even at the Two Swords, she had never mentioned this. It had been inside her, though, whenever she blamed him for her family's misfortune. It still was.

"Do you still love him?" It was hard to ask that question. Harder than it should be. Nor did he like the way he waited for the answer, like a man who would want to be an ass if the answer was the wrong one.

"I could never have married you if I still did. That would not have been honest, for all the practicality of this match. I scrutinized my heart before accepting your offer."

She had a talent for astonishing him. Not many people, if offered luxury and wealth, position and redemption, would worry about the state of old love before grabbing it.

"Should I have told you all about this before we wed? Are you angry I did not?"

"There was no reason to tell me. It is all in the past and does not signify now." Except it did, at least enough for him to ask about it. She was good enough not to point that out.

"That is what Daphne says. It was part of the Rule by which we lived. We did not ask about each other's pasts, because some women have good cause to leave the past far behind."

"Your lack of curiosity is impressive."

"I did not say I was not curious. And one does surmise things. But I never asked."

"It sounds like a stupid rule to me. One of The Rarest Blooms could be a murderer for all you know."

"I suppose so." She rose on one arm and looked down at him. Her chestnut hair fell in disheveled waves around her face and shoulders. "We are not called The Rarest Blooms, you know. Only the trade is called that."

"You are all rare blooms, and I caught the rarest." He guided her head down so he could kiss her. "And the fairest. Now turn around so I can get those stays off you."

"I will call for Nellie."

"You will not." He turned her around and began unlacing her stays. "I am not leaving yet, Audrianna."

Chapter Fifteen

A mong the luxuries showered on Audrianna with her marriage was her own carriage. Three days later she called for it to be made ready, and directed the coachman to take her to The Rarest Blooms.

She found them all in the greenhouse, sorting through pots of lilies and hyacinths. Through the glass she could see the garden coming to life, with rows of fresh leaves poking up through the soil.

They did not make a fuss on her arrival. She might have returned from giving one of her music lessons. The circle opened and absorbed her, as if she had never left.

"With the season starting, we are very busy," Lizzie said, by way of explaining Daphne's distraction with the pots. "We have been asked to replicate what we did for your wedding in two gardens."

"People can be very unoriginal," Celia said. "One lady even wanted the exact same flowers. Daphne had to explain that it would look silly to have daffodils and tulips in pots when they will be growing in gardens freely at the time of the party."

"After two summers ago, everyone fears their own blooms will be small, or not grow at all. It will be a long time before our own garden recovers." Daphne referred to the year without summer, and the hard toll it had taken. She counted out some blooming lilies, pointing to each one as she calculated. Contented, she removed her apron. "They are ready for Mr. Davidson to transport them. Lizzie, please make sure that he gets them all when he comes."

They all returned to the back sitting room. Celia went off to make coffee. Audrianna submitted to a long inspection by Daphne.

"You appear contented in this marriage. Please tell me that you are."

"I am, more than I expected. It has not been without surprises, of course."

"You refer to Lady Wittonbury's interference, I am sure."

She was not referring to Lady Wittonbury at all, but to the rich sensuality of this marriage. It captivated her more than carriages and silks. She forgot who she was when lost in those pleasures. Even the circumstances that had brought her to that bed became obscured for a while.

"She has proven to be a little cloud, but thankfully not as big a one as she might be. And the marquess has become a good friend." Her best friend, actually. Even her only friend in that world. In the light of day, Sebastian remained something of a stranger still, in comparison. She did not speak as freely with him as with the marquess. She did not forget to be careful. Sebastian still dazzled and awed her to the point of disadvantage, and what he did at night only intensified that reaction.

"Is she trying to cow you?" Daphne asked.

"Of course. However, I did not come here to cry on your shoulder or talk about Lady Wittonbury's unkindness. I came to be with dear friends, and to read Lizzie's newspapers and gossip sheets."

Celia arrived with the tray of coffee. "Go and get them, Lizzie. She has quite a stack right now, since we go to town so often with the new trade that your wedding has brought us, Audrianna. Even her headaches do not stop her from reading them all."

Lizzie went to a cabinet and brought back a thick stack of folded papers. "I like to know what is happening in the world. I do not know why you tease me so much, Celia."

"Because she loves you, that is why," Audrianna said. "I am happy to see that you are free of your malady today, Lizzie. I feared I would find you prostrate, and be deprived of your company."

"They strike without warning or reason, is that not correct, Lizzie?" Daphne said. "I think changing weather is the culprit."

They drank their coffee and talked of common things. Audrianna basked in the easy conversation. No etiquette here. No clock ticking away the proscribed time for a morning call. No worry that one laughed too loud, or at the wrong time.

She watched her dear friends, and Sebastian's words came back to her. *Your lack of curiosity is impressive.* She had initially thought the Rule was stupid too, and actually had been very curious. Soon, however, she knew what she needed to know about these other women and their pasts did not matter at all.

And yet, as they chatted, she thought about how little

she really did know. Nothing at all about Lizzie and Celia. And even Daphne, who was her cousin—there had been years when Daphne was lost to her.

Now that she thought about it, she had been the only person in this house whose history was an open book to the others.

Celia picked up one of Lizzie's papers. "What are you looking for? Why did you want these?"

"I knew she would have many more than I have seen. It would be odd if I required the servants to bring back so many every day. I want to see if there have been any notices from the Domino. He has bought them twice now, and I think he may again."

"I do not remember reading any with that name in it, but the last time it was more an allusion," Lizzie said. "We will help you, so this does not take all your time here." She took a stack and handed it to Daphne.

A half hour later, they had finished with no success. The few obscure notices contained nothing to insinuate they had been placed by the Domino.

"Why don't you place one instead?" Lizzie suggested.

"I tried once, but could not phrase it so the Domino would guess it was me, but no one else would."

"She cannot risk that Lord Sebastian would see it," Daphne said. "One does not poke at a sore if one is wise."

Audrianna realized that was an apt metaphor. It explained everything about the tenor of her young marriage. Desire and pleasure formed a balm for that sore, but it did not really heal. Dozens of pokes every day kept it unhealed—the oblique references others made to her father, the obligatory nature of the marriage itself, her certainty that, if he could, Sebastian would prove what the world already assumed.

She wondered what their marriage would have been like if that sore did not exist. It was a pointlessly romantic question. If not for the sore, there would have been no marriage at all, of course.

"Also, I realized that I cannot arrange a series of meetings to which no one else might come," Audrianna said. "My days are not entirely my own."

"Let him come to you," Celia said. "Write a notice that merely asks for contact, and use a shop for an address so the response does not come in your own mail. It is done all the time, by lovers for example. Publishers and book-stores often offer the service, as well as some inns and solicitors."

"Perhaps I will do that." She set aside her curiosity regarding how Celia knew such things. She was no longer one of them and the Rule no longer applied, but it would be a betrayal to pry now.

Could she write a notice that would not catch Sebastian's eyes, but would be spotted by the Domino? It would require very clever wording.

"You might also let it be known at places where foreigners gather that you are looking for him," Lizzie offered. "If you pay an employee to keep an eye out for you, he could direct this man to write to you, if he appears."

"Paying someone would be better than trying to stand watch yourself," Celia said, with a meaningful smile that made reference to their visit to Miller's Hotel.

"It sounds inefficient, but it actually might work," Daphne said. "You provide a description. Your hired helper watches. If such a man appears, your helper would simply ask if he is the Domino. If he is not, the question will be odd but quickly forgotten. If he is, he can be told how to contact you."

"Where should I hire helpers, however? Certain hotels, I suppose." Another smile from Celia. "The Royal Exchange, perhaps?"

"Places of entertainment," Lizzie said. "Theaters, and such. Also shops that sell books in foreign languages." Lizzie tapped her finger against her chin. "What other establishments might attract men away from home with time to spend?"

"Brothels."

Celia's matter-of-fact answer provoked a collective silence.

"While undoubtedly a useful suggestion, and quite possibly an accurate one," Daphne said, "Audrianna can hardly visit them to arrange the hire of a helper."

Celia shrugged. "That is unfortunate. It is very likely this Domino visits one, and those are establishments where everyone is for hire."

Mr. Davidson arrived then. Audrianna helped the others carry pots out to his wagon, for transport to the London flower shops that were The Rarest Blooms' regular purchasers. She enjoyed the familiar chore.

Nostalgia hung heavily when she left The Rarest Blooms to return to London. On the carriage ride home, she composed her advertisement for the papers.

"Lady Ophelia hired The Rarest Blooms to do her garden party. I must admit they transformed what is a very poor garden even in the best of seasons. One did not even notice the odd way she keeps having the boxwood trimmed."

Audrianna did not know if she was supposed to accept the praise as a proxy. Lady Ferris had insisted on talking about The Rarest Blooms despite Lady Wittonbury's efforts to divert the conversation.

She and Lady Wittonbury had called on Lady Ferris together. Lady Wittonbury had decreed that the visit was important to Audrianna's acceptance.

With carefully plotted tactics like this, her mother-in-law moved closer to her goal of procuring a voucher to Almack's for Audrianna, but without demeaning herself by directly petitioning the patronesses of that establishment—women who held social influence that Lady Wittonbury believed she was entitled to herself.

As best Audrianna had surmised, Lady Ferris was a longtime favorite of Lady Jersey, and her good word might be worth these repeated morning calls.

"I was there when Mrs. Joyes arrived to make the arrangements," Lady Ferris said breezily, as if she pursued the subject for lack of another. "She is an elegant, lovely woman."

"All who meet my cousin comment on her grace. Even so, she would be flattered by your kind words."

"I hear she was a governess some years back. One can only pity that circumstances require her to be in trade now. She had a girl with her. A very pretty little blonde. I could see the younger one had a vivacious character by nature, although she acted subdued."

"That would be Celia."

Lady Wittonbury leaned forward just enough to physically insert herself between them. "Will you be hosting your own garden party once the season starts? Last year it was described with admiration for weeks."

"Yes. In the middle of April. I intend to use The Rarest Blooms too," Lady Ferris said. "I recognized her. The young one. Celia."

Audrianna did not know what to say. Neither did Lady Wittonbury. They both sat mute while Lady Ferris savored the caution that entered Lady Wittonbury's eyes.

"I had seen her once, in a carriage. A year ago, maybe two. I was with Lady Jersey in the park and a particular carriage came by. Everyone knows this conveyance. It belongs to—forgive me, my dear, I hope you will not be shocked—a woman distinguished for the highborn lovers who keep her."

"I am sure you are mistaken," Audrianna said. "Several years ago is a long time to remember a face seen inside a carriage."

"It was an open carriage, as is the preference of such women, and this girl's face was not forgettable. 'Who is that?' I asked Lady Jersey—that is how impressed I was by this young beauty. 'That is her daughter,' she said, 'come up from the country now that she is grown.'"

Even Lady Wittonbury, so practiced in poise, could not completely hide her dismay. Her back remained straight and her face an amiable mask, but one could see a little madness enter her eyes.

"Since Mrs. Joyes's companion does not live in town, but in the country still, it appears that you erred," Lady Wittonbury finally said.

"Perhaps." Lady Ferris smiled with delicious contentment.

Lady Wittonbury's eyes shot daggers. She smoothly found a way to end the visit.

Once in their carriage, her composure broke. "It is not to be borne. To be forced to befriend a nobody like Lady Ferris in order to advance your interests, only to have her go out of her way to humiliate me . ." She glared at Audrianna. "You will break with them all, at once. I should have demanded this at the beginning. Now look what my restraint has wrought. Oh, my heavens, what if it becomes commonly known that *you lived there with her*?" That last notion left her eyes wide and mouth gaping in horror.

"Lady Ferris is wrong." Only she was not positive that Lady Ferris was wrong at all. She knew nothing about Celia's life prior to joining Daphne. In truth, the idea that Celia was a courtesan's daughter made all too much sense.

It fit with Celia's worldliness, and the confident way she spoke of society breaking rules in private that they observed in public. And when Celia went to town, she often took some time alone. To visit her mother?

"You will break with them. You must. Do not think that my son will side with you in this. He will use such women freely, but he would never elevate them, or allow his wife to associate with them."

"She did not say Celia was—was a courtesan herself."

"Heaven give me patience. The daughter of a whore— yes, *whore*. Why else would she be brought up from the country, and be shown in the park alongside her mother, if not to become a whore herself?"

Audrianna braved out the rest of the furious scold. She said nothing, and battled to keep from revealing her own dismay. This might be the real reason why Celia had not come to the wedding. Not to nurse Lizzie. Celia may have known that she might be recognized by someone in that church.

Only Celia was not a whore, no matter what logic Lady Wittonbury applied. Celia was a sweet, good friend. She lived with other women in obscurity and peace. Celia had

never even disappeared for a night like Audrianna had
herself. And her happy, cheerful character always brightened the days and made Audrianna laugh.

She hurried to get out when the carriage stopped. Lady
Wittonbury blocked the way with her parasol. "They are
not welcome in this house in the future. You are not stupid, and you know I am correct about how it must be. My
duty is to raise you up to something approaching acceptability for the role you will someday have. I will not allow
you to drag us down instead."

Audrianna pushed the parasol aside and alighted from
the carriage. She ran into the house before Lady Wittonbury could see her tears.

Sebastian entered the sick room. He did not flinch at the
image that the young gunner presented. He had some
experience in this, after all.

The explosion that had almost killed Harry Anderson
had taken a heavy toll. One leg and half an arm were
missing, and the scarred scalp would never grow hair right
again. He had not yet been twenty before the war had done
this to him.

He could not help thinking of Morgan when he saw
Anderson. This young man's future would be as limited
and isolated, here in his sister's house. He could care for
himself, that was true, but he and the Marquess of Wittonbury had much in common now.

Anderson greeted him with a passivity that Sebastian
recognized. So it was for the maimed. Acceptance eventually came, because there was no other choice.

"I am honored that you would see me," Sebastian said.
"I was told that you do not want to speak of it."

"I only agreed to this because Mr. Proctor said you speak for your brother. Lord Wittonbury knows how it is, doesn't he? I cannot refuse him."

"You have his thanks, I promise you."

Anderson moved his half arm. The end of his coat sleeve flapped. "It saved me, it did. And the leg. I was turned just so and they took it instead of my gut. I was thrown, and that probably saved me too. They were aiming for the guns, of course. They did not know they were useless."

"You are the only gunner to survive, so I think you are right. The blast that threw you saved you."

"Lucky me."

Sebastian let Anderson have his bitterness. He had a right to it.

"What do you remember, about the guns being useless?"

"Not very much. We loaded them normal and lit them right. Nothing happened. It could have been sand in there for all the powder did. There were no misfires as such, just some smoke." He shrugged. "So we cleaned them out and did it all again, with new kegs of powder, making extra sure it was dry, all the while under their fire. The same thing happened. We knew then that we were all quail with no brush. Their guns had torn us to shreds before the officers sounded a retreat, I hear. I was half-dead by then.

The remnants of those shreds had made their way home eventually. And told the tale of that rout.

"Will you put your memory of the events in writing? Attest to it officially?"

"As it happens, I don't write anymore, sir."

"I will bring in a scribner who will write your words, and witnesses for your mark."

Anderson hesitated to agree to it. "An officer visited

me while I was in that French convent. I told him what happened. He told me the war was over and nothing good would come from telling the world about this. He said to let the dead rest."

"Do you believe that he was right? If so, I will leave you in peace."

Anderson debated it silently for a good while.

"It just seems to me that the others were killed by someone's mistake as well as by enemy fire," he said. "Doesn't seem right that no one pays for that, although I have heard one man hanged himself over it. And I keep thinking, what if the same mistake is made again?"

"Yours is much like my brother's view, and mine."

"Then I'll put my mark on my story, sir, if you think it will help. You get that scribner here and I'll do it."

Sebastian thanked him. "I have one more question, if you can tolerate it. I would like you to describe those kegs for me. Tell me everything you can remember. Try to recall every marking they had."

S ebastian went up to his brother's chambers once he returned to Park Lane. He finally had information that might break the dam that had held back progress in settling this ordnance matter. He was eager to share it with Morgan, and discuss the next steps.

Dr. Fenwood was not in the anteroom. Sebastian heard some sounds in the library. The door stood open, and as he neared, he heard quiet sobs.

He looked in. Morgan sat in his chair, bending low. Audrianna sat on the floor beside him, her hands to her face, trying to hide her weeping. Morgan spoke quietly to her, so softly that Sebastian could not hear, and patted her crown gently.

The image stunned him. Emptied him. He spied in silence for what seemed a timeless spell. Then a fury erupted from deep in his gut, obliterating the unnatural calm that had claimed him.

He strode away with dark chaos filling his head. The house could not contain it. Maybe the entire world could not. He went to the garden, and the wilderness at its back. Amid the budding trees and emerald grasses, he let the ugly anger have its way.

It crashed and roared and howled incoherently. Eventually it lessened to a steady rain. And in that less obscuring downpour, he knew that this was not simple jealousy turning him mad. This particular insanity had been building since the day Morgan bought that damned commission.

The dark rain demanded truth. It cleansed reality without compromise. His anger would not allow him to put a pretty face on anything right now.

Morgan had been a fool to buy that commission. An idiot. He was no soldier, he had no experience. The army gave no training to him either, but put him in charge of men's lives as if a title conveyed war skills along with property. It was a mercy that more lords and gentlemen had not chosen to make such noble, dramatic sacrifices.

How many had died because of him? Was that the real reason for his interest in the ordnance scandal? Had his own mistakes caused deaths that would never be avenged, so he wanted these other mistakes avenged instead?

And now, Audrianna loved him. Their bond had been palpable in that library. She huddled at his feet, weeping, accepting his comfort. Depending on his affection. She had brought her unhappiness to her dear friend because she had known she would find sympathy and warmth there. She laughed and joked and cried with Morgan, while she still curtsied to her husband.

He could not believe what seeing them did to him. Raw anger kept carving him into pieces. Guilt followed, sickening him. Guilt that he had not thrashed Morgan senseless the first time he spoke of a commission. Guilt that he lived his brother's life. Guilt for begrudging Morgan Audrianna's affection within that diminished existence to which he was condemned.

He normally accommodated the guilt. Right now he hated it, and hated everything attached to it. The obligations. The expectations. The forced discretions. The lost friendships and the tedious compromises.

But he hated even more realizing that he and his brother were sharing Audrianna as they did too much else. While she dutifully gave her husband her body, she had freely given Morgan a part of her heart.

Mostly, however, he hated admitting how much that mattered.

Chapter Sixteen

"It sounds as if Lady Ferris was correct about your friend," Wittonbury said gently. "I believe you think that she was."

Audrianna wiped her eyes. "I believe no such thing. I will write to Celia and ask. When she denies it, I will make Lady Ferris eat the letter."

"What if she does not deny it?"

She knew where he was leading her. She needed no map.

"You will have other friends, Audrianna. Before the season is a month old, there will be sympathetic young matrons who will seek you out."

She leaned against the side of his chair, not moving from the spot where she had hidden when her composure broke on entering this library. She had not wanted him to see her tears, and now she did not want him to see her rebellious reaction to what he insinuated.

The blanket draped beside her face moved and subtly

brushed her cheek. That drew her out of her reverie. She rose to her knees, then stood.

"Thank you, for letting me hide, and for the sympathetic ear. I am sorry that I wept. I hope that I did not—"

The blanket draped beside her face moved.

The significance of that suddenly penetrated her self-absorption. She stared at that blanket and the invisible legs that it covered. His arms remained on the chair's own. He had not tugged or touched that blanket, she was sure.

"Is there a ghost beneath my chair?" the marquess asked. "You are as shocked as if you saw one."

She composed herself. "A thought came to me that took me unawares. I will leave you now. I have imposed on your kindness too long."

"I fear that I did not give you as much sympathy as you hoped for."

"Your advice was honest and fair, and your compassion sincere. I am more grateful than you can know."

She closed the library door when she left. Then she went looking for Dr. Fenwood. She found him in the dressing room, storing linens.

"Madam. Is something amiss with my lord?"

"I just left him and he is well. I want to ask you about something. Can the marquess move his legs at all?"

Dr. Fenwood's expression turned sad. He shook his head.

"Not the slightest amount?"

"The injury was to his spine. He has no feeling below the waist. None at all."

"Is there any chance of recovery?"

"Not without a miracle. There was one physician, a German, who said that with time . . . He claimed to have seen cases where the body healed itself after some years.

The doctor's reputation turned out to be questionable at best upon investigation. No, Madam, I fear that my lord will remain as you see him."

Audrianna left Dr. Fenwood. She would not raise false hopes on such little evidence as a sensation against her cheek. Perhaps she had imagined that blanket moving. Maybe she had done something to cause it to move.

And yet, what if the leg beneath it had actually stirred?

Sebastian did not arrive back to Park Lane until long past midnight. The ride to Greenwich had gone far to relieve his agitation, and for a few hours, while gazing into the heavens through the observatory's telescopes, he had forgotten the fury gripping him. The tempest had not entirely calmed by the time he entered his chambers, but he no longer wanted to put his fist through a wall.

He prepared for the night. He threw on his robe and dismissed his valet. He looked at Audrianna's door.

She was undoubtedly asleep, but being so damned dutiful, she would not complain if he woke her. And if she minded, she could always go cry to his brother tomorrow. He wanted to go in there and take her five different ways, to claim what was definitely his so he would not mind what most certainly was not.

The dark urge alone told him he should not go in at all. Hawkeswell was not here to stop him from being an ass, so he would have to thwart the inclination all by himself.

He threw himself on his bed and turned his mind to his interview with Anderson. He debated what to do with the information he had received. He needed to pursue a new direction, but carefully. He did not want to impugn good men who might be in the way, or raise the hackles of the Board of Ordnance.

He was just seeing a strategy when the door to his dressing room opened. Audrianna looked in, much as she had when she wore that red dress.

This was definitely not the night to think about that dress.

"Do you mind if I come in? I know it is very late."

So much for noble intentions. She had no idea that she played with fire. He should send her away at once.

"Of course you can come in. You are always welcome here."

She padded across the chamber, her little slippers poking out beneath her white nightdress with each step. Nellie had brushed her hair into a dark fall of silk. Erotic images assaulted him the closer she came.

She appeared joyful when she climbed onto the bed. Excited to see him. That charmed him. If she offered him a kiss on her own again, perhaps he would only take her two different ways. Hell, he'd probably recite a maudlin poem while he did it.

"I have been waiting for you to return. I heard you in the dressing room, and when you did not come in, I realized that with the late hour you would not." She smiled. "That was very considerate of you."

"You must remember to tell me that tomorrow. How considerate I am."

Her brow puckered.

"Never mind. It is late and I am not in my senses. I am glad that you came to me since I did not come to you."

"I had to. I need to talk to you about something very important."

She had not come for pleasure, or even company. She wanted something. Three ways, then. Half his mind began sorting through every sexual position he had ever tried, like a connoisseur choosing among rare wines.

"It has to do with your brother."

Back to five. At least.

"Do tell." He would definitely taste her. He had been dying to since that night at the Two Swords. If he had made a bargain to possess a woman's body and nothing more, he might as well possess her fully and stop worrying overmuch about her delicate sensibilities.

"The most extraordinary thing happened this afternoon."

Her eyes sparkled with excitement. He would arrange it so those eyes watched him take her one of the times.

"One of his legs moved. I am almost positive."

A curtain instantly came down on images of her ecstasy.

She had just said something so preposterous that he had no response other than laughter, and that would not do.

"I was with him, sitting next to him, and that blanket moved. A small move, very small, but I have turned it over in my head a thousand times since and I am sure it moved."

"You said that you were almost positive before. Now you are sure. Which is it?"

"Are you angry?"

"I am not angry. But if you are wrong and I pursue it, he will be horribly disappointed. It will send him into a melancholy from which he might never emerge."

She nodded, and turned thoughtful. "I am not almost positive. I am sure."

He just looked at her. If she was sure, she was sure. She was not a woman to have flights of fancy.

He got out of bed and went to a window and threw up the sash. The night air was chilled but he did not care. He looked out at nothing while the cold cleared his head.

"There was a doctor, a German, who said there was hope. He advised certain exercises. My brother could not bear it and stopped soon enough."

"I know. Dr. Fenwood told me."

He looked back at her. "Did you tell him about this?"

"I only asked if the damage was total and permanent. No one had ever explained before, so I thought perhaps some small movement has always been there."

He turned his attention to the night again. "I do not know what to do with this. He is so . . . fragile. His health, his spirit . . ."

"If there is a chance, surely he will want to try and see if he can be whole again."

"One would think so, but I am not so sure." He faced her. "I will speak with him. I must find a good time, when I think he will listen reasonably. Do not tell anyone else about this. Especially do not mention it to our mother."

She nodded. She gathered up her billows of white and began climbing off the bed.

"Where do you think you are going, Audrianna?"

She halted in mid motion. "To my chamber. To sleep."

"I don't think so."

She settled back down. That white froth enclosed her and her hair tumbled around her. Only remnants remained of the storm now, but her silent anticipation drenched the air and his body responded forcefully.

He burned. Not in angry possessiveness now, but with flames that aroused more than his body. He still wanted to take the parts of her that were his right, but this conversation had at least dulled the darkest edges of his desire.

All the same, he was not feeling much like a gentleman tonight.

He just looked at her, with his thoughts deepening the depths of his eyes. Time slowed, its pulse throbbing between them and also inside her. Little beats of rising expectation teased her.

Perhaps he wanted to devastate her with his mere presence. He could still do that. It was getting worse, not better. Or maybe he debated whether pleasure with her was worth the time now. The night had grown old, and the hour was closer to dawn than twilight.

"It is very late," she said, when the anticipation had made her taut. "Perhaps tomorrow—"

"No. You came to me. You do not get to leave yet."

"I did not come for this. You are under no obligation. If you are tired, or . . ."

"Or what?"

"Sated."

She had accepted where he most likely was when her watch passed two o'clock. Stupidly enough, it had come as a shock to her, that sudden explanation. The whole world had warned her. She had accepted the inevitable, and yet when it happened she was surprised and . . . hurt. Terribly hurt. For a long, horrible moment the weight in her heart had been too heavy to bear.

She expected her allusion to it to amuse him. Or anger him. Instead perhaps it surprised him. He looked at her much as he had when she announced his brother's leg had moved.

He turned thoughtful and dark. Brooding. His gaze sharpened just enough to send a thrill down her core.

"Is that what you think? You can be an innocent some-times, Audrianna. I am not convincing myself to want you, out of obligation. I am restraining myself from stripping you and taking you without ceremony, or—"

That "or" hung there, like a dangerous taunt. She rec-ognized the tension in him, visible now in his body and face. He was right. She could be an innocent sometimes. Tonight he found that inconvenient. Still, he had not sought out someone less innocent instead.

She plucked at the bow of her nightdress. "I do not mean to deny you the stripping part, but I would rather this not get torn." She let the fabric slide down her shoul-ders, and slid her arms from the sleeves. It puddled around her hips.

Whatever debate he had been holding ended then. He gazed awhile longer, enough to leave her flushed and titil-lated. Then he walked to the bed. He did not get on it, but stood tall beside it, the dark silk of his robe in front of her face. His hand reached and lightly stroked one nipple.

That was enough to make all the tantalizing sensations collect into a focused hunger. It was wanton, really, how easily she succumbed now.

"Look at me."

She gazed up while that light caress teased her merci-lessly. Her body savored the pleasure trickling down.

"Touch me."

She reached for the dark silk. She ran her palms over it, following his chest from shoulders to waist, feeling the edges and swells of his torso. Still he maddened her. Both hands touched her now. Wicked fingers did their worst until her own touch needed more. She slid her hands be-neath the silk and caressed him more surely, relishing the skin beneath her fingers.

"Kiss me."

They were not requests or little instructions. He spoke commands that he expected her to obey.

His face and mouth were too high. He did not bend to her. She realized he did not mean his mouth at all. She leaned forward, until her lips touched the warmth of his torso. She flicked her tongue, to taste. A new pleasure flowed, warm and dark, like a deep current beneath the others.

Fascination now, with the feel of him. With the soft velvet surface of his skin and the hard form it covered. She drew her legs beneath her and kneeled so she could caress more freely. She traced muscles and arms and shoulders with her hands and mouth.

She pushed the robe off his shoulders so she could feel more of him. It fell to the floor and he stood there, more naked than she had ever seen, his strength and male beauty and arousal fully visible to her.

She extended her arms and caressed up the length of him while she looked. Her gaze reached the beauty of his face, harsh now from passion's tension.

"Touch me." His gaze penetrated her. Knowing. Demanding. She could not pretend that she did not understand what he meant. She looked down and tentatively laid her fingertips on the tip of his phallus. It hardened even more. His whole body did.

Breathless from both arousal and her own audacity, she slid her fingers up and down its length.

He pushed her shoulders and she fell back on the bed. He joined her, bracing himself over her while his head dipped to kiss her deeply, then use his mouth on her breasts.

She clutched his shoulder with one arm and continued stroking him with the other. The pleasure and intimacy were heavenly, and she fought not to lose herself and her awareness of it.

He looked down at what she was doing to him, then in her eyes. "That day in the garden, when I gave you the necklace."

"Yes?"

"What did you think would have happened if I did not stop?"

Her mind went back to her surprise that day. To the way he kissed her leg, then her thigh.

"What did you want to have happen?" he asked.

She had wanted nothing. Not really. But her scandalous woman's body had anticipated something very wicked, and too shocking to say.

He saw it in her eyes. She could tell he did. He kissed her cheek, then her breast. His body lowered. Her breath shortened with each second. Her physical reaction stunned her. The sensations of the night lowered too, and pooled into a vital and erotic sensitivity.

When he spread her legs, she closed her eyes, to hide from him and herself. She instinctively moved her hand in a gesture of modesty.

He kissed her thigh. "You will not stop me. You are mine. All of you."

He lured her with kisses that softened his command. Devastating touches ensured she would not stop him and prepared her for the rest. When it came, she no longer was shocked, no longer wanted to retreat.

She abandoned herself to a forceful, inconceivable pleasure that had her helpless, and crying out her madness until a glorious release obliterated all her other senses.

Then he was with her, in her, in a furious, feral joining

that kept the pleasure trembling through her in a long, beautiful echo.

Dawn broke with Audrianna still in his arms. He still lay entwined with her, where he had fallen after that climax ripped through him.

He eased himself off her as carefully as he could. It still woke her. She turned on her side and opened her eyes. A deep acknowledgment showed in the glance she gave him, and also a touch of confusion and embarrassment.

Her awkwardness passed soon enough. Nakedness breeds familiarity, and she found the accommodation of both that had marked their marriage from the first afternoon.

They would go their own ways soon. He to his day's plans and she to hers. Right now, however, he put that off and drifted in the stillness of early morning.

"The season will start soon, and we will both be busy day and night. Before it gets under way, I want to bring you to the family's seat, and introduce you to the people there. They will expect me to."

"I would like that. I do miss the country, now that I am in town all the time again."

"We will linger if you like it there. We will depart at the end of this week."

"Next week would be better."

"I have something I must do on the way, and it should not be delayed. Why would next week be better?"

"Your mother has some plans for me at week's end."

"She can change the plans. We will go on Thursday, so tell Nellie to prepare."

She was in no hurry to depart this bed. That pleased

him. Yesterday's storm was miles away now. The night had banished those clouds for a few hours at least.

"There is something else that I have to tell you," she said.

She was not in the habit of chatting in bed. Her overture raised a very male, instinctive caution. If she were a different kind of woman, now is when she would wheedle for expensive gifts.

"Something else about my brother?"

"No. Much worse, and it grieves me. Lady Ferris told your mother yesterday that Celia is a courtesan's daughter, brought to town a few years ago to join her mother in trade."

A memory nudged at him, of a country-bred daughter of a celebrated woman of pleasure, being trained by her mother. There was an auction for her virginity that was all the talk at the clubs. He had not participated, but many had. The girl was reputed to be lovely and went for a high sum.

"I am going to write to Celia and ask her if it is true," she said.

"That is the wisest course."

"If it is true, I will not invite her here. I will respect your mother's wishes on that, and not entertain her or be seen with her."

"I regret to say that in this my mother is correct. I am sorry it must be that way."

"I understand why it must be. However, I wanted to tell you that I will not break with her and the others completely, the way that your mother demands. I will visit them privately, and call no attention to myself, but I will not abandon my friends."

He did not miss that she was not asking for his permission or advice. "Did my brother suggest this option?"

"Not at all. He agreed with your mother on every point."

"As do I."

"They did not forsake me because of my father's disgrace, but accepted me into their home. They did not turn me out when our scandal threatened to stain them by association. I must be as loyal to them as they were to me."

"And if I forbid it?"

"It is my hope that you will not make such an unreasonable command."

He could probably command all he wanted and she would do as she chose.

At the moment he did not give a damn about that. She knew it too. She had planned this announcement's timing very carefully.

He reached for her. Right now he was more interested in commanding in ways that she enjoyed obeying.

Two days later, Sebastian told his brother about Anderson's story. The news subdued Morgan, as all reports about that massacre did.

"I will give this to the army, of course, and to the Board of Ordnance. I am also going to trace that gunpowder to its source, however."

"It is unlikely that you will find its source."

"The keg had markings. I will see what I can learn. It is not much, but more than I had a month ago."

"Do not feel that you must play the runner for my sake. I know that is why you have not let this go."

"At first, yes, but I have other motives now. I am now doing it for Anderson. And, I confess, I am hoping that I learn that Kelmsleigh was innocent."

"And if he was not?"

"He has already paid, and it will be over in any case."

"That would be good. For it to be over."

He said it wistfully, but not in the vague, sad tone that he so often used to use.

"Your spirits seem to have improved of late, Morgan. You have been spared those deep melancholies."

"As the weather warms, I have convinced Dr. Fenwood to move me to the window in the afternoons. Even a few minutes of fresh air have improved my health, I think."

"I am glad to hear it. I want to talk to you about that too. I am curious. Has there been any change in your legs?"

"No. Of course not."

"None at all? No sensations? Nothing?"

"These are odd questions. Why would you ask them?"

"Your spine was not crushed or broken. There is always the chance that—"

"There is no chance, damn it. You sound like that German quack."

"His theories were controversial, but he was a celebrated scientist." He waited until Morgan's burst of anger calmed. "Audrianna was with you a few days ago. Sitting on the floor beside your chair."

"She was distraught because she learned one of her friends is not what she thought. You must tell her to break with the girl."

"Why she was there is not why I mentioned it. She told me that as she sat there, the blanket moved. Which means the leg under it might have moved."

"She is wrong." His face tightened again. "She said nothing of this to me. If she had, I would have quickly disabused her of the hopeless illusion."

"No, she told *me*. Do not be angry with her. And while she has great affection for you and prays she is correct, she is not given to illusions. Did you see the blanket move? Do you know another explanation, of which she is not aware?"

He glared like a man who wanted to strike a blow.

"I ask again. Have there been any sensations? Any at all?"

"No, damn you."

"I think that you are lying."

"Why would I lie to you?"

"Not to me. To yourself. And I have no idea why." He got up and walked around the table. He grabbed Morgan's chair, pulled it out, and swung it around.

"What in hell—?" Morgan yelled.

He pulled the blanket away. "You could not walk now even if you were completely healed, so even the slightest change will be subtle. But try to—"

"The hell I will. Get out."

"You will try, damn it. If there is even the smallest chance, you must try."

"Chance? There is no *chance*, you fool! And who are you to decree that I must try? I am the one stuck here. It is my damn life we are talking about!"

Sebastian strode to the door. "Fenwood, come here."

Fenwood hurried in.

"Throw him out," Morgan commanded, pointing at Sebastian.

Fenwood eyed Sebastian warily.

"Fenwood, my wife says that there was movement. Small, almost imperceptible. Call the physicians to examine him. And keep this blanket off him unless he needs it for warmth. Watch for movement yourself."

Morgan was almost apoplectic. "I will not stand for this!"

"I'll be damned if I will let you accept this if there is a chance for better." He grasped the arms of Morgan's chair and leaned in close. "You will let the physicians examine you, and if they find any sign of hope, you will fight for that chance. I will make you."

Chapter Seventeen

Sebastian rode through the Waltham Abbey Royal Gunpowder Mills. Four years ago the streets would have been busy and the canals full of barges transporting materials and kegs of powder. Since the war's end, however, this elaborate factory in Essex produced only one-tenth of its former output and the yards and buildings were quiet.

It still operated, however. Men still carried sulphur into the mixing house. Others burned charcoal to go there as well. Smoke still came from the melting house where the saltpeter was prepared. Coopers sawed and pounded kegs into shape.

The men with the most dangerous jobs loitered outside the mill house. Inside the carefully mixed ingredients were ground together by the edge runner mill. Beside the brick structure a huge waterwheel in the Millhead Stream did the labor.

One of the men darted inside to pour water on the big stone, so the volatile gunpowder would not stick on the mill surface. Everyone here, in the factory and the town, risked the disaster of an explosion every day, but none so much as the men who worked the actual mill.

Down the lane and over a canal, Sebastian found the offices. He entered and introduced himself to the clerk.

Another man, tall and wiry and thin, with a heavy brow and deeply chiseled features, came out to introduce himself as Mr. Middleton, the storekeeper. He ushered him to the inner office. His rough-hewn face frowned with worry.

"We had nothing to do with that business, sir."

Sebastian had not yet named his business, but he was not surprised that Mr. Middleton had guessed. The managers of all the royal mills would be aware of who had taken an interest in corrupted gunpowder.

"It is my hope that you can help me discover who did. I am not here to put you under a quizzing glass."

"It would not help if you did. I am only lately come to this appointment. Mr. Matthews was here before me."

"Then how do you know this mill had nothing to do with it?"

"We are a royal mill, sir. Owned by the Crown as you know, along with those at Flavesham and Billingcollig. Mr. Congreave's father made it his life to ensure our army and navy had the best gunpowder, and we are proud of the quality we produce here. Better than the other Crown mills. That has been proven by science."

"Mr. Middleton, you are the storekeeper. You bring in the materials, and you send out the gunpowder."

"That is correct."

"Do you know all the processes, and the transport?"

"I do at that."

"Within that knowledge, can you guess how this bad gunpowder reached the front?"

He pondered the question. "It can't happen."

"It did happen. It did not fire, and it was not wet. The only explanation is adulteration by bad material or incorrect milling."

The reality was too foreign to Mr. Middleton's sight of the world. He kept shaking his head.

"It cannot happen at the mill, whichever mill it was," he said emphatically. "There are too many involved. Too many checks and too many tests. Too many eyes."

"What if it was not this mill, or another royal mill? During the war, private mills were also used. All of the powder did not come from mills owned by the Crown."

"Most did, but no, some did not. However, our standards were demanded of them. Even if a terrible mistake were made, it would be caught at the arsenal. It is tested there."

"Each keg?"

Mr. Middleton's mouth folded in. "Not each and every keg, I expect. Each batch. Each day's production. We test here, then they test there."

"Is it possible that, knowing it is tested at the factories, someone might get careless and not test as scheduled at the arsenal?"

"Negligence, you mean. Possible, but there are others about. Gunpowder is serious business, sir. Not much is left to chance with it."

Sebastian removed a piece of paper from his pocket. "This gunpowder was in kegs with these markings. Does that tell you anything?"

Middleton peered at the paper and the drawings on it. "That one is the mark of the Ordnance Board. It means it went through the arsenal and was checked." He looked up and flushed. "The batch was, as I said, not perhaps this very keg."

"And the other mark?"

He shook his head. "I do not recognize it— No, wait, maybe . . ." He lifted his pen. On a sheet of paper he copied the keg's mark, then drew two more lines. "See here. This could be what that mark was. It could have faded, or just been marked carelessly." He handed over both sheets. Sebastian saw how the two extra marks had turned D & F into P & E.

"There is no D & F mill," Middleton said. "But P & E refers to the Pettigrew and Eversham Mill. It was one of several that popped up during the war, to make a profit. And to have some bad explosions. The private ones are not always so careful about that. We can control the quality of what they make, but not how they make it. This is not a hobby for amateurs."

No, indeed. There had been some bad explosions and fires at these mills. It was one reason he had left Audrianna at the inn they had used last night, a few miles upriver. He doubted the workers here ever forgot that one spill, one slip, and they all would be blasted to heaven.

The puzzle had captured Middleton's interest now. He took the papers back, and mused over the one Sebastian had brought. "They put their mark on fast, I would guess. Careless."

"Possibly not. That derives from a gunner who survived. It is from his memory, which might be inaccurate or incomplete."

"Did he remember anything else?"

"Not with certainty. He only said that the keg was easy to open. More than normal. Is that significant?"

"That is impossible to know. It suggests that the keg had been opened before, though. Most likely at the arsenal."

Middleton did not have to spell it out, nor would he. If the keg had been opened at the arsenal, it would have been for testing. In which case, someone looked the other way when it was reported to be of bad quality.

"What is the location of this mill? Pettigrew and Eversham?"

"The property is in Kent," Middleton said. "However, with the end of hostilities, it, like several other small upstarts, closed. I think the mill was sold."

"Thank you, Mr. Middleton. You have been most helpful."

Middleton's face fell. "I did not tell you anything of note, sir. I trust you realize that and will not be reporting to anyone on my helpfulness."

"As far as the Ordnance Board will ever know, should they even become aware of this meeting, you merely impressed on me the impossibility of bad gunpowder leaving a royal mill."

Sebastian tied his horse to the carriage, climbed in next to Audrianna, and told the coachman to begin.

He had not told her where he was going when he left her to wait at the inn and rode away. He could have had an urge to tumble a milkmaid in a nearby field for all he let her know.

"While we are at Airymont, I will have to tour the property," he said. "Do you ride? You can join me. The tenants will appreciate it if you do."

"I ride. I also sing, sketch, and play the pianoforte passably. My mother, like most others, believed all young ladies should know such things."

He glanced at her, as if checking to see if she had been insulted by his question. She smiled to let him know that her response had been a little joke. Mostly.

He settled in for the remainder of their journey. Thoughts obviously occupied him, but he did not appear inclined to share them with her.

"Did you learn anything interesting at your meeting?"

He shrugged. "It was a brief business conversation."

"Your business is politics and government. You probably feared boring me, and left me here to spare me. That was kind of you."

He actually looked pleased with her gratitude. And relieved?

"However, I would not be bored to hear of it. Not at all. I am very curious about government."

"It was nothing interesting, I promise." He turned that smile on her, to encourage her to think about other things, or even about nothing at all except him.

"The Essex countryside is beautiful," she mused, gazing out the window. "It is hard to believe that a factory exists a few miles away that has the potential to destroy everything we are looking at right now. The Waltham Abbey works are downriver."

"I believe they are, now that you mention it."

"Now that I mention it? Had you forgotten so quickly? Why, it cannot be more than an hour since you were there."

Chagrin flashed, then resignation that she had figured it out. "I learned absolutely nothing of interest," he reassured her again.

"I explained that I was going to decide what was of interest to me in this matter."

"You are becoming vexed for no reason. I merely spoke

with the storekeeper, and learned something about how gunpowder is kegged and transported. I did not bring you because it is dangerous there."

She coaxed her rising anger down to a low simmer. She studied his handsome face. Smiling. Appeasing. Innocent.

He was lying. Not directly, but she should have been there. He had learned something from that storekeeper that occupied his deeper self. That was in his eyes whenever his gaze moved away from her.

She reached over and laid her glove on his. "I am asking you, please, to tell me what you learned."

No longer smiling. Serious now. He lifted her hand and kissed it. "Do not ask."

"I must."

He sighed, with the exasperation of a man cornered. "I learned that the gunpowder could not make it to the front unless someone deliberately allowed it, after learning it was useless."

Her heart thickened. Not negligence, then. "It was a conspiracy. A plan. As you suspected."

He nodded.

The implications were too disappointing to accept. "This is why I wanted to be with you. I think that you hear what you want to hear, to confirm your own theories."

His gaze penetrated hers. "Do you really believe that I would go out of my way to hurt you, and put mere pride before your happiness?"

She did not want to think so, but he hungered for culprits as much as she did for justice. "You are better than that. However, I think that you pursue this for reasons besides pride. I think—I think that you do it because of your brother, and the life you must now share with him,

and the way he was hurt. I do not think that my happiness
signifies in this quest of yours at all. I am, after all, a late,
unexpected, and inconvenient addition."

His angry reaction stunned her. Frightened her. She might
have slapped him. Challenged him. His glare told her she
had said something she should not.

She looked away, to end the argument. It was not to be.

"Is there anything else you want to say?" he asked tightly.

She collected her courage. "Even if that is how it
happened—a plan—my father was not involved."

"Quite possibly not."

"Assuredly not."

He just looked at her.

She let the carriage put some miles between them and
the row. Then she asked a question about Airymont, to
change the subject. He answered at length.

They conversed about small, unimportant things for an
hour, and she tried to ignore how the sore between had
been poked so hard that it was bleeding.

Chapter Eighteen

Airymont's house sat atop a rise of land, swept by sea winds from the Essex coast a mile away. Like the London house, it displayed the grand opulence of the last century's great manors, with two wings embracing a grand courtyard and an elaborate staircase leading to the entry in the center of the main block of stone.

The servants greeted them like Sebastian was the master. They lined up to meet Audrianna. She was shown to her chambers, then the housekeeper gave her a tour while Sebastian met with the steward.

She returned to her rooms. A servant had been assigned to be her maid, and the woman was unpacking her baggage. Audrianna looked out the tall window onto the courtyard. Down below Sebastian was mounting a horse. He had changed into riding coat and boots, and another man already sat astride nearby.

A footman arrived at her door with an explanation. Lord Sebastian assumed that she would want to rest after the journey, and a matter on the estate required him to go out with the land steward. He would return in the evening for the dinner party that had been arranged.

"Will you be wanting this dress this evening, Madam?" The maid held up her rose satin dinner dress.

"No. The white one."

She watched the two horses trot out of the courtyard. Her perspective dwarfed them, as did the massive wings of the house. No doubt there was a matter on the estate that required attention. On an estate this big there always would be. The carriage ride here had been full of brittle silences amid their small talk, however, and she suspected he had not been sorry to be called away.

S ebastian broke into a gallop once outside the court-yard. The speed did not ease his mood. It matched it.

He should have left her in London. He had been a fool to find reasons why he should not. He had to introduce her to the country at some point, but it did not have to be right now.

She addled his senses sometimes. That was his only excuse, and it was a damned sorry one.

Of course she would know where the royal gun-powder mills were located. Kelmsleigh probably spoke of such things in his home as casually as Wellington described warfare and other lords discussed horses and clubs.

Under the circumstances, it had been stupid to think she would let him go his own way in the morning the way she did all the time in London, and not quiz him about it. She would have ignored it if she thought he visited a lover, but she could not keep silent about her suspicions that he had gone to that gunpowder mill.

The temptation to lie to her had been strong. Not to avoid a row, but to avoid seeing the hurt in her eyes. If he had known she would so calmly name her insignificance, as if it were a truth generally accepted, he would have lied. If he guessed that she would say the rest of it—

"Sir!"

He reined in his horse abruptly and turned. His steward had hailed him, and now pointed to the left.

"You wanted to go to the Mulder farm, did you not, sir?"

Did he? He couldn't remember. Addled, that was what he was for certain. All because a woman was unhappy.

He trotted back and turned his horse onto a forest path that would lead to the farm. There were tenants to talk to and improvements to inspect. He would fill his time and his mind with useful things, not the accusing green eyes of a woman who could never trust him.

The dinner party went well. It was not Audrianna's triumph, however. The steward and housekeeper had planned it and Sebastian had invited the guests. Audrianna did not have to do anything except attend as hostess.

The guests were all new to her but close acquaintances of Sebastian and each other, as happens among country neighbors. The mood turned informal and gay. She received enough attention as the new wife to feel included, but not so much as to feel conspicuous.

Sebastian made an excellent host. Witty. Smooth. Warm. He was relaxed with these people he had known his whole

life. The only awkwardness—and she did not think anyone else noticed—was between him and her.

The sore still bled. She tried to cover it, soothe it, but
the implications of their row created soulful pains that she
could not master.

She did not want this invisible rift that she felt between
them. She did not want to lose the familiarity that had
begun and that truly made life more than tolerable. And
yet she also could not bury her fear that he was going to
condemn her father to more disgrace yet, and that good
man would not even be able to defend himself.

She looked down the table at him, while silver clinked
on china. Ladies spoke of dresses bought for the season
and men discussed hunting and politics. His gaze met hers
briefly, and he smiled.

Not one of his winning smiles, designed to mesmerize
her. Not even the smile of a friend. It was a reassuring one,
that was all. An approving smile, which said the unsuitable bride was acquitting herself well enough tonight.

He did not come to her chamber that night. A moment
arrived, a distinct moment, when she knew he would
not.

That pained her. Frightened her. Her heart hollowed out,
as if something vital had been removed.

She considered the little argument that had created this
estrangement. For all its brevity it had produced a chaos
of strong emotions. Anger and hurt and fear on her part.
And on his?

Anger too, when she said he would see it through even
if it hurt her. His reaction to that played on her mind now.

His expression—not just anger. Also startled and . . . insulted? Dismayed?

Suddenly that row appeared very different to her. In this new perspective she was not the only one aggrieved. A little panic fluttered in the void, as she imagined how she had looked and sounded to him.

That meeting at the mill had troubled him. He had not wanted to speak of it. He had not wanted to tell her the direction it pointed. He had tried to spare her for a while at least. In return she had accused him of indifference to her happiness.

She found an undressing gown and slipped it on. She wrapped herself in a long shawl. She would go to him and apologize. Not for being hurt. Not for being afraid or angry. She would apologize for forgetting to wonder why he was angry and hurt too.

He was not in his chamber. She gazed around the room, disappointed. She had plucked up her bravery with every step here, and for naught.

Sounds in the dressing room advanced to the door. Her heart flipped while she watched the door open. Her reflective mood made her wonder at her reaction. Not fear. Not at all. Excitement and joy and anticipation of setting things to right. That was what she experienced.

It was not Sebastian. The old servant acting as his valet peered around the door at her.

"He has gone to the observatory," he said. "There is no telling when he will return, Madam."

"Where is this observatory?"

"It is not an observatory proper. It is a gardener's hut.

It is beyond the main garden and straight through the little woods there, in a clearing on the other side."

She left and went down the stairs. The night was not too cold, and her shawl was warm. She would find him, say what she felt obligated to say, and leave. And perhaps in the morning they would no longer be strangers again.

The cosmos often calmed him. Its vastness absorbed whatever darkness he carried in his soul. A drop of poison has no potency when put in the ocean.

Tonight, as on some other nights long ago, it affected him differently. Its beauty moved him profoundly. He lost track of scientific facts, of astronomical concerns, and just looked until he floated up there. The telescope and the hut, the distance and his physicality, ceased to exist for a long moment.

Such sublime occurrences happened rarely now. He was grateful to experience it once again, like a vivid memory of a childhood friend.

The world always intruded, however. A breeze. The metal against his face. A sigh or breath. It did not take much to break the spell.

No sound did it this time. No touch. Just an awareness that he was no longer alone. He turned his head away from the stars.

Audrianna stood outside the open door, watching. She wore an undressing gown festooned with lace flounces that contrasted with the wool shawl that wrapped her. The moonlight picked out the fire hidden in her hair, but it also cast her face in shadow.

"Come in, Audrianna."

She stepped up from the grass, onto the board floor. No

lamps burned, so only the doorway and the roof's hole let in the dim light of the half-moon.

She looked around the simple hut. Not even a cottage, it had served gardeners as a place of respite during long hours. Sebastian had put the telescope here ten years ago, when he realized that it was ideal with the height of the land and the break in the trees.

She ran her fingers along the shiny metal of the telescope. "Does it just stay here, poking toward that hole? What if it rains?"

Her practical concern charmed him. "I take it down when I leave, and cover the hole." He grabbed a thin rope dangling from the roof. "It slides either way when I pull this."

She admired the telescope, bending to see how it pointed at the patch of heaven. "It is very impressive."

"Would you like to look through it?"

"Very much, if I may."

"Come here, then."

He pointed the lens toward Mars, then lifted her onto his lap. "Put your eye right there."

She peered tentatively, as if she feared breaking something. Then she pressed her eye and gasped.

"It is amazing," she whispered. "Glorious."

He sensed it absorbing her as it did him. He slid his arm around her so she would not be distracted by balancing on his knees. Silken strands of her hair teased his face and the shawl's wool nestled his hand against her body.

"Wait." He eased her head to the side while he aimed the scope to another spot and checked the view. She spied again and gasped again.

The stars had gone far to dispersing his black mood. Holding her lessened it too. Not totally. Resentments that he did not want to name still rumbled deeply, lowly—incoherently—as they had for two years, but at least he could ignore them again.

"Do you ever get used to this?" she asked. "Does it become commonplace with repetition?"

"Never." The response came quietly, low and male. Calm.

She understood now why none of the day's turmoil had greeted her when she looked in the door. This hut offered a type of escape unknown to most people. He could look at the stars and every emotion would seem small in comparison.

She had interfered with that. She had intruded. It had been kind of him to allow it, and to show her what really lay within the glittering night sky.

She relinquished the glory. She slid off his lap. "Thank you. That was astonishing."

"Someday I will take you to Greenwich, and sneak you into the observatory there, so you can look through a larger one."

"I would like that. The looking. The sneaking might be fun too."

She crossed the wooden floor and hopped down into the grass. She looked up at the sky, so different from what she had just seen.

"Audrianna, why did you come here?"

She turned. He had not returned to his escape. He stood at the hut's door.

"You are not given to night walks," he said. "Why did you take this one?"

"I was looking for you. I wanted to apologize. Not for

how I felt, or for protecting my father's name. Not even for fearing that you would not."

"For what, then?"

"For only thinking about my own feelings and fears. And for not being kinder. I think that I said something that cut in ways I do not intend or comprehend. If so, I am sorry."

He stepped down. "You cannot be blamed for seeing something quickly that it took me too long to recognize myself."

"I do not even know what you mean. I think that you misunderstood me."

"The life you must share with your brother. It was the reason you gave me for the investigation. You named an uncomfortable truth."

"I did not mean that the two of you live one life."

"Except we do."

"I do not see—"

"Then look again. I wield his influence. I have his power. I play the lord on his estates and I sit at his place at tables. I have molded my life and myself to this duty of standing in for him, but not replacing him. Had he died in the war, it would have been a more tragic reason to take his place, but the duty and role would have been a natural inheritance."

His tone grew harsher as he spoke. Not for her. The thoughts and words themselves angered him.

"You are not— You are admired in your own right, and any power comes from your own character and good judgment."

"If true, that is worse. I live his life, I take his place, and *he is still alive seeing me do it, damn it.* If he thinks I live his life better than he could— Bloody hell, this joint existence causes moments of misery for me, but it must cause many more for him. I am the thief, after all. The loss is his."

She did not know what to say. She understood his tenacity about the gunpowder now, however. She understood why he would not give it up. The half in the chair could not do it, so the half that walked in the world would. Out of love or out of debt, he would give his brother some kind of justice.

"You do what must be done. You steal nothing."

"Whether I steal or he gives, we indeed share a life due to fate." He reached through the night and touched her face. "We even share you."

Her breath caught, and only partly owing to the charge that entered her with that touch. "What do you mean?"

"You know what I mean."

She feared that she did. A notion entered her head that had entered before. Only now it took on new meaning. "That day at your house—your brother's good spirits in my company—is that why you proposed again? For *him*?"

"Perhaps, in part. I did not realize it. However, his delight in your company may have encouraged me to press you more than I might have." He folded his arms and turned his gaze to the stars, as if seeking distraction. Or escape again. "Two halves of a whole. It has become so normal I do not even notice unless the truth cannot be avoided. Of course, I did not expect—well, I did not plan to share you quite so literally."

Shock cleared her head to a state of precise clarity. Memories marched through, of comments and questions, of reactions and moods. She feared that she understood all too well what he implied.

"If you think that I hold romantic feelings for your brother, and deplore his infirmity for that reason, you are very wrong."

He looked at her. Darkly. Tensely.

"He is a friend," she said. "A dear friend. I do not love him except as a brother. Certainly not like a husband or lover. Whatever the two of you share, it does not include me."

She embraced him, so he would perhaps believe her. His arms pulled her closer and he looked down as if he could see her thoughts in the dark. She reached up and cupped his face with her hands and guided him down so she could kiss him and maybe he would know that even when he was a stranger he had not only excited her body.

The result was inevitable. She knew that kiss would be like fire to oil tonight. Another escape perhaps, but it would bridge the awkward chasm forming today.

The moon provided just enough light to create a magical night. Dark trees draped the clearing, and with their first kiss it became a private, intimate chamber of nature. The stars hung low in a canopy of brilliant dots.

The passion built in a rush of grasping embraces and furious kisses. She welcomed the assault, encouraged it. Within its power and hardness a sweet emotion flowed, born of his confidences, and now of her relief that this complicated day had not left her alone after all, watching him stepping back instead of forward.

His embrace clutched her, supported her, controlled her. He lowered to his knees and his kisses claimed her stomach and hips, her thighs and mound. They burned through her garments and into her blood until tongues of fiery pleasure licked her skin.

He pulled her shawl off and threw it down, then pulled

her to it with him, until she lay atop him on the ground, entwined in an embrace so taut they might be trying to break into each other's souls.

He set her up on her knees and caressed down the front of her gown. "Open it."

She worked the buttons impatiently, rising up so she could reach them all. He unfastened his own garments. Her body quaked at what was coming. A deep, low pulse begged.

He pushed the fabric of her gown aside so it gaped wide, exposing her. The stars entered his eyes while his hands began their luscious caresses of her breasts. Soon she rocked to that lower throb of need as it became unbearable.

She pulled the fabric out from beneath her so that pulse could feel his hardness and warmth and promise. It was delicious kneeling up like this, straddling him, being teased in the most physical ways in the moonlight.

He drew her down toward him so his tongue could torture her breasts. He entered her just enough to taunt and make her crazed. Her breasts were so sensitive it seemed that every lick on them sent a jolt of pleasure down to where they joined.

She was almost weeping by the time he thrust into her fully. She threw back her head and opened her eyes and saw the stars falling and entering her. Then she collapsed into his embrace while he ravished her.

They slipped through the garden before dawn. Sated and dishabille, they stole into the house like two servants having a clandestine affair.

He left her at her chamber door. She kissed him before opening it. Was it her fourth kiss given freely, without him luring her into abandon first? He was losing count.

"You could change it if you want," she said. "We could move out of that house. You could leave government. I will do whatever you require." She smiled. "We could go to Brazil."

Her concern touched him. He kissed her one last time before he left, to let her know that. "You are too good, and I am grateful. But I do not know how I want my life to be anymore. I do not know what I want."

Except her. He knew he wanted her. Both her passion and her heart.

There it was.

How unexpected.

Chapter Nineteen

After four days Sebastian concluded that even an agreeable and passionate wife would eventually grow tired of a husband's nonstop use of her. Since he could not restrain himself in this idyllic setting where nothing interfered, he gave the word to the servants that he and Audrianna would return to London.

She fell asleep in his arms almost as soon as the carriage left the courtyard. He should feel guilty for exhausting her. Instead he only knew the devil's contentment.

After a night at an inn, she was more herself the next day. She noticed, therefore, that they were not on the same road as when they went down to the country.

"We are in Middlesex," she said after examining the passing farms and buildings when they approached London. "We are not far from Cumberworth."

"As long as we are out and about, I thought you might like to see your friends."

She smiled with delight. He felt like a magnanimous king giving his approval to her petition to maintain these friendships, even though she had made it clear that she would do as she liked. Thus did women turn sane men into their fools.

Her smile soon waned, like a flag brought to half-mast. "It will not be a happy visit. I will have to talk to Celia. I had not written to her before we left. I could not find the courage or the words."

"It may be easier if you see her. It will certainly be kinder."

Mrs. Joyes emerged from the house when the carriage stopped. She embraced Audrianna and welcomed them both. "Lizzie and Celia are in the greenhouse. You must go to them at once. They will be so happy you have come to us."

"I will go. I need to speak to Celia privately, Daphne." She glanced back at him.

"Then be off with you. I am sure that Lizzie will allow the privacy you seek."

"I will remain out here and enjoy the fair day," Sebastian said. "You will find me in the garden when you are ready to leave. Will you join me for a turn, Mrs. Joyes? I believe there is a portal over here."

Mrs. Joyes strolled beside him to the portal and into the garden. He could see Audrianna in her pale, crepe bonnet enter the greenhouse and greet her two friends with embraces. The glass's distortions did not permit a clear view of their features, but he knew Celia from her blond hair. The other dark-haired one must be Lizzie.

Soon that dark head moved away and Audrianna was alone with Celia.

"It will not be a pleasant conversation, will it?" Mrs. Joyes asked, pulling her concerned gaze away from the glass panes.

"No. Do you know what is being said, and why?"

"I think so. You have learned about Celia's mother and have forbidden Audrianna to be friends with her."

"No doubt you find that harsh. Audrianna understands even if you do not."

"I understand too, Lord Sebastian. Even people who fight the world have to choose their battles. Audrianna is ill-equipped to fight this one, and must retreat."

"I believe she intends to continue visiting here. The friendship will not end completely."

She raised her eyebrows, impressed. He let her believe he had agreed to this, instead of being given little say in it.

"I am surprised you guessed what this was about," he said. "Audrianna says none of you know the full history of the others. That there is a rule against inquiring."

"I know more than most. It is my home, after all. I bring them here. It is a good rule, although I think that you do not approve."

"As developments indicate, it is a rule with risks. You might at least have warned Audrianna."

"You mean warned *you*, don't you? There was a very good chance no one would find out. I owed Celia discretion more than I owed you an explanation."

She stopped to examine a climbing rose on the wall of the conservatory. She muttered something to herself about it needing trimming, and they strolled on.

"Do any more surprises await?" he asked. There were two other women here with vague histories, including the one beside him now.

"Possibly. One never knows. Women often leave their

pasts behind for very good reasons. If the past finds them despite their best efforts . . ." She shrugged.

"As long as none of you are murderesses or pirates, I suppose my wife's reputation will survive more revelations."

She did not find his little joke amusing. "I will tell you a story that explains why even I do not know everything. When I first came to this house, I had a servant. I then hired another. This second woman was new to the area, and of vague background. She seemed honest to me, but very meek, so I took her on. She became like a sister to me. One might say she began The Rarest Blooms. The greenhouse that you see is to a large extent due to her knowledge of horticulture and what she taught me. I also learned from that sweet woman's friendship that a woman without family need not be alone."

"That was good of you to take her in, and you both benefited. However, one fortunate experience does not mean all will follow the same path."

"Hear me out, sir. She became friendly with the other servant and one day confided to her what I already had been told. That she had run away from a husband who beat her. She revealed her real name. The other girl was not discreet. She meant no harm, but the secret was out. The brute of a husband arrived here and dragged her away, as was his right by law." Her face tensed. "I will never forget the terror in her eyes. I was powerless to help her."

She took a deep breath and swallowed the emotion that had crept into her voice. "He hit her, twice, right in front of me. With his fist, and on her face. He drew blood and— Anyway, now when one of my sisters does not want to speak of her past, I respect it, Lord Sebastian, and I expect all the women here to do so as well."

There was nothing to say in response to a story like

that. However, it confirmed his belief that the ambiguities in this household could be potentially dangerous. "I hope that your goodness and generosity are always rewarded in kind, Mrs. Joyes."

"The day will come when they will not be, I think. Thus far my judgment of character has protected me, however." She looked past him, toward the greenhouse. "Here comes Audrianna. She looks close to weeping. I must go and comfort Celia. I will leave your wife's sorrow to your care, Lord Sebastian."

Sebastian's time soon became absorbed with government and the start of Parliament's sessions. Audrianna's time became occupied with navigating the demands of a rapidly increasing social schedule.

She began receiving callers. She chose Tuesday afternoons, when she knew Lady Wittonbury left the house. She received the curious and the cruel, the friendly and the grasping. There were more of the last than she anticipated. Far too many people were under the illusion that the wife of Lord Sebastian could influence him to their husband's and family's benefit.

Most of them were women, but some were men. The former could be very blunt, but the latter hoped flattery and time would win her over. She wondered what Sebastian would think if he heard some of the poetic appreciations sent her way during those calls.

Then again, he might not find it at all odd. Perhaps he was calling on the wife of some lord or MP while he was gone, casting his own lures to engender favor for one of his bills.

Two weeks after the visit to Airymont, she brought a

book to the drawing room to await the cards and visitors. Outside the streets were busy with carriages and wagons. The annual influx of the best families to London had begun in force.

She slipped a letter out of her book. Celia had written. They had agreed to continue this communication, as well as Audrianna's visits. She looked at the familiar hand on the address and thought about that meeting where she asked Celia if Lady Ferris's story was true.

Celia had displayed no embarrassment. No shame. That was a relief. And she had known at once what it meant to their friendship. No rancor there. No hurt that was visible. Audrianna had been the one to weep, and Celia the one to comfort.

Now Celia had written, and a very cryptic note it was too. Perhaps she thought Sebastian would be reading it, and dared not write plainly.

I have cause to believe that your queries will receive some answers soon. She meant the queries about the Domino. Thus far no letters had arrived for her at the office of Mr. Loversall, the solicitor whom she had arranged as a mail drop. Nor had the employees at the hotels and theaters that she had approached contacted her with information either.

It was unlikely that Celia herself had met the Domino, so her allusion was too mysterious to make much sense.

She rather wished Celia had written about other things, like the state of Lizzie's health and the garden's resurrection with spring growth. She found herself visiting the flower shops supplied by The Rarest Blooms, and purchasing bouquets that made her nostalgic.

"Madam." The voice startled her out of her thoughts. The butler stood in front of her, salver in hand.

She read the card and her mood clouded. Roger had called. Now, that was bold.

She agreed to see him and braced herself for echoes of those old pangs of sorrow. Instead, when he entered the drawing room, she experienced nothing at all except a mild irritation that he did not have the good sense to stay away.

He was in his uniform and looked very smart. His gaze swept the drawing room, then settled on her lone figure. His eyes sparkled with a familiarity that he should not show anymore, even if they were alone.

"Up from Brighton again?" she asked.

"Yes, a short leave. I expect we will all be enjoying much of the season here. There is not much to do down there, except when the Prince Regent visits. The French aren't going to invade now, are they?"

"I am sure there will be invitations aplenty in both towns. Hostesses always like having young men in uniforms about."

They chatted about upcoming balls and parties. "It is my hope to meet individuals in government who can help my career in peace time," he explained. "The country requires many fewer officers and I do not fancy living on half-pay."

Audrianna had come to recognize the overture. She pretended she had not.

"Perhaps you will put in a good word for me," he added when she did not offer herself.

"Roger, only a stupid woman would ask her husband to help a man to whom she was once affianced. You are no rival, but men are men."

Her response truly surprised him. "Your husband? Lord Sebastian? I would never request such a thing of you. It was my hope that you would speak on my behalf with the marquess."

"Wittonbury is an invalid. He never leaves the house. His influence is nonexistent now."

"He is not a hermit, is he? I am told he enjoyed considerable influence before he went to war, and engenders even more sympathy now. A well-directed letter from him would find favor with the recipient, who would want to do him a good turn. He was a friend of the army and still is, and the War Office will not treat his recommendation of an officer lightly."

"He does not even know you. Why would he so recommend you?"

"He knows you, doesn't he? How else do you think this happens? Someone knows someone who knows someone who does a favor in kind." He looked amused and sly. "It is said he has affection for you. If so, he will be glad to write a letter."

"It is said? By whom?"

He shrugged. "It is known. It is around. I heard he let his affection be known in order to ease your way, so that being caught with his brother near Brighton would not cause you too much disdain."

She had underestimated the marquess. He might be a prisoner of those chambers, but as Roger said, he was not a hermit. He still received a few friends and he could write letters. It touched her that he had tried to ease her way.

"If Wittonbury favors me, I am flattered. I think that it would not do for me to overvalue my good fortune, however. I can only dip from that well so often, I expect."

Roger heard the rejection of his petition buried in her musing. His face assumed a severe passivity. He masked his disappointment beneath formality, and soon took his leave.

Deciding she had awaited callers long enough, Audrianna went up toward the marquess's apartment. She had not visited him as much the last weeks as before. In part that was due to the increase in social obligations, but his days had altered as well.

One of those physicians called in had detected some sensation in Wittonbury's legs. Sebastian had ordered exercises be resumed. Most afternoons, if one passed those chambers, one could hear Wittonbury cursing while Dr. Fenwood forced flaccid muscles to move.

When she entered the apartment's library, those exertions were finished. The marquess sat near the window, his face to the crack of fresh air.

"Ah, my dear sister. I am relieved you are here. Fenwood won't dare interfere with me now."

She could not help but glance at his legs. The blanket never covered them now, unless he had guests. It seemed to her that they showed more mass. They no longer resembled thin bundles of rags stuffed into trousers.

"Do not ask," he said. "It is all a fool's errand, and I weary of talking about it."

"Then we will not. Should I read to you, or would you like a chess match?"

"Pettigrew and Eversham. P & E." Mr. William Holmes, Treasurer for the Board of Ordnance, muttered the name over and over while he perused his account books in his Tower office.

It had taken two weeks and considerable political capital for Sebastian to procure this meeting. Mr. Holmes, like all of the Board, held his office from the Crown and felt no obligation to accommodate a mere member of the House of Commons. Only when the Prime Minister had intimated that the Crown might be persuaded to reconsider Mr. Holmes's recently attained position, and the handsome salary he drew, did Mr. Holmes finally decide time could be found for this inquiry after all.

"Ah, here it is. A small mill, from the looks of it. Fairly late to the game. It appears that powder was purchased from them beginning in 1811. Maybe seventy thousand was paid overall. That may sound like a handsome sum, but for an industrial affair it is quite small. It is a wonder we bothered with them, but the need for reserves was severe."

"And the last payment?"

Mr. Holmes ran his thick finger down the page. "May 1814. They probably thought the war would last forever. One wonders if they even realized their investment back in three years."

Perhaps they had not. That thought opened a new path in Sebastian's mind. "Do you know who owned P & E?"

"The records do not say. I could probably discover the name of the person to whom the money was sent, but it may not be the owner. The name itself implies a partnership, although neither Pettigrew or Eversham are familiar names to me. My predecessor, Mr. Alcock, might have known them, but of course, he is not available."

"If you were to find to whom the payments were sent, I would appreciate it. I will await your letter."

Sebastian rode back to the City. He visited one of his solicitors. He had charged the man with learning what he could about P & E, and now he had a date when the company might have been formed. That alone should make digging for information more productive.

Chapter Twenty

"That fellow is flirting with your wife again." Hawkeswell made it a point not to look in Audrianna's direction while he spoke.

"So he is." Sebastian did not look that way either. All the same, he had been keeping an eye on things.

"I trust that the passing weeks have reduced the novelty of marriage and that you will not want to be an ass this time."

That remained to be seen. "That Fellow" had called on Audrianna last week, according to his valet, who heard about it from the butler. It appeared That Fellow had friends enough to be invited to more parties than expected too. What was the good of having a regiment at Brighton if the officers never stayed there?

"His name is Major Roger Woodruffe. I found out about him for you," Hawkeswell said. "His introductions come through an aunt of his mother. The aunt is married to a baronet, and Roger there mines the connection for all it is worth."

Hawkeswell had checked rather thoroughly. Which meant Hawkeswell probably knew Major Woodruffe and Audrianna had once been engaged.

"I expect he will be underfoot all season then," Sebastian said. He did not mind that too much. Audrianna said she no longer loved Major Woodruffe. He was inclined to believe her, if only because the alternative was wanting to be an ass, as Hawkeswell put it.

However, Woodruffe's presence reminded him of the odd caprices of fate. He had assumed that if not for her father's disgrace, and a cryptic notice in the *Times*, and a disastrous first meeting that resulted in scandal, he would have never met Audrianna.

Only, most likely he would have, it turned out. He could have been at a party like this and seen her after she was married to this army officer.

What if she had captivated him then? He would have been faced with seducing another man's wife. Since he did not much like Major Woodruffe, from what he could see, that would not bother him too much. Unfortunately the Audrianna he knew might very well have refused to be seduced.

"Lord Notorious has arrived, I see," Hawkeswell mused.

That explained the little agitation that flowed through the garden party. Heads turned and whispers buzzed as Castleford made his entrance. He smiled like a man amused by the attention, but who also considered it his due. Mothers beckoned their virginal daughters to come admire The Rarest Blooms' artistry at the other end of the property.

"At least he is not drunk," Sebastian said.

"He could not enjoy the fame if he were. Nothing like being a dissolute rogue to make one popular. When the book of scandal is written, he will get a whole chapter, and you and I will be reduced to footnotes, despite our concerted attempts to make our mark. Thus does even mild discretion breed obscurity."

While the girls were pulled away, the young men gravitated toward Castleford like he was a magnet.

"He has a talent for making one feel old and boring, I will give him that. I may go and bask in the glow of his outrageous infamy myself," Sebastian said.

"No need. It appears he is coming to us. Promise to keep me from hitting him if he unleashes that sarcastic wit of his. I will do the same for you."

"I need to apologize, Audrianna. I was too bold at your house when I called."

"You are too bold now. You must not address me with such familiarity anymore. Especially not where others can overhear."

Roger glanced about and flushed. "Of course. It is just . . ." He labored over his words, keeping one eye on the bodies milling around them. "I should have known that you could not speak freely there. I was relieved to see your notice."

Notice?

"In the *Times*," he whispered. "Did you not receive my response? I left it as instructed."

Suddenly she understood. She had been placing notices for the Domino. In an effort to be cryptic, she had perhaps been too much so. Roger had concluded, stupidly, that the message was for *him*.

She had not been to her mail drop in several days. Whatever note Roger had written still waited there.

"I do not know to what you refer. I placed no notice for you." She had never lied so baldly in her life, but she saw no alternative. And she had placed no notice *for him*.

"'*A.K. requires a meeting with D to discuss matters most confidential. Send response care of Mr. Loversall of number 7 Portman Square.*' That was not you?"

"Indeed not. Why would you think it was for you?"

He flushed. "You know I was called Dumpfry at school. I assumed . . ." He glanced in the direction of Sebastian. "You could hardly use R.W., could you? That would be blatant."

"There must be a thousand A.K.s in London. I am sorry that you misunderstood."

"Zeus. He is coming this way," Roger hissed.

Sebastian was striding through the tunnel of blooms devised by Daphne, aiming their way. Hawkeswell was with him, and another man that she recognized as the Duke of Castleford.

Roger turned away. "I will—"

"You will stay right here," she said. "You will be introduced. If you avoid my husband, he may misunderstand your interest and our friendship, and I'll not be explaining your cowardice to him for the rest of my life."

Sebastian had come to introduce Castleford to her. The Duke was blessed with a tall, lean elegance and a beautiful face. Yet, despite his almost courtly bearing, he exuded something that raised an alarm in her feminine instincts. As he bent to kiss her hand, warning bells sounded loudly. *Bad. Dangerous. Trouble and heartache,* they tolled. Only the most foolish woman would not run and hide if this man cast his eyes upon her. The duke's smile implied, however, that the world was full of very foolish women.

"I have been negligent in my friendship with your husband, and not done my part to welcome you to society," Castleford said to Audrianna. "Such a beauty you have caught, Summerhays. I understand your willingness to be domesticated, if this sweet lady was the lure."

Sebastian could tell that Audrianna viewed Castleford with veiled skepticism, but the flattery still made her blush. As always, she acquitted herself well in the conversation of pleasantries that followed.

That Fellow had not left and had gotten an introduction to everyone too. He did not seem to notice that Castleford had forgotten he was there now. Major Woodruffe kept reacting to the duke's witticisms as if the duke was watching for it.

Sebastian sidled over and claimed Woodruffe's attention. "You are an old friend of my wife's, she tells me."

"Yes, from years ago."

"Childhood friends?"

"Not quite that long ago, but a goodly time now."

As they chatted, Sebastian moved Woodruffe away from the others, just enough for some privacy. "She says that your regiment is in Brighton. I expect we will see more of you this season then."

The fool brightened at what he interpreted as a friendly overture. "I hope so. I look forward to it."

Of course he did, the blackguard.

"You will have to forgive me, Major Woodruffe. I am new to marriage, and perhaps more given to jealousy than some of the more experienced husbands that you know. It is possible that you seek only friendship with my wife. If, however, you entertain any other—"

"I assure you that such a thing is the furthest idea from my mind."

"Come now, Major. We are both men. Such ideas are never far from our minds at all. But if you do anything that causes me to think that your mind dwells long on that particular idea, I will thrash you, I will ruin you, and I will probably kill you."

Woodruffe just stared at him, aghast at the bald threat. Sebastian smiled.

"The letter was a mistake, sir, I assure you, if she has it and you discovered it," he rushed to say. "I misunderstood her notice. It will not happen again." Woodruffe quickly took his leave.

Letter? Notice? What an odd and interesting thing for Woodruffe to say.

Hawkeswell had noticed the private conversation. He left Audrianna to fend for herself with Lord Notorious's attentions and strolled over.

"He left fast."

"He did, didn't he?"

"He appeared a little sick there as he ran away."

"I think the cakes don't agree with him. Cream icing is to be avoided when the days get warmer."

Hawkeswell watched the diminishing scarlet coat. "You were an ass, weren't you?"

Sebastian sighed. "Yes, I fear that I was."

And it had felt damned good.

Audrianna told her coachman to stop at the corner of Portman Square. She then walked down to the building that held the chambers of Mr. Loversall.

It was not an imposing structure, but then Mr. Loversall was not an imposing solicitor. The few shillings he earned by serving as a mailing address were probably important to him. That was why he executed these duties with all discretion.

She greeted the clerk who filed the mail. She had been in often enough over the last few weeks that she did not have to identify herself as A.K.

The clerk checked the files, then shook his head. "Nothing again, Madam."

"It has been four days since I visited to claim letters. Are you certain none are there from several days ago? I am very sure that one should be."

He checked again, and shook his head.

That was odd. Roger's letter should have arrived right after her last visit. Perhaps he had addressed it incorrectly.

"I was not here Monday," the clerk said. "I can inquire of Mr. Loversall if he misplaced letters in my absence."

"Would you please? I know there was a response."

The clerk disappeared into the solicitor's office. Mr. Loversall himself emerged, apparently confounded. He gave Audrianna a good look.

"*This* is A.K.?" he asked his clerk. "*She* paid for the service? You are sure?"

The clerk confirmed her secret identity.

"This is most irregular," Mr. Loversall fussed. "Another A.K. arrived yesterday and took what was here. I just assumed if he knew of the arrangement, he was indeed A.K. The correct A.K., I mean."

"He?" It seemed that Roger had retrieved his ill-considered love letter. "Was he a tall man, handsome, young, with red hair?"

Mr. Loversall nodded on each point, except the last. "Dark hair, Madam. Very dark. My abject apologies for the confusion and error." He glared at his clerk. "If I can make amends, please let me know. I assure you that no future mail will be handed to anyone except you."

She barely heard him after the first two words.
Sebastian had Roger's letter.

Audrianna braced herself for a scold at best and suspicions at worst. Instead Sebastian acted so normally for the next two days, so lacking in jealousy, that she began to wonder if perhaps someone else had taken Roger's letter.

It entered her mind that, having interfered with any assignation, he considered the matter over. Or he may have released any jealousy or anger at Roger instead of her. While that would only be fair, she did not like to think that Roger would pay too dearly for his misunderstanding, conceited and presumptuous though it had been.

She grew tired of waiting for the sword to fall. Therefore, while they strolled through Hyde Park three days later, joining the hundreds of others seeing and being seen during the fashionable hour, she broached the matter.

"Do you have a letter of mine?"

He appeared perplexed by the question.

"A letter addressed to me," she explained. "Do you have one that I have not seen?"

"I have no letter addressed to you. I do not purloin your letters from the servants. What a rude thing to suggest."

That reassured her, and she turned her mind to what other tall, dark-haired man might have interfered. Then his words repeated in her head.

"It is not exactly addressed to me. Not in the proper way. Only my initials would be there."

"Ah." He waved to a friend who greeted him. "That letter."

"You knew which letter I meant, I think."

"I did. Are you sure that you want to talk about this here and now?"

She heard a warning. That concerned her enough that a decision to put off the conversation only lasted a few minutes.

"How bad is it? How indiscreet?"

"Bad enough for me to call him out and be acquitted, if—"

"A duel! You must not!"

"I was going to finish by saying if I thought he was a true rival. You said he is not. I choose to believe you."

Two days of worry lifted from her heart. "Thank you. I am grateful for your trust. I feared asking you, but it is clear that you are a reasonable man and not given to rash reactions."

He smiled vaguely at her compliment. "Audrianna, if I had concluded he were a rival, I would not be so reasonable. Just so you know."

"I do not mean to distract us from the topic at hand, but—I remind you that you agreed that you would accept rivals, and be reasonable. Quite specifically. Once a child was born. That was part of the settlement, in a way of speaking."

He stopped walking and faced her. He smiled in that bedazzling way. "I did indeed say that you could have lovers. But I never promised that I would not kill them."

He acknowledged the greeting of a passing matron. They strolled on. Audrianna considered that she should upbraid him for bargaining in bad faith that day, but this truly was not the time.

"How did you know about the letter?"

"Major Woodruffe himself told me about it and said that it was all a misunderstanding."

"Roger told you himself?" Stupid, *stupid* Roger.

"Yes, the day of the garden party. How else would I have known where to find it?"

How else indeed? She decided all was well that ended well, and left it at that.

The circumstances of that letter nudged at her the rest of the evening. Their conversation played in her mind at the theater and dinner party that they attended. After he left her bed that night and sated bliss had passed, a few ambiguities in what he had said presented themselves and begged for explanation.

The next morning, she waited until eleven o'clock when his breakfast with Wittonbury would end, and presented herself at his door. She waited for his valet to finish, then asked the man to leave.

"I would like the letter," she said.

"I burned it. I could recite the poetic parts if you like. I have forgotten the rest—where he arranges an assignation."

Again that note of warning. For all his good humor about this, he did not like what he had read.

"I find it odd that he told you where to find the letter. If he thought someone should retrieve it, he could have done so himself. I cannot hear him giving you directions to Mr. Loversall's office."

"He only alluded to newspaper notices. I found the address in one of them."

Which meant he had read the notice and, because of Roger, knew who had paid for it. "Were there any other letters besides Roger's waiting for me?"

He looked at her, exasperated, amused, and annoyed all at once. And so she knew.

"There were, weren't there? How dare you not tell me. I paid for those notices and Mr. Loversall's service out of my pin money, and if someone besides vain, foolish Major Woodruffe responded, I have a right to know."

"There was one more," he said with resignation. He strode into his dressing room and returned with a letter. He placed it in her hand.

"It is still sealed," she said.

"Yes."

"Why?"

"I was deciding what to do with it. Give it to you, keep it from you, or burn it unopened."

"Burn it unopened? That was a mad thing to consider."

"And yet I considered it."

She broke the simple seal and took the letter to the window. "It is from him! Look, he identifies himself with a drawing of a domino, so I will know for certain." She read the scrawled message. Sebastian came close behind her and read it too, over her shoulder.

Covent Garden. Church Portico. 2 o'clock, a week hence.

She checked the date at the top. "That is tomorrow. Thank heavens I did not delay in asking you about this, or I would have missed this meeting."

"You are not going."

"Of course I am going."

He snatched the letter away. "No, you are not. He is dangerous. We know nothing about him. He may want to silence your curiosity, not satisfy it. I will go and I will tell you what transpires."

"That is not fair. Nor is it practical. The last time he tried to arrange a meeting, your presence ruined it. He thinks you are a man who waited for him at the Two Swords with a pistol. The piazza is full of people and he can hardly drag me away in secrecy. Why, a hundred men would be at my beck and call with one shout."

"You are *not* going."

His insistence vexed her. Husbands could be very inconvenient sometimes. "If not for my notices, there would be no meeting at all. You are just jealous that I thought to do as he had done, and realized that a man who posts notices probably also reads them."

"I am not jealous. I am full of admiration. You posted notices so ambiguous that an *old lover* thought that you sought an assignation with *him*. And yet our friend still understood, and here we are. Brava." He tucked the letter into his frockcoat and folded his arms. "You are not going."

Arguing was getting her nowhere. She did not want to accuse him of desiring to keep the truth from her. She did not want to believe that. However, this was not some clerk at a powder mill being met. This was the Domino, and she needed to hear what he had to say.

Sebastian had turned very stern. His expression was uncompromising. She moved in close to him. Very close.

She looked up at him. "You only want to protect me, I know. However, I will be safe if you are with me. I knew I had to bring you. That was my intention, to find him so we could both meet with him and learn what light he might shed."

"You planned to bring me along?" He sounded incredulous, and insulted that she thought he was fool enough to believe her.

"Of course." She wrapped her arms around him.

"You intended to be a good wife and give me this letter so we could both hear what he had to say?"

"Absolutely."

He frowned down at her. She smiled up at him. He wavered just enough, which annoyed him worse.

"We will talk about it later. I must get to Whitehall." He extricated himself from her embrace and left.

She went to her chamber, sat at the writing table, and began listing the questions she needed to ask the Domino.

Sebastian would allow her to go with him. She would make sure that he changed his mind.

Nor had she lied to him. She would have shown him the letter and asked him to accompany her. She *did* require his protection.

She also expected the Domino to demand much more money than she had herself.

Chapter Twenty-one

By morning Sebastian admitted to himself that his wife had vanquished him.

First, she used logic that was so damned good it cornered him. The Domino had arranged the meeting with her, not a man, and would disappear if she were not there. Also, she was the one who would know if the man who came was really the Domino.

After grinding him down with her good sense, she had then turned her feminine wiles on him. A promise had been extracted at the moment of defeat, when he was too preoccupied with pleasure to care about the morrow.

"It would be best if you are not with me at first," she said as their carriage approached Covent Garden. "He might bolt if he sees you."

He did not give a damn if the man bolted. She was excited and optimistic, and certain the day would end with her father's good name restored. He was not convinced it would go that way at all.

He was going to regret not burning that letter the way every instinct had urged. He might regret even more allowing her to be here today. But she wanted to know what he knew, all of it, because she still did not trust him to give appropriate weight to the evidence of her father's innocence when he heard it.

It was not really the letter he had wanted to destroy. He had wanted to burn this entire episode out of their pasts.

"I will let him speak to you first, but I will not be far away." The piazza and market stalls would be very busy in the afternoon. Too busy for Audrianna to inspect every man. They had to count on the Domino finding her.

The carriage stopped and they got out. Sebastian escorted her along the side of the church. Before they rounded its side and entered the piazza, he explained the plan. "Go and stand on the west side of the portico, near the second column. Do not move from there. Even if he beckons you, even if he wants to seek more privacy, do not leave that spot without me at your side."

She nodded and walked away. He called for her to stop. He eyed her reticule.

"Did you bring a pistol? I swear if you did that I am going to—"

"Do not be silly. It is in Cumberworth. The pistol belongs to Daphne, not me. Nor would it fit in a reticule. I counted on you to have the weapon this time."

As she turned the corner, a handsome man strolled into the piazza from the west. He ambled along like someone with time on his hands, looking for a diversion. He nodded in Sebastian's direction. Sebastian nodded back, then turned to circle the building and enter its front portico from the other side.

Audrianna took her place next to the second column from the most western one in St. Paul's portico. She hoped Sebastian would be discreet. If he was too visible, their friend might disappear.

A throng of humanity milled in the piazza. Fruit sellers and vendors of baskets, flowers, and even used garments hawked wares from beneath the wooden roofs of their rough shelters. Women of all stations shopped alone or with gentlemen in high hats. Dirty children and dogs ran between everyone's legs.

The portico was quiet in comparison. Only she stood here. The Domino had chosen well. He could watch from amid that crowd, and wait until he was sure it was safe before approaching. Even if he did not recognize her from the Two Swords, her mere presence announced herself as A.K.

A gentleman strolled along the nearest stalls, looking finer than most here but not finer than all. She recognized him as Lord Hawkeswell. He noticed her and raised his hat in greeting, then strolled on.

She could not see Sebastian anywhere.

"Pardon, madame." The voice addressed her with French words and an accent. She jolted alert and looked over her shoulder.

A man entered the portico from its arched side. He wore high boots and pantaloons, and a cloak over his brown frockcoat. Red curls were visible beneath his low-crowned broad hat. His face was fuller than her brief memory, and fairly ruddy in the light of day.

The cloak was odd. It was really too warm for one to-day. It gave him a dramatic appearance, the way he had it thrown back. The white lining on the black fabric looked theatrical and, along with his hat and pantaloons, made him appear like someone in a costume drama.

Then she realized the cloak was his calling card.

He took a position to her right and looked out over the piazza. "Forgive me for being forward, but that is a very handsome cloak," she said. "Black and white, like a dom-ino."

He beamed at her. "It was said that cloaks like this, worn by the clergy in France, inspired the name for the tiles."

They acknowledged each other with their eyes more than words.

"The man whom you wanted to meet at the Two Swords was my father. He has been dead a good while now. I was there in his place, as I am again now."

"I know that he is dead. Now I know. I did not then."

"Why did you want to meet him?"

"I had heard he was having some difficulties. I thought perhaps I could help."

"Did you know him?"

He shook his head. "We never met."

His accent no longer was French. More Germanic. "Are you from Holland?" she asked.

"*Madame*, it is not in my interest to identify myself."

"Of course. My apologies. My father can still use your help, if you are still inclined to give it." As she spoke, she saw Sebastian step into the far end of the portico.

The Domino caught her glance there. His head jerked around. Alarm entered his eyes. He stepped toward the western arch, but stopped in his tracks.

Audrianna looked over. Lord Hawkeswell stood there, framed by the arch.

"You have laid a trap for the Domino, *madame*."

"I have not. I brought protection, that is true. I am a woman, after all." She spoke fast to keep him from running. As she did, yet another familiar face appeared.

The Duke of Castleford staggered into the piazza, rubbing his eyes and buttoning his coat. He looked as if he had just rolled out of bed. Considering the infamous trade that filled many of the surrounding streets, most likely that was exactly what had happened.

He squinted and recoiled from the sun in the piazza. Collecting himself, he set his hat on his disheveled hair and walked directly across the stones in front of her.

He spotted Sebastian and came alive. He paused and his gaze scanned the portico. It came to rest on her and the Domino.

"Lady Sebastian, good day to you. Is something amiss? Is that actor bothering you?"

The Domino glanced to either side, then peered at this new player. She could see him calculating how to dodge into the crowd.

"We would like this fellow to stay where he is," Sebastian called, walking toward her but trying not to alarm the Domino more. "If he comes your way, Castleford, I would be obliged if you discouraged him from leaving."

"Do you mean catch him? Block him?"

"Yes."

"To hell with that." The duke yawned. He fumbled beneath his coat. His hand emerged with a pistol in it. He aimed it right at the Domino.

"I would not move if I were you, sir. I am an excellent

shot, but my head hurts so bad right now that I would probably aim for your leg and shoot off your balls."

The Domino looked like a man trapped. He scrutinized Sebastian as he approached. "You."

"Yes, me. Do not be concerned. My arm is healed and I am not looking for revenge. I do not even have a weapon, and I will not stop you if you choose to leave after you hear us out." He looked out at Castleford. "I cannot speak for him, however."

"If you arrange for him to point that pistol elsewhere, I will hear what you have to say."

"We are fine now, Castleford. I appreciate your help," Sebastian called. He looked over at Hawkeswell. "Yours too, Hawkeswell."

Lord Hawkeswell tipped his hat to Audrianna, pivoted, and walked away. The Duke of Castleford let his arm fall so the pistol aimed at the ground. Forgetting he even held it, he looked around the piazza as if he had never seen it before. He walked away, muttering to himself.

"Your strategy was elaborate," the Domino said to Sebastian.

"After you disappeared upon seeing me the last time at the bookstore, I thought I should discourage you from doing so again."

"Are you with the authorities? The military or customs officials?"

"I am with the government, but I am not interested in you. Only what you know."

"I think the risk is too big. I would not want what I know to land me in prison."

Which meant it could. Which meant it was important. Audrianna looked at Sebastian desperately. Here she was, face-to-face with the man who might clear her father, and he was going to *walk away*.

"There is no risk," she said. "I am grateful that you saw my notice and recognized it was for you. I have been hoping to meet you for a long time."

"I did not chance upon your notice. I was directed to it."

Sebastian found that far more interesting than she wanted. "How were you directed to it?" he asked.

The Domino smiled boyishly and blushed. "I was at a"— he glanced at Audrianna and blushed harder—"a place of, um, entertainment and someone asked if I was the Domino. Imagine my surprise. I was told to look in the paper for a notice of interest to me. Now it would be good if I go, I think."

He bowed to her, to take his leave. She wanted to scream for Castleford to come back with that pistol.

"One hundred pounds," Sebastian said. "Speak freely and it is yours."

The Domino froze mid-bow. He looked up, impressed. He straightened. He looked out at the piazza. "We must do this where I say. Not here."

"Wherever you choose," Audrianna rushed to say.

He gestured for them to come with him, and walked away.

They followed the Domino out of the piazza and south through the streets of Covent Garden. "What do you mean, you did not bring a pistol?" Audrianna whispered to Sebastian.

"He would never have believed I would use it in broad daylight in town. I did not need a weapon to protect you anyway."

"He believed that Castleford would use it."

"That is because Castleford wears bad judgment like a medal. He sweats recklessness."

"And you are not reckless? One hundred pounds? He would have been glad for fifty."

"You speak to me of recklessness? That is rich. You did not only put notices in the papers, apparently. You paid people to watch for you, didn't you? Did you just walk into these places and wave pound notes around and ask who wanted to be a spy?"

"It was not like that at all. I was very discreet. And it worked. He said he was told about my notices at a place of entertainment. Probably one of my theater spies found him."

"I do not think that he learned of your notice at *a theater*. From his blushing and hesitation to speak of it in a lady's presence, I suspect that it was an establishment of a different sort of entertainment. There are an abundance of them in this neighborhood."

She stopped walking. "Surely not."

"Probably so."

"But I hired no watchers at br—" Two thoughts caught her words in her throat. Celia recommending just such watchers, and Celia recently writing to say her queries might soon bear fruit.

Sebastian took her arm and hurried her along to catch up with their leader. "You are due a long scold. One thing at a time, however."

The Domino took them to one of the small docks on the river, where private craft were moored. He climbed onto one of the sailing vessels. Sebastian followed, then grabbed her waist and swung her aboard.

"Is this yours?" Audrianna asked. She received no acknowledgment of the question, let alone an answer.

The Domino removed his cloak and spread it on some boxes, to make a seat for her. Sebastian made himself comfortable on a barrel.

"One hundred, you say. No matter what you learn from me."

Sebastian nodded. "You have been looking to sell information. I am prepared to buy it."

The Domino settled himself on a box. "I did not ask to meet this lady's father only to sell information. I also intended to sell him my silence. For one hundred, I will throw that in for you as well."

Chapter Twenty-two

Sebastian experienced no surprise at the insinuation of blackmail. Audrianna, however, looked as if she had been slapped.

He could see an objection forming. He sent her a glance to warn her to swallow it.

"Why would your silence be of value to Kelmsleigh?" he asked. "And while I understand you do not want to give us your name, can we call you something besides the Domino now? It makes me feel I am part of a farce."

"You can call me Frans. It is as good a name as any other."

"I wish you had used Frans from the start," Audrianna said. "Why the Domino?"

"To suggest why I wanted that meeting, *madame*. A common child's game is to line the domino tiles up in long rows, then . . ." He tapped his finger against air. An invisible row of dominos began falling with the first one. "I anticipated that the others involved would help your father find some money for me, if they comprehended that his exposure threatened them too." He pointed to Sebastian. "When, at the Two Swords, I saw that pistol in his hand, I thought a different means of obtaining my silence had been chosen."

He removed his broad-brimmed hat. His red hair gleamed in the sun. "So now I am just Frans. Less important than who I am is what I am. I practice a profession not welcomed by governments and customs officers, but my trade improves the purses of everyone involved."

"You are a smuggler," Sebastian said.

"Call it what you will. As with all trade, it is most profitable if a ship or boat carries cargo both ways. Wine in, wool out. I pride myself on my efficient use of every vessel at my disposal."

"You must have thrived during the war."

"We always thrive during wars, but yes, Napoleon ushered in a golden age. I do not think I will see the likes of it again before I die. What made it especially profitable was the size of the French army. They needed so many things in such quantity, and their merchants could not begin to procure it all from friendly nations. Cloth. Food. Iron."

"Gunpowder."

Frans nodded. "You can imagine my delight at learning that I could send French luxuries into England, and leave with gunpowder that I could then sell to the French. In both cases, I first took the goods home so the source from an enemy was not too obvious. With the gunpowder, my brother sold it to a Frenchman who had friends in that army." He sighed contentedly. "Like kegs of gold, they were."

"Except they contained powder of bad quality," Audrianna objected.

"*Madame*, I would never sell false goods. A bad reputation would put me out of business. What I took from these shores was of high quality. It had been removed, a few cupfuls here and a few there, from kegs of powder made under the most exacting standards, for sale to the English military."

Sebastian stood and paced the boat while he rearranged his thinking. He had suspected a conspiracy, but not like this. He had assumed that the bad powder had been made on the cheap. Inferior materials had resulted in lower costs, but the kegs were sold for the standard price after manufacture.

Instead someone had taken perfectly good powder, and skimmed some off. He looked at Frans. "Those kegs that were tampered with—there would have to be another substance mixed in, so they carried a full weight. That is what ruined the powder."

"Exactly. During transport to the arsenal, the wagons and barges would be diverted and the kegs opened for all of this."

"It was a damned dangerous scheme. Opening those kegs, tampering with the contents—it was a mercy there was not a huge explosion."

"It was dangerous in many ways. Much too complicated also. I had assumed the kegs were stolen from an arsenal. When I was told about this elaborate deception, I was shocked. It was only a matter of time, I said, before we were all found out. Armies do not send just anything to their troops and call it gunpowder. There are procedures to ensure its quality. I could see myself meeting my contacts to collect these kegs one night, and there would be a regiment waiting to shoot me." He slapped his knee for emphasis. "I was ready to end it, right there, when I realized the full risks."

"And yet you did not," Audrianna said, with censure in her tone. She had been listening closely, and quietly. A good deal of apprehension had entered her eyes.

She knew where this was going. Sebastian cursed himself for allowing her to come with him today. He doubly regretted Frans speaking of blackmailing Kelmsleigh at the start. But for that, there might still be a way to protect her from what was coming.

"I did not end it, *madame*. They convinced me it would not be found out. They explained how adulterated kegs would not be discovered until they were opened on the field, and by then who would care? One keg is bad, they open another. The evidence would be washed away by the rain."

"Who were they?" Sebastian asked, as much to avoid the most logical next question as to obtain the identities. "The managers of the mill?"

"If my contacts had been so indiscreet as to tell me, I would not have dealt with them. I have not thrived by doing business with stupid men. I met with intermediaries. Transporters. But—this could not have happened without someone in authority at that mill being aware. This was not a scheme devised by thieves and smugglers."

"How did they convince you?" Audrianna blurted out. "You said that they convinced you by explaining how it would not be discovered."

Frans looked at her long and hard. He probably saw what Sebastian saw. She appeared dismayed while she braced herself for the answer.

"They told me that their kegs went through one arsenal, *madame*. They had a man there, among those who check for quality. He had been paid to pass all the gunpowder coming from this mill. When he sometimes could not arrange to handle these kegs and another man did, and some bad powder was found, they had paid an official here in London handsomely to make certain that those reports disappeared."

She barely reacted. Sebastian could tell that she was not really seeing this little sailing vessel or the two men with her anymore. She maintained her composure, but her sadness filled the air.

"Word reached me that some of that powder had unforeseen consequences," Frans continued, speaking only to Sebastian now. "I heard enough to know that the government here was suspicious that a London official responsible for ensuring quality in ordnance was being investigated. So, when next my affairs brought me to your shores, I attempted to meet with this man." He held out his hands. "You know the rest."

"You were going to bleed him."

"I was going to inform him of facts with which he might be aware or unaware, for a price. Whether he chose to bury those facts, or use them to exonerate himself in some way, was not my concern. However, once he had bought these facts, they would no longer be mine to sell elsewhere. It would have been much like my arrangement now with you, no?"

Sebastian retrieved one hundred pounds in notes from his pocket. He had brought more. He had expected to pay dearly for this information. In the end he would, but not with pounds.

He pressed the notes into Frans's hand. "Is this your vessel?"

Frans smiled noncommittally.

"If it is, cast off. If it isn't, go back the way you came.

You should avoid plying your trade on the English coast for a long while."

Frans bowed to acknowledge the threat. "There is one more thing you may find interesting. I tell you for the lady's sake."

"What is that?"

"I left England immediately after our unfortunate meeting near Brighton, and I only returned two weeks ago. I never disappeared from a bookstore. I never went to a meeting at one. I have no idea where this bookstore is, or what meeting you are talking about."

Audrianna hardly noticed their path back toward the piazza. The sounds of this busy part of town sounded like a far-off din. She felt as though someone had bludgeoned her heart to where it bled in her chest, swollen and hurt.

Summerhays guided her. He said nothing the whole way. He stayed very close, however, with one arm across her back, as if he guessed that her mind might not remember to put one foot in front of the other.

He handed her into the carriage and settled beside her. They rode west in silence.

Her daze slowly lifted. She looked down and saw her hand in his. It touched her that he tried to comfort her. Her throat burned and she swallowed the emotion with difficulty.

"How much do you think he was paid?" she asked.

"Who?"

"The ordnance official in London who fixed the reports. What is the cost of such things these days?"

"I have no idea. It is an odd question, Audrianna."

"As much as you paid Frans? If you sought to buy such a man, what would you offer?"

"Audrianna—"

"Please tell me."

He exhaled heavily. "I would probably offer at least half his annual salary, maybe as much again."

"Then less than you just paid Frans." She worked it through. "I expect that if that man had a wife and family always wanting things, always asking for dresses and diversions, he might be tempted even for so little a sum. I expect that if his wife thought it humiliating not to have a carriage, and his elder daughter needed a settlement for the good marriage she hoped to make, and his younger daughter coveted fashionable clothes, he might convince himself it was a small thing."

She tried to imagine her father rationalizing it. She could not. Even harder was picturing him taking the step. However, she had no difficulty at all seeing him plagued by guilt, when it turned out the rain had not washed away that powder in one terrible situation. If he had done this— he would never have forgiven himself.

A man born a thief like Frans might brave it out. A man who knew he had sold his integrity, his good name, and caused the deaths of others never could.

Her thoughts turned chaotic, and horribly sad. She had been so very sure of Papa's innocence of even the least of the accusations. Now she found herself fearing that the truth might be far worse than she ever thought possible.

Sebastian's hand squeezed hers. "Frans was never given a name. He did not know who the official in London was. He only assumed it was your father when our attention settled on him. You should not assume the worst."

Her vision blurred. It moved her that he would pretend the evidence was not damning, in order to lessen her disillusionment.

She found one tether on her composure and held tight. It was bad enough he had felt obliged to marry Kelmsleigh's daughter. He should not be obliged to defend a criminal on her behalf, even in the confines of this carriage.

"Let us speak of other things," she said, forcing a smile. "Tell me about your misspent youth, getting into trouble with Hawkeswell and Castleford."

He regaled her with stories of three young bloods ignoring decorum and good sense. She appeared to pay attention, and even laughed on occasion, but he doubted she truly heard him.

She kept her composure and poise, however. All the way home, and as they entered the house and walked up the stairs, only her eyes revealed the depths of her sad astonishment. Her bravery both impressed him and broke his heart.

The door to the library flew open while they passed it. His mother sailed out. "You are returned. Thank heavens. You must go to him at once. You must see. You must make him admit it and call the physicians and—"

"Becalm yourself. What has happened?"

She inhaled deeply. "Your brother's leg moved while I was there. Most distinctly. We were having a . . . conversation and he was exercised while making a point and his right leg moved to one side. It was very clear to me. There could be no mistake. He denies it, however, although Dr. Fenwood said the physicians came last week and indeed they found he had some sensation. You must go up there at once and talk to him."

Audrianna touched his arm. "I am going to retire to my chamber and rest. Go to him."

She continued up the stairs. Sebastian watched her go while his mother waited impatiently.

"Morgan's leg moved some weeks ago," he said. "Fenwood has been forcing some exercise. I am glad to hear there are more signs that he may recover someday."

"Why did no one tell me there had been this change? I think that I had a right to know."

"Only if he chose to let you know did you have a right to know. Apparently he did not so choose."

"Well, I know now. Come, we will go to him together and convince him to make more effort. We will make him try harder. He needs us now more than ever."

He looked at the stairs and pictured Audrianna mounting them. Back straight and head high, gracious and poised, she had put on an impressive performance.

"I will visit Morgan this evening. Right now I have something else that I must do."

He left his mother gaping at his dismissal of her demands. He went up to his chambers and entered the dressing room. He stood at the door to Audrianna's room and listened. No sounds came at first. Then he heard feminine voices exchange a soft rumble, and a door closing. She must have sent Nellie away.

Silence then. Perhaps she was spent from the day's drama, and had fallen asleep.

He turned away, to find his own silence so he could think about what they had learned, and decide what to do with it. Or whether to do anything at all. In particular he wanted to consider the implications of the last thing Frans said.

If the Domino had not advertised that meeting at the Muses, and Audrianna had not, who instead had?

A sound suddenly penetrated the wall. A musical crash, like china breaking, accompanied by an anguished feminine curse. Then muffled, strangled sobs.

He opened the door. Pieces of porcelain littered the floor. The drapes had been pulled against the daylight. Audrianna lay on the bed in her white undressing gown, her face buried in a protective pile of pillows.

She wept violently. Her emotion wrenched his heart. Anger sounded in her sobs, along with a disappointment too devastating to bear.

He went over to her. If she wanted her privacy, she would let him know, but he could not leave her like this unless she sent him away.

She startled when she realized that he stood beside the bed. She only wept harder, as if he reminded her of another grief. He slid his arms under her. He lifted her, turned and sat on the bed, and held her on his lap while she huddled in his embrace and cried out her heart.

His embrace freed her. She stopped fighting the horrible heartsickness and let it flow. She turned half-mad at one point, became so lost in the sorrow that nothing else existed. He held her more firmly and pressed a kiss to her temple that made her sane again. Such a small gesture, really. A small touch of care. Yet it created a peaceful breeze that stirred her alive and pushed out the dark clouds of this storm.

She calmed under that breeze and the comfort it brought. Spasms wracked her as the worst emotion ebbed. He handed her his handkerchief and tucked her snugly against him.

"I have made a scene, haven't I?" she asked when finally she could talk at all. "I even broke something. I do not even know what I threw."

"You were angry."

"I do not know why, or with whom."

"Perhaps you were angry with him. And with me."

"Not you. Please do not think so." Not him at all, although he had not been far from her emotions in the madness. She had hated the way that sore had been there in this marriage, and how the mention or thought of her father poked at the wound until it hurt.

"Him, mostly," she admitted. "And myself, for being so sure and for assuming the worst of you."

She had also released the last of a different kind of anger, she realized—that born of the self-righteous certainty that her father had been wronged. She had buried her grief within it and now, today, that grief had finally been freed and had its day. The grief had become more tragic, though— and terribly confused in its memories.

The certainty was gone, but she could not completely give up her belief in Papa. She could not accept he had been responsible for those young soldiers being killed and maimed. She could not bear the thoughts of his fear if such a sin hounded him. A horrible truth beckoned and nibbled at her mind, but her heart would not, could not, acknowledge it.

Sebastian made no move to release her. He just held her in a comforting embrace while she sniffed and dabbed her eyes with the handkerchief.

"You are supposed to be with your brother," she muttered.

"No, I am supposed to be here. For as long as you want."

She tipped her face and kissed his cheek. She laid her head against him and let his strength hold together emotions that still wanted to shatter.

Within their peaceful silence a new emotion filled her, one whole and confident and sweet, not brittle and furious. Freed too by the death of her certainty, it touched her heart with memories of the intimacy of their nights. It forced her to acknowledge the importance of this embrace.

She looked up at him. The old bedazzlement descended, only now it filled her heart with an ache of glowing warmth, and moved her in ways that she suspected she would never be able to deny after this day.

She kissed him again, because she had to. Her spirit was too bruised to pretend she did not need him to hold her like this. Eventually she would be able to face all these truths on her own, but she wanted to hide in the protection of his care a good while longer.

He looked down at her, so deeply that she wondered where his thoughts were.

"Aren't you going to kiss me back?" she asked.

"I was waiting to see if waiting would lure you into kissing me a few more times."

She thought that a sweet little joke, just light enough for their mood and closeness. Then she realized it was not a joke at all.

Another truth. There had almost been too many today. She sensed that there was more to this one than she understood. She heard an invitation to express the warm, beautiful ache in her heart, though.

She slipped off his lap, then climbed back on, facing him, with her knees bracing his hips. She circled his neck with her arms and kissed him yet again. Longer this time. Her gratitude for his comfort, her sorrow about her father,

her vulnerability within this newly acknowledged love—
the kiss moved her profoundly because all of her heart's
emotions poured out while she pressed her lips to his.

She unfastened her undressing gown and let it fall off
her body so he would know what she wanted. He lightly
trailed his fingertips over her skin, along her neck and
breasts and chest, while she plucked at his cravat.

"Are you sure?" he asked. "You are very sad."

"I am not only sad. I am very sure. I need this now."
She threw aside his cravat and worked on the buttons of
his shirt. "Touch me and kiss me while I do this. Lightly.
Very lightly, so I am not overwhelmed."

He obeyed. His fingers and mouth coaxed the gentlest
arousal to flow like warm water. It filled her sweetly while
she removed his garments so she could caress him.

She closed her eyes so she could feel the warmth and
texture beneath her hands better. She savored every touch,
every physical inch. Then she rocked forward so he fell
back on the bed, and straddled him so she could watch her
hands move.

Caressing him felt so good. Love sparkled all through
the pleasure it gave her. She could tell it pleased him to
accept this slow care. She leaned forward and kissed his
mouth, then his neck and shoulder. She tasted, tasted, and
wondered at the way the sensations of her body touched
those of her heart.

He rolled them both over and did for her as she had just
done for him, kissing her body carefully, caressing gently.
A more frantic excitement began beckoning, but she held
it at bay. She did not want to lose herself. She did not want
anything obscuring the deep poignancy that her emotions
created right now.

He released his lower garments while he kissed her.

She took his phallus in her hands and caressed him as carefully as he had her so they might share the exquisite intimacy she experienced.

Then she wanted nothing else but him. In her body and in her arms. She told him so. She asked him to take her then, right then, so she could bind herself to him and know a fulfillment of this emotion drenching her soul.

He settled in her deeply. Perfectly. She let him fill the rest of her too, all her senses, and lost herself finally, in him and his scent and strength. And as she held him closely and accepted both his need and his care, she was moved so profoundly that she wept again, only not in sadness this time.

Chapter Twenty-three

"Show them. It is a small request from friends who have affection and concern for you," Sebastian said.

Morgan glared at him. "I am not an animal in a menagerie that does tricks for the crowd."

Kennington reacted with surprise. "Animal? Tricks? My apologies, to be sure. I mean no insult. If in my joy at the news I showed disrespect, I am undone."

"It is not your fault," Sebastian said. "It is mine for being indiscreet. I had no idea my brother had not informed both of you of this progress."

"Let us finish our game and speak no more of it," Symes-Wilvert said.

Everyone picked up their cards. Kennington and Symes-Wilvert silently peered at theirs, trying to appear indifferent but communicating their hurt by the subdued angles of their blond heads.

Morgan threw his cards down. "Move the damned table," he said with exasperation.

Sebastian stood up and pulled the table away. Morgan's legs no longer appeared so lifeless in his trousers. The exercises had been restoring their mass. Except for their complete immobility, one might never know about his infirmity on seeing him like this now.

"Do not expect me to get up and dance," he snapped. "This is a very small thing that my brother celebrates, and it will probably never amount to more."

His friends nodded, but their eyes remained on those legs.

Morgan closed his eyes. His jaw clenched in concentration. His right leg vaguely flexed beneath the trouser's fabric, then moved slightly to the right.

"By Jove, it is a miracle," Symes-Wilvert whispered. He turned to Kennington. "Did you see that? Did you?"

"I did indeed. Ha-ha! Damnation, how could you keep this a secret? Why, it is astounding. A miracle, as Symes here said."

"Do not make more of it than it is. Do not go telling the world about it either. I'll not be performing for curious bastards who suddenly remember that I am still alive."

"Of course. Certainly. And yet—what do the physicians say? When did this happen?" Kennington asked. "We are all ears and you must tell us about it."

The card game now forgotten, Sebastian slipped away, to take care of private affairs in the City. He called for his horse, mounted, and aimed east.

Morgan's secrecy about the improvement in his condition had been peculiar. It was almost as if he refused to believe it was happening.

The neglect in informing their mother had been understandable. She had been visiting Morgan every day since learning the truth, and any man can be excused for avoiding that as long as possible. Kennington and Symes-Wilvert, however, were friends, and Sebastian truly had assumed that they knew.

When he arrived in the City, he visited his solicitor's chambers near Lincoln's Inn. Mr. Dowgill was not the family lawyer. Instead Sebastian became Mr. Dowgill's client when, as a young man, he concluded that having privacy in certain affairs required him to use a lawyer other than the one who oozed flattery on the too curious and too ruthless Lady Wittonbury.

Dowgill had proven more than competent in those early duties. A bland, pale man of unimpressive appearance, he possessed a knack for convincing even the most obstinate mistress that Sebastian's offered parting settlement was the best she would ever get.

Dowgill greeted him with his usual mild manner. They sat down in his inner chamber. Dowgill set some papers on the small table between them.

"As you requested, I looked into this company, P & E. I had difficulty learning anything more than you told me. It built a mill in 1810 and began making powder in the next year, which was sold to the Board of Ordnance. After the war ended, it ceased operations."

"Did you find any information regarding the owners of P & E?"

"At first, almost nothing. From what I could ascertain, it was a partnership, not a syndicate. I communicated with an astute colleague in that county, and—I found this provocative, if I may say so—he indicated that while he had no particular knowledge of this business, he had formed the opinion that the owners were not named Pettigrew and Eversham at all, despite the mill's own name."

"That is indeed provocative."

Mr. Dowgill pressed the fingertips of one hand against those of the other. He gazed over the construction thoughtfully. "It is impossible to know why such a deception occurred, of course. No one in the county ever met the owners. They did not avail themselves of the sort of hospitality that they could enjoy as proprietors of so significant a business. I found myself contemplating this oddity, for surely it might unlock the answers you sought. The most logical explanation was that the owners were gentlemen, and did not want to affix their names to a place of trade."

Sebastian could think of an even better explanation. The owner or owners intended that scheme with the powder from the first, and hid their identities to try and save their hides in the event it became known.

"And then I soon learned that the mill had been sold for certain, as you told me you had heard," Dowgill said. "The solution became obvious and simple. One cannot use a fictitious name in buying or selling property. A signature must be written and witnessed. I therefore wrote to Mr. Skeffley, the fuller who bought the property, and asked from whom he had obtained it." He looked meaningfully at the papers on the table.

"You have a name for me?"

"I do, sir."

Sebastian waited. Mr. Dowgill tapped his forefinger on the papers.

"Lord Sebastian, I find myself in a peculiar circumstance. I am your servant, but even so I am a counselor. I do not know the reason you wanted this information. However, unless your goals are the most benign, I advise you now to reconsider whether I must hand this name over to you."

"I am very sure that you must."

Although not the answer he wanted, Dowgill had resigned himself to hearing it. "Quite so. I am therefore required to ask you to keep my name out of any discussions that you might have with the individual in question. Not only my name, but my involvement even by reference to your solicitor. There are those who know I have been of service to you in the past."

Dowgill was conducting some elaborate negotiations. That alone piqued Sebastian's curiosity all the more. "Of course, if you require it. However, you have only done your duty to me, as my solicitor."

"Any reasonable person would see it that way. Regrettably, this individual is not known for reason. Rather the opposite."

"You know him, then?"

"I only know of him. His circles are more elevated than I will ever attain. You see, he is not only a gentleman, as I suspected. He is a peer."

The solicitor's long preamble and deliberate caution suddenly made more sense. "He will never learn from me that you pursued this on my behalf. If he discovers it some other way, I will make sure that no ill fortune falls on you as a result."

Dowgill expressed silent gratitude with his expression. "I must sound like a coward to you, and counseling you to be one as well. Had it been anyone else— He duels, you see. It is commonly known he does, and—"

"His name, Mr. Dowgill. I would appreciate knowing it now."

He slid a paper out from amid the rest. He handed it

over. "Sir, as you will read, Mr. Skeffling reports that he bought that mill from the Duke of Castleford."

Sebastian did not pay a morning call on Castleford. He wrote and requested a private meeting on a matter of great import. Since they had known each other for many years and were once good friends, he included a suggestion that it would help enormously if Castleford were sober, and if no pretty bottoms were nearby to distract him.

The reply came two days later:

If you are determined to be boring, come to my house at two o'clock Tuesday. Since that is the day when I schedule my weekly descent into tedium, I will not have to endeavor too hard to be boring too.

When Sebastian arrived, he was brought to the library. There he found Castleford conducting business with his secretary. The neat stacks of documents, and the sharp commands peppering the desk's young occupant, revealed that when he descended into tedium, the duke could be as boring as any other man with significant responsibilities.

"I have discovered that if I make one long day of it, then I can go to hell the other six," he said when Sebastian's presence interrupted. "Leave us, Edwards, but do not go far."

The young man took his leave. Castleford sat on a divan and stretched out his legs. "I hope this is not about some bill. If so, your masters are asking you to dip from the well too often."

"It is not about any Parliamentary matter."

"Thank God for that. You love that game so much there

are some who think you will be Prime Minister before long. My money is on an impressive scandal taking you down first. One that you can't marry your way out of. Does that sweet woman know what she has in you?"

"Government is not a game. Neither is law."

"Politics is. Part chess, part gambling, part horse race, part lottery. You would not have taken to it so well if it were not. Now, what do you want with me?"

Sebastian had debated most of the night how to approach this. There had been some anguish in that vigil along with a good deal of anger. He and Castleford no longer faced the world shoulder to shoulder as in the old days, and a sharpness had entered the relationship they still had, but being obligated to make this accusation troubled him.

"As you know, I was looking into that bad gunpowder. I have found its source, and learned how it became adulterated. I know that you were responsible."

Castleford barely reacted. He just looked at him.

"I felt that I owed it to you, to let you know that it was all going to come out."

"What the hell are you talking about?"

"That powder came from your mill. I want to believe your managers arranged for the rest, for the skimming and replacement of powder from the kegs with another substance that rendered the powder useless. If you say that was how it was, that you knew nothing of the scheme, that is all I need."

"All *you* need? An apology is all *I* need. Now, or I swear that I will call you out." He stood and paced away, furious. He ran his hand through his hair and pivoted to glare. "Have you gone mad? This is *me*. I don't own mills. Why in hell would I want one? Let alone one that could blow up. As for skimming and whatever else you think I did, why would I bother?"

"For the fun of it? You also like your games."

"If you believe I would have risked those soldiers' lives, you are an idiot. I might fuck their sisters, but I would not do this."

"You owned the mill. I have seen the indenture by which you sold it recently. It is your signature."

Castleford froze, astonished. Then he strode to the door and yanked it open. He bellowed Edwards's name.

The young man hurried in. Castleford pinned him with a stabbing glare while he jabbed a finger in Sebastian's direction. "Edwards, explain to him that I do not, nor have I ever, owned a mill."

Edwards looked like a man trapped by a lion. His wide-eyed, wary glance darted to Sebastian. Then he took the duke's measure and blanched.

"Well, tell him," Castleford roared.

"Uhhhh—my lord—actually . . ." Edwards swallowed hard. "You did own a mill, briefly. Remember? It was signed over to you in payment for a gentleman's debt. I recall writing the letter to your solicitor telling him to sell it off for whatever he could get."

Castleford turned a black expression on the young man, who stepped back a pace.

"I could dig out the letter's copy if you like, my lord."

"Who in hell gave me this mill?"

"I do not know. I only remember that letter to the solicitor."

"Go find this letter's copy."

Edwards was happy to do so. "It would be in the study. I will search for it forthwith."

Castleford threw himself back on the divan. "I will speak with my solicitor and send you everything he has, Summerhays. If I owned this place during the time in question, he probably knows the names of the managers and whatnot." His expression showed a degree of dismay. "If this scheme that you describe happened while I owned it, I will of course take full responsibility."

The irony was not lost on either of them. Castleford taunted society every day with his behavior. He devoted his life to walking along the wrong side of the line of acceptability. His excesses were so indiscreet that scandal no longer could be bothered to erupt around him. Yet this advocate of calculated rebellion might finally be brought low by an incident of which he was completely ignorant.

"There is no hurry on this," Sebastian said. "I will wait to hear from your solicitor or you about the particulars."

"That is too good of you." His sardonic tone reminded Sebastian of a younger Castleford, one just as bad but less enthralled with sin.

Sebastian had to smile as the memory of their old friendship passed between them. "I hope that I was not too boring this time."

"Not at all. I could have done without finding myself checkmated in a match I did not even know I was playing, though."

"I have decided that I will not be taking lovers," Audrianna said.

She spoke into the night, during the peaceful aftermath of passion, at that exact moment when bliss turns to contentment and speaking will no longer destroy the holy awe that suspends time.

Sebastian's lazy brain turned over what she said. "I did not know that you were intending to."

"I was not, in any specific way. However, we agreed that I could later, if I chose."

"And now you have decided that you will not so choose?"

"Do not worry. You already know that I am not like your mother, harping at you with jealous questions and resentments."

He sorted through his reactions. Boyish glee, of course, that his singular possession of her would be eternal.

Relief that she comprehended the poison that resentments and jealousy could drip into a marriage.

Dominating them all, however, was an inexplicable annoyance with the assumptions she alluded to.

"It is not, perhaps, a decision that one can make for the future," he said. "Ten years hence you may—"

"No. I will not." She looked right in his eyes. "I will not."

He was not going to argue with her certainty. If she had decided to be faithful, it was not in his interest to convince her otherwise. However—

"Is it because I said I would kill them?"

She laughed. "Of course not. I know you would not really kill them."

Once again, it was not in his interest to explain that he very well might. She had probably saved him a duel or two with this decision. All in all there was no disadvantage here to him that he could see. And yet—

"What did you mean, I already know you are not like my mother when it came to jealousy and resentments?"

"Is it not obvious? I have not expressed either so far, have I?"

"No. But . . ." He had assumed that she knew she had

no cause for either or both. It sounded like she thought that she did, though.

He found himself balancing on an odd precipice. He could tell her she had no reason to be jealous so far, and therefore had not really been tested when it came to jealousy. Or he could be grateful that even early in their marriage, his wife had accepted the wandering ways of men.

Common sense said that in the interests of peace and harmony in the coming years, he should leave the subject alone now. Definitely.

Then again—

"Why the hell would you think you had any reason to express jealousy so far? I have hardly been neglecting you. Damnation, woman, I haven't had a solid night's sleep in over a month."

She went still, then sat up. She peered down at him. "I am astonished. I work up the courage to tell you that I have decided to be faithful, and now you are angry."

"I am not angry."

"You sound angry. I do not see why you would be. In a manner of speaking, this has nothing to do with you."

"Of course it has to do with me. You are going to be faithful to me, aren't you?"

"Would you rather I were not?"

"Of course not. I only want to know why you think I have already been unfaithful."

"Why would I not? A rake does not cease being one upon an obligatory marriage. There are those who say he does not cease being one ever, no matter what marriage he makes. When you do not return to this house until early morning, you do not say where you were and I do not ask. I am capable of drawing some conclusions, however. I am not so innocent that I do not know how marriages like this go."

He pulled her down, and braced himself above her so he looked down at her face. "You drew the wrong conclusions. I have been with no one else for a long time. Months." Not many months, but at least not since they met. There was no need to get too fine on the point, however.

"Truly?" she asked in surprise, wonderment, and disbelief. He heard a wavering note too, as if the answer mattered to her a great deal.

"Truly. As for how marriages like this go . . ." A part of him shouted for silence now, before something regrettable were said. He ignored that voice and forged ahead. "Why did you tell me that you will break the mold?"

"I wanted you to know."

"Why? If not for a pledge in return, why did you want me to know?"

She gazed up at him. "It was important for me to say it, that is all. So you would know, and could be sure of me, if it ever mattered to you when you wondered."

If it ever mattered to you when you wondered. That took the wind out of his stupid indignation. What a sad thing for her to say or think.

She had actually been very sensible. She expected nothing from this union except those terms in the settlement and agreed privately between them, and his right to do as he pleased had been both explicit and implicit in it all.

Her "if" just hung there, though. If her having a lover did not matter, then she did not matter. It bothered him deeply that she took for granted that she did not.

"It would matter a great deal if I ever wondered, so you have given me a gift in saying this," he said. She really did have a right to know that.

He had been jealous, after all. He had even been an ass because of her. He kissed her, and tasted a faint salty moisture on her cheek. "Has it mattered to you, when you wondered?"

She nodded, but did not speak.

Kiss her, give her pleasure and be silent now, you maudlin fool. He knew full well he should end this conversation. However, he did not like to think of her wondering, and assuming she could not even ask without being thought an unsophisticated scold.

The vows that they had exchanged were supposed to take care of this question, but of course they usually did not.

"It seems only fair that we exchange gifts, I think. I will not take lovers either."

She looked so astonished, so utterly amazed, that he almost laughed. But something else in her eyes touched him deeply, and he would never forget the way she looked at that moment.

"It will be very nice not to wonder anymore," she said softly. "However, if one day you—"

He touched her lips to silence her. He did not want her to release him from this promise before he even discovered if he could keep it.

"If someday one of us regrets this choice, we will talk about it, Audrianna, and try to remember when it mattered."

And why.

Chapter Twenty-four

Morning was not very old when Audrianna alighted from her carriage. However, she had a full day planned and could not put off this visit. Fortunately, a woman need not be too particular about proper calling hours when calling on her own mother.

Mama was happy to see her. As they walked to the morning room, Audrianna noted a new carpet in the library. She wondered if Sebastian was still doing penance.

Mama was full of talk about friendships renewed and relatives rediscovered. Her willingness to let bygones be bygones both heartened and saddened Audrianna.

Since that meeting with the Domino, Mama's stoical reaction to Papa's disgrace had been taking on other potential meanings, as had so much else in Audrianna's memory of that long, terrible time.

"Sarah has a young man dancing attendance," Mama confided finally. Glints of delight sparkled in her eyes. "A gentleman."

"That is wonderful, Mama. Does he live in London?"

"He must, mustn't he? Although he has property in York-shire. His profession requires his presence here, however. He is a barrister."

"That is impressive indeed."

"I promised to obtain an invitation to Lord Sebastian. I knew you would not mind."

"Of course not."

Mama was not stupid. She heard the resignation. She also probably saw the evidence of resentment that Audri-anna felt about being so "useful," despite Audrianna's attempts to hide it.

"I do have high hopes about this." Mama cast down her eyes and spoke apologetically, like a petitioner who had stepped over a line surrounding the queen. "Perhaps more than are warranted. We could put him off if you like, until his intentions are more explicit."

"No, that is not necessary. I will arrange an introduction whenever you like. I will be happy to do this." It was unlikely that this barrister's intentions would become more explicit unless her usefulness became so first. This was why she had married, wasn't it? She should not allow her heart's new discoveries to obscure that.

It was those new discoveries that had brought her here. That and her new lack of certainty about Papa, and the emotional confusion regarding him that would not go away except when passion banished it for a short while. She looked at her mother's soft, gentle face, framed so nicely in her lace-edged white cap, and summoned the courage to broach a subject never before discussed.

"I have been thinking about Papa recently," she said. "And about those accusations made regarding his negligence."

Mama said nothing, but a new stillness entered her even

though she had not been moving anyway. Her gaze remained down, as it so often had in Papa's presence those last months.

"Do you think that he was involved in any way, Mama? You have never indicated that you did, I know, but attention settled on him for a reason. He was the person who saw all the reports on the powder's quality. He gave the word that it could be distributed. You defended him, I know, but . . ."

Mama sighed deeply, as if a burden recently removed had just been replaced on her spirit. She looked up, but not with a mother's eyes. Her gaze was much more honest than that.

"He worried. I could see the entire scandal take a toll on him. He shrank before my eyes," she said. "He had always been given to periods of melancholy. He hid it from you and Sarah, but he could not hide it from me. The war had done that to him. Such a mood settled on him, and this time it did not lift. He stopped talking to me, due to that darkness."

"So he never told you that he was innocent?"

"He feared he was not, I think. Very early, even before the stories came out, the army knew and he spent weeks picking through his memory with me, trying to remember if he had made such an error. 'The mistake must have been at the arsenal,' he kept saying. 'My office approved no bad powder for distribution.'"

"Then he did deny it." Audrianna's heart lightened at this small evidence. Mama did not describe a guilty man, fearful of being found out in a crime, but of an honest one who was worried he might have made a mistake.

"He was not certain in his own mind, Audrianna. The worry did not go away. The melancholy came and stayed."

"He was being hounded and disgraced. Of course he would be melancholy. Surely you believe he was innocent of all of this."

She waited, her heart beating hard, for Mama to join in the old defense of Papa. The heaviness in her chest grew painful and her composure turned a little desperate when the silence stretched.

"You do believe that, don't you, Mama?"

Mama's eyes filmed, as if she looked in her mind and heart to see what she believed. Then her eyes warmed and brightened, and her gaze returned to that of a mother looking at a daughter.

"Of course I believe that. I am his wife, after all."

"You should not have done it," Daphne scolded, while she cultivated the soil around a rosebush with a hoe. "What were you thinking, Celia?"

"She said it worked," Celia replied from where she pruned on the other side of the bed. "You owe me ten pounds, Audrianna, to repay me for what I gave my mother."

"Your mother paid ten pounds to those brothels to look for the Domino for me?"

"I do not know what she paid *them*. That is what we must pay *her*."

Daphne stopped working and studied Celia from beneath the brim of her straw bonnet. Audrianna suspected Daphne was thinking what Audrianna herself wondered.

"Where did you find ten pounds, Celia?" Daphne asked.

Celia's attention became absorbed by her examination of the bush's stems.

"I hope that you did not borrow," Daphne said. "You know the rule. We do not go into debt."

Celia sighed dramatically. "You cannot go into debt to a *mother*. She paid them, and I will pay her back. She was so happy to hear from me that she did not mind at all."

They returned to the gardening. Audrianna had come to visit on this most glorious day, knowing it would be spent working like this. She had worn old half boots and a simple dress, and borrowed an apron on arriving.

She needed the company of her friends today, while her mind turned over yesterday's conversation with Mama. She had told herself she went to Mama for the truth, but now she realized she had gone to have her own certainty reinforced again. Only now, despite Mama's dutiful last words, Audrianna suspected that the only person who had ever truly been certain that Horatio Kelmsleigh could not be guilty of anything regarding that gunpowder had been Audrianna herself.

Now his one champion was not so sure anymore. Quite the opposite, as much as she wanted to be. Nor could she resolve the matter in her heart by accepting his guilt.

At least another part of her heart was not confused anymore. She took great comfort in that.

The sun shone very warm, and they all bent to the labor amid the plantings, protected by bonnets and gloves. A thick row of big tulips flanked the rose bed where they pruned and weeded. Their velvety cups showed the exuberant display that flowers manage just prior to petals falling.

Lizzie could be seen through the greenhouse glass, working her magic on a tray of seedlings she had coaxed to life. She would come out soon, and they would no longer be able to speak freely of this. Lizzie still did not know about Celia's mother.

"I am sorry that you were disheartened by what you

learned from your Domino, Audrianna." Daphne kept working the soil with gentle hacks. "I know that you chose to believe in your father."

How like Daphne to know what occupied her mind. Yet, Audrianna realized that Daphne touched on an important lesson regarding the human spirit. For all of one's instincts and emotions, one had to choose what to believe about someone else. Perhaps the worst part about disillusionment was how it made one feel like a fool for believing in good things. Maybe that was why she still could not accept the evidence for what it appeared to reveal.

The greenhouse door opened. Lizzie stepped out with the tray in her hands. She went to a cold frame in the sun, opened it so the top hinged back and lay on the ground, and set her tray inside it. It was time to harden off the vegetable plants that would be planted in mid-May.

Lizzie then joined them, looking very lovely in her simple lilac bonnet and light blue muslin dress. She had been free of her headaches for several weeks now, and appeared healthy and very fresh.

Audrianna looked at her friends. The marquess had been correct, and a few young matrons had sought her out within her new world. She had begun to be absorbed into some circles. She laughed sometimes without wondering if she ought or not.

It would never be like this, however. No friends would ever replace these.

She bent to pull an intrusive clump of turf out of the bed. "I think that I have fallen in love." Saying it, putting it into words, both thrilled and frightened her. She could only tell these women, of course. She could never dare such a revelation with anyone else.

Silence fell around her until only the chirps of birds

and the rustle of autumn's old leaves were audible. She looked up to see three pairs of eyes on her.

"Oh, dear," Lizzie said. "That is probably unwise."

"Considering the unpromising reasons for this match, you are probably right. Still, there it is," Audrianna said.

"Not unwise. Not necessarily," Daphne said.

"It is only unwise if you expect love in return," Lizzie said. "That is not what marriage is about, not really. And his name is still linked with women in the scandal sheets. If you are prepared to accept an unbalanced marriage in this area, life can still be tolerable, I suppose."

"I think that falling in love is a good thing," Celia said. "Even if it hurts, at least you know you are not dead. So I am happy for you. I say throw caution to the winds and fall passionately in love and lose nine-tenths of your heart." She gave a dead piece of her rosebush a solid clip. "Just do not lose your head too, and hold that last one-tenth for yourself. It is fine to tell us, but do not tell him or he will make you his slave."

Audrianna rather wished she had not learned about Celia's heritage. She could not help but think she was hearing Mrs. Northrope speaking, teaching her daughter the ways of the world. Unfortunately, as a woman who served as mistress to other women's husbands, Mrs. Northrope probably possessed a wisdom about men that few women could duplicate.

"I feel very old," Daphne said with a little laugh. "Or very young. I am not sure which. I am the only one, it seems, who thinks it is very beautiful that you have fallen in love, Audrianna, especially since you had good cause not to. It appeals to the optimist in me, I suppose."

Celia examined the bushes near her. "We are done. They are as ready for blooms as they will ever be. Let us go in."

They all walked to the house, pulling off gloves and aprons as they went. Inside they discarded their bonnets and boots.

"I have a new song," Audrianna announced. "I brought it so Celia could sing it for us."

"Have you given this one to Mr. Trotter?" Lizzie asked.

"I dare not. He would want to publish it under my name and I do not think that would be wise, considering my marriage, and the infamy of 'My Inconstant Love.' I do not want to resurrect that scandal in any way."

"He would probably put another engraving on it, of you and Lord Sebastian in bed making love," Celia said. "Give it to me. I will sing it and we can imagine the image he would provide."

Audrianna took the page from her reticule and handed it over. They all sat in the back sitting room in their stocking feet, while Celia read through the song and notes.

"It is your best one yet, I think," she said as her eyes moved down the page. "It would require a very tender image, I think."

"Thank you. I think it turned out well. I think I will title it 'My Heart and My Soul.'"

Celia looked over with that mature expression she could assume sometimes. She held the sheet high and began singing.

It was very special for Audrianna to hear her songs sung by someone else, and not only in her own head. She had written this one the day after meeting Frans—the Domino—and while her heart still seemed exposed to emotions both painful and beautiful. She had found solace in the melody, and release in putting words on the intimacy she had experienced in Sebastian's arms.

Daphne and Lizzie listened in stillness. Celia's clear,

young voice lent poignancy to the words. It sounded far better than Audrianna had ever expected.

Silence hung for a five count after Celia ended the last note. Daphne smiled a little sadly. "It is beautiful. It is such a pity that you dare not give it to Mr. Trotter."

Lizzie dabbed her handkerchief to her eyes. "I fear that you have lost all of your heart, Audrianna, if that song is telling of your emotions. Yet who can hear it and not long to know the same sweet heartache? It makes me regret not being in love myself."

Celia looked long and hard at the music. "It is wrong that this will never be performed again. It deserves a large audience."

"I am content to have heard you perform it, Celia. If it never has a larger audience than the four of us, I can bear it."

"May I keep it, and sing it again later? When you are not here, it will bring you to us in spirit."

"That copy is yours, to do with as you please. Perhaps of a night I will hear it in my head, and know you are singing it again." She stood, and bent to kiss each one in turn. "Now, I must leave you all, much as I wish I could stay longer. Lady Wittonbury is hosting a dinner party tonight and it will take me hours to prepare for her inspection."

The day after the dinner party, Audrianna visited the marquess. The season's schedule meant that she called on him less frequently now, and when she did, she had a long list of parties and balls to describe.

To her surprise, Sebastian joined them after half an hour. He sat in the private library listening to her along with his brother, as if he did not have a dozen other places to be.

"Your descriptions are so vivid that I feel as if I were there," the marquess said by way of compliment. "I would have liked to see Halliwell's face when the beeswax from the chandelier landed right on his quizzing glass."

He mimicked the shock he imagined and they had a good laugh.

"Would you?" Sebastian asked. "Liked to have seen it?"

Wittonbury's mirth died. The two brothers looked at each other in a way that caused Audrianna to feel she had just interrupted an argument.

"I ask because you resist every effort that might one day allow you to see it. The physicians say you must try to stand or you will never stand, and yet you refuse to try."

"If I could stand, I would. I cannot, so I don't."

"It does not happen that way. It has been explained to you that if the muscles are not worked, they will never work."

"You are becoming as tedious as our mother. I have told her she cannot come here anymore unless I invite her. I should have taken your advice on that months ago."

"Kennington and Symes-Wivert are banished too, I have heard. So the only guest you welcome now is my wife, because she is too good to make you feel like a coward."

Audrianna stood to excuse herself from what had become a very private conversation. The marquess objected.

"No, he will go, not you."

"I am not going anywhere, until you try to stand."

"Then you can sit there until you go to hell."

Sebastian crossed his legs, as if that would suit him fine. "You will not try for yourself, or for our mother or me. Will you try for her?" He angled his head in her direction. "If she requests it, will you do it?"

Wittonbury glared at him.

"Ask him, Audrianna."

Wittonbury let out a sad, resigned laugh. "You bastard."

"Ask him. I command it."

She wished he would not demand this. It was not fair to use her friendship with his brother this way. Nor did she care for the unspoken parts of this conversation, the parts that she did not understand.

"Would you try?" she asked quietly. "It would be wonderful if you could leave these chambers one day. I do worry about you. If there were a fire— If you fail, it will not be worse, and in trying so far, it has already become better."

He said nothing in response. He did not blame her, she could tell. All of his anger was with Sebastian.

He braced his hands on the arms of the chair. He forced his body up a few inches. Then his arm's strength could not hold his weight and he sank down hard.

Sebastian stood, walked over, bent, and slid his arms under his brother's at their top. He straightened and lifted the marquess until he held him upright with two boots planted firmly on the floor. It all happened so fast that Audrianna was startled at the abrupt activity.

Then Sebastian stepped back and left his brother without any support. The marquess's mouth gaped in shock. Then he fell again, backward into the chair.

"Are you mad?" he yelled.

"They held, damn it. Briefly, before they buckled, they held. Do not tell me you did not feel your muscles rebel and give way."

The marquess closed his eyes and composed himself. Rage ceased distorting his face. "It was unseemly for you to do this in front of Audrianna."

"I needed a witness that you know to be sympathetic. Ask her if they held or not."

He did not ask. She knew then that her husband was correct, and that his brother resisted doing what he must to regain his life.

She went to him, and kissed his cheek. His eyes were still closed, as if he had retreated from both of them and from the truth.

"I should go now. I will always come and tell you about the season's balls, for as long and as often as you like," she said. "However, I confess that one day I would like to dance with you at one instead."

T wo weeks passed and Sebastian did not hear from Castleford's solicitor. That was not a good sign. Perhaps the information had been unearthed on a day other than Tuesday. Tristan might well conclude that he did not have to take responsibility after all if duty did not conform to his pleasure.

And so, three weeks to the day from when he had that meeting, it surprised Sebastian when a letter from the duke was delivered by messenger.

Either be here this afternoon before five o'clock, or wait until next Tuesday.

It meant sending regrets to two other men with whom he was scheduled to meet, but at three o'clock Sebastian made the ride to Castleford's palace on western Piccadilly Street.

When Sebastian entered the library, Castleford was snapping orders to poor Edwards. He pointed to the divan by way of telling his guest to sit and wait.

Fifteen minutes later, after a letter had been dictated to his land steward, Castleford deigned to address Sebastian.

"Come with me. He is in the drawing room."

Sebastian followed him. "Who is in the drawing room?"

"Mr. Goodale. One of my solicitors. He takes care of inconvenient, personal matters for me, much like your Mr. Dowgill does for you."

"You made him wait the entire afternoon?"

"He has refreshments and books and good air from the garden, and he can bleed me for the whole day. He does not mind, I am sure."

It appeared Mr. Goodale did not mind at all. He had settled his plump, short body in the largest chair, had pulled up a footstool, and was reading by the light of the open window with a glass of brandy in his other hand. It was a wonder he had not cast off his shoes. He expressed annoyance with the interference when the door opened, but jumped to his feet when he saw Castleford stride in.

Castleford sat in the chair Goodale had vacated, leaving the balding solicitor to perform before him like a schoolboy. "Tell Summerhays about that mill."

"My lord sold that mill to Mr. Skeffley in October of 1816."

"He knows that part. Tell him about my acquisition of that mill."

Goodale cleared his throat for his recitation. "The mill came into my lord's possession as payment for a gambling debt in the amount of seven thousand pounds. The gentleman and I held protracted negotiations, because he felt the property was worth rather more than that and hoped, I believe, that the difference would be paid to him. My lord was not involved in this bargaining, needless to say."

"Which is why I did not remember anything about it," Castleford said.

"My lord merely signed the documents once I had drawn them up, along with a number of other documents I brought to him that day."

"It was a Friday," Castleford inserted meaningfully. "Goodale here has been known to miss Tuesdays."

Goodale flushed. "My continued apologies about that, my lord, but I must meet with barristers and they are jealous of their time too."

"I merely emphasize that if you had brought these documents on a Tuesday, I would have remembered signing them." He made the point for Sebastian's sake.

"When did this acquisition take place, Mr. Goodale?" Sebastian asked.

"Earlier that same year. May 1816."

After the war, then.

"Goodale, you can leave now," his master said.

The solicitor left at once.

"My apologies for implying more involvement on your part than there could have been," Sebastian said.

"Apology accepted. I will not call you out and kill you."

"It took him a long time to find this information."

"Not at all. He had it in my hand the evening of your last visit. I did not give it to you until today because my Tuesdays were full of other business."

"Of course. There are only so many Tuesday hours in a week, after all. Are you going to tell me who paid off this debt with that mill? It is important."

Castleford eyed the decanter of brandy, but clearly thought better of it. "As it happens, that was the other business filling those Tuesdays. I did not like that someone had buried his crimes behind my name in this way.

No doubt he assumed that when evidence pointed to me, any investigation would end. Such special consideration is the sort of unfairness that makes it very nice to be a duke, but it is bad form to take advantage of the advantage, so to speak, if you are not a duke." He stifled a yawn. "Sit, please. You are reminding me of my old tutor, hovering there."

Sebastian sat. "His name?"

"You are truly disliked at the Board of Ordnance. Did you know that? They use strong language when talking about you. Oakes burned my ears, and Mulgrave doesn't trust you at all."

"You spent the last two Tuesdays talking to the senior officers of the Board of Ordnance?"

"Something did not make sense, and I thought they might clear it up. I find that I like things to make sense on Tuesdays."

"That is what sobriety does for you."

"Hence the tedium." He leaned forward with his forearms on his knees and looked very soberly at Sebastian. "Here it is. It seems—and I do not recollect it at all—that I got that mill in payment of a gambling debt from Percival Kennington."

"Kennington?"

"Odd, isn't it? Who would have guessed he had gone into trade. And according to Goodale, not alone. His friend Symes-Wilvert was in it too. Two solid sons of barons, putting their shoulders to the grindstone together, literally, to manufacture gunpowder for the great cause."

Sebastian was as surprised as Castleford wanted. He never guessed that Pettigrew and Eversham were actually two men he knew. Bloody hell, what had they been thinking? Whatever they had gained financially had not been worth the risks. And to now live with the knowledge they had caused the deaths of innocent men— Jesus, he had wanted to hand Morgan justice on this matter as a gift, but now his closest friends—

"You set out to be an avenging angel, but find yourself on the devil's path, I think, Summerhays."

Castleford was watching him closely. Not with glee. His eyes were those of a friend from years ago, who had just read his mind, and who had sent Goodale away for a reason.

"Why did you really speak with the officers of the Board of Ordnance?"

"To express my severe displeasure. Everyone knows those two are fools. Would you buy gunpowder from them? Damn, I would not trust a flint if they sold it. I don't care if they tried to be sly by naming the company after their great-aunts or favorite horses. Men on the Board had to know who owned that mill. Yet they still contracted with them." He sat back in his chair. "One wonders why."

Castleford would say nothing more. That last sentence spoke his opinion. His expression conveyed an old friend's concern.

They both knew that there was no way that Kennington and Symes-Wilvert would obtain a contract from the Board on their own.

Someone had interceded on their behalf.

A woman knows when a man's mind is not on her. Especially when they are in bed.

Audrianna realized that while Sebastian's caresses were the same and his kisses just as passionate, an essential part of her husband was not paying attention.

Her own desire ebbed as a result. She covered his hand with hers, and held it to her breast.

She had never stopped him before, but she could not pretend that something was not alive in this chamber besides the thrills of mutual pleasure.

He did not seem to mind. He stayed in their embrace for a long time, his hand beneath hers. Then he sat up and reached for his robe. "I am sorry."

He left. She heard sounds in the dressing room next door. She rose and went to look in. He had thrown on clothes and was pulling on boots.

He noticed her. "I need some air to clear my head."

He appeared sad and subdued. She had never seen him like this before. "What is it that so preoccupies you?"

He forced a smile and came over and kissed her forehead. "Go to sleep."

That would never happen now. She did not even try. She returned to her chamber and ducked beneath the drapes so she could look out. Soon she saw him in the garden, just standing there in the moonlight. Perhaps it was the night, or the mood she had felt in him, but he appeared tragically solitary down there.

She draped her sensible shawl around her and put on her slippers. Taking a taper for light, she went down the stairs and out into the night.

He did not even notice her at first, so absorbed he was in his thoughts. She doubted he knew he had not moved from the same spot for a quarter hour now.

He finally saw her. He stretched out one arm and she went to him. He wrapped his arms around her and his mood enclosed her too. The sorrow within it was unmistakable now, and her own heart saddened too.

"What is it?" she asked again.

He kissed her crown. "I am on the horns of a dilemma. For the first time I do not know what to do. I never expected—I have misunderstood something so profoundly that I should be shot for stupidity."

"Not about me, I hope."

"Not about you. You are all goodness and honesty. It is about my brother. I think—I do not want to suspect it but—I think that he has known the truth all along about that gunpowder. I fear that—I believe that his interest in the matter all this time was not that of a man seeking justice, but of a man seeking reassurance that his own role would not be discovered."

He tensed as he spoke, but calmed once he finished. The latter mattered more to her than her shock at what he said.

"You must have good cause to think this, or you would not. It is almost inconceivable, however."

He turned her under his arm, so they could stroll among the plantings. The night's damp made the scents of spring hang heavily around them, mocking his wintery spirit.

"The powder was made at a mill owned by Kennington and Symes-Wilvert, the two friends who visit him each week. He has known them since they all were boys. God help me, I even question their devotion to him now."

"If his friends did this, he might be unaware."

"He may not be certain, but he is not unaware. I am seeing so many things in my mind again. His questions, even his concern about you—I think he knows, and it preys on his mind."

"Do you think he invested? Gave them the money? Surely he did not plan the smuggling and the rest. I will not believe that of him."

"I think he used his influence to ensure that mill's powder was bought for the war. The rest, I hope, was not of his doing." They paced on slowly. "But I think he knows. I think he has known a very long time."

She understood the chaos in him, because it was in her too now. And perhaps she also understood the marquess's own moods, and the melancholy that could descend on him.

"What are you going to do?"

"I do not know. Perhaps nothing. Or try to find out for certain. To broach this with him—I cannot do it unless I am sure. I want to forget the entire matter. I am tempted but—"

She said nothing. It was not for her to lead him to any decision.

"But that would not be right, or fair," he continued, but not with a lot of conviction. "Not fair to those men, or to that maimed gunner who finally had the key to the truth. Or to you."

How much did that last fairness weigh on him? Her father's name carried the full burden of this scandal now, and if there were others, that was not fair.

However, she did not want to picture him confronting his brother with his suspicions, or even with the truth. That would destroy something between the two of them that would never be replaced. She feared it would also destroy something within each of them too.

"He only sought to help friends, most likely," she said. "There is no crime in that."

"That is true, there is no crime in that, if that is all he did. However, if I bring this all to light, he will share the disgrace no matter what his role. I think he knows that. And fears that."

The hell still tormented him, but he no longer seemed lost in it. She stopped and embraced him. "You seem more yourself now. Still distracted, but not so darkly. It seems the air has indeed cleared your head."

"It was not the air, but your good heart and sympathy." He looked around. "Do you realize where we are?"

She glanced over her shoulder. They had found their way to that private spot where he had taken her the first day she visited this house.

"I think that I have some unfinished business with you here," he said. "I think that I should take care of that, and escape hell for a while."

"Are you sure that you can escape it enough?"

"You will have my complete attention this time." He led her over to the bench.

"Perhaps I should see that I do." She closed her hand on the evidence that she already had most of his attention. "What would it take for you to escape completely tonight? For me to turn hell into heaven, the way you did for me when I was lost?"

"If you sit on that bench and lift that nightdress, I will have us both in heaven soon enough, I promise."

"That can wait. I am enjoying this. I want to lead the way, and not only follow. I am allowed to take care of you sometimes too, am I not? When you are sad, or faced with dilemmas."

She sat on the bench so she could unfasten his trousers. She released him and took his length in her hands and caressed. She took her time so he would have the best pleasure and forget the harsh world.

He let her care for him. He did not try to stop her or even caress her back. He stood there while her hands smoothed and stroked, his dark eyes watching her.

It aroused her too, even though she only gave. She pressed a kiss to the side of his shaft to express that. His whole body tensed in response, and his stance turned as taut as a bow. She playfully kissed the tip. A low, strangled sigh escaped him and his hand lightly touched her crown.

She understood then. She just knew. She flicked the tip with her tongue. She boldly enclosed it with her lips.

The remnants of his distraction lifted. He relinquished himself to her. He threw his head back while she led him into ecstasy.

Chapter Twenty-five

Confusion poured up the staircase. Lady Wittonbury's voice could be heard rising above it all. Then a louder voice, this time Sebastian's, ordering the marchioness to be silent.

Audrianna went down to see what disaster had struck. She came upon Sebastian executing tactics that would impress a field marshal.

Wittonbury sat in an armed wooden chair at the top of the stairs. Four footmen flanked him. Two more stood halfway down the staircase, facing the marquess.

Lady Wittonbury hurried over to her. "He has asked to be taken out to the garden. I do not know whether to be overjoyed that he desires the change, or distraught that he might get ill."

"I do not think fresh air will harm him. We should choose to be overjoyed, I believe."

"Yes. Of course. And yet . . ." She watched the preparations with worried eyes.

The footmen moved as a unit. They grasped the chair in various places ordained by Sebastian, and at his signal lifted the chair and began carrying it down.

"You are very sure that all the servants are gone," Wittonbury said. "I look a fool and do not want those girls to be gossiping about it to servants in other houses."

"They have all made themselves scarce," Sebastian promised. "We will have you outside in a thrice, and back up even faster when you want to return."

Audrianna admired the care Sebastian took with this expedition. He was, as always, very solicitous of his brother's health and pride.

They had not spoken again of the dilemma regarding the powder. She knew that Sebastian had not brought the matter up with Morgan, however. The distraction was still in him, and yesterday, when they were with the marquess for a few minutes, she had seen how Sebastian looked at his brother in a pensive way that reflected how the decision troubled him.

The chair reached a landing and turned a corner. Wittonbury could see his mother and her now. "Well, come along," he called. "I don't intend to contemplate nature all alone."

Lady Wittonbury glided to the top of the staircase. He noticed. "You too, sister. We will have a garden party."

They followed the chair out to the terrace and out onto a patch of grass flanked by two stone paths. The footmen set it down. Dr. Fenwood tucked a blanket around the marquess, then walked away to take a position a good fifty yards away.

Footmen and gardeners hurried to move some iron chairs close. A small table emerged from the house. Sebastian had been carrying two books, and he set them down.

He checked his pocket watch. "For all the drama, that

barely took fifteen minutes. In the future it can be done faster, and they can have you back up in your chambers in less than ten even today. Just have Fenwood call for the men."

Wittonbury nodded. His mother sat her iron self in an iron chair and beamed approval. Audrianna strolled toward the house with her husband.

"Was this his idea?" she asked.

"He was at the window and admired the garden. I said he should go down and did not hear him object."

"He seems contented enough."

"He knows that his old life is within reach. He can taste it. He refuses to hope and yet he has begun to hope all the same." He gazed over at the quiet conversation between mother and son. "It would be a hell of a thing if scorn waits for him when he can finally leave this house."

"Have you decided what to do?"

He shook his head. "My courage fails me whenever I try to speak to him about it."

He left to go about his day. The marquess beckoned her to one of the chairs. Lady Wittonbury encouraged her to feel like an intruder with the tight smile of forbearance that she wore.

Audrianna sat as an observer, not a participant. She watched the marquess's animated expressions and talk. He was delighted to be out here. Maybe even excited. Yet from deep within him she sensed, as she always had, a melancholy that was too quick to accept fate.

"It was good of you to occupy me for a while," he said to his mother after a half hour. "I know that you have calls to make, and you should do that. Audrianna will keep me company for a while longer before I go in."

Any other woman might have missed the dismissal for

what it was. Lady Wittonbury did not. She possessed the ability to exude grace that had a razor's edge, and she took her leave with an invisible but cutting huff.

Wittonbury tilted his head so his face received full sun. He closed his eyes. "The warmth is peaceful. It makes me deliciously lazy."

"Rest if you like. I will stay here while you do."

It appeared he would, but after a few minutes he spoke. "Are you happy, Audrianna? Are you making friends?"

"I am happy. I have some new friends."

"I am glad to hear that you are. My brother has been preoccupied with something of late. I am glad it does not touch on you."

"Actually, I think it does. He has learned quite a bit about that gunpowder. We discovered that my father was probably complicit, but that there were others involved too, in worse ways."

He did not move. His eyes remained closed. She felt an alertness claim him, however. "That is interesting. What else has he learned?"

She told him about the young gunner, and the marks on the kegs, and the discovery of the company's name. She described the scheme to take good powder out of kegs and sell it to a smuggler, and how a man at the arsenal and one in London had been paid to ensure that the tests cleared the bad powder, or that the reports of bad powder were lost.

She went no further. She did not say that Sebastian knew who owned that mill during the war. She had said enough for him to guess the rest, however, if he knew the truth already.

He opened his eyes and looked around the garden. A little sadly, but also very thoughtfully.

He inhaled deeply. "Then he will know it all soon, if he

does not already." He shielded his eyes with one hand. "Thank God."

His composure wavered and he shielded his face yet more. He collected himself and looked at her. He appeared truly relieved. Also frightened and desperate.

Her heart hurt for him. "He recently learned about your two friends. He is not sure that he wants to know all of it now."

"No, of course not. But he will decide that he must. It is the honorable choice." He looked down at his lap and legs. "I believed this was my punishment. When I learned what Kenny and Symes had done, and how I had aided them— a man does not send his oldest friends to prison or worse. So, I went to fight, to make amends. When fate decided a higher price was required, I accepted my loss as fair."

"Is that why you have fought that healing? Because you thought fate would exact a higher price instead?"

"No, dear girl. I deserved this punishment, and so I did not believe there could be any healing in the first place."

She reached across the little table. He took her hand in his.

"Do your friends know that you know?"

He shook his head. "They thought they were very sly, but if you have known a man most of your life, you can tell when something is up. So it was with them. Little comments between them, spoken out of turn. A new carriage that Kennington could ill afford. Reckless gambling when there had been none in the past. I suspected they had some scheme with that mill. There was a third partner, a man I did not know. He had lured them into it with promises of great riches. Neither one is wealthy, so they were enamored of this investment and insisted it was pouring out money beyond their dreams."

"Perhaps it was. Their good fortune was not a reason for you to know what they were doing."

"So I have told myself. But I knew. Within their joy at all that money to spend, there was also fear and guilt. I could smell it. I was concerned, because I had put in a good word for them. My name obtained the contract, not theirs. And then, the earliest reports drifted back about that massacre—long before the war ended, long before the first word in the papers, the army knew something had gone very wrong on that hill for those men. And I learned of it, the way powerful peers often do."

He looked away and shook his head. The hold on her hand gripped tighter. She almost told him not to speak of it because his distress was so plain. Having started, however, he seemed determined to finish.

"I told Kenny and Symes that there had been this horrible mishap with some powder, and asked them how it could happen with all the quality checks. I sought their expertise. After all, they owned a mill that made the stuff. Not possible, they swore. And yet it had happened." He looked at her, with eyes as intense as his brother's could be. "And I knew. I just knew it was their powder, from their mill. It was on their faces and in their voices, as they feigned ignorance. They are neither one sly by nature, nor good at lying. I had convinced the army to buy ordnance from two fools who had done something that got good men killed. And I also knew that I would never forgive myself."

And so he had accepted the imprisonment of infirmity when it came, as a justice. She imagined him waiting for the truth to come out these last years, hoping his brother learned everything but also dreading that day at the same time.

What had Sebastian said? *I do it for him*. And he did, but in ways he had never guessed.

"Tell Sebastian what I have just said, when you know he has decided to go forward," he said. "I do not want him to ask me about it. He deserves better than having to interrogate his own brother about such a thing. Nor could I bear to face him that way. I might as well end this in moral cowardice, as I began it, I suppose."

"You were not a coward. This was not your crime. You were duped by two good friends."

"I should have guessed they were up to no good. Kenny and Symes invest in a mill? My brother would have been duly skeptical, as I should have been. I should have demanded to meet and know the man who proposed this to them. I should have told Sebastian where to look when he began his search, rather than fear that what little I had left of my dignity would be taken away by disgrace."

"And yet you did not stop him. You encouraged him. He would never have pursued it otherwise."

"I expect that murderers half hope that they will be caught too, so the fear of capture will end. Such are the contradictions of the soul. I have come to know mine too well." He raised her hand, kissed it. "I am sorry that your father's name was pulled into this, Audrianna. When it was, I asked them if they knew him to be a man who could be bought. They both said no, and I am sure that they spoke the truth."

"My father gave the final approval before powder was distributed. If reports of bad powder came from an arsenal, he would have seen them. I would like to believe that you can be so sure of your friends' opinion of his honor, but suspicion fell on my father for a reason."

He vaguely shook his head. "Whoever was their man at

the offices of the Board of Ordnance, it was not him. That was perhaps the worst part—to see another good man suffer and die because of my weakness. I never thought he would kill himself. Kenny and Symes probably did not either. Thus did three idiots and cowards hurt your family."

She dared not believe him. He lied to make some good of this for someone; that was all. He had nothing to lose now. Yet her heart filled with hope, and affection that he had said it, even if it were not true.

He released her hand. He found his handkerchief and wiped his face. "The papists say confession is good for the soul. Perhaps they are right."

He called for Dr. Fenwood, and told him to bring out the footmen.

That night she gave Sebastian as much love as she could along with pleasure. She let her care burn in each kiss she gave his body, and his scent and touch burn her soul. She finally took him into herself, absorbing him deeply, holding him tightly, and moved in the hard rhythm that would allow them the ultimate escape together.

She collapsed on him, with her heart bursting with the emotions that she had brought to this bed. A memory came to her, from not long ago at all, of wanting to make him admit he was wrong about her father. Of blaming him for her pain. Then another memory, of his sweet care when she realized he had not been wrong at all.

She remained in the embrace that held her to his body. She turned her face so her mouth was beside his ear.

"I have been thinking about your dilemma. I think that it would be best to allow this investigation to die."

His embrace tightened. He rolled, so that she was on her back and he could see her face.

"You think that I should walk away, now that it touches on my family?"

She wished he would not view it that way, even if that is exactly what she meant.

"Whatever your brother did, he has more than paid, has he not?"

"They are two separate things. His condition is tragic and he has suffered, that is true. But it was not in payment for his negligence."

He thinks it was. The marquess had given permission for her to convey his confession, but she would rather not. If Sebastian knew for certain of his brother's involvement, he might believe he could not let this die at all.

"If you ask him about this, accuse him of this—you will create a chasm, no matter how honest you have been, and no matter what he says."

"Damnation, do you think I do not know that?" He rolled again, without her. Away from her. He lay on his back with his tight profile limned by the glow of the lamp on the far table.

"Would it not be better, then, to just not know?"

"I thought you wanted to know everything. To have the truth. There is no chance of exonerating your father, if he was innocent, if I end this now."

"Frans said—"

"Frans found a name in a newspaper," he interrupted. "Now that I know the truth of this scheme, the planning and the dangers—I am not convinced your father had a role. Quite the opposite."

So this also preyed on his mind, as he weighed and balanced duty against the brother he loved. And yet, his opinion only pained her because it put her at the center of the grief that might come to this family.

"They would go to someone they knew and trusted, not approach a stranger. That would be much too risky," he said. "We may have indeed hounded an innocent man to the grave, as you always thought. There can be no compensation for that, certainly not to him but even not to you, but at least his name can be cleared. My brother's embarrassment would be a small price to pay for justice."

The sore could still hurt if poked, even if it no longer bled. A good deal of guilt had plagued her as she decided what to do, especially since the marquess had said that her father would indeed be exonerated. But her old quest seemed very small when she saw the anguish that this decision gave Sebastian.

"I will remember my father as he was. I do not need another victim to take his place. Whatever decision you make, please do not make it because of me."

His head turned so it faced hers. He looked over at her for a long time. The mood between them became drenched with the kind of intimacy that normally existed right after passion's soul-baring ecstasy.

His hand sought hers between their bodies. "You humble me sometimes. You offer gifts of yourself in ways that—"

He moved on top of her, so his skin touched hers from torso to legs. He gazed at her so thoughtfully, so intensely, that she feared what he perceived.

"Why would you try to give me this when the truth was so important to you?"

Her throat burned. Her heart filled with the best ache. "Because you are more important now."

"Is it a gift of love, then?" he asked quietly.

The invitation was unexpected, and harder to accept than she thought. "Yes. It is a gift of love, Sebastian."

Still thoughtful. Still intense. But that smile now, that could still dazzle her silly. "Then I accept it with love, Audrianna. More love than you will know. So much that it staggers me."

Her ache transformed to joy at his words. Blissful, resplendent joy such as she had never known. It spilled through her and out of her and made her laugh with delight. He laughed too, at her surprise and at his own, and they shared the sweetest kiss.

He moved just enough. She spread her legs to accept him. He entered her so their bodies mimicked their hearts.

He became thoughtful again. "I am deciding if it feels differently, now that I know you love me. I think maybe it does. Interesting."

"How so? How is it different?

He pondered it. "Unbearable desire still, that is certain. Only also . . . perfect contentment." He shifted a little and she giggled. "And also unexpected happiness within the desire. Also . . ." He closed his eyes, savoring and naming. "Also the smug satisfaction of being totally sure of complete possession of all of you."

"That last does not sound very romantic."

He arched so his mouth could reach down to her breast. "I may be besotted by love, but I am still a man, Audrianna."

His tongue circled in its torturous paths on her nipples. It did not take long until he had her close to raving. She let her love cry out along with her pleasure. She held back nothing, so he would know and indeed be totally sure of that possession he craved.

Soon all that mattered was how he filled her. The joy

centered there, in the beautiful sensations while he moved. Long, deep strokes stretched her, completed her, and made the pleasure intensify slowly until untold tiny thrills pulsed out to the rest of her body.

She never escaped into abandon. She remained alert to him through it all, feeling him, loving him. Even at the end, when those thrills collected and tightened and screamed, she remained aware.

He was with her too, in that clear acknowledgment that it must be that way, that they must never forget this loving, or any moment of it. Still amazed by the pure beauty of their unlikely, mutual love, they gazed into each other's eyes through the perfect cresting of their passion, and the breaking bliss in which they were totally as one.

"Did you tell him? He has not said a word to me. He sits at breakfast as if he is ignorant." The marquess quizzed her several days later. He had even summoned her just for this purpose.

"I did not tell him," she said truthfully. "It appears he has decided to handle it another way."

The marquess frowned at that. She wondered if the complexities in his soul regretted being left alone with his private guilt. Perhaps he truly wanted public disgrace.

"Whatever he decided, he will not accept your sacrifice." She pointed to his chair. "He will fight with you about it, because he believes you can one day walk again."

"If I ever do, it will diminish him."

"No other man can diminish him. He does not want your life, either as a gift, or due to your infirmity. He will gladly return whatever is yours when you are ready to take it back."

He did not appear convinced. "Did he tell you this?"

"He did not have to. I know."

He smiled skeptically.

"I know," she repeated firmly, with some annoyance.

That took him aback. He ended the subject by fishing out his pocket watch. "Kennington and Symes-Wilvert will be here soon. Call Dr. Fenwood so I can sit by the window for some time before they come. Do not leave. Come back in when he is done."

She went to the anteroom and sent Dr. Fenwood in. When he returned, she went back to the marquess. He sat near the open window.

"The world is so beautiful," he muttered. She stood beside him and looked out the window, down into the garden with its bursts of color amid the green plants and trees and gray stone paths.

While they admired it, a head moved into view. Then two others. Three men walked into the garden and down a path. They stopped and chatted.

The marquess's eyes narrowed on them. "What is he doing? Why would he pull Kenny and Symes out there with him?"

She did not know. Sebastian was doing most of the talking, even if they could not hear what he said. The other two men only listened. Soberly.

"It appears you were wrong," the marquess said. "It looks like my brother will demand that justice have its pound of flesh after all."

Kennington and Symes-Wilvert had nothing to say. They did not even try to defend or excuse themselves. They just looked at the ground in dismay.

"We did not think . . ." Kennington began. Whatever he intended to say must have sounded poor to his own mind, so he stopped.

"I am sure that you never imagined that there might be soldiers in battle left with only that adulterated powder," Sebastian said.

"Exactly," Kennington said. "Those kegs all get mixed together in transport, we were told. There would always be good powder when one of these was found to be bad."

"Who told you this? I do not believe this scheme was of your making." It was not their character that he trusted. Sebastian just did not believe for a minute that these two men were smart enough to concoct and execute such an elaborate deception.

Symes-Wilvert looked at Kennington with some fear.

Kennington chewed his lower lip. "A fellow broached the idea of a powder mill with us. He had it all planned. I had that bit of land near the river in Kent, and it would be perfect, he said. Symes here invested some money as his share. Borrowed it from his brother."

"We thought at first it would just be a normal mill," Symes said desperately.

"Except it wasn't," Sebastian said.

They both stared at their boots, miserable.

"Who was this man? This third partner?" he pressed.

Kennington cleared his throat. "Name was Patterson. He had worked at the Waltham Abbey Works so he knew how it was done. That was his contribution in it."

"We haven't seen him in over a year," Symes muttered. "We heard a rumor he took his profits and went to America."

So there it was. Two fools lured into deep water by someone much smarter than they were. This Patterson had chosen his partners well. Perhaps he picked them because their best friend was a marquess with connections at the War Department and Board of Ordnance.

"There was an advertisement some time ago, about a meeting at the Temple of the Muses. My wife thought it was for her. I think now that it was an attempt by the two of you to locate the man who shot me in Brighton."

Kennington turned very red. "I was shocked to see her there. I thought the notice was very cleverly worded and only he would—"

"You only knew about that episode in Brighton, and why I was there, because of my brother. He described it, and you sought to find the Domino before I did, in order to buy his silence on whatever he might know."

"Wittonbury may have mentioned something," Symes-Wilvert said. "But as soon as that scandal broke, and we saw it was you and Kelmsleigh's daughter involved, we thought it would be wise to know what you knew." He cleared his throat. "As it were."

"You used my brother most ignobly. I trust that your visits have been out of friendship, and not only to keep aware of what he learned and did not about your crime, or out of guilt that you had so badly betrayed his friendship."

"There has been guilt enough, but I'll not hear insinuations that our friendship is not honest," Symes-Wilvert said with some umbrage.

Sebastian contemplated the two men. They had confessed fast enough. They had probably been waiting to do so for years. And the instigator, this Patterson, was probably living in luxury in America.

"I think that it will not serve the country, or the army, to have all this—" A commotion interrupted him. A very small one, but it could not be ignored.

Four footmen came out on the terrace, carrying a chair in which Morgan sat like a king in a royal litter. Dr. Fenwood and Audrianna walked behind them.

Kennington and Symes-Wilvert were distracted by the spectacle. Morgan gestured to the garden and spoke to the footmen. The chair descended the terrace steps. The entourage moved down the stone path to where Sebastian stood. The footmen set the chair down.

Kennington smiled with delight at his friend's emergence from his prison.

Morgan did not smile back. "My brother has been telling you what he has discovered about your gunpowder, I think. I have decided that it is time to stop pretending that it did not happen, and that I did not know about it."

No one moved. Kennington's expression shattered. "You have known? Oh, dear God."

"Yes, you fool, I have known. And I have regretted allowing friendship to sway me to do something that good judgment said I should not, and then swaying me more to keep silent when I should have spoken." He shooed away the footmen. "Audrianna, come here, please. I require your help, if you will give it."

She glanced in question at Sebastian, but approached the chair.

"Closer, dear sister."

She stepped closer.

Morgan eyed his friends. Then his concentration turned inward. He shifted in the chair, braced his hands against its arms, and slowly, painfully, rose.

His legs almost buckled when they took his weight. He grasped Audrianna's shoulder to steady himself. Face taut, eyes blazing, he stood on his own legs and faced his astonished friends.

"You were both looking relieved when I came out of the house. Was my brother offering us absolution? How generous of him. Regrettably, it is not his to give."

Kennington and Symes-Wilvert cast down their eyes again. Their faces flushed. They knew it was not a friend who spoke to them now. Morgan was all marquess as he stood there through force of will and little else. All Lord Wittonbury.

"I told this dear lady that I believed that her father's name was disgraced by mistake. That was not my brother's blame, or the newspapers, or anyone's except ours. His death is on our hands alone. You will now tell her the truth, whatever it may be, so she finally knows it."

Sebastian looked at Audrianna. She tried to avoid his gaze, but finally met it.

She had known. When she offered her gift of love, she had known it all. She had spoken with Morgan and learned the truth. And she had also learned that the truth might clear her father.

Sebastian was glad that this was his brother's conversation now. He could not have spoken himself without betraying his emotions. It moved him profoundly that she had tried to protect him from the hell of exposing his own brother, to the point of sacrificing her own justice.

"There was a man at the Tower, who was paid. He dealt with the records and stores. It was not your father, but a clerk who was beneath him and who could remove reports of bad powder if any came in on our mill, and also change things in the records after your father made his approval," Kennington said quietly.

"Our sincere apologies, Madam," Symes-Wilvert mumbled.

"Apologies are due, that is certain, to her and many others. But they are not enough. You know they are not," Wittonbury said. "You will give the name of the other man to my brother, along with all the names of all the men who conspired with you." He looked at Sebastian. "Then he and I will do what must be done."

Kennington and Symes-Wilvert looked as if they had been bludgeoned. Not daring to speak, they bowed and took their leave. They hurried back up the garden path.

Wittonbury raised his voice and told them to stop. He could not turn to see them, so he spoke into the air. "No matter what happens, you will always be my friends."

He did not see their astonishment. Thoroughly cowed, they turned and walked out of the garden.

Morgan grimaced. His balance wavered. "Help me to sit, Sebastian. Quickly, before I fall on my face and take your dear wife down with me."

The garden was silent except for the sounds of spring and the gentle falls of her feet. Audrianna meandered along the stone paths while she absorbed the drama that had just unexpectedly unfolded. Sebastian had gone in with his brother. They probably would talk privately for a while.

She also needed to have some private conversations. She would go visit Mama tomorrow. Mama deserved to know that her loyalty to Papa had not been in vain.

Audrianna let the old memories come as she strolled. They did not provoke anger now, or fear. She did not want to weep. She pictured her father in better times, and it brought joy, not pain. A lovely peace had settled in her with the confession of Wittonbury's friends. The marquess had been correct that these two men were not good liars. They told the truth when they exonerated her father, she was certain.

Her father's face came to her vividly, more clearly than it had in months. It seemed to her that his dark eyes warmed in recognition. Then he smiled and nodded, and his image began dimming in her imagination.

Boots fell into step beside her. She had not noticed that Sebastian had returned to the garden. He took her hand, and they walked on, enjoying the new peace together.

"Your gift that night was even more selfless than I knew," he said. "Morgan had confided everything to you, hadn't he?"

She nodded. "He wanted you to know. He wanted me to tell you. I could not. I hoped you would find a way to spare him the disgrace. If you knew for certain, perhaps honor would not permit that."

"I was going to try. He did not allow it." He smiled a little ruefully. "He asked about that German physician. As we brought him up, he spoke of going abroad, once this matter is settled and aired. Then he called for our mother."

Audrianna glanced to the window of Wittonbury's library. Would Lady Wittonbury be overjoyed to see her husband's heir reclaiming his life and authority? Or dismayed by the disgrace that would diminish her influence along with his?

"I think he was very brave," she said. "And very kind to his friends at the end, in what he said."

"They stood by him when he was forgotten. He will not abandon them." He stopped and pulled her into his arms. "I am glad that your father will be vindicated. Glad for you and me, and for our love. And I am grateful that you believed in him when everyone else did not."

"Grateful?"

"If not for your determination, you would have never gone to the Two Swords that night. I might never have met you, or stolen that first kiss."

"You would have stolen one from another woman instead, and been well contented," she teased.

"It would not have been the same."

"You are a charmer, my love. Far be it from me to discourage your flattery, however."

He smiled his enchanting smile. As she grew dazzled and dizzy, his expression turned more serious. "You distracted me badly that night. It was—unexpected. It occurred to me, as we awaited the justice of the peace, that if you were transported, that kiss might indeed have to sustain me forever, the way the poets say the important kisses can."

This was not flattery now. His tone said it was not. She did not laugh or treat it as playful banter either.

"I quite lost myself in that kiss," she admitted. "It was very hard to hate you after that."

"Much as you tried?"

She laughed. "Yes."

"Well, at least you never found me boring."

She wrapped her arms around his neck. "Never that. And now I love you too much to contain it. Kiss me, so that I can release some of that love before I burst."

He kissed her, and it was a kiss for the poets to talk of, a kiss never to be forgotten for the rest of her life.

Read on for a preview of the next novel in Madeline Hunter's ravishing quartet . . .

Provocative in Pearls

Available from Jove Books March 2010

Chapter One

A good friend lets one spill bile, even if he finds it boring. So it was that Grayson, Earl of Hawkeswell, took advantage of Sebastian Summerhays's friendship while they were both trapped in Summerhays's carriage this bright August morning.

"I curse the day my cousin introduced me to the bastard." He heard his voice snarl with anger. He had sworn to himself, *sworn*, that he would not do this, but here he was fuming like a chimney at the idiocy of life and pouring woe into Summerhays's ear.

"Thompson was not at all willing to cooperate?" Summerhays asked.

"Hell, no. But, her trustee has agreed to join me in pressing for a new inquest, and with the help of Providence and the courts, I will be free of this complicated disaster by year's end."

"It makes no sense to interfere with the inquest. The man is not rational if he tries that."

"He wants the connection. Or rather his wife does. She is mining it for all it is worth while she can, hoping the new ties hold once the connection itself is severed. He is also comfortable with the way things stand. He has control of that company, which is what he wanted. If we end this impasse, he risks losing that."

"It is good for you to be going down to the country, then. You can use some peace."

Summerhays smiled over like the good, understanding friend that he was. There was something of the physician's sympathy in his expression, as if he worried for the health of the man he placated.

Hawkeswell saw his umbrage the way Summerhays must, and his anger turned to bitter amusement. "I am a comical figure, am I not? Such are the punishments for selling oneself in marriage for some silver, I suppose."

"Such matches are made all the time. You are the victim of an odd circumstance, that is all."

"Let us hope the circumstances change soon. I am in dun territory up to my eyebrows and have sold what I can. It will be porridge this winter, I think."

The talk turned to other things, but part of Hawkeswell's mind remained fixed on the marital conundrum that had plagued him for two years. Verity had drowned in the Thames, but her body had never been found. How she got there on her wedding day, why she left his estate at all, remained a mystery. There were those who wanted to blame him.

His old reputation for a bad temper fed that speculation, but any fool could see it was not in his interest for Verity to disappear that day. An unconsummated marriage was an ambiguous marriage, as her trustee had so clearly explained when he refused to hand over her income from her trust. The Church would have to decide if there had been a marriage at all if she was ever declared dead. In the meantime . . .

In the meantime, her husband—or maybe not her husband—could wait. He could not remarry while she was still officially alive. The money that led him to the altar was out of reach, however. He was in limbo.

That powerlessness goaded him. He resented being a pawn of fate. Worse, this could go on for years.

"I appreciate your company, Summerhays. You are too good to tell me I am tedious. It was generous of you to suggest I accompany you out of town before taking to horse for Surrey."

"You are not tedious. You are on the horns of a dilemma and I regret that I have no solution. Since you will not allow me to lend—"

"I do not want one more debt, least of all to a friend. I have no expectations of being able to repay what is gone already."

"Of course. However, if it does come down to porridge, perhaps you will accept my offer for the sake of your cousin and aunt."

"I cannot accept." Except he could, of course. If it got that bad he probably would. It was one thing to suffer this himself, but even worse to watch it affect those for whom he was responsible. He carried considerable guilt already, not only for his aunt and cousin, but also for the good people who lived on his entailed lands and who deserved more care and generosity than he could afford.

"Did you tell your wife that you were coming down a day early?" he asked. Summerhays had married in the spring, and his wife visited her friends in Middlesex with some frequency. Her stays this summer were often extended, to avoid the heat in town.

"I cleared my affairs so late yesterday that there was no point. I will surprise her. Audrianna will not mind."

Hawkeswell admired the security with which his friend said that. Generally women did mind when husbands interfered with their plans. If Summerhays were another kind of man, and his wife another kind of woman, showing up unexpectedly, a day early, at a country house party could lead to some awkward explanations.

The coach rolled down the main lane of the village of Cumberworth, with his black gelding trotting along on its tether. He would have to visit his aunt once he reached Surrey, he supposed, and tell her that he would soon have to let her town house go. It would not be a pleasant meeting.

Even worse would be the consultations with his steward, who would again advise enclosures of the common ground on the estate. Hawkeswell had long resisted following the modern practices on that. He had sought to avoid the hardships that enclosures would bring to the families whose lives depended on that land.

People who had not seen the roofs over their heads maintained properly by their landlord should not now be deprived yet again, and in worse ways. His finances had become dire, however, and unless they improved soon, everyone would suffer anyway.

The coach took a turn outside the town. A half mile along it carefully made another turn onto a private lane. A sign marked the property: THE RAREST BLOOMS.

The coachman stopped where the trees fell away in front of a pleasant stone house surrounded by a handsome perennial garden of free, rustic design. Summerhays opened the coach door. "You must come and meet the ladies. Audrianna will want to see you."

"I will take my horse and be off. It is you she will be happy to see."

"The horse needs to rest. I insist you come with me. Mrs. Joyes will give you some refreshment before you begin your ride, and you can see the back garden. It is among the finest in Middlesex."

Since the duties waiting in Surrey did not encourage haste, Hawkeswell fell into step beside his friend and they walked to the door. A thin woman opened it and curtsied when she saw Summerhays.

"Lady Sebastian was not expecting you today, sir. She is not packed, and is in the garden."

"That is fine, Hill. I will not mind waiting. I can find my own way to the garden, if you have other duties."

Hill curtsied again, but walked with them through the house. They passed a sitting room and a cozy small library crowded with stuffed chairs. Hill left them when they entered another, more informal sitting room in the back.

"Come with me," Summerhays said. He guided the way down a corridor that gave in to a large greenhouse. "Mrs. Joyes and the ladies have a business here, called The Rarest Blooms. You have seen their artistry at my wedding, and at many parties last season. This is where they work their magic."

The greenhouse was impressive, and large. Citrus trees and ferns, plants and vines, filled it with greenery and scents. High windows had been opened and a cross breeze fluttered leaves and petals.

They strolled to the back, where a grape vine laden with clusters of fruit hung over some iron chairs and a stone table.

Hawkeswell looked out the wall of glass. Distorting waves in the rectangular panes made the scene beyond more a watercolor wash than a Renaissance oil, as colors paled and blended and blurred. Even so, one could identify four women out there, at what appeared to be an arbor near a brick wall on the far side of the property.

Summerhays opened a door and the images clarified. It was a rose arbor covered with white blooms. Audrianna sat on a bench under the arbor, beside the pale, perfect Mrs. Joyes of the dark gray eyes. Hawkeswell had met Daphne Joyes at Summerhays's wedding.

Two other women sat on the grass, facing the bench. One was a blonde with elaborately dressed hair. The other wore a simple straw bonnet, and its deep brim obscured her profile.

Mrs. Joyes noticed the gentlemen emerging from the greenhouse. She raised her arm in greeting.

The two women on the ground swung their heads to see whom Mrs. Joyes hailed. Then that bonnet turned back and the woman wearing it gave her attention to Audrianna.

An odd sensation vibrated in Hawkeswell, like a plucked string of a soundless instrument. That patch of grass was shaded, and that bonnet made deeper shadows. And yet . . .

He peered hard at that bonnet, so still now. It did not turn again, even as Audrianna and Mrs. Joyes called for Summerhays to join them. The tilt of the head, however, made that string pluck again.

He walked toward them with Summerhays, along sand paths that meandered amid thousands of flowers.

"Who are the others?" he asked. "The ones sitting on the ground."

"The blonde is Miss Celia Pennifold. The other is Miss Elizabeth Smith. Lizzie, they call her."

"You have met them before?"

"Oh, yes. I am well acquainted with all the rarest blooms."

Hawkeswell exhaled deeply. Of course Summerhays would have met them all. The alarm in his instincts was uncalled for.

"Well, not Lizzie, now that you mention it. I had never realized it before, but while I have seen her in the garden and through the greenhouse glass or even passing by in that bonnet, I do not think that we have ever been introduced."

They approached the ladies. The bonnet's crown remained resolutely turned to them. No one else seemed to notice that, or consider it rude in the chaotic exchange of greetings and introductions that followed.

No one seemed to realize that Lizzie had never been introduced to Audrianna's husband, either, just as Summerhays himself had not. But an earl had entered the garden for the first time, and that head's immobility could not last forever in the courtesies that followed. Eventually Audrianna began the official introduction to Lizzie.

The bonnet rose as Lizzie stood. Blood pounded in Hawkswell's head as that lithe body, hidden beneath its shaft of simple blue muslin, turned. Head bowed modestly and deep brim shadowing her face, Lizzie curtsied.

The pounding eased. No, he had been wrong. And yet his memories of the particulars were so vague. So shockingly vague. But, no, his mind had played a trick with him, that was all.

"I will go ask Hill to bring out refreshments," Lizzie said quietly. Very quietly. Like a whisper.

She curtsied again, and walked away. The circle of women and the buzz of talk did not much notice her leave.

The tilt of that head again. The manner of walking. The pounding began again, savagely.

"Stop."

Everyone froze at his command and stared at him. Except Lizzie. She kept walking and did not look back. Her gait altered, though. She looked ready to bolt.

He strode after her and grabbed her arm.

"Lord Hawkeswell—*really*," Mrs. Joyes scolded, her expression one of stunned surprise. She looked with distressed curiosity at Summerhays.

"Hawkeswell—" Summerhays began.

He raised a hand to silence Summerhays. He stared at the delicate nose visible beyond the bonnet's brimmed profile. "Look at me, please. Now. I demand it."

She did not look at him, but after a long pause she did turn toward him. She shook his grasp off her arm and faced him. Long, thick dark lashes almost touched her snow white cheek.

Something shivered through her. Anger? Fear? He had never before felt someone's spirit react like he did in that moment.

Those lashes rose. It was not the face that told him for certain. Not its oval shape or her dark hair or rose of a mouth. Rather it was the resignation and sorrow and hint of rebellion in her blue eyes.

"*Damnation, Verity. It is you.*"

Chapter Two

"If she is not down here in two minutes I am going up there. I swear that I will tear this house down with my bare hands if I have to and—"

"Calm yourself, sir. I am sure there has been a misunderstanding."

"Calm myself? *Calm myself?* My missing wife, assumed dead for two years, has been living the sweet country life here, mere miles from London, knowing full well the world was looking for her, and you say I should *calm myself*? Let me remind you, Mrs. Joyes, that your role in this borders on criminal and that—"

"I will not listen to threats, Lord Hawkeswell. When you have composed yourself enough to have a civil discussion, send word to me. In the meantime, I will be at the top of the stairs, with my pistol, should you think to be brutish." Mrs. Joyes floated her ethereal, pale elegance out of the sitting room.

Summerhays had been poking in cabinets. "Ah, here is

some port. Stop that infernal pacing and get that temper of
yours under control, Hawkeswell. You are in danger of
being an unforgivable ass."

He could not stop pacing. Or looking at the ceiling toward where *that woman* had taken refuge. "If ever a man
in the history of the world had an excuse to be an ass, Summerhays, it is I. She has made a fine one out of me anyway, so I lose little in playing the part."

"No glass. This will have to do." He held a delicate
teacup in one hand and poured the port. "Now, drink this
and count to fifty. Like old times, when you got like this."

"I will look idiotic drinking out of that— Oh, what the
hell." He grabbed the cup and downed its contents. It
didn't help much at all.

"Now, count."

"I'll be damned if—"

"Count. Or I will end up having to thrash sense into
you and it has been many years since your temper forced
that on me. One, two, three . . ."

Gritting his teeth, Hawkeswell counted. And paced. The
red drained out of his head but the anger hardly dimmed.
"I don't believe that Mrs. Joyes did not know who she
was. Or that your wife did not."

"If you dare to imply again that my wife lied in saying
she was ignorant, I will not finish with you until you need
a wagon to bring you back to town," Summerhays said
dangerously.

"Don't forget, as you remember old times, that I give
as well as I get, or better." Hawkeswell bit back his fury
and paced out his count. "What the bloody hell is this
place?" he asked when he got to thirty. "Who takes in a
stranger and does not even ask her history. It is insane.
Mad."

"It is a rule here, not to ask. Apparently Mrs. Joyes has cause to know there are often good reasons why women deny their histories and leave their pasts behind completely."

"I can't imagine why."

"Can't you?"

Hawkeswell stopped pacing and glared at Summerhays. "If you imply that she had reason to be afraid of me, I swear that I will call you out. Bloody hell, she barely knew me."

"That alone might make some women fearful, I expect."

"You are talking nonsense now."

Summerhays shrugged. "You are only at forty-five."

"I am fine now."

"Let us keep it neat."

Hawkeswell stomped five more steps. "There. Now, I am all becalmed. Go tell Mrs. Joyes that I *demand to speak to my wife, damn it.*"

Summerhays folded his arms and inspected him carefully. "Another fifty, I think."

Lizzie sat on her bed, listening to the bellows of indignation coming from below. She would have to go down there soon. She could be forgiven, she thought, for taking a few minutes to prepare herself, and to accommodate herself to the notion of prison before the gaol door actually closed.

She had been a sentimental fool. She should have left as soon as Audrianna agreed to marry Lord Sebastian last spring. Or at least last week, after her twenty-first birthday passed. She had known that she had a war to fight once she came of age. Now she might not be able to fire a single shot.

Hawkeswell would have found her eventually when she returned to the world. There would have been no way to avoid that. However, she had planned to be among people who knew her and who would help, and she would have been prepared for him. Dallying in this house had brought catastrophe, and she might find herself imprisoned by that marriage after all this effort to avoid it.

She stopped castigating herself. It had not been mere sentiment that made her put off her departure. She had not really been a fool. Love had kept her here, more love than she had known in years. She could be excused for surrendering to the lure of spending one final week with her dear friends, all of them together one last time. The news that Audrianna would visit had come the very day she planned to say good-bye, and it had been enough to vanquish her weak resolve and growing fear.

Stomping shook the house. Another curse penetrated the floorboards. Hawkeswell was in fine form.

That was to be expected of any man making such an unexpected discovery, but she had always suspected he had more of that male fury than most. She had surmised at once that they would not suit each other when they first met. They never would now, that was certain. He was in league with Bertram in all of this, of course. And she had humiliated him by running away and not dying for real.

A delicate rap on her door sought her attention. She did not want to face her friends any more than she wanted to face the man spilling curses below, but neither could be avoided. She bid them enter.

They came in wearing expressions much as she expected. Audrianna was wide-eyed with astonishment beneath her fashionably dressed chestnut hair, but then she was too good to imagine a woman daring such a thing. Celia, who probably could imagine women doing any manner of things, appeared merely very curious. And Daphne— well, Daphne was exquisite and pale and composed, as always, and did not seem very surprised at all.

Daphne sat beside her on the bed. Celia sat on the other side. Audrianna stood in front of her.

"Lizzie—" Audrianna began. She caught herself as the name emerged, and flushed.

"I have thought of myself as Lizzie for two years. I suppose that you should call me Verity now, however. I expect I had better get used to it again."

Audrianna's face fell, as if she had clung to the belief that this was all a mistake.

"Then he is correct," Daphne said. Her tone indicated that she had rather hoped it was a mistake too. "There has been no error. You are the missing bride of Hawkeswell."

HUNTER   Hunter, Madeline.

              Ravishing in red.

$7.99

DATE			

BAKER & TAYLOR